Elephants and Butterflies

AMJ Dykes

Book Cover by Esté Mathee
First edition 2025

ISBN 978-0-646-72798-1

This book is dedicated to those who knew how to turn on my light when I had no idea where the switch was.

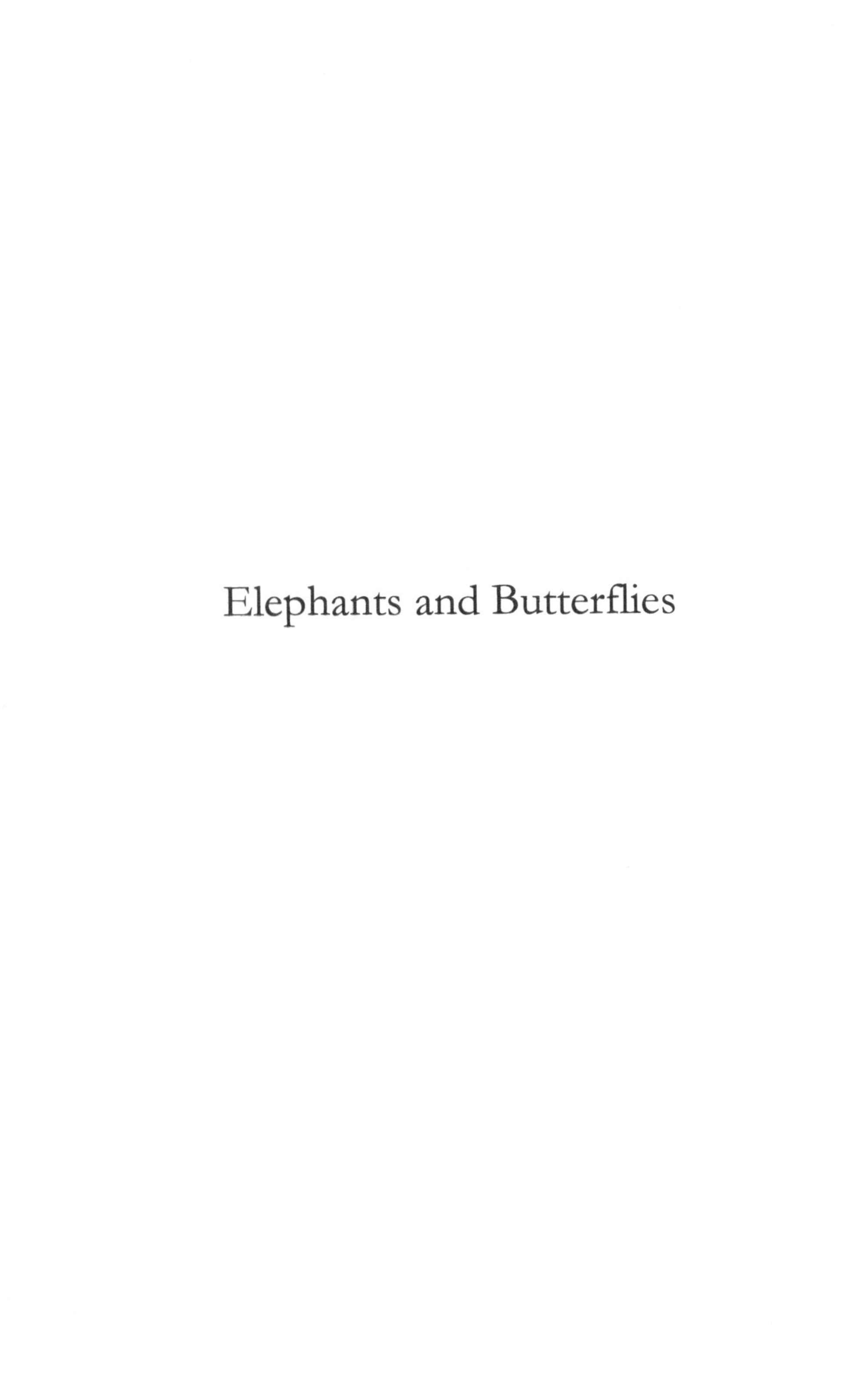

Elephants and Butterflies

CHAPTER ONE
The Party

It had been three weeks since I caught him cheating on me. Well, since my best friend Andjela caught him. She had sent me photos of him with another girl. They were at the bus station together kissing. It twisted the knife a little more knowing I had to walk past the scene of the crime on my way to and from school every day.

I used to love the bus station. I would see people getting on buses and it felt like they could be on an adventure anywhere. To a business meeting in Belgrade. To visit their boyfriend in Montenegro. On a holiday to the other side of the world. Some place so far away it may as well be on another planet. Some crazy place like Australia.

I was walking home from school in my small Serbian town called Požega. Looking down at my favourite black Converse shoes, as I tried to avoid all the cracks in the pavement. Somehow in my seventeen years that game still hadn't grown old. Ed Sheeran playing for the bajillionth time through my broken headphones, with only one of the buds working. I thought the game helped me feel better; a tiny bit less awful anyway, but who knows. I needed to run the study on it to discover if it really helped. *'Could I actually do that research?'* I wondered.

When I got dressed that morning, I made sure I had my favourite clothes and shoes on because it was the lowest period of my life. Wearing my favourite blue jeans, white long-sleeved shirt, and yellow hoodie.

Catching my reflection in a Yugo car window as I passed, I saw my hair was falling over my shoulders, all the way down to my stomach. Brown with some natural highlights flickering through like the sun trying to force its way through the branches of a one-hundred-year-old oak tree. I could never dye or cut it short; it was my favourite part of my body. I loved my hair, but that day even I hated how it looked. I was surprised at how skinny I appeared, which wasn't ideal, but it was hard to worry about trivial things like eating with how I was feeling. My shoulders were slouched; I never stood my full height even though I was quite tall. 'Walk with your shoulders back and your head held high. You are a Draganić!' my father's voice rang in my ears. Classic Balkan pride.

Suddenly, I felt a tap on my shoulder. I took out the one working headphone, leaving the broken one in my ear. I wasn't sure why I had both in when only one worked. It was my best friend Andjela Marjanović. 'Nina, why didn't you turn around? I was shouting out to you,' Andjela panted to me.

Andjela had her tennis bag on her back and was sweating. She must have just come from the courts. She trained every day and got time out of class during the winter to practise. Practice never went long, but it was always intense. 'If I can't accomplish what I want in ninety-minutes then it's not worth doing,' she would always say. It must have worked for her because she was the number three ranked junior girls' player in the world.

'Sorry, had my headphones in,' I said, as I pulled the broken headphone out that was just for show, and put them in my pocket, hitting pause on Ed's soothing melodies. *When I press play, I'll go back to the beginning; I can't listen to just half the song, that's insanity,* I thought. 'What's up?' I asked, struggling to act like I cared about what was happening at all.

'There's a big party tonight. Everyone's going. I want you to come with me,' Andjela said excitedly with a smile on her face, bouncing on the balls of her feet as if ready to return serve.

Andjela was possibly the most beautiful woman God had put on our green earth; even standing there without makeup on and sweating. She had an easy beauty about her. A kind of grace, and she carried that in her movement on the court. Her legs looked like they went up to her armpits. A skinny, yet powerful frame with those long limbs. Long blonde hair, and green eyes, which she would always use to say how special she was. 'Look at these eyes! This is two percent here. Never forget that you seventy-five-percent brown eyed basic bitch,' she would say, and we couldn't help but burst into fits of laughter. In my eyes, making fun of each other is a staple of any healthy relationship. It was my love language.

She was going to make an endless amount of money through tennis if she kept caring about it. It was strange that someone could be as beautiful as her, but it wasn't her best characteristic. It was her heart. It said a lot about how loyal and kind she was. Sometimes kind to an annoying level. She was amazing. I really loved her.

'I don't know. I'll see how I feel later. I'm pretty tired and have a lot of studying to do. Can I let you know?' I asked, trying to avoid her two percent eyes, hoping she would let something go for the first time ever.

'Yeah, sure thing. Just see how you feel, but I really want you to come with me,' she said, with a concerned look on her face.

'Nina, are you okay?' Andjela asked, trying to catch my eyes. When she did, I could see a concerned look that permeated her tone.

'I'm alright, just lots of work to do,' I said in a clearly unconvincing tone. It's difficult to lie to someone who has been your best friend since you were four years old. Also, I was the worst liar on the planet. It never stopped me from trying though.

'Well, I'm always just a phone call away. Remember that,' Andjela said. 'I'll see you later tonight…hopefully,' and she hugged me tightly.

'Thanks for the sweat,' I said, grossed out and feigning wiping it from my face.

'Sharing is caring,' she laughed as she turned and ran in the opposite direction towards her mother's car. Her mother Ivana waved to me as we caught each other's eye. I gave a half smile, waved, and turned towards home.

I continued my way home putting my half working headphones back in and let Ed's sweet lyrics flow through my heavy brain. My mind had been on a constant loop trying to figure out what I did to make him cheat on me. Maybe it was because I wasn't ready to sleep with him. Maybe he found his hoe. My mind constantly whirring like that had me desperate for a nap. Just to give me some respite from thinking.

The leaves were turning brown as trees fell asleep with autumn taking hold. I found trees and plants fascinating. The way they know to go to sleep to survive the winter until spring, where they come back to life in all their beauty. It's as if they say, 'yeah you forgot I was here, didn't you? Well, here are some beautiful flowers for you to see, just to remind you who I am'.

I looked up and saw the sun falling behind the mountains in the distance. They were completely covered in trees, but before long, they would be predominantly white with snow.

'Whoa,' I said, extending my leg out in a very uncoordinated way to avoid stepping on a crack in the pavement. The last thing I needed was to step on one and take another loss.

In Požega the trees ran along the side of the main road into town called Nikole Pašića, with their branches hanging over the sidewalk. The fallen leaves doing a great job of hiding all the cracks in the road. The street split ahead. If you turned left, you went towards Čačak, a town not too far from Požega, and if you turned right, you headed towards my house.

It was unusually warm for a November day. It would have been at least twenty-three degrees Celsius. Two young boys, maybe nine-years old, ran past me with a basketball. They must've been heading towards the basketball court near my house. It's the second most popular sport behind football in Serbia. Before long, it would be too cold to play basketball outside, when the snow hit our town which sat in the shadows of the mountains.

To the right there was a house and their corn field. As I looked left, I saw a field where there were a group of boys, including my brother Jovan playing. He had taken his shirt off for some reason. *'He has real problems keeping his shirt on. I hope he grows out of this phase, it's becoming weird,'* I thought, shaking my head with a wry grin. He was only eight-years old. He would get home later when he was finished playing with his friends. Jovan was always outside playing.

My mind drifted back to my ex, and the picture Andjela sent me that I hadn't yet deleted from my phone. Anytime I thought about him through the lens of rose-coloured glasses I would look at it to remind me of the boy he really was. When I looked at it, I felt like someone was twisting my stomach, like they were wringing out a wet towel. It hurt, but I couldn't delete it just yet.

I kept walking, but I had lost focus on the path and accidentally stepped on a crack in the pavement. I swore loudly in English, hoping that no one understood what I said. I was furious at myself. *'Everything bad happens to me,'* I thought, and kicked a small stone lying on the footpath, watching it bounce in front of me before veering onto the road. I fought off the urge to walk back to school and start again, instead choosing to take my loss and continue towards home.

I walked past the basketball court where there were a group of boys playing, and some girls waiting to get onto the court. *'I hope they get to play the boys and kick their butts,'* I thought, as one of the boys that ran past me air balled a three-point shot.

Travelling along the road that led to my house, below the train track overpass, I felt cold in the shadows. Unable to recall the last time I saw a train on those tracks, I wondered what route they travelled instead of that path now. A car arrived on the other side of the underpass, and they waited as I jogged to the other side. There wasn't enough room for a person and a car to go through at once.

Everyone was out the front of their houses enjoying what was likely the last of the warm weather before the cold days took hold. 'Hi, how are you? Good thanks,' I said to every house as I walked past. I had put my head down and just walked by the houses ignoring them before, but I heard about it from my mama later.

'Don't be rude, be polite to your neighbours,' I could hear Mama's voice softly in my ears.

A couple of street dogs ran down the street, but I had no idea what breed they were. Probably a mix which was normal for street dogs. I wanted to adopt them. All of them. When I was younger, I would bring home dogs from the street. 'You don't know where they've been,' Mama would say to me.

'Yes, I do, the streets,' I would snap back, upset I couldn't keep them. I hoped one day I could have a big farm and adopt them all. *Who needs boys when you could have dogs? At least a dog is loyal,'* I thought coldly, as the picture of my ex floated through my mind once more.

I finally turned left into the laneway that led to my house. It was a very faint shade of green, a colour which my brother, sister and I all picked out when Mama asked our opinion. It was two storeys, but we only lived on the bottom floor. The stairs to the top level were outside, next to the front door, and we only used it for storage, and the washing and drying machines. The house had a flat front, made from concrete, which helped to keep it warm during our freezing winters. There was a single four paned window on the second level looking over the laneway. We had a nice, big yard where my brother was normally playing, and a little table under the stairs where I would sit and drink my morning coffee, if there wasn't a metre of snow.

I opened the front door, but before I could take my headphones out or my shoes off, Mama was there greeting me just as I crossed the threshold of the house.

'Hi honey, how are you? How was school?' she asked immediately while taking my jacket and bag from me to hang on the hook next to the front door. Somehow, she did that without making me feel smothered. Mama was shorter than me, but that wasn't helped by her slouching. She had perfectly symmetrical eyebrows above her kind, brown eyes. Her face was framed by her chocolate brown hair, which looked like curtains to her stage. Her smile was one of calm, telling me that things would be okay.

'Okay,' I mumbled, answering both of her questions in one.

'Your tata called. The job's running long so he's going to be gone for at least another month,' Mama said, beginning her news of the day. My father was working on a construction project in Montenegro and had been gone for seven months. 'Don't forget we're going to Baka's house for lunch on Sunday. Make sure you don't make plans for that day,' Mama continued. We went to my grandmother's house almost every Sunday for lunch. 'What's wrong?' she asked in the same tone that Andjela asked with earlier, not taking a breath between the subjects.

'Nothing, I'm just tired. I saw Jovan on the way home. Where's Milica?' I asked, not seeing my sister's shoes inside the front door. Milica was twelve and like Jovan, always seemed to be out with her friends.

'She's studying with a friend,' Mama replied.

'I think I'm going to have a nap now,' I told Mama, feeling all my emotions weighing on me.

'Okay, honey. I'll come and wake you for dinner then?' she said, half asking and half telling.

'No, it's okay. I'm exhausted and I'm not hungry. If I don't wake up then just let me sleep through,' I said, failing to keep the defeated tone out of my voice.

'Well, just get a good sleep and you'll feel much better tomorrow,' Mama said. She hugged and kissed me on the cheek.

I walked to my room and closed the already open door behind me. The unmade bed I had left behind that morning was still there, but there was a notebook on it. *It must be a gift from Mama,'* I thought, feeling a surge of affection for her. I loved notebooks. I examined it closely and ran my hand across the cover and its binding. It was a calming royal blue, blank cover. Like my clothes, I liked things that weren't compromised with brands. *I can't wait to use this,'* I thought, smiling and staring upon it. Lifting it to my face, I closed my eyes and let the scent of new paper waft over me. So many associations of love are through our noses. We know what home smells like, or Baka's house smelling like everything she had ever cooked. Or that unique scent of a person you love. I walked across to my desk and placed the notebook down gently.

I took off my shirt and socks. I balled my socks up and shot them towards the dirty clothes basket, watching them in flight closely as they fell gently into the basket. I threw my shirt over the back of the chair at my desk and slid my jeans off before placing them on top of my shirt. Finally, I took my bra off saying aloud to myself, 'goodbye boobie prison'. I put on a big t-shirt and crawled into bed.

Pulling the covers all the way up to my neck I grabbed my spare pillow, my cuddle pillow. Lying on the right side of the bed, turning away from the drawn curtains where a small amount of light snuck into my room, I cuddled my pillow and drifted off to sleep. A stressless sleep.

'Nina! Nina! Come on, get up. We're going to the party,' Andjela said, as my eyes barely cracked open to see what was happening. She had turned the lights on and was already rifling through my closet. She pulled out my white jeans, black short-sleeve top that was cut down to the bottom of my sternum and threw them onto the bed.

'What are you doing?' I asked sleepily, trying to push myself up with my right arm. She was wearing a classical little black sleeveless dress. Her black leg strap heels added another ten centimetres to her already impressive height. It was no wonder she could cover the court so well.

'I'm taking charge and dragging you to the party. If I don't, you'll just lay here and feel sorry for yourself. That's not what we do. You need to get out and talk to people. Come on. Let's go and flirt with boys and give them fake phone numbers. I've already memorised the number from the pekara,' Andjela said, turning back from the closet having looked through the rest of it and concluding that there wasn't a better option than what she had already tossed on my bed. I knew she wouldn't let it go, but I just expected to wake up to twelve text messages and three missed calls from her.

I picked up my phone and saw that there was only one message, it was from my ex again. *I'm sure it's just the same rubbish about how he's sorry, it was a mistake, and he misses me. Blah, blah, blah,'* I thought bitterly. I opened the message and deleted it without reading it. I wanted him to see the read receipt and that I ignored him. The time read ten-twenty-six pm.

'Can't you just let me sleep? You should let me feel sorry for myself. I'm getting really quite good at it. The only party I want to go to is my pity party,' I drowsily said, dropping my head back to my pillow, wondering if I could somehow turn self-pity into a career. There's probably some position in the government for people that have that skill set, seeing as most employed at government level are useless.

'Nope. Here. You're wearing this. We're going and will be the two hottest girls there. Put your clothes on; I'm going to have the tea that your mama has made. You have ten minutes. Your time starts…now,' Andjela said as the seconds hand on my clock hit twelve, and she walked from the room before I could mount another protest.

I swore at her under my breath as I sat up on the edge of my bed. Standing up I looked at myself in the mirror. I looked like a mess with my hair going all over the place. Walking towards the mirror I closely examined my face. I had a small mole on the underside of my lip on the left. I liked that part of my face. I loved distinctive features. Things that others looked past I found interesting. And to me interesting is attractive. Naturally pink lips lying below a small nose. Freckles on my forehead, or as I liked to call it, fivehead. In my brown eyes you could see speckles of green. Maybe my eyes weren't as basic as Andjela joked. No one had ever noticed that detail before apart from my mama. The only person I let get close enough to see would be my ex, and he wouldn't notice if the Northern Lights made an appearance in his living room. *'Asshole,'* I thought, proud of myself for not looking at that photo again.

I put my jeans on first, struggling to get them over my hips and butt. *'I'm not sure how I'm so slim yet have this butt. I look like a Pixar mama,'* I thought as I buttoned them. Searching through the closet for a bra which Andjela had kindly let me select on my own, I put it on hoping that she didn't want me to go without one. The shirt was too low cut and had put my cute bra on display. I opened my closet and selected a different black shirt, slipping it on. I picked up my phone, ID, and heels, and walked to the kitchen. Passing the bathroom and my sister's room, I saw her door was open, but she was on her phone and listening to music.

Walking into the kitchen Andjela and Mama were deep in conversation while Jovan played with mama's phone. Jovan had a thick, strong body, and happy brown eyes. His smile spreading his big cheeks brought a joy to my life like nothing else. The TV was playing some Bollywood soap opera in the background that my mama loved.

'Oh Nina, please. Your hair. You could at least comb it. Sit down,' Mama demanded, and she opened a drawer to pull out a hairbrush. She stood behind me and combed my hair while Andjela finished her tea. There was a sponge on the table.

'I was going for a, I don't want to go look. Mama, why did you let her in? I was asleep,' I said as Mama continued to comb my hair and Andjela laughed from across the table looking at my miserable morning face.

'Well, you trying to hide your moods is like when you play hide and seek with a toddler. They will stand behind a chair giggling in the same room you started in thinking you can't see them. You think you have hidden it but you're miserable Nina. You need to go out with your friends and have a good time,' Mama said, as she finished brushing my hair.

'Okay, there. What do you think Andjela?' Mama asked, standing back to analyse my freshly combed hair.

'Beautiful. Come on, let's go,' Andjela said as she stood up and walked towards the front door.

'Nina, here,' Mama said as she handed me a two-thousand dinar note. 'Have fun, stay safe, and be careful. I'll leave my phone on, so if you need a ride please call. I love you.' Mama kissed me on the cheek.

'I love you too, Mama,' I replied with a forced smile, and I picked up my shoes and headed towards the door where Andjela was waiting.

'Thanks for the tea,' Andjela said to Mama, as I put my shoes on. Mama waved goodbye and closed the door behind us.

'Ready?' Andjela asked as we began to walk up the driveway.

'I hate you,' I replied, staring daggers at her out the corner of my eye.

'I love you too,' she said, wrapping me in a big hug and kissing me on the cheek.

'So where is this stupid party?' I grumbled to Andjela, while I looked up at the sky. It was a beautiful, clear night. So many stars in the sky. You couldn't help but feel small when you looked at the stars. It was the kind of night you would want to lay on a blanket with someone you love, starring at the sky, talking about life; well with someone or your dog. *'Now I would probably favour the dog,'* I thought, picturing the two dogs from earlier that day.

'The Sunshine Café. It's Marko's birthday. Did you get him something?' Andjela asked me jokingly.

'I didn't even know it was his birthday. His gift is my presence, and he should be eternally grateful that I'm coming because it's ruined my sleep,' I said, finally taking my eyes off the beautiful night sky. Andjela couldn't help but laugh.

'So, what did you do after tennis?' I asked.

'Have you ever heard of a site called worldvidcam.com?' she asked.

'Nope. What is it?'

'Basically, it matches your webcam with another random person's around the world. I go on there and talk to people sometimes. Spoke to a guy from England today. I even got his phone number. I won't text him though,' Andjela said, as if the whole thing was boring to her.

'Why not?'

'Why would I get close to someone in another country? What if I fall in love with him? That just sounds like a miserable existence. I'm not going to do that to myself,' Andjela finished as we continued to walk towards the café.

Fifteen minutes later we walked through the front door of the café and I felt like I had been punched in the face, the sensory overload was so significant. Music was blasting, lights were flashing, and people were squeezed in like sardines. There was a smell of sweat and alcohol mixed into one. It was impossible to move without bumping into someone. *I know Marko's popular, but I didn't expect anything like this. I'll have to start paying more attention,'* I thought, as I squeezed through the crowd, following Andjela. My heels stuck to the floor as Andjela and I worked our way through the room. We saw Marko and some of our friends on a raised platform, considered the VIP area, so we tried to wind our way towards them, battling through the packed bar. The VIP area had a rail around it, with a small set of stairs the only access to it.

It was hard to believe The Sunshine Café was a quiet café during the day considering it was a wild nightclub after dark. Normally at night I prefer a kafana. Serbian music being played by a live band that perform for different tables in turn. You see people standing on chairs, singing along and dancing. It's a festive atmosphere instead of the wild nightclub scene.

'Do you want to get a drink first? Then we can go upstairs and say happy birthday,' Andjela yelled directly into my ear, the only way to be heard over the music.

'Okay. I'll get the drinks,' I yelled back. Manoeuvring through the packed nightclub, I reached the bar. I leaned over the bar and the bartender turned his head to hear my order over the chaos. 'Can I have two rakija's please?' I asked, holding up two fingers.

He returned with a bottle of rakija and held it up to confirm he got the order correct. I gave him the thumbs up, so he proceeded to put two shot glasses down on the bar and poured the rakija. I handed over the money and I took both glasses, handing one to Andjela who had made her way to the bar to join me. 'Živeli,' we yelled in unison, clinking our glasses, and taking the rakija down in one, trying not to gag. Normally you sip rakija, but I needed a quick mood changer. Warmth spread through my body, all the way to my fingertips as I tried to shake the burning sensation in my throat. We placed our glasses on the bar before we navigated our way through the sea of people up the stairs to get to Marko and the VIP area.

'Hey! You guys made it!' Marko slurred as he saw Andjela and I appear at the top of the small set of stairs on the platform. He hugged us simultaneously. The smell of alcohol on his breath was overpowering. He stumbled backwards and looked me up and down as if he were a cyborg scanning my personal information in his database. It was as if he had never seen me before, even though we had known each other since we were six years old.

Marko stood a head above Andjela, his bulging muscles were setting a huge challenge to the buttons on his shirt, which looked like it could burst open at any moment. He had a serious face, short dark hair and brown eyes. Almost every girl at school thought he was hot, including Andjela….and I guess myself as well. If you could create in a lab the perfect physical specimen, Marko was what you would finish with. Marko and I were always the top two of the class in biology, so our professor put us together for a lot of group work. A person shouldn't be that attractive and smart, it was not fair to other people. The girls at school laughed at everything he said, but those were probably fake laughs because they were thirsty. I thought it was pretty embarrassing the way they acted around him.

'Happy birthday, Marko. Are you having a good time?' I asked, leaning in so he could hear me and touching his arm.

'Yeah, it's so much fun. Everyone came, it's crazy here. You two look great,' Marko yelled over the music. 'There's a couple of bottles here, just help yourself,' he gestured towards the table. His family was quite wealthy, so it was no surprise he was buying drinks for the party.

'Thanks heaps. We'll catch up with you later, man,' said Andjela, and she grabbed my arm and pulled me away towards the table of drinks. She poured each of us another rakija and we drank them quickly. 'How are you feeling?' she asked me.

'I'm alright. The rakija is definitely helping,' I said laughing. 'Do you want to go and dance?' I asked.

'Sure, let's go,' Andjela replied, and we walked back down the stairs to the dance floor.

I hated to admit when I was wrong, but Andjela and Mama were completely right. I needed to go to the party. It was so much fun dancing with Andjela. Not having to talk about what I was feeling. Whatever his name was being the furthest thing from my mind. Just enjoying being around my best friend.

I looked up to where Marko was standing with a gaggle of thirsty girls all hoping to be the one to gain his attention. I could see them fake laugh and toss their hair, looking embarrassingly desperate. He met my eyes for a moment and broke into a smile. I began to pick nervously at the ends of my fingers and turned quickly back to Andjela.

We continued to drink and dance as the night went on. We could have been doing it for twenty minutes or three hours, I had completely lost any idea of time. I sang horribly at the top of my lungs with everyone else in the café. 'I'm just going to the bathroom. I'll be back in a few minutes,' Andjela shouted, and she disappeared into the ocean of people.

I turned around and Marko was standing there, almost hovering over me. I absentmindedly resumed picking the ends of my fingers. 'Hey, having a good time?' he asked with the same strange look as when our eyes met before. His eyes looked glassed over and distant.

'Yeah. Andjela and I are having so much fun,' I replied. As I continued to dance, he closed the small space between us so that his body was pressed against mine. I was feeling increasingly uncomfortable but didn't feel like I had anywhere to go as I was surrounded with people. I wanted him away from me, but I didn't want to be rude to him on his birthday.

'I'm sorry to hear about you and your ex,' Marko said, leaning down and speaking into my ear. He was so close that I could feel his breath on me. I felt a cold shiver down my spine. I could smell his cologne that was masked earlier by alcohol. A musky scent assaulted my nasal cavity and made me feel immediately nauseous. My skin crawled while he placed his large hand on my hip. I peered into his eyes and he didn't look the slightest bit sorry about my ex, he almost looked happy. I was beginning to feel claustrophobic and could feel my breathing become shallow. I needed to get outside into the cool November night air.

Then he did it. He grabbed my face with one hand, while the hand that was on my hip reached around and groped my butt. He tried to kiss me, but I was able to pull my face away and wriggle free before he could force his mouth upon mine and then smacked his hand off my butt.

'What are you doing!?' I shouted angrily, pulling away from him, trying to put as much distance between us as possible. People continued to dance behind me and buffeted me back towards him.

'What do you think I'm doing? Come on. It's my birthday, give me a present. I mean, you've been looking at me all night. You touched my arm. You want it. I know you want me,' Marko said, trying to grab a hold of my body again.

I pushed him away, using all my restraint not to punch him. 'I don't want you. I have never wanted you, and I have no interest in you. Just leave me alone,' I screamed at him. All I wanted to do was go home and disappear under my covers for a few days. As I turned to leave the Sunshine Café, Andjela returned and saw the tears welling in my eyes and looked at Marko.

'What's going on here?' she asked angrily. Andjela looked like she was about to breathe fire through her flared nostrils as the heat rose in her cheeks.

'Nothing. Nina is just a tease... Bitch,' Marko said with spittle flying from his mouth.

In a flash Andjela stepped forward, as if jumping on a short ball and punched him flush on the nose. Blood exploded all over Marko's face. He grabbed his nose and fell to the ground with a thud that could be heard above the blaring music.

'You're the bitch, Marko. Loser,' Andjela said with contempt, looking down upon him with disgust as she grabbed my arm and marched me from the café before he could respond.

'I'm sorry, Nina. He's just pathetic,' Andjela said when we reached the salvation that was outside. I walked towards home, wanting to put as much distance between myself and that pig. Despite her long legs, Andjela struggled to keep up.

'It's not your fault,' I said, as I stopped walking and turned to face her. 'You were just trying to help me, and I love you so much for it. I really was having a great time until that. I just want to go home though. I'll see you at school on Monday,' I said, kissing Andjela on the cheek, and I turned to walk home.

I can't believe he thought that about me. Does everyone have that opinion of me or is it just him? The boys here are proving that they don't even have a basic level of respect. I don't think girls are really that hard to figure out. All I really want is someone that treats me with respect, and cares about me. Blue eyes would be nice as well though, now that I think about it,' I thought as I continued along the path towards home. Hot tears began to fall from my eyes. I let them fall freely, hidden in the night.

Without paying attention, I was walking through the front door. I took my heels off with a groan. *'Why do I do this to myself?'* I thought, looking at them with disdain and tossing them onto the pile of shoes just inside the front door. I walked into my room and shut the door behind me. I felt dirty, desperately needing a shower to wash the filth from me, but it was after one am, and I didn't want to wake the rest of the house.

'There's no way I can sleep right now after that,' I whispered to myself.

I threw my clothes of the day from the chair and sat at my desk, opening my laptop. It sprung to life with its wake-up sound. 'Shhhh. Wow that was aggressive,' I whispered to my computer, as if it would listen to me, and I loaded up the internet.

I had no idea where I wanted to go, but the site that Andjela mentioned earlier came to mind. I typed worldvidcam into the search engine. It appeared immediately. I clicked on the link and proceeded to press the connect button on the site.

'Waiting for stranger' the page read. I waited patiently with no idea what I was about to be confronted with. I looked at the box showing my face on the screen and saw my eyes glistening with the night's tears.

'I hope their internet connection is poor so they won't be able to see my tears. At least I didn't put makeup on tonight,' I thought, trying to wipe the proof of my sadness from my eyes.

A man popped up into the previously black box. The most beautiful blue eyes I had ever seen looked at me. No, not at me, into me.

'Hi,' he typed, with a beaming smile spread across his face.

Wow,' I thought, feeling the misery of the night disappear in an instant and be immediately replaced with butterflies exploding in my stomach.

CHAPTER TWO
The Funeral

'Are you ready, Luka?' asked my mother Milena as she adjusted my tie. I was wearing the same suit we bought for my Year Twelve Formal five years earlier. Mum thought I would fill out and grow into it. Oh, how wrong she was. It was hanging off me like I was freshly released from prison and going for a job interview to stack shelves at the local supermarket. Even though at twenty-two years of age I should have probably just bought myself a new one.

'Maybe tomorrow's the day that I magically begin to look like a twenty-two-year-old man instead of a seventeen-year-old secondary school student. It's okay though, I have a new black tie for the occasion,' I thought sarcastically.

'Yeah,' I replied. I wasn't really, but that didn't matter. It was time. Walking up to the microphone in front of a church full of people, I closed my eyes and took a deep breath. It felt like the most important thing I had done in my life.

As I stood behind the microphone and looked upon the coffin of my beloved Nana, six pallbearers from my family walked towards it. I caught my father John's eye, and he gave me an encouraging smile. Dad was at the front. Pretty regulation for Dad, he never wanted to follow anyone. The six pallbearers stood waiting for me to begin.

Nana had been sick for a long time, but that didn't make it any easier. The matriarch of the family had passed on. I looked down at the guitar that was hanging from a brown strap across my shoulder and could see my heartbeat causing it to move. *This might be a convenient little metronome,'* I thought.

I loved playing songs for Nana. I remembered when I got that guitar for my birthday, she made me play a song for her immediately. She even heckled me to hurry up because I was taking too long to tune the guitar. The guitar was tuned perfectly already though; I was just buying time because I was so nervous my hands were shaking. She requested 'You Are My Sunshine'.

I would visit her as often as I could. She would make us both a cup of tea, bring out the sweet teddy bear biscuits, and we would talk. Whenever I had a song to play, she would be the first one to hear it. Nothing could ever make me feel better than seeing her smile at something I had created. *I miss her. I loved her. No, that's not true. I love her,'* I thought, with a twang of pain in my chest.

With each passing second it felt increasingly difficult to not completely fall apart. It was my chance to tell everyone in the church how special Nana was to me. How special she was to everyone. How things couldn't possibly be the same without her.

I hit the first chord, and as I did, in unison, Dad, and five members of my extended family lifted my beloved Nana's remains to their shoulders. Supporting each other, they carried her down the aisle of the church. It was a strange scene watching six men cry together. It showed just how amazing she was.

'This is for you Nana,' I said to myself, careful to not say it into the microphone, as a tear rolled down my cheek and landed on my guitar. I sang with every ounce of passion and emotion I had in my soul.

Happy endings don't exist,
They always end with tears like this.
But I choose to stand in memories,
Where your face shines happy.
Serenity lived in talks with you,
Over bowls of veggie soup.
And while my world is just not right,
I know you're looking down from paradise.

You'll be in the tea I make Mum,
And my walks in the sun.
You'll be in every lyric I write,
And every song that is sung.
You'll be in the eyes of my children,
And the hearts left beating.
Alone I know I'll never be,
Because my guardian angel lives with me.

I think of all the things I'll miss,
It feels like a never-ending list.
Your soothing hugs,
Reminding me I'm loved.
In your presence I always felt safe,
And saw that things would be okay.
I hope one day to be like you,
And find love in every day anew.

You'll be in the tea I make Mum,
And my walks in the sun.
You'll be in every lyric I write,
And every song that is sung.
You'll be in the eyes of my children,
And the hearts left beating.
Alone I know I'll never be,
Because my guardian angel lives with me.

You always saw beauty in the world,
No matter how large, or how small.
I hope I'll make you proud of me,
Until the day we enjoy another tea.

You'll be in the tea I make Mum,
And my walks in the sun.
You'll be in every lyric I write,
And every song that is sung.
You'll be in the eyes of my children,
And the hearts left beating.
Alone I know I'll never be,
Because my guardian angel lives with me.

I put down my guitar, wiped the silent tears from my cheek and followed the rest of the congregation from the church. I stepped outside. It seemed overcast above the church on Ballarat Road. I looked up and there was only one cloud in the sky blocking the sun. *'God must be watching this,'* I thought smiling. People were crying, talking, hugging, and passing along condolences to one another.

Mum walked up to me and hugged me with Dad standing beside her. 'She would have been so proud of you. Every time you visited her, she would call me right after you left and tell me that you visited. I could hear how happy you made her. You made her feel so special,' Mum said with tears in her eyes.

Mum and Dad were older than most when they had children. My sixty-year-old mother Milena had a slight build but was quite tall. Those kind hazel eyes bearing contact lenses. Her dyed auburn hair fell to her chin in a bob cut. Well, I assumed she coloured it; she was sixty after all.

My dad John with his wavy hair that was mainly grey being sixty-four, still had the remnants of the black hair of his youth that he claimed to be brown. 'It's just really dark brown,' he would say to me. Yeah, so dark it was black. He was an average height for a man and had a slim build. An incredibly happy face that supported a pair of glasses.

I couldn't hold it in anymore. The emotion of the day and singing my nana's song was too much for me. That was that. I cried my eyes out as Mum hugged me. I cried on my Mum's shoulder with Dad's hand on my back. It was one thing to think you knew what you meant to someone, but hearing how special I was to Nana made my soul glow. People can say don't give me words, give me actions. Well, I had always thought we needed both. We need actions that follow through on the words.

I stood up straight and wiped the tears from my eyes, hoping that no one else would see. I didn't like people knowing I had feelings, which was tough to convince people of after singing that song. My younger brother Aleks and younger sister Maja walked over to us, breaking away from a conversation with my cousin James.

Aleks clapped me on the shoulder and Maja kissed me on the cheek. 'Cool song,' said Aleks with a grin on his face.

'It was so beautiful. When did you write it?' Maja asked.

'I wrote it last night. Not ideal to leave it to the last minute, but I feel like I need the stress of time pressure to write. I think it worked out okay,' I said, shrugging my shoulders with a half grin. Maja laughed along with Dad.

'Left it to the last minute huh? I guess the clutch gene runs in the family then,' Aleks said. He was an elite basketball talent. Standing head and shoulders above the rest of us at just eighteen years old, with broad shoulders, long and slim arms, as if God personally sculpted him to play basketball. He was skinny, but that wasn't going to last long. He had a full scholarship to play basketball in America. He delayed it twelve months due to how sick Nana was. His eyes were firmly on playing professionally in the States.

'Well two of you are then, think I missed that one,' said Maja.

'That's not true at all. You routinely get into trouble at school and somehow under the pressure of a teacher's questioning, manage to talk your way out of it. I think you all have this crutch gene. Thank your father and I, you obviously got it from us,' Mum said, with a tone of stating the obvious.

Maja, Aleks and I chuckled shaking our heads. Dad stifled a laugh. 'It's a *clutch* gene Mum. What on earth is a crutch gene?' Aleks asked, still laughing.

'Oh, I don't know. Close enough is good enough,' Mum said, slightly embarrassed, her cheeks turned a rose red, as if she had one glass of wine too many.

Maja's face had lit up from laughing and you could really see how beautiful she was. Still only sixteen years old, but already taller than Mum. Long dark hair with light blue eyes. Maja and I looked more like siblings than we did with Aleks.

'You are all talented,' said Dad dismissively, looking at his watch. 'Okay, Robertson's, I think it's time that we went to the wake. We need to help finish setting things up at Nana's house. Luka, go and grab your things and meet the rest of us there, okay?'

'Sure, Dad,' I replied, and walked back inside the church. It was empty apart from the support for the coffin and a large photo of Nana. I walked past the photo, unplugged my guitar, and put it back in the case. I began to make my way out of the church but before I did, I stopped and turned to look at her photo.

Nana had come to Australia with my Pa and Mum, who was the eldest of four children. Three girls and one boy. They arrived from a town called Požega, Serbia when my Mum was just one year old. It was extraordinary to me the life they built together. Arriving in a country where they didn't speak the language and had little money; working hard to make a new home, and there was a church full of people to say goodbye. It was a church filled with love.

'Goodbye Nana, please watch over me. I'll try to make you proud,' I said aloud to her photo, turning on my heel and walking from the church.

I decided to take the scenic route and walked through the side door because I felt like I needed some time to be alone. Most people had probably headed to the wake, but I didn't want to risk running into anyone. The sun had come out from behind the cloud and all of a sudden, I felt very warm. *'I guess God's moment of mourning for one of His favourites is over,'* I thought.

Maidstone was a working-class area. Lots of immigrants lived there and they formed their own little communities inside the larger Melbourne area. I crossed the busy Ballarat Rd and continued down Studley St towards Nana's house.

I walked through the front door and people were everywhere. Striding purposefully down the hall, I placed my guitar in Nana's bedroom. Making my way from the bedroom, I was greeted by my entire family with a hug, congratulations on my song and a look of consolation for our loss. I barely made it two steps before being stopped again. And again. And again. I really didn't want to be there. There were so many people it was making me feel anxious. That combined with the emotion of the day, it all just felt like too much.

Continuing to work my way through the packed house, I searched for my cousin James. There were people laughing and telling funny stories about Nana. Nana never drove, so the story of Pa trying to teach her while they were on holiday was being told in different versions throughout the house. In one Pa grabs the wheel from her, in one she hits the accelerator instead of the brake and collides with a tree. 'Don't let the truth get in the way of a good story,' Dad would always say.

I finally found James sitting at a table in the backyard looking at his phone.

'Hey, how's it going?' he asked, dragging his eyes away from the basketball game he was watching.

'Yeah alright. This day's just a lot to deal with. For everyone. How have you been?' I asked.

'Yeah alright. Finished uni last week so haven't been doing much. Watching television and going online. Have you ever heard of a site called worldvidcam.com?' he asked.

'No. What is it?' I replied curiously.

'Just a site that matches your webcam with random people around the world. I spoke to some guy in America about basketball. A girl in Sweden too. In unrelated news, I will be moving to Sweden. It looks nice. Wow,' he said winking, and I couldn't help but laugh.

'Nah I haven't heard of it before. It sounds cool,' I replied absentmindedly.

'That was a great song, Luka,' James said in mild surprise. 'I didn't even know you played. How long have you been keeping this secret?' he asked. It was weird that I never told him or my other best friend Michael that I played. Maybe I liked having my own thing that I could do just for fun without being asked to perform. Different rules applied for Nana though.

'About five years. To be fair to you, the only person outside of my house that knew I played before today was Nana. I would just play in my room alone,' I told him.

'Are we still talking about the guitar?' James asked, playfully punching me on the shoulder.

'You're hilarious,' I said sarcastically.

James and I grew up together. He was a cousin by marriage when his father married my aunt. He was tall, strong, and there was no other way to put it, had a beautiful face. Did I mention he was incredibly intelligent too? He was almost finished studying to be a physiotherapist. Sometimes God does give with both hands.

'So, you've never played in front of a crowd before today? Why?' James asked.

'Yeah. Well, it's pretty terrifying getting up in front of a crowd of people and playing a song that you wrote,' I replied.

'Then why would you do it today? That was a big crowd and an incredibly emotional time. I think that would be harder than playing in front of a group of drunks in a bar.'

'This was the last time I could play for Nana,' I said, lowering my head. He put a hand on my shoulder, and I looked up to see him smiling. We always made fun of each other but knew the moments to be supportive. He wasn't just my cousin; he was one of my best friends.

'Good point. I'm sure she loved it. Everyone else did. Well, everyone apart from Great Aunty Ellie, but she still maintains to this day that penicillin was a mistake. People are just soft,' he finished with a spot-on impression of ninety-two-year-old Aunty Ellie.

'Seriously Luka, you need to play in front of people. You have a gift, and you need to share that with everyone. I have a friend that runs a bar in the city, and he's always looking for people to play. Every time I go there the band really sucks. I think he'd want you to play there. Actually, I recorded your song in the church. Your Mum told me before the service you were singing and asked me to record it. I'm going to show it to him, and I know he'll be begging for you to play. I'll talk to him; just please tell me you'll think about it?' he finished imploringly.

'Okay, I will,' I said softly. I could see why he dated so many beautiful women. He was difficult to say no to. 'I think I'm going to head home now. It's been a pretty long day.'

'Yeah, sure thing. I'll give you a call during the week and we'll hang out,' James said.

'Sounds good,' I replied as I stood up. James stood up with me, shook my hand and pulled me in for a hug. James was a hugger, but I wasn't, so obviously we hugged. James turned his attention back to the basketball game he shouldn't have been watching, and I headed towards the house.

I walked back into the house and saw my dad there pouring a glass of red wine. 'Hey Dad. I've had enough. Just letting you know I'm going home now,' I told him.

'Okay, mate, no problem. Just make sure you see Mum before you go,' Dad said.

'Do you know where she is?' I asked.

'No idea. She could be anywhere. She couldn't have gone far though,' he said as he went back to his wine. As far as Dad was concerned there was only red wine. White wine was just a waste of a good bottle. If a waiter asked him whether he wanted red or white, he would say, 'there's only one kind of wine,' and then heartily laugh at his own joke. The sign of a great joke is when you tell it, and you are the only person laughing.

'See you at home, Dad,' I said, and made my way through the rest of the house on my search for Mum. I walked towards Nana's bedroom to get my guitar. I tried to slip through the packed hall without touching anyone, the same game I used to play in secondary school. Sliding through the small gaps with my slight frame between the different groups of chatting people, I made it to Nana's room. I gave a small fist pump in celebration of my victory.

Next to the window looking out upon the white roses in the front yard was Mum sitting alone, in Nana's old chair. She saw me come into the room out of the corner of her eye and gave me a half smile with a glistening tear, threatening to fall down her cheek. I walked over and sat on the ground with my back to the wall, hoping a spider wouldn't climb onto me from the windowsill.

'Are you okay, Mum?' I asked, and she turned to look at me.

'Not really. She was sick for a long time, but it's still a shock. Someone that you spoke to almost every day of your life is no longer here. Every night like clockwork she would call at eight. This last week I've still found myself taking the phone to the couch so I wouldn't have to get up to get it when she called. As it turns out, when a person dies, they don't call anymore. Your grandfather would always walk down the side of the house and through the back door. He died fifteen years ago, and still when I hear a sound outside, I look around half expecting to see him coming through the back door. I will never get used to this. At different times in your journey things happen that change your life forever. Meeting your spouse, having children, and when someone who's so close to you that they feel like a part of you is no longer around. Things will never feel the same again,' she finished, and looked back out of the window.

'It isn't easy for anyone. She's your mum so I can't imagine how hard it is for you. I'm heartbroken, but I feel lucky. Lucky that I got to spend so much time with such a special woman. I mean look at the church today. It was completely packed. She touched so many lives, and we were a couple of the lucky few that got to be really close to her,' I said quietly, taking hold of Mum's hand and squeezing.

'Thank you. I love you,' she told me as I stood up.

'I love you too. I think I'm going to go though. I've really had enough and just want to go home. Is that okay?' I asked.

'Sure. Drive safely,' Mum said as I kissed her on the forehead, picked up my guitar and walked towards the door.

As I reached the door I paused and turned around to look at my mum staring through the window upon Nana's beautiful white roses. 'Do you know how I know that Nana was a great mum?' I asked, and Mum shook her head. 'It's you. You're the best mother someone could ever have, and I have no doubt that a lot of that came from Nana. Never forget that while she isn't here, her imprint will be here forever. Through you. I'll see you at home,' I said, and walked from the room before Mum had a chance to respond.

I put my head down and walked quickly from the house. Straight to my car, putting my guitar on the back seat and I drove home.

I walked through the front blue gate of our Williamstown family home as the afternoon sun had begun to fall, it was hard to see the two-storey weatherboard house which had been home for as long as I could remember. A white house with blue trim. Remnants of an old tree house in the one-hundred-year-old blue spruce tree that made it almost impossible to see the house from the street. I placed my guitar just inside the front door which I had no doubt would draw the ire of my mother, but sometimes it was better to ask for forgiveness than ask for permission. Getting it up the stairs felt like a problem for future Luka.

I headed straight for the backyard where my dog would be looking over his territory. Down the hallway I passed my parents room and their bathroom on the right, the lounge and dining rooms on the left, continued past Maja's room next on the right and the stairs leading to Aleks' room and my room. The hallway led into the kitchen and living room in an open plan.

In a time of great emotional stress, I just needed to pat my dog to ease the tension of life. I walked through the kitchen and living room and opened the back door. As if expecting me, our little white and light brown Cavoodle stood at the backdoor with his tail wagging. He didn't notice that I was gone but he was excited to see me.

'Hi Monty, missed you today buddy,' I said, as I crouched down to pat him, and he immediately rolled onto his back wanting his belly rubbed. He was always a tripping hazard because he would throw himself in front of you and if you weren't watching you could be lying on your back next to him.

As I sat down on the deck he sat beside me quietly, very mellow. Dogs have an incredible innate ability to match your emotional energy. At that time, I just needed a friend to sit in silence with, and he knew exactly what to do. Normally he would fall asleep in no time, but not that day. He wanted to make sure he stayed awake to keep me company. 'I love you, Monty,' I said, continuing to stroke his soft coat.

We sat for what felt like hours with no real thoughts going through my mind while night fell. I was in almost a fugue state, my hand running up and down Monty's spine. It felt like the first time in forever that my brain had stopped for a minute. *This is what it feels like when your mind isn't racing. It's nice,'* I thought, closing my eyes, wishing I experienced it more often.

I listened to the rustling of the cherry plum tree as the wind blew its branches and finally, I felt like it was time for bed. I gave Monty one final pat, stood, and walked through the back door.

Up the stairs, I walked into the bathroom to brush my teeth and wash my face, then went into my room. It was relatively small with just space for a bed, bedside table and a mirror in the corner. I took off my ex-convict suit and threw it on the floor. Another problem for future Luka to worry about. I was left in just my underwear and caught a glimpse of myself in the mirror. I turned and walked towards it, stopping an arms-length from the mirror and looked at myself. I felt a sudden electrical pulse surging through my body all the way to my fingertips. I hated the person in the mirror. A boiling hatred for him as if I had just witnessed him murdering my mother. *I'm so ugly. Disgusting,'* I thought with a burning loathing. Short and messy brown hair sat atop my head, my blue eyes the only thing I liked about myself. A slightly large nose, small mouth and large teeth. Below average height and a very skinny body with shoulders slightly rounded. Moles spread across my body from the dangerous Australian sun. I felt sick looking at that repulsive face and body.

'Maybe that one will turn into a melanoma and kill you,' I said to the creature that stared back at me in the mirror with my finger on a mole on my shoulder. 'That won't happen though, you're not that lucky. No wonder no girls want to date you, I mean look at you. You are disgusting. Better get used to rooms like this because you're going to be on your own forever. You are a loser, Luka,' I spat, finishing my pep talk. I continued to stand and stare at myself with a look of repulsion for a couple more minutes because I was a glutton for punishment. Finally, breaking away from the mirror, I turned the light off and crawled into bed like the creature I was.

I heard the rest of my family come into the house soon after as I laid there staring at the back of my eyelids. I could feel it was going to be a sleepless night. My heart was racing with hatred for myself, and I had no way of slowing it down. I felt like I wanted to cry to release the pressure I was feeling on my chest, the weight of an elephant sitting on me, but I couldn't let it out.

The minutes turned into hours as I laid there. I couldn't switch my mind off, but there was nothing coherent running through it. The little self-loathing pity party I threw myself before bed was always a great way to have a sleepless night. I just wanted a break from feeling terrible. Some respite from what I was feeling. I was tired of feeling like that. I turned on my bedside lamp and found a packet of sleeping tablets there. I took two from the packet that said one tablet per dose and swallowed them down in one gulp with the water that always sat on my bedside table; a staple of someone who breathes through their mouth when they sleep, constantly waking up with a mouth bone dry. I turned off the lamp and looked at the time; it was just after one. I rolled over and closed my eyes.

I must have fallen asleep immediately after swallowing the pills because when I opened my eyes and grabbed my phone it was ten past nine in the morning. I sat up and took off the covers. Knowing that if I decided to lay there for the coming hours my brain would revisit that place of verbal self-abuse I knew too well.

I got out of bed and threw on a grey hoodie and navy tracksuit pants. Walking downstairs there was no one to be found. I had finished university for the year where I was studying a Bachelor of Sport Science. I loved sport but picked that degree to buy myself time to figure out what I wanted to do with my life.

The rest of my family must have been out. A note was sitting on the table saying Mum, Dad and my sister were out for brunch and my brother was at basketball practice. I poured myself a glass of orange juice and walked into the dining room where Dad's laptop was set up. I opened it and immediately found myself on Dad and my favourite footy team's website. That club may be the greatest sign that I liked to psychologically abuse myself. Dad and I always went to games together and saw them get killed. You know you're ashamed of your club when people ask who you follow, and you look at your shoes while uttering that dirty word in footy, 'Melbourne'.

The site I heard James mention at Nana's house floated through my mind, worldvidcam.com. Curious, I entered the URL and hit enter. I clicked connect and it said, 'Waiting for stranger,' as I waited for it to load.

'Next, next, gross, why is he doing that?' I thought, as I continued to skip through people, unsure as to what I was looking for.

A woman appeared, with an angelic face and the most beautiful brown eyes with flecks of green I had ever seen. It's as if I could see them sparkle through the screen. It was probably the fastest anyone had ever pressed three buttons on a computer before when I typed 'Hi,' and enter. I couldn't help but smile.

CHAPTER THREE
The Meeting

There was a dejected and broken expression on his face that immediately changed into a beaming smile when I smiled at him. There is something beautiful about seeing someone look down, and then that expression change as soon as they see you. I felt a warmth spread through my entire body seeing his face light up. He had the most beautiful blue eyes I had ever seen. I felt like they were staring into the deepest part my soul. So often you can feel like a man is looking at you in an objectifying way, but not him. He was staring at me like he was seeing me, like he really saw me, causing me to twirl my hair around my finger. No one had ever looked at me like that before. I will remember that first look for as long as I live.

'Hi,' I replied, almost as quickly as he had typed to me.

'What's your name?' had appeared on my screen in no time. He was either the fastest typist to ever live, or incredibly enthusiastic. I liked enthusiasm, especially when it came from a smile like that.

'I'm Nina. What's your name?' I replied immediately.

'I love that name. It's beautiful. It suits you. My name's Luka. It's great to cyber meet you,' he said, and looked to be laughing at his own horrendous joke. I felt worried that he had kids, because a joke like that could only come from a dad.

'Thanks, you're sweet. I like your name too. It's very European,' I said, trying to figure out where he was from. The sun was shining through the windows behind him, where lots of family photos sat on the windowsill. Clearly, he wasn't in Europe, it was after midnight in Serbia.

'Where are you from?' he asked, trying to figure out the same thing as me, but giving up on the investigation.

'I'm from Serbia. It's a small country in Eastern Europe. Do you know of it?' I asked. His face dropped. *Did he hate Serbia?* I worried. Concern washed over me because his smile had disappeared.

'No way, that's unbelievable. My grandparents moved to Australia from Serbia when my mum was only one. Where in Serbia are you from?' Luka asked, that beaming smile returning to his face. Relief spread through my chest, seeing his joy return.

'I'm from a small town a couple of hours outside of Belgrade. It's called Požega. It's nice and quiet, but sometimes I think it would be nice to be closer to the city. It can get a bit insular at times,' I finished typing. As I was looking at the keys to type, I hadn't noticed his mouth was hanging open as if I had just spontaneously combusted on screen. 'What?' I asked Luka. I was really confused. He wasn't moving so maybe he had frozen. *He's so cute, please don't tell me his internet connection has gone,'* I thought stressfully.

'Please tell me you're lying. Is this some sort of practical joke? Are you even a real human?'

'Yes, I'm real. What's wrong?' I asked, not sure whether to laugh or be annoyed.

'It's just that you're the most beautiful woman I've ever seen, and you're from Požega. Are you a hacker that's somehow found out my entire family history in five minutes?' Luka asked, looking like he was having a mild stroke. He sent each sentence in a separate text. I had to mute my laptop as each text prompted a small bing noise. I liked that he texted in that way. I always texted in the same fashion.

'No. It's really where I live. Wait,' I said while I reached for my purse and pulled out my ID. I banked on him not being an international predator that was going to write down my information and then travel to my house to attack me. It seemed like there would be more convenient targets if that was his game.

I held up my ID to the camera to show him an address that said Požega. 'Do you believe me now?' I asked, still confused as to why he was acting so strangely.

'Yeah. Sorry if I came off like a jerk. You probably won't believe me either, but that's where my grandparents lived before deciding to move to Australia.'

'Really?' I asked, unable to keep the look of scepticism from my face. Sometimes guys will lie to make you think you have things in common or a connection just to get closer to you.

'Yeah. Mum was born there. My grandfather died when I was young, so I didn't know him too well, but I spent a lot of time with my grandmother. She always spoke about going back and seeing Požega again, but it just never happened. She passed away a week ago and we had her funeral yesterday. I've always wanted to go and see where my family came from,' Luka finished. There was a look of sincerity on his face, in his eyes, and I knew that he wasn't lying.

I was lost for words for a moment, which didn't happen often. I had always thought that when something seemed too good to be true, that it was. *Is this another one of those occasions? He does feel genuine though. It could all be a ploy of his to get me to open up. That would be crazy though, wouldn't it? This is the internet after all, the home of crazy. Who knows, most guys have awful game,'* I thought, unable to come to a conclusion, but I was intrigued enough to want to keep talking.

'I'm really sorry to hear about your grandmother. If you ever come to Požega, we'll have to try and find your family's house here. Was she sick or was it a surprise?' I asked.

'She had a stroke and struggled for a while until she finally gave in. She fought an incredible fight.'

'That must have been devastating when you found out. I can't even imagine,' I texted, leaning forward in my chair. Luka's eyes drew me in; I wanted to jump through the screen and sit at the table with him to talk so I could feel those eyes in person.

'Something like that, even when you're expecting it every day, it comes as a shock when it finally happens,' Luka said, and I could see the sadness in his face.

They must have been close,' I thought, feeling a twang in my chest. 'I've been lucky that no one close to me has passed away. I can't imagine how I would handle it. I'm sorry your family is going through that,' I texted, hoping he could feel my sorrow for his loss in the words on his screen. I felt the need to put a consoling hand upon his arm. It must have been why he looked so broken at first. If it was my grandmother, I would be hidden in my bed for weeks.

'Thank you. You're very kind,' Luka said, and while he was smiling, I could see the hurt, the sadness in those perfect blue eyes.

We looked at each other for a moment as I tried to think of something to say. 'So, you're Australian then?' I asked, deciding to move the conversation to something less hurtful to him.

'Yeah. We live in Melbourne. It's where my grandparents decided to come.'

'Why Melbourne?" I asked, determined to learn as much as I could about Luka.

'I actually asked Nana why they decided to move here, and she told me that she was born for the sun, not for the snow,' he texted, and I saw the joy return to his smile at the memory of talking to his grandmother. 'So, how old are you?'

'I'm eighteen,' I lied to him. *What if he's twenty-something and doesn't talk to me if I tell him I'm seventeen?'* I wondered in a panic. I wanted to continue talking to him. I needed to know him better. It was a reaction, but I wasn't going to correct myself. The kindness I saw in his eyes and that cute smile couldn't disappear from my life, not yet anyway. I know it sounds crazy, but I already felt something special. I knew he would be important to me.

'How old are you?' I asked. *Please don't be younger, please don't be younger,'* I prayed silently to myself.

'I'm twenty-two. I hope that's not a weird age difference for you.' Luka looked a little anxious. I felt vindicated in my decision to lie. He looked nervous about the age difference, but that wasn't an issue to me.

'No. The boys at my school are immature and disrespectful. I had an experience like that tonight at a birthday party, so it's nice talking to someone who is mature for once.'

'I've lied well if you think I'm mature. You can tell me in a month if you still think I am. Are you in university or school?' Luka asked.

'My last year of high school. I don't know if I'm excited or sad to be finishing. If I decide to go to university, I'll have to move to Belgrade. It's a scary idea to move a couple of hours away from home, leaving your friends and family. I don't have to worry about that for a while so I'm going to try and avoid thinking about it,' I said with a wry smile. I hadn't spoken to anyone about that. I already felt like I could tell him my deepest fears and secrets. Those kind eyes made me feel safe, that he already cared about me and would listen to any concern on my mind.

'That sounds daunting. Change is never easy. It does sound scary, but it sounds exciting too. Just because something is different doesn't necessarily mean that it's going to be worse. It could be the best thing you ever do.'

'I didn't think of it that way,' I texted, feeling a calm wash over me.

'I live with my parents so you're more of a grown up than me. I think my parents will change the locks on me soon if I don't move out. I know that I would if I was them,' he texted, and he began laughing.

'I should apologise to you though,' he said, his smile changing to a serious look suddenly.

'Why?' I asked. He hadn't done anything to be sorry for, well maybe just not believing that I lived in Požega, but he had already apologised for that.

'I feel like such a creep staring at you like I am.' I covered my mouth to stifle a laugh. He had me worried for a moment. 'I just can't seem to look away. You are so beautiful. I can't help it,' he said, nervously looking off camera as if wanting to know what his next line was. I got the feeling he didn't have a lot of experience with women.

'You are cute. I had a tough night, so talking to you has been the highlight of my day. You can keep looking at me like that all you want. You're not making me uncomfortable at all. Quite the opposite actually,' I texted him reassuringly. Usually, I had my walls up and it would take a long time for me to feel comfortable around someone new, but there was something different about Luka. An immediate comfort and trust. That was dangerous with a new person because I was ready to spill my life story and that could scare him off. I knew Andjela would say that I should reign myself in and play it cool, but I didn't want to, I wanted to share the real Nina with Luka.

'Thank you. You're really kind. You may or may not have noticed but I have barely stopped smiling the entire time we've been talking. There isn't anything medically wrong with my face, I just love talking to you,' he said.

'His face must be getting sore with all this smiling,' I thought, hoping it would never disappear.

He tried to make a serious face. Maybe he thought he seemed too interested and wanted to play it cool, but that lasted about half a second before he broke into another wide jubilant grin. I had been trying to figure out what was different about his smile than everyone else's, and then it clicked. It was the eyes. He smiled with his eyes, and that is where the beauty in a smile lies. That is the true magic in a beautiful smile.

I was a generally sceptical person. People will tell you what they think you want to hear to get something from you, but I didn't get that feeling from Luka. He was real. He wasn't rare. He was unique.

'Hang on one second,' I typed. I couldn't believe myself. We had been talking for a long time and I hadn't heard his Australian accent. I liked accents. British, French, Irish, but my favourite had always been Australian. I raced to my bedside table and grabbed my half working headphones, slightly concerned that when I got back to my laptop he would be gone. I plugged them in to the headphone jack, looked up and felt relieved as he was waiting patiently for me.

'Okay, so you claim you are Australian. You wanted proof before that I'm from Požega, now I want proof that you're Australian. I want to hear your accent,' I typed, smiling. I don't think that there is a woman on this earth living outside of Australia that doesn't think it's attractive.

'I don't even know what I should say. You're really putting me on the spot here,' Luka texted, looking nervous.

'I couldn't care less what you say. You could say my butt hurts from the huge pimple on it for all I care,' I said, wondering why I had to pick that particularly graphic example. I was glad that it was tough to read tone through text because it would have come out a bit too aggressively if I had said it out loud, so strong was my desire to hear his voice. Feeling like he might need a little extra nudge, I gave him a flirty smile. Well, what I hoped was a flirty smile. I saw in the box of my video that I was twirling my hair around my finger again. *Why do I keep doing this?'* I wondered. I wanted to hear him say my name but thought it would be strange to ask him to say it.

'No, that's not fair. That's a dirty trick, Nina. How am I supposed to say no to a smile like that? Okay, fine, for you. Under one condition, you need to reply to what I say by speaking as well. I want to hear your voice too,' he texted, negotiating what I thought was a fair deal. 'And let the record show, I do not have a pimple on my butt, just so we're clear,' he added, much to my amusement.

'Okay that's fair. Now stop procrastinating and get to it,' I typed, sitting forward in my chair, resting my head on my hands.

'Wow, are we married already? Yes dear, here you go,' appeared on my screen and I waited with anticipation to hear his voice. 'Nina, would you like to go on a cyber date with me?' Luka asked. A soft, yet deep voice. A clear accent but not a heavy one. An almost melodic tone to his voice. I loved his voice from the very first note. And the way he said my name, wow. It caused an involuntary flutter in my stomach.

'*Damn, I might be in trouble here,*' I thought. 'Oh my gosh, that was so cute, Luka,' I told him, with a nervous quiver in my voice that I prayed he didn't pick up on as a smile broke across my face. 'I really love your voice,' I confessed to him.

'I love yours too, but why are you whispering?' Luka asked, whispering in response to me.

'Everyone here is asleep. I don't want to wake them,' I responded, and feigned falling asleep.

'You're very thoughtful.' He was so smooth in his conversation transitions. I felt like we could have sat up talking the entire night.

'I like how you say my name. There's something soothing about your accent to me,' he said, looking as though he was pondering the reason as to why.

We had given up on typing and were just speaking to each other. I had to try hard to control the volume of my voice as I was so excited talking to him. The flutter in my stomach had settled causing my voice box to relax. *Hopefully when I speak next the quiver will be gone from my voice,'* I thought.

He looked confident and sounded self-assured, but I didn't think he believed that. As if he was faking confidence. While I got the impression he didn't have a lot of experience with women, I wasn't sure why. He was engaging, handsome, and caring. Everything I could hope for in a man. Well, apart from living in Australia.

'So, what is a cyber date, Luka? I've never heard of that before,' I said, both unsure and excited. *Now that I think of it, I don't think my ex and I ever went on a real date. We just hung out after school and on weekends, but he never planned a date for us. This cyber date might be my first official date,'* I thought.

'We dress up in nice clothes, well I will, you can wear what you want, and then do whatever we decide to do. We can have a meal together; so, sit on video chat and eat our meals. Or we can have coffee, so we each make a coffee and have that on video chat. Just sit and talk to each other,' he said as if it was the most obvious thing in the world. He looked anxious that I hadn't said yes yet.

'Now, before you say anything, I know it's kind of weird, but I think the line between weird and sweet is whether you like the person or not. So, I'm hoping you like me enough to think that it's sweet,' he continued, trying to sell his idea. He didn't need to sell his idea though. I was sold on Luka, so I was ready for whatever date he proposed. Well, any legal date.

'That makes sense, and it sounds very sweet to me,' I replied, and I could see the relief break out across his face. Whether he was faking confidence or it was real, it was present in normal conversation, but when it came to putting himself on the line, his doubts were obvious to see. Maybe that's why he didn't have a lot of experience with women. *How could he think I would be anything other than over the moon to go on a date with him?'* I wondered.

'I guess that means you like me,' he said with a bowed head, looking up at me. He looked so adorable I could feel my heart melt.

'I guess so,' I said, and we sat there in an uncomfortable silence for a moment waiting for the other to start a new topic. 'So, what time is it there?' I asked, saying the first thing that popped into my head. *Really Nina? That was the best you could come up with? Time?'* I thought, mentally smacking a hand to my forehead.

'It's eleven-thirty am Saturday. What about there?' he asked, snapping back into life.

'It's one-thirty am Saturday morning,' I told him.

'Oh, so I'm in the future then. Want me to tell you your future?' he asked, grinning as if he had some line up his sleeve already.

'I didn't know you had the gift, the Sight. Please tell me what I'm in for so I'm prepared, share your knowledge with me, Gifted One,' I said, sitting forward in my chair putting my elbows on my desk, placing one hand on top of the other and my chin on top, playing along. I was interested to see what rubbish he was going to come up with. He closed his eyes and put two fingers to each of his temples as if to summon his power.

'You will meet a guy who is special to you. You will make each other incredibly happy. I'm seeing a plane, and I'm seeing, oh yes, the Eiffel Tower. The Sight has shown me that you will go to Paris together. I'm also hearing, hmmm, some kind of accent. Sounds somewhat like mine which is very bizarre,' he finished, finally opening his beautiful eyes.

I was glad I said I wanted to hear his voice, talking is so much nicer than typing. There's a connection you can get through talking that you don't get through typing. I could see more of his mannerisms where I felt like I was getting to know him more than if he said the exact same things via text.

'Make of that information what you will. It's not for me to interpret, that is for you,' he said, shrugging his shoulders and once again breaking into that smile with his eyes sparkling.

'So, am I allowed to break down the flaws in what you said, or should I just play along? I'm torn because it does sound like an amazing future,' I said, knowing full well that I was about to tear through his story even though it was adorable.

'Is it possible to do both?'

'Well, I'm not sure, but I definitely feel like trying. Here goes. So even though you are only ten hours ahead, I'm supposed to believe that you have seen this trip that I'm to have with a man that has an accent remarkably like yours. And this will be happening in the next ten hours?' I asked. I wanted to see how quick he was on his feet. Find out if he could fire back at me or just wilt away.

'Who am I to question the will of the Sight? Maybe that is why I was bestowed with this huge responsibility, and you weren't. I don't think you should be worried about how and when. You just always must ask yourself why not? Why couldn't it happen? As far as I'm concerned, there's never a good reason not to take a beautiful woman to Paris,' Luka said.

'*Okay, well played Luka, well played,*' I thought, trying to suppress a grin. He had passed that test with flying colours. 'True. You can always find a reason not to do something. Thank you for sharing with me your gifted vision. People should find more reasons why they should do things. Why shouldn't it be me that goes on the beautiful trip with the handsome blue eyed Australian man?' I said, my voice rising. The excitement of the idea was causing me to speak louder, and I heard my sister stir in the next room. *'Quiet, Nina,'* I thought sharply.

A picture floated through my mind of walking hand in hand with Luka past Notre Dame and along the Seine River. I felt the heat rise in my cheeks, unable to help but blush at the thought.

'The Sight didn't say anything about blue eyes.'

'Yes, that was my little wish, Genie Man,' I replied, feeling the heat in my cheeks continue to grow.

'Oh Nina, do you need a cold towel? You look pretty red there,' Luka said, as he gave me a look of mock concern. I made a rude gesture with both of my hands, and he broke out laughing.

'And here I thought you were a sophisticated woman. Not such a lady after all then.'

'Surprised I fooled you for so long.'

'Who knows what's going to happen in the future? I may just turn up there one day and surprise you with a trip to Paris. We have already done the most unlikely of things,' Luka said.

'What's that?' I asked, wondering what could be more unlikely than a boy from Australia turning up randomly to Požega to take me on a trip to Paris.

'We met. It's obviously just the first time we're talking, but you seem different to me. Different is interesting, and I know that I want to keep talking to you. I want to get to know you. I just hope that I'm not alone in feeling like this,' Luka said.

'You aren't. I feel it as well. You might wake up tomorrow and decide that you never want to talk to me again. Talking to you has been my highlight of the past month, not just today. I think I've smiled more during our conversation than during the last four weeks,' I said. It was a strange feeling to feel so comfortable with someone so quickly. It was a dangerous thing to trust someone new, but it felt amazing. Then again, it could be both.

'So, can I have your phone number? I do genuinely want to talk to you again and have our date,' Luka asked, his voice shaking slightly. He looked nervous suddenly, but he had no reason to be. Like I thought earlier, I didn't think he had a lot of experience with women and asking that was probably a huge deal for him, putting himself on the line.

'Hmm, I don't know,' I said, just teasing, but his face dropped immediately, so I had to correct it quickly. 'I'm just kidding, of course you can have my number. If you didn't ask within the next two minutes, I was going to just give it to you,' I whispered in a rush, so he didn't have to feel bad for a second longer. The beaming smile returned to his face, and I typed out my number, checking three times that I hadn't made a mistake.

'That was a good one. You really had me going. I liked it,' he said laughing. 'I was genuinely worried you would say no. Can I have your number has two answers, so until I get the answer I want, the answer I don't want is the one I assume I'm getting. We live so far away and I'm just a stranger on the internet. A face on a screen. Now that I have your number, I don't know, it just seems a bit more real. I'm just happy you gave it to me,' said Luka, and the relief was written all over his face. It wasn't just relief though; it was also gratitude.

He thinks way too much, just like me. Spending all that time in our own heads. If his brain moves as quickly as mine does, it must be a tough place to be sometimes,' I thought empathetically.

He held his phone up and I laughed asking, 'what are you doing?'

'You know, just taking a selfie to commemorate the moment of meeting you,' he said, posing with an adorable grin.

'I didn't really take you for a selfie guy, but here we are. Well anyway, it's getting late here, I better head to bed,' I said, feeling a bit disappointed that our conversation had to end, but I knew there would be many more to come. He must have felt the same way, because the smile that had been painted to his face almost the entire conversation had disappeared.

'Send me a message now just so I know that you have the right number,' I said, wanting to leave no room for error. My phone buzzed and up popped a number that I was safe to assume was Luka's. He had sent the photo of the two of us on the screen together and had written 'Our first photo together'.

'Thank you for talking with me. I'm so happy I jumped online and came here. I only just heard about this website yesterday from my cousin, and you are the first person I've spoken to here,' he said.

'That's so crazy. I only heard about this website earlier tonight from my best friend, Andjela, and you were the first person I spoke to on here too,' I replied. *I don't believe in coincidences. Everything happens for a reason,'* I thought smiling.

'Maybe we were meant to meet. I better let you get some rest though. Sleep well, and you can bet your life on me texting you. Can't wait for our cyber date,' Luka said, giving me one last perfect, eye sparkling smile.

'Maybe we were.' I smiled back and couldn't help but blush again. I waved and closed my laptop, feeling both happy and a little sad. Happy because I had met such a special and interesting man, and sad because I wasn't looking at that smile, or those eyes anymore. Although, I knew the moment I closed my eyes I would see them again.

As I got myself ready for bed, I was still thinking about Luka. The boys I knew were full of fake bravado and toughness when around a girl they liked. Trying to get anything honest from them was like trying to get blood from a stone. *Not this man. Maybe that was the difference, they are boys, and he is a man,'* I thought.

As I laid my head on my pillow, I had a strange feeling about having seen Luka's face for the first time. I was so hurt by what had happened in the previous few weeks, including that night, but there was something about his face. Soft and sweet. I felt like I had met a genuine gentleman. The way he looked at me with those magical blue eyes, I knew he felt things deeper than any person I had ever met. It was the face of a man that I knew would hurt himself before he hurt me. The kind of face that if he fell in love with the wrong woman, it would destroy him. He didn't have to worry about that though. I knew it was only a first meeting, but it felt different. It felt special. He was safe with me.

CHAPTER FOUR
The Return

I kept sitting there staring at the screen after Nina's face disappeared. I could still see the outline of her head in the black box where she had been just moments before. I didn't know what to think because it was so incredibly bizarre. As soon as her face left my computer screen, it was as if I forgot what life was like before we met. Already, I was trying to resist the urge to text her, not wanting to seem like a needy puppy dog and scare her away. *'There will be plenty of time for that. Let's give it at least a couple of hours,'* I thought.

I stood and caught a glimpse of myself in the mirror that was on the wall to the left of the dining room table and turned to face it. An ornate frame painted gold around the two-metre-wide and one-metre-tall mirror. The smile Nina put on my face was still spread from ear to ear. It didn't look like me, my factory settings face was one of a perpetual look of misery. It seemed like the settings had finally been changed. *'I better wipe this away or else I'll make everyone suspicious. Luka doesn't smile needlessly like this. Luka happy? Don't be silly,'* I scoffed, still looking at myself. I tried to bury my smile, which lasted half a second before the Nina joy broke out across my face again. I hadn't used those muscles that much in living memory. *'This is what it must feel like after going to the gym. I'm going to be sore tomorrow,'* I thought. Only ninety minutes after seeing that angelic face for the first time and I already knew the fall was going to hurt.

I walked to the front door to grab future Luka's problem, the guitar that I left there the previous night, and carried it to my room. Eighteen steps, or nine if I was feeling energetic. *'I'm going to write a song about this,'* I thought as I rushed towards my room. I felt like it would be nice to write about something happy for once. I needed to get all that joy swirling around inside me out and onto paper. Then maybe I would be able to process it properly. I needed to understand what that feeling meant. I had no understanding of what was happening inside me. A feeling stirring that I had never experienced before. *Was this normal when meeting someone for the first time?'* I wondered.

I ran down the small hall at the top of the stairs to my room as if those feelings would escape my body and never be recoverable if I didn't write them down immediately. Like when you have a crazy dream about someone, you wake up thinking I need to tell them, but within twenty minutes you can't remember a single detail. As if trying to catch smoke with your bare hands. Closing the door behind me I put the guitar case flat on the ground. I pulled my guitar from its case, tuned it, and then picked up my song scrapbook and pen. I flicked past countless songs about what it might feel like to be happy, self-loathing songs, to find a blank page about halfway through the book.

As soon as my pen hit the page my mind went into a haze. It felt like I didn't have to think of one line. As if the pen was dragging my hand across the page, writing the lyrics itself. *What sort of musical sorcery is this?'* I thought, watching the pen race across the paper, as if smoke was going to begin emanating from the page. The lyrics had never flowed so smoothly, and within ten minutes I had them all written down. No lines crossed out. My handwriting looked messy because of the rush for the words to escape the pen.

The only time the pen left my hand was to put together the chord progression. That was always where I struggled most when writing songs. Putting into words how I was feeling was the easy part. I was not a great guitarist though, so pairing lyrics with the right progression to communicate the wordless emotion so that someone could feel what I felt in my soul within the first four bars was a challenge.

'That must be the feeling of being in the zone that my brother talked about,' I thought. An out of body experience where things just work. A perfect amalgamation of all my previous song writing efforts mixed with the perfect muse. Nina. Without even trying it just happened. You can be out of it as quickly as you got in it, with no more idea about how you got in the zone, than how you got out of it. Like a moment, it is fleeting.

Fifteen minutes later I put my pen and guitar down and walked to the bathroom with my towel humming the melody of the song about Nina.

Stepping into the shower I started to sing the chorus to myself. *'Should I share what I wrote with Nina? It might be a bit too much at this stage. I mean we have only spoken once. Yes, I think the best decision is that I don't share the song with Nina…. just yet anyway,'* I thought as the water fell over me. I would one day. I wouldn't be able to help myself. It was like when you bought someone a birthday present, and you got so excited that you couldn't wait until their birthday to give it to them.

While I adjusted the temperature on the shower, James' idea began circling around my head. Once I found the perfect temperature and water pressure, I stood beneath the steady stream and let the hot water fall over my head and body. It was the way I imagined world leaders made important decisions that affect the fate of entire nations. If it was good enough for them to make decisions like that, it was good enough for me to decide whether I should play in front of a crowd of people that I didn't know.

'Why not?' I asked myself. As James had said, if I could play in front of my family at my own grandmother's funeral, then surely, I could play in front of a crowd of drunk people in the city. *'What's the worst that can happen? That I get booed off stage, ridiculed and abused as I forget the lyrics and completely embarrass myself in front of a room full of strangers? It would only be the secret dream that I*

had been harbouring being crushed. No big deal,' I thought, chuckling to myself. Strangely that gave me some comfort. To hope for the best and expect the worst. At least then I would know if it was something I was capable of, and I could stop sitting around wondering about it. As my nana would say, dreams are goals without a plan, and I needed to make that a goal for my own sanity.

The weight that I had been carrying on my chest had melted away. I didn't realise how hard I had been working to breathe until I felt the suffocating weight of an African bull elephant walk off my chest. The elephant had been with me for as long as I could remember and had finally given me a moment of respite. *Was it Nina? Was it deciding to finally give performing a go? Maybe it was both. I don't know,'* I thought. What I did know was that it was the best I had felt in longer than I could remember, and I wanted to make sure I spent as much time feeling like that as possible.

I reluctantly got out of the shower, grabbed my towel, and dried myself off as well as I could with the towel that was still damp from the day before. *'I should probably start hanging it up instead of leaving it lying on my bedroom floor,'* I thought. I walked back to my room with the towel wrapped around my waist to get dressed, with the melody of Nina's song still playing on a loop in my mind.

I picked up my phone and had another urge to text Nina. Hopefully she had the sense to put her phone on silent when she went to sleep. There was a voice in my mind telling me to text her, and a pressure beginning to build on my chest again. It felt like the only way to be able to relieve that pressure was by giving into that urge and texting Nina. I opened our conversation thread. I typed 'Hey' and my thumb hovered over the send button, unsure whether I should pull the trigger…. *'No, I better not yet, it's too soon,'* I thought resolutely. I exited immediately from the conversation, wanting to give it more time before reaching out.

Instead, I called James. There was no point hanging over the idea of performing in public, it was better to tackle the idea head-on. To turn the idea into a reality. Our friend Michael was arriving back in Melbourne that night from a nine-month trip across Europe, so I also wanted to see if James would come to the airport to pick him up with me. I dialled James' number and counted each ring as it passed. The count reached six when James answered. 'Hey Luka, what's up?' he said half yawning.

'Not much. What's happening? I mean apart from you just waking up,' I replied. I laid down upon my bed, staring at the light fixture hanging from the roof. The glass light shade was opaque and in the pattern of blooming roses. The attention to detail on the shade was truly a work of art. *The talent some people have is extraordinary,'* I thought.

'Got it in one. Probably a good thing you woke me up or else I could have slept until noon,' he said with another yawn, sounding like a lion's roar.

'Yeah well, if you looked at the time, you would've noticed that it is past noon. Anyway, I didn't call to make sure you didn't sleep all day. Michael's landing tonight. Do you want to come with me to pick him up from the airport? We can get dinner after and then drop him off at his folks' place,' I said.

'Umm yeah sure, that sounds good. I don't think I have anything planned, and if I do, I'm sure it's less interesting than that,' James said, still struggling to wake himself, releasing another huge yawn. I doubted coffee would be enough to wake him up, he needed a bucket of ice water poured over him.

'Okay, cool. The other thing I want to ask you is if that idea of yours, for me to play at your friend's bar was a real thing or just talk?' I asked trying to sound aloof. I felt like I was standing on the edge of the ten-metre high-dive, about to step from it and take the fall.

'I mean he's complained to me before that the only people he can get to play at his pub are old guys or terrible wannabee DJ's. I think a young guy playing an acoustic guitar set would be right up his alley. I can't see why he wouldn't jump on it but let me give him a call and talk to him. I'll send him the video of you singing and then I'll let you know. He should have an answer for me by the time you pick me up tonight,' James said, sounding like he had finally woken up. Maybe his mum had come into his room with that bucket of ice water.

'Awesome. Okay, so I'll pick you up at seven tonight.'

'Cool, and Luka, I won't even charge you a management fee for hooking you up with this gig,' he said with a laugh, and hung up the phone.

I felt nervous. I said that I wanted to do it, so as far as I was concerned, I had made a commitment and there was no backing out. *What if James was wrong though? What if he wasn't looking for anyone and I was about to get rejected when I finally put myself out there?'* I asked myself. All of that was terrifying, but the most important thing was that I was trying. I needed to relax and let things take their natural course. To not worry about something that was out of my control. 'Yeah, because you've become such an expert at that through your life,' I said aloud to myself. If the opportunity didn't eventuate, then there was nothing stopping me from pursuing other options. I felt a steely resolve to pursue it and see what happened.

I headed downstairs and found my mum sitting at the table reading the newspaper. 'Hi Luka, how are you?' she asked, looking up from the newspaper lying in front of her.

'I'm okay, would you like a cup of tea, Mum?' I asked, bouncing into the pantry where the kettle was waiting.

'If you're making one then I would love to have one with you,' she replied, with a smile on her face, turning her attention back to the newspaper. She exhaled in frustration reading an article about another failure of leadership from our government. Obviously, they weren't making enough decisions in the shower.

I filled the kettle and turned it on. I walked to the drawer to pull out our favourite cups with prints of Monet's water lilies on them. One had a chip in the top of it, so I made sure that was my cup or else I would hear about it. I put a tea bag in each cup and poured in the boiled water, setting the timer on my phone for four minutes and thirty-five seconds. Mum was a bit particular about her tea.

'So, how are you feeling after yesterday?' I asked, as I sat down in my seat, directly across from Mum at the table. I sat in it every day for the twenty years we had lived there. We all had our spots at the table. My parents may have paid for that seat, but my butt owned it.

She let out a sigh as if releasing her stresses before speaking. 'I'm alright, I guess. I feel better now that it's over, and somehow also worse if that makes any sense. It feels like I can move on, but I'm also denigrating my mother if I do. Like if I'm to move on and live my life without being constantly sad that I've now lost both my parents, that I'm forgetting them in a way. Like I'm disrespecting them by not having them constantly on my mind. Each day that passes is a day longer since I've seen them.'

'That makes sense, but they wouldn't want you to be weighed down by the sadness of them being gone. It's one thing to be sad, I am too, but you're focusing on the wrong thing,' I said.

'What do you mean?' she asked with a quizzical look. I checked how long was left before the tea was finished drawing.

'I mean that you're focusing on the bad memory of them dying, instead of the good memories that you had while they were alive. It isn't as easy as just flipping a switch in your brain, and all of a sudden it doesn't hurt to think about them being gone, but that's what I'm going to do. I'm going to remember playing cricket with Pa in the front yard, or him making me cry because he was aggressively combing my hair into a part like his. It's funny now even if it wasn't then. Or making vegetable soup with Nana. It's how I want to remember them,' I finished, looking down at the table. I felt like I had been transported back to those moments as they wafted through my mind. I could smell the grass while playing cricket with Pa, and the vegetable soup in the kitchen with Nana.

'When did you get so wise? Being the parent, I thought it was meant to be me putting your mind at ease,' Mum said, shaking her head and glancing across at the tea, silently wondering if it was time yet for it to be poured.

'It's okay Mum, we're all wrong sometimes,' I said, smiling as the timer went off. *Now it's time to focus because the Tea General needed to have her precious leaf water relaxer prepared perfectly,'* I thought, turning my focus to the steaming cups.

Firstly, I took the tea bag out and threw it in the bin. Secondly, I poured a small amount of milk in and was careful not to overdo it. Just a dash because I didn't want it to be too 'milky'. I would see my work disappear right down the sink in the blink of an eye if it wasn't correct to the millilitre. Thirdly, one flat teaspoon of sugar sprinkled into the tea, and then stirred exactly twelve times. I would worry about mine after I got the feedback from Mum's cup. I placed the cup in front of Mum gently and waited with bated breath as she raised the steaming tea to take a sip. I waited for what felt like an eternity as she stared over her cup, letting the tea wash over her taste buds. 'Perfect, thank you, Luka,' Mum said, and I could finally breathe again.

I poured some milk in my cup and dropped in a teaspoon of sugar. I stirred a couple of times and retook my seat at the table.

'So, Luka, we need to talk. What are your plans? What are you going to do with university? You only have one year to go, and you need to start thinking now about what you'll do after,' Mum hit me with out of nowhere. She didn't even look at me when asking, still looking through the newspaper. I didn't know I was about to be up for that conversation, but that was her skill. You never knew what you would be forced to think about. It felt like sometimes she cared too much.

'Umm, I'm not sure, Mum. I mean I don't really like uni, and don't see the point of it anymore if I'm honest. I was starting to think about leaving. After playing yesterday at the funeral I thought about giving music a go,' I said, my entire body clenched for the dragon fire about to be spit in my face. *Just close your eyes and it will all be over soon,'* I thought, holding the scalding hot Monet cup so tightly it could break.

'Don't be ridiculous. You can't leave. You only have one year left. All that time and money wasted. Pursuing that is a waste of time, barely anyone makes it in that industry,' she said incredulously. It wasn't the answer she was expecting. I should have been more diplomatic the day after the funeral. It had been started though, so we needed to have the full discussion.

'I don't think it's a waste at all. I feel like the real point of university is to figure out what you want to do. This is what I want to do. It's the thing I'm most excited about. Sport Science isn't exciting to me. I just picked it because I didn't know what else to do,' I said, feeling my heartrate increase, and the adrenaline from the discussion coursing through my body as if I was in a physical fight.

'Well, if you gave music a try what would that even look like?' Mum asked. She was at least giving me a chance to make my case.

'Don't blow it, Luka,' I thought. 'Getting as much live experience as I can and see what opportunities come my way, if any.'

'Won't most of these be at night?' Mum asked.

'Yeah, I suppose they would be,' I replied, knowing she was setting me up for her knockout point.

'Why can't you go to university and finish your last year while also playing in those places at night? Classes are during the day, so you should be able to do both,' Mum said. She was right. I would be able to do both without cutting any options off.

'I mean, I guess that would work. It wouldn't be the worst thing in the world to have a degree,' I said sheepishly.

'Exactly! And at the end of the day, if you change your mind and want to do something with your degree then you can. Just finish it and have that piece of paper. It's really only six months once you take all the holidays into account. You'll be finished in no time,' Mum said, as she finished the last of her tea and took the cup to the dishwasher.

'Hello, hello,' Dad said, as he walked into the kitchen, returning from whatever it was dad's do when they go places.

'Where are the pots?' Mum asked, as she completely ignored his chipper greeting, bringing the temperature in the kitchen down a few degrees.

'They didn't have the one's you wanted at the Altona shop. I'll go to the Maribyrnong store tomorrow,' he replied quickly. He was probably at the driving range and practiced that lie in the car on the way home.

'But you have club championships tomorrow,' Mum said, with the frustration being clear and breaking through her calm voice.

'Okay, if he has the club championships tomorrow, he was definitely at the driving range. You must take that B grade club championship first round very seriously,' I thought, shaking my head in amusement.

'I've already called the store and got them to put the pots on hold for me to pick up tomorrow. I'll pick them up on the way home. Don't worry, Milena, I am capable of doing things,' Dad said, knowing he was off the hook and that Mum clearly hadn't noticed the golf glove slightly sticking out of his pocket.

'So, Luka,' Dad started, and turned his attention towards me following his victory against Mum. 'Now you're on holidays I think you should start to work. It doesn't have to be full-time, but you need to do something. I'm not going to have you sitting on your butt watching TV for the next four months. I don't need you moping around all day,' he said in his ever-sensitive tone. It would be nice if there was a bit more care, but it was a plus that he noticed I had been struggling.

'Well actually, I'm going to start playing in bars and pubs, Dad,' I said, knowing that I was about to have to win the same argument again. Or more accurately, negotiate another compromise.

'Play? Play what? You're going to hustle drunk middle-aged men out of their precious beer money by playing them in darts? What do you mean 'play'?' Dad said, ridiculing me, even though he knew what I meant.

'I'm going to sing in a bar and see if I can make something of that,' I told him, with as much conviction as I could muster.

'That's adorable, but I mean an actual job, not the profession of a hobo. Do you have a lot of gigs lined up?' Dad asked, pressing on with the questioning.

'Well, James might be able to get me one to play on weekends in a bar in the city. He said his friend might be interested,' I told him, frustrated that I couldn't get any support, and that Mum wasn't jumping in to help me.

'Might? Okay, so that's a no then. If you want to play on weekends, then go for it. Have your fun on the weekend, but you need a proper job during the week. I think you should come and work for me. Just come in three days a week. That way you can still have some holiday time, play your little gig things on the weekend, and save some money. I need the help at the market anyway. I want someone that I can trust, and I know I can trust you,' Dad said. Dad ran a fruit wholesale business, selling to fruit shops and providores.

Neither were taking it seriously, but there was no point in arguing the point now. They were right that it was a long shot, but it was my long shot to take. There was only one way for them to take it seriously, and that was for them to see me making genuine progress. I had fought with my words. I needed to fight with my actions.

'It might be a good thing for you. Remember what the psychologist said? You need to fill your time and stay busy. I think it's best for you,' Mum chimed in. It felt like they had spoken about it. Little did they know that my ability to overthink knows no bounds, and I would still be able to easily do that even if I was busy.

'Fine, I'll come in,' I said, unable to come up with a reason that I couldn't apart from not wanting to wake up at midnight to work. *I guess making a bit of money wouldn't be the worst thing. It would give me more freedom. Freedom to visit someone,'* I thought.

'Okay great, and if you like it you might want to come in full-time when you finish uni,' Dad said. He had been pushing for me to work for him full time ever since I finished school at seventeen.

I got up and walked back to my room. I felt drained. I had spent a lot of mental and emotional energy that morning meeting Nina and then having those conversations with Mum and Dad. I needed a nap, but I had never been able to relax my mind enough to take naps.

I walked into my room with a strong urge to reach out to Nina but felt that it was still too soon. I needed distance between my phone and my hands for safety, so I threw my phone on my bed. A distraction was necessary, so I picked up my guitar that was leaning against my bed and began practising the song I wrote that morning.

For the next three hours I played my new song on repeat until the progression was second nature. Until the lyrics were burned into my brain like a nun in the fifties teaching the times tables by rote. If I were too much of a coward to say hi to Nina, then I could at least play the song that I wrote about her. I loved playing it. I loved how it made me feel. I felt like I was someone special. I felt important to her. There was a kind of euphoria inside my chest for the first time, where only anxiety had sat before. Finally, that anxiety had left me alone. For the moment.

I couldn't take it anymore; I had to text her. I felt like a drug addict trying to resist the urge to take their next hit. There was only so long I could distract myself before the urge became too much. It engulfed my entire body and there was nothing else I could think about. It crippled me from doing anything else because of that one thought, and the only way to stop it was to give in. Give in to its power over me and do what my entire being craved.

I picked up my phone, deleted the message 'Hey', that still sat waiting to be sent, and texted, 'Hello from the other side'. I immediately regretted saying that. 'You just can't help yourself. She's going to think you're an idiot,' I said aloud to the empty room, picking up a pillow and covering my face before muffling a scream into it. I blamed my dad because clearly dumb jokes were hereditary. Of all the things I could have said, I texted her the stupidest thing of all. I hoped she would laugh but there was a much higher chance she would think I was a complete loser. *'She could do both, the two aren't mutually exclusive, I guess,'* I thought.

I threw the pillow off the bed and silently screamed at the ceiling trying to let the awkwardness out. It didn't work.

Fortunately, I didn't have time to sit and stew on it as it was time to go and get Michael from the airport. At least there was something to occupy my mind and stop me from constantly checking the world clock to see if she was awake. The last thing I wanted to do was double text. That would put me on the fast track to getting my number blocked.

My hands craved to be occupied, so I collected my wallet and headed downstairs counting the steps as I went again. *'I really need to stop this incessant counting, it's annoying,'* I thought frustratedly. Continuing to the kitchen, I stuck my head into the room. 'I'm going to get James and then pick Michael up from the airport,' I said to Mum and Dad.

'You're not going to give your mother a kiss goodbye?' Mum asked, turning her head and pointing to her cheek.

I walked quickly up to her and kissed her on the cheek. 'Love you.'

'Love you too,' Mum replied.

'Tell Michael we said hi,' Dad said after me, as I walked quickly from the room, collected my keys at the front door and jogged to the car. I checked the time in the car and saw I was a few minutes late, but I always was for everything I did.

James lived close by and stood waiting out the front of his house when I arrived. He jumped into the car, and we headed to the airport.

Forty minutes later we were walking into T2 at Melbourne Airport in Tullamarine. There were many people waiting for loved ones just outside the doors that international travellers returned through. Entire families waiting with signs and flowers for someone to come home. There were two doors where arrivals walked through, so those in the terminal had their heads on a swivel like at a tennis match looking from one door to the next. Taxi drivers circled around the fresh arrivals like vultures looking for the weak one to feast on.

A guy about the same age as me, paced closely by clinging to a bunch of flowers. He looked nervous. He checked his watch repeatedly and the flowers shook in his hand. *'Probably waiting for someone he met on worldvidcam.com,'* I thought. He was wearing a black jacket which was weird. It was a very warm night.

I always loved the airport growing up. My father would take me just to look at the planes and have lunch. It seemed like a magical place, a hub of possibilities. People flying all around the world to family, friends, partners. Going to see places that pictures would never, and could never do justice. People travelling on their own and people travelling in a group. People coming back home and people coming to see the city where I lived for the pure enjoyment of it. I wondered what it would be like walking through those doors for the first time. How different eyes could see the exact same thing in a completely different way.

'I spoke to my mate at the bar. He watched the video I sent him and he's keen to give you a go. If you're still into the idea he wants you to play Friday night,' James said, as we leant against the rail separating those arriving and those waiting.

We watched the arrivals come through the doors and their eyes scan the crowd trying to find those who were waiting for them. *'I could stand here all day and watch people's faces light up when their eyes lock onto their loved ones,'* I thought. The sheer joy and love in the room as I watched the embraces was special. Just upstairs resided the departure gate, how strange that the antithesis of what I was witnessing was so close. Like having the palliative care ward and the birth ward next to each other.

'Yeah, that's cool. I'm definitely still wanting to do it,' I said, only half paying attention to him because I was more interested in watching the people interacting. They were all so happy. It must be a special place to have that much happiness in it. I couldn't help but wonder what it would be like to see Nina walk through those doors. I quickly looked at my phone to see if she had replied…. nothing.

The young guy was still pacing back and forth nervously. He craned his neck at each door to see if the person he was waiting on had arrived. He looked anxious.

'He said he'll give you a call tomorrow to sort out all the specifics. I'm getting paid a talent finder's fee of free drinks for the night, so I think I'm the real winner here. I'm looking forward to seeing my client play,' James finished, feigning taking a drink.

'That's great,' I said absentmindedly. I felt my phone vibrate so I grabbed it immediately to see if it was Nina. There was nothing there at all. I felt like the people inside my phone were playing with me at that point. I checked the time in Požega, it was ten-am. *Well, she had a late night, so she probably wants to sleep in,'* I thought.

'There he is!' James said excitedly, pushing me and pointing to our right, finally getting my full attention. Sure enough, there he was. Michael looked dishevelled, like he hadn't shaved or had a haircut in months. With his long red hair and beard, he stood above the rest of the crowd. He was impossible to miss. He spotted us and a beaming smile spread across his face. His powerful frame moved the crowd out of his path and ran towards us, pulling us both into a tight embrace at once. He smelt as he looked, that personal hygiene was only an option while he was away, an option he declined.

'Thanks for picking me up, guys. I'm so happy to see you,' he said, his beaming smile still on his face. He was the most positive guy I had ever met, so it was tough to work out why we were friends sometimes. I guess we balanced each other out and James sat in the middle. 'Have you been waiting long?' Michael asked, as he adjusted the large military green bag hanging from his shoulder.

'Maybe fifteen minutes? That's about right, isn't it, Luka?'
James asked, but my attention had been drawn away again.

The young guy who was pacing back and forth was running
towards a young woman. They embraced each other and when
they broke apart, he kissed her and handed her the bouquet of
flowers. Then he did it. The reason for his nervous and anxious
energy became clear. He put his left knee on the floor and
reached inside his jacket pocket. Both Michael and James were
staring too. A quiet fell across the terminal as it had drawn the
attention of most of the people there. I didn't know if it was
madness or beautiful. It could be both. It would have to be if
they were in a long-distance relationship. I could never propose
publicly, but I envied his courage.

We were too far away to hear what they were saying to each
other, but he seemed to be on his knee for a long time. 'In the
movies when I've seen these scenes, the man seems to be putting
the ring on by now. Do you think the long wait is a good or bad
thing?' I asked the other two.

'Umm, she doesn't look as happy as she did a minute ago.
She looks freaked out,' said James, louder than he planned as
numerous heads turned to see who had spoken.

'And look at his face. I don't think he's getting the feedback
he thought he was going to get,' Michael said in a hushed tone.

Suddenly, she hurriedly walked towards the exit with her bag
and flowers and left him there on one knee in the middle of the
arrivals terminal with what would have felt like the entire world
staring at him. His eyes were stuck on the floor in front of him
where his partner was standing just a moment before. He wiped
his cheek with the sleeve of his jacket and stood up. The ring
disappeared into his jacket pocket, and he walked towards the
same exit that she walked through.

'Do you think he's going to talk to her?' James asked at the
same volume as before, but the terminal had sprung back to life.

'I hope so,' replied Michael.

'I don't understand it. He was going for some Hollywood moment but if you're going to put yourself on the line like that, surely you have to be positive the answer's going to be yes,' I said.

'He probably did think it was a guaranteed yes. No one plans to humiliate themselves like that. Maybe it was just the forum in which he did it that freaked her out. Who knows?' Michael said.

'Well, if he thought those things, then he didn't know her that well, and it's probably best they don't get engaged yet. I'd want a bit of a clue before I asked a woman to marry me. Just a little sign, like her asking me, are we going to get married? Or when are we going to get married? You know, just a small indication,' I said, and they both laughed.

'You boys hungry? After being in Italy I could really go for some pasta,' Michael said, and all three of us walked back to the car.

We drove to Lygon St, famous for Italian restaurants and sat down in a restaurant called Lonzaretta's at a table by the window. I placed my phone on the table facing up so I could see the moment Nina replied. I knew it was rude, but I needed to know. As hard as I tried to push it from my consciousness, it wouldn't leave me alone. We took our menus from the waiter and quickly analysed them without saying a word to one another. Before the waiter could even walk away, we ordered our meals and a bottle of Heathcote Shiraz to go along with it.

'So, Michael, tell us about your trip. What was your favourite part?' James asked.

'How long do you have? I saw so many amazing places. Drinking coffee and reading in a Parisian café. The Sedlec Ossuary in the Czech Republic was incredible. Sagrada Familia in Barcelona was even bigger than I thought. I bought paella and ate it staring at that building for hours. I couldn't take my eyes off it. St Peter's Basilica in Vatican City. Just sitting there and appreciating where you were was so serene. Walking through Kalemegdan Park in Belgrade was beautiful during the spring. The cobbled streets around and the old fortress; it felt like I was on another planet because we have nothing like that here. Everything here is so new; we just don't have the history that these places have. I couldn't get enough of it. I'd go back right now if I could,' Michael said.

I saw my phone light up sitting on the table and the name Nina appear on it. My heart jumped and the Nina smile was back on my face. I grabbed my phone and read her message. 'Hahaha you're silly. Good morning.' Relief washed over me.

'How are you?' I replied quickly.

'Who was that?' James asked, trying to read my screen.

'No one,' I shot back quickly. 'It sounds like it was amazing. Did you get home sick at all?' I asked, keen to keep the attention on Michael's trip.

'Not really. Your days are so full, and you always have something new to see. I didn't have a clear plan of how long I was going to stay in each place, so as soon as I'd seen enough of a city I moved on. I did get sick of staying in hostels though. The rooms with four beds weren't too bad, but I was in a room with eighteen beds in Malmo, Sweden. If I got thirty minutes of sleep that night I'd be surprised. There were tag team snorers in that room. Any time I was in there, day or night, there was someone snoring. I left there after one night because of that,' Michael said, shaking his head. He looked like he was still bitter about it.

My phone vibrated again. I knew I shouldn't look at it because it was rude, but I couldn't help myself. 'I'm okay. Slept well but I'm still a bit upset about last night. Thanks for talking though. You cheered me up. How are you?' Nina replied.

'I'm sorry you're still upset. Glad I could cheer you up even if it was just a little. I'm alright. Having dinner with Michael and James,' I texted, and put my phone down on the table again.

Seeing as I was staring at my phone replying to Nina, I hadn't noticed that the other two were looking at me. 'Who was that?' James asked again, this time more forcefully. As I was about to reply, he put up his hand to stop me from talking and continued. 'And don't tell us no one, because you had this stupid smile on your face while replying. What's her name?'

'How do you know it's a girl?' I asked, with a furrowed brow.

They looked at each other and laughed. 'Because no man has ever had that look on his face while texting their dad. You've met a girl and if you're going to be rude and text her while having dinner with us, then the least you can do is tell us who she is. So, I'll ask you for a third time, who was that?' James asked. Both Michael and James had leaned forward in their seats waiting for me to reply. Apart from telling them about what celebrities I thought were hot, I had never told them about a woman I liked. I always kept those things to myself.

'Her name's Nina. I just met her this morning on that site you told me about, James. She is way out of my league.'

'Oh, I love it when they're out of my league,' James said, with a smile on his face shaking his head.

'So, where's she from?' Michael asked.

'Serbia. Požega actually,' I answered, emphasising it to James.

James and Michael gave each other a concerned look and then turned their attention me. 'Are you sure this is a good idea? I mean, she lives on the other side of the world, mate. Aren't you worried that you're just going to get your heart broken?' Michael asked.

'It's a heart, not a face. You can get your heart broken from anywhere, she just can't break my face from there. I mean, it's a possibility, but isn't that the case with any person you meet? No matter if you live next door to them, or if they live on the other side of the world. They can still break your heart. Proximity isn't everything. We've only just met each other so let's not get carried away. I do like her though, so hopefully we can keep talking and I don't blow it,' I said, fully expecting myself to ruin it by saying something stupid by text at any moment.

'Oh, don't talk like that. I mean of course you're going to blow it at some stage but at least fake some confidence. Girls respond to that. Put yourself in the headspace that you did when you sang at Nana's funeral. That was confidence,' James said. He had a way of making me laugh about the things I was self-conscious about but also building me up out of that. It was a special skill to have.

'Maybe meeting someone in that way isn't the worst thing in the world either. I mean, you can get to know her without having to worry about the physical elements that go along with it. In a way it's purer,' Michael said.

'I don't know about that. I like the physical elements... a lot,' James said, as the waiter returned with the bottle of wine and poured out a glass for each of us. A sly smirk appeared on the waiters' face at hearing what James said.

'Perfect. Thank you,' Michael said to the waiter.

'Sorry for the delay with your wine. Your main course will be served soon,' the waiter said, before turning and walking towards the kitchen.

'Oh, that sounds nice. Who are Michael and James?' Nina texted.

'James is my cousin, and Michael is my friend from primary school, but we went to different secondary schools. They're my best friends.'

I want to see her again. Tonight,' I thought. I rolled the dice and sent another text to see if she was available. 'So, I was wondering, would you like to have a cyber date when I get home?' I asked, making multiple spelling mistakes and correcting them, as my hands shook slightly as nerves took over asking Nina on a date.

'So, how do you plan on making this work?' Michael asked.

'Haven't really got that far. Just have video chats, text, phone calls, and then visiting each other I guess,' I said, thinking on the run.

'Well, you can keep talking to her when you get home. You know our rule, when we hang out, no phones. That's not changing no matter how hot she is,' James said.

My phone lit up again and an urge impossible to resist struck me again as I felt my eyes go to Nina's reply. *The first time I've asked a girl on a date in two years, and James expects me to wait another two hours to find out if she said yes? No chance. Hopefully there's a better answer waiting for me than last time, when Caitlin told me she wasn't attracted to men. Two weeks later I saw her holding hands with a guy down the street,'* I thought.

'I just need to see what she said, and then I'll put it down,' I said, picking up my phone once more.

'I'm not sure that's a great idea….' she texted, and my heart sank. I knew it was too good to be true.

My head dropped. I felt my phone vibrate in my hand. 'I'm just kidding. How could I say no to seeing those blue eyes again? I'd love to but can we have it when you wake up?' Nina asked.

My heart did a summersault. *'She said yes!'* I celebrated to myself. I knew she said yes when we first met, but to have a positive answer again felt like it was Christmas in my chest. I had no idea how I was going to sleep with our date waiting for me when I woke up.

'I would have thought quite easily haha. Great. I'll text you when I wake up. Can't wait to see you,' I replied, and put my phone on flight mode.

The waiter placed in front of James a pizza, a ravioli dish in front of Michael, and a marinara pasta in front of me.

'Welcome home, Michael,' James said, raising his glass.

'It's great to be home,' Michael said, and we put our glasses together.

We enjoyed the rest of the night eating, drinking, and laughing. I was ecstatic that Michael was back. He had been away for so long that I had forgotten what it was like for the three of us to be together. I had missed him.

CHAPTER FIVE
The Date Preparation

I awoke but didn't want to open my eyes. I could sense the sun coming through my window, but I didn't want to accept the day that was waiting for me. I felt dirty. Cheap. I could feel Marko's groping hands on me as I lay there.

Slowly I forced my eyes open to see my blinds were up and my door was wide open. Mama must have come in and woken me, but I had fallen asleep again without it registering. I had missed days of school because of this phenomenon. It was a gift. My clothes were folded on my desk, and she was the only person that would do that.

I could hear Jovan's cartoons playing loudly on the TV from the living room. I had no idea how that didn't wake me up. We should probably get a special fire alarm because there was every chance I would sleep through a house fire.

With each passing second, I felt worse and worse. I wasn't sure if I should get up and try to break the cycle, or stew in the horrid feeling constricting my chest. *'Maybe I'll have a nice dream of beaches in a foreign land,'* I thought. While that was tempting, I needed to wash myself. I didn't shower when I got home and needed to cleanse my body and hopefully my soul. Let the steaming hot water and soap take away the filth of the night before. I doubted there was a soap that could stop my heart from feeling dirty though.

Using all the energy I could muster, I took off my blankets, grabbed my towel and headed straight for the bathroom. I hadn't looked at the time yet, but I could hear SpongeBob on the TV so it must have been before twelve. *Before twelve? Urgh, so disappointing,'* I thought, trudging towards the bathroom. I turned the water on as hot as I could handle, hoping that I would come out looking like a lobster. I closed my eyes and tilted my head back to let the steaming water fall over my face and through my hair. I couldn't help but run through every interaction I had with Marko, searching for the smallest possible sign that I had been asking for his advances. *'He said I was asking for it, so, was I? Most people say I look cold and unapproachable, not that I'm some crazy flirt. Was there something in the look when we made eye contact? No way! Well, I don't think there was. I should talk to Andjela and find out if she thinks I did anything to provoke it,'* I thought.

Lathering my hair with the apple scented shampoo that didn't smell anything like apples, I stopped abruptly as if someone had hit pause. Since I woke up, I had been consumed by thoughts of that vile pig Marko. I was furious at myself. I hadn't even thought about meeting Luka since I woke up. My heart rate quickened as my arms returned to motion massaging the shampoo into my scalp.

I hadn't looked at my phone yet, so I didn't have any idea if Luka had texted me while I was asleep. I thought he liked me, he had asked me on a date after all, but you couldn't really know from meeting someone once, especially through a computer screen. He had the entire day to re-think and come to his senses while I slept, so maybe he didn't want to talk again. I rushed through my second application of shampoo and then applied my conditioner. I watched the second hand of the clock on the wall do two rotations, my anticipation for what could be waiting on my phone rising with each tick. I rinsed out the conditioner, turned off the water and jumped out of the shower.

I didn't even dry myself. I just wrapped myself in my towel and walked quickly to my room, leaving a trail of water behind me. I picked up my phone from my desk and hoped to see his name waiting for me. Dead. I swore under my breath and took two big steps to my bed where my charger laid in wait, hungry to be put to work and plugged it in. I waited impatiently as the charger pumped life into my phone like a defibrillator, sitting on my bed in my towel with my hair dripping, urging the charger to speed up. *'If he hasn't texted me then I'm not texting him. The sperm swims to the egg, not the other way around,'* I thought defiantly, while I waited for my phone to turn on.

'No, come on. Not an update. Later! I pressed later! Why are you updating?' I groaned at my phone in frustration. I busied myself with my post shower hair routine to keep distracted from the torture my phone was putting me through. Hair as long as mine needed a lot of care or else it could go badly. *'I'm not sure how Rapunzel managed with hers stuck in that tower for so long,'* I wondered. I applied my leave in conditioner and silicon drops, ensuring that there was an even distribution from the root to the tip.

Finally, the update finished, and my phone sprang to life. 'Thank you,' I said sarcastically, as my phone revealed its wallpaper of Jovan and my sister Milica. After a moment I unlocked my phone, opened my texts, and there it was. His smiling face and comforting blue eyes were staring into mine from his profile picture next to a message reading, 'Hello from the other side'. *Wow. A simple hi would have done the trick, but hey, way to go for trying to be interesting. At least one man was trying to make me smile,'* I thought.

Luka and I exchanged texts. I made sure to wait a moment before replying to each of his messages. I didn't want him to think I was a loser staring at my phone with no life because I was replying before he could even put his phone down.

Each time I saw the notification light on my phone flash, my heart involuntarily jumped into my throat. *'I wasn't this excited and giddy when I started to date my ex,'* I recalled. A couple of times the notification was an email asking for my bank details to deposit the four million euro left to me by my great aunt that lived in

Switzerland, and the other in Ethiopia. It was quite amazing that my family was so successful across the world. I wondered how much money I had left on the table by not replying with my bank details. Each email was a frustrating tease. The only thing I wanted to see on my phone was a text from Luka.

I broke into a smile reading the message from Luka asking me on a cyber date. *I'll tease him and pretend I think it's a bad idea, and as soon as it says read, I'll take mercy on him. He may as well get the full Nina experience immediately,'* I thought, smiling as I typed out the text. I wasn't able to have the date when he asked, but I suggested one for in my evening, his morning.

I felt ecstatic that I would be seeing Luka in a few hours. I continued to sit on my bed in a towel and dried my hair with a comb and dryer. I decided to dress up as if we were going out to a restaurant for our date. I wanted him to know that our date was important to me, and I wanted to look nice for him. *He'll have just woken up when it's time for our date, so let's hope that he has a shirt on. Well for the first date anyway,'* I thought, smiling to myself.

I walked from my room to the living room and sat next to Jovan on the couch. He was so focused on what he was watching that a T-rex could have sat next to him and he wouldn't have noticed. Kissing him on the forehead and hugging him, his eyes didn't break from the TV for a moment, but he hugged me and kissed me on the cheek.

Mama walked over to the table with a plate of pancakes and a cup of warm coffee which she placed in front of my usual spot. 'Come and eat, honey. How was your night?' Mama asked, taking the next chair. I stood up and took my seat in front of the pancakes.

'Interesting. It had its moments,' I said, making sure to focus on the TV. I wanted to be as vague as possible about the events of the previous night without lying to her. I was normally very open with my mama; I told her everything. She was like a friend, but I wasn't ready to talk about what happened yet. Mama could read me like a book, so if I made eye contact with her, she would know that something was wrong, and something was also great.

Jovan walked over to the table and as soon as Mama's gaze drifted out of the window just for a moment, he took a pancake from my plate. With half a pancake hanging from his mouth, Mama turned back catching Jovan. 'Jovan, you have already eaten six this morning and now you're taking one from your sister!? You have had enough. Let your sister eat her breakfast,' Mama yelled.

'Can I at least finish this one?' Jovan mumbled, through a mouthful of pancake.

'Don't be disgusting and talk with a mouthful of food. Fine, but let Nina have the rest of her breakfast. Okay?' she said, leaving zero room for any answer that wasn't some form of affirmation.

'Okay,' he said, and he inhaled the rest of the pancake without chewing, like a pelican.

'It will be scary to see how much he eats when he grows up. He might put Serbia into a famine on his own,' I thought, beginning on the pancakes Jovan hadn't stolen.

I finished my breakfast, then carried my phone and coffee back to the couch. Sitting next to Jovan, I started to scroll through my phone looking at the waste of time that is social media. I opened my text thread with Luka and scrolled up to the picture he sent me the night before of the two of us on the computer screen. I tried to stifle the small grin that was forcing its way to my face as I looked at it. Seeing visual confirmation that it wasn't a dream, and I did meet that beautiful man made me deliriously happy. I felt butterflies flutter in my stomach.

A text came from Andjela. 'Hey, I'm coming over now. I'm leaving tennis so I'll be there soon.'

'Okay,' I replied. I didn't really want to see anyone not named Luka, but telling her no would be as successful as trying to say no to going to the party.

'Where's Milica?' I asked Mama, as I put my phone face down on the couch.

'She went to see some friends. She'll be back at... well I don't know when she'll be back. You know what your sister's like, she can't sit still for two minutes. I'm guessing she'll be back for dinner tonight though,' Mama said.

Jovan's cartoon ended. He kissed Mama and walked from the house without saying a word. 'Take your coat, Jovan,' Mama screamed after him.

'Can you please clean up, Nina? I need to do some washing,' Mama said.

'Sure. Just letting you know that Andjela's on her way over,' I said.

'Well, you better do those dishes quickly. I don't want her seeing our messy house,' Mama said, walking out of the room towards the laundry.

I looked around the living room and kitchen and saw the only things out of place were the dishes in the sink. Unless the house was as clean as an operating theatre, Mama considered the house to be messy. I shook my head and began to clean the dishes. The thought of the date with Luka was forced from my mind by cancerous thoughts of the night before. Marko.

The scene played on a loop in my mind and no matter how hard I fought to push Luka back into my focus, I couldn't break the cycle. I could feel Marko's slimy hands on me causing my body to give an involuntary shudder. I felt dirty all over again, like I hadn't showered at all. I realised that no matter how I looked at him, it didn't mean I asked for what he did to me. That he decided to take my body because he wanted it, not because I wanted him, was not okay. That my consent or my desire for him was a secondary concern to him. Or not a concern at all. All that mattered was what he wanted in that moment. He didn't see me as a person; he saw me as a thing. A thing he could take because he wanted. Something to conquer. I couldn't let him force me to turn on myself though. He was at fault, not me.

There was a knock on the front door just as I placed the last dish in the drying rack. I walked to the door and saw Andjela's outline through the frosted glass. I opened the door and greeted her with a kiss on the cheek. The kind where you make the kiss sound and press your cheek to the other person's. She had her tennis clothes on and a big tennis bag on her back, which she put down as she slipped her shoes off just inside the door.

'How are you?' Andjela asked, as she walked by me into the living room.

'I don't know. I'm alright, I guess. How are you? How was practice?' I asked, as I followed her through to the living room.

'Going to tennis practice the morning after a party was not the greatest decision I've ever made. I think going out last night was bad for both of us,' Andjela said, as she sat on the couch.

'Yeah, last night was equally bad for both of us,' I said, with as much sarcasm as I could muster.

'Well, it could be if I get arrested for punching Marko considering the news I just got,' Andjela said smirking, as she jumped off the couch and walked back to her bag at the front door. She rushed back into the room with a letter clutched in her hand.

'What's that?' I asked, as she handed me the letter. Removing the letter from the envelope, I began to read. 'Is this for real?' I asked, with my mouth hanging open and eyes wide in disbelief.

'Well, the Australian major tennis tournament is in a couple of months. I was meant to just be playing in the juniors, but I've managed to get into the qualifying tournament for the main draw. It's going to be my first attempt at getting into the main draw of a major. I didn't think this was going to happen for another twelve months,' Andjela said, grinning like a Cheshire cat and bouncing on the balls of her feet as if she was back on the practice court.

I squealed in excitement and launched myself at her. I hugged her as tightly as I could, and we started jumping together in jubilation.

'This is unbelievable. I... I... I'm speechless. I'm so happy for you. How are you feeling about it?' I asked. Even though she was incredibly talented, I was shocked. I had been to Belgrade and watched her win the junior national championship at fourteen. She had won three of the four major championships in juniors but had never been to Australia. The possibility of her entering the main draw was another thing completely. 'This is the big time,' I said, with all thoughts of that pig momentarily pushed from my mind.

'I'm nervous and excited. This is what I've been working for my entire life. It's what I've wanted to do ever since I can remember. Maybe I'm ready, maybe I'm not, but what I do know is that I'm going to bust my butt to get into the main draw. Can you imagine if I get through and get to play on Rod Laver Arena? I'm ready to leave now and practise in Melbourne to prepare for the tournament,' Andjela said, taking a seat at the table bouncing both of her legs with excitement.

'They better have live streaming of qualifying because I'll be watching it. I don't care if it's at four in the morning,' I said, leaning over and giving her another huge hug. 'Do tennis superstars drink tea?' I asked, walking to the sink, filling the kettle, and putting it on.

'I don't know about them, but future superstars do,' said Andjela, as she followed me to the sink. 'I leave in about six weeks, so I just need to get my visa done as soon as possible. I haven't played in Australia before so hopefully it won't be an issue. It's going to be so much fun to see Melbourne as well. It looks beautiful when I've watched Novak dominate that tournament on TV.'

'I'm so jealous you get to go there. I really wish I could go with you,' I said, as I leaned against the kitchen counter waiting for the water to boil. I put the fruit tea bags into the cups and poured the boiling water into each. I passed a cup to Andjela and carried mine back to the table, taking my normal seat.

'That wasn't the real reason I came over though, it was to see how you're holding up, Nina. I mean really, how are you holding up?' Andjela asked again, as she leaned forward in her seat towards me, not breaking eye contact. It felt like she was staring into my mind to try and get the answer that way, knowing I would try and downplay what happened.

'Really, I'm okay. I mean it was awful at the time and I'm confused, but it's no big deal. I'm over it. Plus, hearing your news has helped me feel better as well. I'm so proud of you,' I said, although I was positive that I hadn't convinced her I was okay.

'That means a lot to me, but I don't know how you expect me to believe that you're okay. You were sexually assaulted last night,' Andjela said, a bit too loudly as the front door opened.

'Shut up,' I mouthed at Andjela, and I looked towards the door, listening carefully.

'What!?' Mama screamed from just inside the front door. There was a bang on the ground as Mama dropped what I assumed to be the washing basket and came charging into the room. 'What are you talking about? What do you mean you were sexually assaulted? Nina? Andjela? Would someone please tell me what happened?' Mama yelled, as her eyes darted from Andjela to me. Her face was a mix of rage, fear, and confusion.

Andjela gave me a look that said, 'if you don't tell her, I will'. I gave Andjela a dirty look and sighed, turning to face Mama. 'Fine. It's not a big deal, so please don't freak out, but last night at the party Marko grabbed me on the butt and tried to force me to kiss him. I don't want you to worry about it though, it's over,' I said in a casual tone, trying to calm Mama down.

'Umm actually, I think I will worry about it,' Mama snapped back.

'You didn't really think your mama would hear that and say sure thing, no worries. Let's forget about it and move on with our lives, did you?' Andjela asked, as she took a sip of her tea.

I looked away from her and back to Mama who was about to completely lose it. 'Marko? Not Marko Petrović? You've been going to school with him since you were six. I thought you two were friends. Why would he do something like that to you?' Mama asked, getting more worked up with each word she spoke.

'Yeah, that Marko. I mean we were never great friends. We were more like acquaintances. I don't know. I keep changing my mind about whether I encouraged it or not. I don't think I did, but I must have done something without being aware of it. I'm not sure what I did, but it had to be something for it to happen. Or is he just a pig? I don't know. I mean people don't just do things like that, do they?' I asked, turning from one to the other. I had tried to rationalise it in my mind, but I wasn't able to believe what I had reasoned as a plausible answer for him to do that. Other than he didn't respect me.

'Yes, they do,' Andjela said. 'There are some men in this world that think just because you exist that they're entitled to you. That you should be grateful purely because they're interested in you. I see it all the time when I travel for tennis. Most men in this world are great people; ninety-nine percent of the men are terrific and genuine. Then there's that one percent that have no respect for women, and by extension themselves.'

There was a quiet knock on the door and as Andjela got up to see who it was, Mama pulled up a chair next to me and sat down, placing her hand on my arm. 'Not all people in this world are good, honey. Sometimes things happen that have nothing to do with you, you're just in the wrong place at the wrong time,' Mama said in a soothing voice, finally able to relax after the initial shock of hearing what happened.

'What are you doing here?' Andjela asked aggressively from the front door. I almost heard the spittle fly from her mouth as she spoke.

The voice that replied made my heart sink. 'I came to apologise to Nina. Can I talk to her?' said Marko in a muffled and miserable voice.

'No. She doesn't want to see you. What you did was disgusting. If you don't walk away right now, you're going to get hit a little bit lower,' Andjela said, and I could hear her voice quiver with rage. She slammed the door, and I could feel the house reverberate with her fury.

'Thank you,' I whispered to Andjela, as she sat back at the table. I looked to Mama and my eyes started to well up. I thought I was fine. I thought that if I told myself it wasn't a big deal then I would believe it, but hearing his voice broke something inside me. Hearing his voice took me back to the bar. I felt nauseous at the thought of his hands on my body again. Except this time, I didn't have alcohol to numb the feeling like I did the night before. I couldn't hold it in anymore. 'I don't know what I did wrong,' I squeaked, unable to hold my tears in and placing my head on Mama's shoulder, I began to sob.

'Honey, shhh,' Mama said soothingly, with her arm wrapped around me, gently rubbing my shoulder. 'You did nothing wrong. It doesn't matter if he was drunk. Being drunk doesn't turn you into a completely different person, it just brings out who you really are. It lowers inhibitions, so people can't fake their true self. It has nothing to do with who you are, Nina; it says everything about him. He is a bad person.'

'You've had a bad run the last few weeks, Nina, but it's just a coincidence,' Andjela said. 'Just keep being you. You're not doing anything wrong. If you were, I would tell you.'

'Well, it hasn't been quite as bad as you would think,' I said, wiping the tears from my cheeks, a smile breaking through.

'What do you mean?' asked Andjela, puzzled.

'I met a man last night. We actually have a date tonight,' I replied.

'Right back on the horse, hey? That's my girl. Who is he? Did you meet him in the bar before… 'the thing'? Spill, Nina,' Andjela said, a big smile on her face as she took a sip from her cup.

I took my head off Mama's shoulder and wiped my nose with a tissue. 'I can lie, and you don't judge, or I can tell the truth, and we pretend it's a completely normal way to meet someone,' I said, looking from Mama to Andjela.

'Obviously we want the truth,' Mama said.

'You know the site you told me about yesterday? The one that connects you to a random webcam around the world?' I asked Andjela. She nodded, and Mama sat there silently. 'Well, I didn't feel like going straight to sleep, so I went on there when I got home last night. I met a boy named Luka. He's actually from Melbourne.'

'That's great, honey, but please enlighten me as to how you plan to go on a date with a boy from Australia? That's only about a day on a plane away? I doubt he'll be swinging by here tonight to pick you up and take you to dinner,' Mama said with scepticism.

'He texted me before and asked if I would go on a cyber date with him, so we're going to do that tonight. He's going to tell me when he wakes up and we'll do a video chat.'

'That's so cute. I'm going to see my grandparents with my mama today, but I'm coming back tonight to help you get ready for your date. I'll help with your makeup, and we'll pick something cute for you to wear,' Andjela said. She looked just as excited for my date with Luka as she was for her Australian tennis tournament news.

I couldn't possibly say no to her. I didn't want to say no to her either. Andjela helping me get ready for my date sounded like a lot of fun. 'That sounds great,' I said, as she took her hand off her cup, and placed it on my hand.

'Can we not make a huge deal out of this though? I'm just going to be talking to a man on my computer,' I said, trying to get my excitement under control. The bigger deal they made of it, the more pressure I was going to feel. The more pressure I felt, made me feel like I was more likely to make a mess of the date. I was more excited for it than I had been for anything in a long time. It was a strange feeling, balancing the hurt of the night before, and the excitement for my date that night.

'Well, I better get going. I need to take a shower, see my grandparents, and get started on that biology homework. I'll be back at about nine to help you get ready,' Andjela said, as she stood up and gave me a hug.

'Oh geez, a shower really would be a great idea,' I said laughing, smelling her intense training session. She smiled and gave me a gentle tap on the cheek. 'Thanks for coming over. It means a lot to me.' Andjela headed for the door, picked up her bag, and slipped on her shoes, before beginning her walk home.

I spent the next few hours trying to distract myself from any thoughts about guys. I spent time reading, studying, even doing some work in the garden. Anything to make that clock tick a little bit faster. I didn't want to fall into an emotional hole by thinking about what happened with Marko. Thinking about the date was not any more of an option, because I didn't want to have the date in my head before it even happened. I wanted to be able to enjoy Luka's company and be present. Be in the moment. Concocting a rehearsed conversation in my head was no way to have a good time with Luka.

By late-afternoon I was studying outside in the failing sunshine when I looked up and saw Jovan turn the corner at the top of the driveway. He was walking with his football under his arm and his head down. The closer he came, the clearer it became that he was upset. With Tata travelling so much for work, and me being nine years older than Jovan, I had a major hand in raising him. Seeing him upset was like someone punching my soul.

'Hey Jovan, what's wrong?' I asked, grabbing his hand as he tried to walk by, pulling him towards me.

'Nothing,' he said in true Draganić family style, not convincing anyone.

'Come on, you can tell me. It will be our little secret. I won't tell Mama a thing. I promise,' I whispered into his ear, and kissed him on the cheek as he took a seat next to me.

'Well, my friend Bogdan and I went to the football pitch to play. We were playing and then some older boys came along and told us to get off the pitch. When we said no, they took my ball and kicked it off the field. We sat and waited for them to let us back on the pitch, but they didn't. They didn't let us play at all. Bogdan and I just wanted to kick some goals and we couldn't do it,' he finished, dropping the ball dejectedly.

'I'm sorry that happened. People can be very mean and selfish. We both know that they are nowhere near as talented as you are. One day those boys are going to be watching you score a goal for Serbia in the World Cup. Never stop practising.

Never stop working. Okay, Jovan?' I said, as he listened intently with his sorrowful look beginning to soften.

'You're wrong, Nina. They aren't going to watch me score a goal in the World Cup,' Jovan said, looking down at his shoes, a steely resolve appearing on his face.

'Come on, you have to be positive,' I replied.

'No, they won't see me score a goal. They will see me score *goals* for Serbia in the World Cup,' he said, raising his head and smiling at me.

'Well before you get to that point, you're going to have to show that you can beat me first,' I said, standing up and kicking the ball in between the pot plants set up in the yard to act as goal posts.

For the next hour Jovan and I played football together. Making sure Jovan kept score because it wasn't the right score unless he was winning. Milica returned home part way through our game and sat in the chair I had left empty. Milica looked like a young version of our mama. Her hair was the same shade of brown, and her shoulders were slouched like Mama's. Her eyes were a chestnut brown which expanded like a cartoon character whenever she smiled. Whenever I saw her smile, it looked like Mama was smiling. Hearing all the yelling and laughing, Mama came out to see what was causing all the commotion.

'Come on Jovan, she is slow moving to her left, go hard to the right,' Mama said, as he dribbled the ball right and kicked a goal. 'Great goal, Jovan!'

'What happened to, oh I could never pick one of you as my favourite?' I asked, as I dribbled the ball back between the goals to restart play.

'Well, you have a couple of years on him, so I thought I'd try and level the playing field a little by giving him some advice. Plus, he knows you can't go left. You haven't been able to since you hurt your ankle a few months ago playing basketball. Even the birds sitting on the garage know you can't go left,' Mama said.

Mama thought I hurt my ankle playing basketball at school, but what really happened was that I went over on a pair of heels when Andjela and I were drunk one night trying to find our way home. I told her it was basketball because she wouldn't have let me go out the next weekend if I hurt it drinking. What she didn't know wouldn't hurt me.

'Well, instead of standing on the sidelines, why don't you two come out here and show us what you can do?' I goaded Mama and Milica.

'Okay then. Jovan and I against you two. First team to ten wins,' Mama said.

'Fine with me. Are you ready, Milica?' I asked my sister.

'Always. I think we should put something on the line though. Nina and I always have to cook dinner on a Saturday. When we win, we get tonight off. If we lose…, which we won't…, then we have to cook dinner twice this week. Do we have a deal?' Milica asked Mama.

'Okay then, I could use an extra night off this week. Just make sure it's up to my standard. Keep it simple, like your chicken, that's always nice. I don't want to have to send it back to the kitchen like I did with last week's attempt at lasagne. That will not impress your Australian,' Mama said. Jovan feigned throwing up behind Mama as she grimaced at the memory of the failed lasagne.

'Well, if it was that bad then you might want to lose the game, so we all don't have to suffer again,' I said to Mama, laughing.

'No, you two need to practise. Ready, Jovan? Let's go,' Mama said, and Jovan nodded, with a look of determination on his face.

For the next twenty minutes we competed like our lives depended on the result of the game. To be fair, with how poorly the previous week's lasagne went, our lives may very well have been on the line.

Mama played a defensive midfield role and set Jovan up for goals the entire game. Milica played a defensive role while I played more up the field trying to score. Jovan was excellent with the ball at his feet, but he was only eight so we could push him around. Normally I would be okay with him winning, but I knew we didn't have any chicken left in the house, and I didn't want to have to go to the shops to make crumbed chicken, my best dish.

We went goal for goal. I had almost forgotten that Mama was a supremely talented junior player, but she fell pregnant with me at eighteen. After that, pursuing football was no longer a priority for her. Her only dream was to be a mother. Some people grow up knowing they want to be a doctor, or a police officer, she wanted to be a mother.

'It's tied. Nine all. Next goal wins. Think you've got one more in you?' I asked Mama, trying not to show her that I was exhausted.

'I've been taking it easy on you. Jovan and I will end it right now. Isn't that right, Jovan?' Mama said, and he drew his thumb across his neck like he was the Grim Reaper.

I dribbled the ball towards goal with Milica running on my right. Mama was marking me, and Jovan on Milica. I faked left just as Milica made a quick run to get past Jovan. I passed the ball towards Milica with the outside of my foot, but the ball hit a small lump of dirt and sat up ever so slightly. Jovan managed to block the pass with his foot and Mama collected the loose ball. Now they were two on one. I was caught in the middle with Milica trying to make it back into the play. She was too far behind. Mama passed the ball to Jovan who on the first touch kicked it towards goal. Looking like it would bounce off the pot plant from where I stood, it proceeded to strike the inside of the right pot, bounce back to the left pot plant and just cross the line. We had lost. Jovan took off his shirt and was swinging it around his head like he had just scored the winning goal for Serbia in the World Cup. Mama ran after him and picked him up to celebrate.

'Well girls, better get to the store. They won't be open for much longer. Let me get you some money. Please keep it simple, we don't want to go to bed hungry tonight,' Mama said, and she walked inside to get money from her purse.

Milica and I returned home thirty minutes later in complete darkness, feeling lucky that we got the final four chicken breasts. Trying to keep it as simple as possible, we got lettuce, tomato, cucumber, and carrot for a salad, and some potatoes to roast too.

'Can you peel the potatoes while I take a quick shower, please?' I asked Milica.

'Yeah. I'll peel the potatoes and do the salad. We can do the chicken and roast the potatoes together,' she replied.

I returned to the kitchen ten minutes later with the salad prepared and the potatoes peeled. We mixed two eggs into a bowl and put the breadcrumbs on a plate, mixing in my grandmother's chicken spice. I didn't know what made up Baka's secret recipe, I just knew it was magic. Milica and I covered the chicken in flour and then in egg before crumbing it. We then cooked the chicken, roasted the potatoes, and prepared the table. We enjoyed our almost family dinner together, with Tata still in Montenegro for work.

'What do we say to the chefs, Jovan?' Mama asked, as we placed the food on the table.

'Thank you. It's delicious. It tastes like victory,' he said through a mouthful of chicken. Mama gave him a light smack to the back of the head, unable to keep the smile from her face.

As we cleaned up there was a knock on the door, and Jovan ran to it. Andjela was back to help me get ready for my cyber date.

'It's okay, Nina, I'll finish cleaning up. Go and get ready for your date,' Mama said.

Andjela and I went to my room to prepare. Milica had followed into my room, not wanting to be left out.

'Do you have any ideas about what you're going to wear?' Andjela asked, as she opened my closet and started to sift through the clothes hanging there as she did the night before. My closet was jammed full of clothes, but I somehow still only wore about four different things.

'What do we think about what I'm wearing now?' I asked, turning on the spot, causing Milica and Andjela to shake their heads and laugh.

'Nina, as much as what you're wearing now would be the 'real you', I don't think wearing sweatpants, a stained hoodie, and no bra is really going to put out the first date vibes you want. Let's maybe leave that particularly hot ensemble for the second date, and make a different impression tonight,' Andjela said, as she turned back to the closet.

I laid on my bed next to Milica, who got up and started to help Andjela look. My phone, which was laid next to me suddenly buzzed. I snatched it up immediately. It was Luka.

'Hey, hope you had a good day. I'll be ready in fifteen minutes. Does that suit you? Can't wait to see you,' he texted.

'Perfect, see you soon,' I replied immediately, and jumped up to help Andjela and Milica look through the closet. Shutting down every idea they had, from dresses, different shirts, from formal looks to casual. I needed to show him that I cared but not look like we were going to a wedding. I was running out of options, and out of time.

'I can't believe how hard this is. What if he's wearing something nice and I'm looking super casual? What if he's wearing something chill and I show up in a cocktail dress? I'll look like an idiot,' I said frustratedly, trying not to hyperventilate. I walked back to my bed to check the time on my phone. 'Great, only ten minutes left. I don't have anything to wear and haven't done my makeup yet. Let's do the makeup now and worry about what to wear in a minute,' I said, my voice becoming progressively higher pitched as I opened my makeup bag.

'I'll help you with your makeup, and Milica, you keep looking for something for Nina to wear. I think we should keep it basic, a natural look. What do you think?' Andjela asked me, as I took a seat on my desk chair, and Andjela laid my makeup upon my desk.

'Yeah, let's just use BB cream and some lip gloss. I think that would work. Plus, it'll work with whatever outfit we decide on, so it will give us some flexibility,' I said, with an eye still on the time, noticing it was down to eight minutes. I wanted to be a couple of minutes late, so he had to wait for me, but not so late that he got frustrated and bailed on our date. *If I can't decide, I might have to wear my stained hoodie,'* I thought, feeling desperate.

'Okay, so let's take a breath. What kind of look are you aiming for, Nina?' Andjela asked, as she started to apply the BB cream.

'I want to look like we're going for afternoon drinks on a nice summer day. Something cute, but not over the top,' I said, as Andjela evened out the cream across my cheeks and nose.

'That means dresses Milica. Don't look at pants and shirts anymore,' said Andjela, applying a small amount of cream to my forehead.

'I've got it,' Milica exclaimed. Andjela and I turned immediately to find Milica was holding a sky-blue dress with flowers printed on it. It was an off the shoulder dress, layered over my chest and went to halfway up my thigh fitting my figure snugly. It was an old favourite of mine. I loved it.

Andjela put the BB cream away as Milica laid the dress out on my bed. 'What do you think?' Milica asked, intently looking upon the outfit.

'How did we not see this before? It's perfect Milica. Thank you. Andjela, can you hand me the lip gloss? I'm supposed to be online now,' I said. I applied my lip gloss, and I pulled a strapless bra from my closet. I incarcerated myself and quickly put my dress on. 'What do you think?' I asked, putting my arms out and turning around.

'I love it,' said Milica.

'You look beautiful. He won't know what hit him,' Andjela said, as Mama walked into my room with a glass of red wine.

'Here. You're on a date after all,' Mama said, placing the glass next to my laptop. 'Have a great time with Luka. Come on you two, let's give her some privacy.'

'But Mama, I want to see him and say hello,' Milica whined, as she was dragged from my room by Mama.

'I really think I should stay and listen. I need to get used to hearing the Australian accent. It's purely educational,' Andjela argued futilely, as the incoming call from Luka appeared on my laptop.

My heart began to race. I tried to downplay it during the day, but my body told the story of how I truly felt. I was over the moon excited to see him again. All the bad thoughts of Marko were expelled from my mind. Luka was the only thing that mattered.

I pressed accept on the call and his smiling face appeared before me. *Those eyes are even more beautiful than I remembered,'* I thought, awestruck.

'He's cute, Nina. Find out if he has a brother,' Andjela whispered, as I shooed her from my room. I turned back to the laptop to look at Luka. Our first date hadn't started, and I already felt like I had known him for a long time. It didn't feel like a first date.

CHAPTER SIX
The Cyber Date

Normally when I woke to my alarm it took my brain a couple of minutes to figure out what time it was, what day it was, and where I was. Before falling asleep I would lay there for what felt like an eternity, turning my mind over thinking about every uncomfortable thing I had done in my life before finally, eventually, drifting off to sleep. So, by the time my alarm woke me, I was only just falling into REMS. That morning was different though. I woke up picturing Nina's beautiful smile, those cute freckles on her face, her eyes the perfect shade of brown with flecks of green, and her incredible flowing hair. Normally I would be wracking my brain for an explanation as to why someone like her would be going on a date with me, but not that morning. That morning, all I felt was joy and excitement.

When my alarm rang at seven, I felt like I'd had four long black coffees already, like waking up on Christmas morning. I sat bolt upright as my eyes snapped open, I reached for my phone to turn off my alarm, and texted Nina saying that I would be ready for our date in fifteen minutes. For a moment a little voice in my head said she would cancel. That voice was thankfully immediately shut down by the excitement and joy that I woke up with. She texted back quickly agreeing to be ready by then. *'Is she as happy and excited as I am? I doubt it. She couldn't possibly be feeling this excited,'* I thought, the feeling of elation consuming me to the point I could even feel it in my toenails.

I threw a pair of shorts on and went to the front yard to find a row of white rose bushes planted just inside the front fence. I took a moment to feel the warmth of the November morning hit my face. I could hear a bird singing, so I looked up and saw two rainbow lorikeets in the gumtree of our neighbour's front yard. Their rainbow colouring looked like they were created in a children's story. Nature truly is extraordinary.

'Good morning,' said a woman, as she was dragged past the front fence by her German Shepard.

I found the most exquisite rose on one of the bushes, broke it off and walked back inside the house making sure to lock the security door behind me. Mum always thought there was about to be a string of brutal day murders in our upper middle-class neighbourhood in Williamstown.

I walked to the kitchen and with each passing moment I felt my heartrate increase. I poured a large glass of wine hoping it would help me to relax, thinking that drinking at seven in the morning could be the beginning of a beautiful drinking problem. *'It might be a bit cliché if I become a musician and am an alcoholic as well. Maybe I should consider another addiction to be less of a stereotype,'* I thought.

I peeked through the back window and saw my parents sitting at the table, sharing breakfast. Almost every weekend during the warmer months they got up before seven and had breakfast together in the backyard. Mum saw me and gave me a smiling wave, which I returned with a touch less enthusiasm. I was glad they weren't in the kitchen to interrogate me as to why I had a rose and was pouring myself a glass of wine. Heading back to my room, I walked up the stairs as if I was in an egg and spoon race, being careful not to spill a drop of the very full glass.

I entered my room and gently placed the wine glass on my bedside table, resting the rose on the right side of the bed, out of view of my laptop. While we couldn't share a meal together at a restaurant, I wanted to make sure I looked like I was going on a first date in person. If I wasn't dressed nicely then she might think I wasn't taking it seriously. I knew the exact shirt I was going to wear. There were a limited number of options for nice shirts in my wardrobe, so it wasn't like I was going to need a fashion task force to help me pick the perfect date outfit. My sky-blue shirt stood out to me, and unlike my suit, it fitted me properly.

There were only a few minutes until my date with Nina, so I quickly ran to the bathroom to brush my teeth. I was convinced that using teeth whitening toothpaste for the first time in weeks was going to turn my teeth pearly white instantly. I brushed before I put my shirt on, knowing that by Murphy's Law, I would drop toothpaste on my shirt and need to change it.

I rushed back to my room, put on my shirt, and buttoned it quickly. I turned on my laptop and placed it on my lap as I sat on my bed. My hands were beginning to shake, and I could feel them getting clammy, so I picked up the wine carefully with two hands. I took a sip to try and calm my rising nerves as my laptop sprung to life. I didn't think I could be more nervous than I was walking to the altar at Nana's funeral, but as the moment drew closer, my nerves flew to all time heights. As the computer finally loaded, my heart was almost beating out of my chest. Tightly clutching the wine in my left hand, my shaking right hand extended to press the call icon next to Nina's profile picture. The screen turned to a large version of her profile picture, and I could see myself in the bottom righthand corner. I didn't look as nervous as I felt which was a relief. The screen continued to read 'calling' for what felt like an eternity, and just as I started to worry that she might not answer, calling switched to connecting. There she was.

I was in awe. You build someone up in your mind and think surely they can't be that beautiful; it's not possible for anyone to be that beautiful. Then you see them and realise you were wrong. I was wrong. She was even more beautiful than I remembered. My mind went blank as I drank in the angel in front of me. She didn't look like she was trying. She was wearing a beautiful blue floral dress. It was hanging off her shoulder and

I could see that she had a long and elegant neck which flowed perfectly into her collarbones. Almost like she was made of porcelain. *How is it possible for a woman like this to be on a date with me? Stop it, Luka, don't question a good thing. Just enjoy your time with her,'* I chastised myself.

She wore a big smile as she saw my hand clap over my mouth. She looked nervous. Or maybe that look was excitement. They are the same sensation; it just depends on if you think it will go well or poorly. Nina looked unsure of herself, her hands moving strangely like she had just grown them, until one found its way to her hair and began twirling it. Nina looked like she didn't know what to say, which relaxed me. Maybe, just maybe, she felt that same something special I was feeling.

'You are so beautiful. You look amazing, Nina,' I said, before I could even say hi. The words just slipped out of my mouth. Playing it cool was apparently not in my dating game. By the look on her face, she appreciated my cheesy comment because she laughed. She looked off camera and shooed away someone before her focus returned to me.

'You look really nice, Luka. I like your shirt,' she said, which made me smile so widely I thought my cheeks were going to split open. I could feel the heat rise in my face and I didn't know how I was supposed to respond to the compliment. I didn't know whether to acknowledge it or move on to another topic. I thought that I should just open my mouth and force speech, hoping that it would come up with something intelligent.

I placed the wine glass on my bed side table after taking another sip. I saw that Nina had a wine glass also and mirrored my action, taking a sip of her wine and putting it down on her desk.

'I'm really happy to see you, Nina. Normally I struggle to sleep because I have a million things running through my head, but last night it was just because I was excited to see you. I'm trying to not scare you and I feel like I'm doing a poor job of it,' I said, and immediately wished that I didn't just open my mouth and hope for the best. *'What am I doing with my hands?'* I wondered, looking down at them, seeing them strangely hang in space. I grabbed my glass of wine and had another sip just to occupy them.

'Don't worry. You're not scaring me. I was excited to see you as well,' Nina said, with a coy smile, looking off camera and reaching for her wine again.

'What is that wine called?' I asked, trying to sound like a normal person on a date. So far, my dating experience had been what I had seen on television, so I wasn't sure what people talked about on a first date.

'I think it's called Kovačević,' Nina said, holding the wine glass out to examine it. 'What's yours called?' Nina asked, pointing to my glass with hers.

'I'm not sure of the brand name. I just know Dad loves his Heathcote Shiraz, so it's probably from that region. I'm trying to learn more about wine, so I'm not just drinking to get a buzz, but I don't have a particularly refined palate. I think if someone put a one-thousand-dollar bottle in front of me and a ten-dollar bottle I wouldn't be able to tell the difference,' I said, shaking my head, and resting the glass on my lap.

'Well, here's to a first date buzz,' Nina said, raising her glass, holding her little finger outstretched as she took a drink.

'Cheers,' I said. I raised my glass and tapped it on my webcam. 'That little finger held out means that you're fancy.' Nina's hand was covering her mouth and her eyes looked like she was laughing.

'As Patrick taught us, when in doubt, pinkie out,' Nina said, in a bad Patrick Star impression. I laughed trying not to spill any of my wine.

I looked around Nina's room to try and find out a little bit about her. She had a corkboard full of photos of her with whom I assumed were her friends and family. *I hope to find a picture of us together on there one day,'* I thought, dreamily. There was a bookcase over her left shoulder overflowing with books, but I couldn't read the titles as I didn't speak Serbian, much to my nana's disappointment. On one of the shelves there was a framed photo; it looked like it was her and her family. It must have been her most prized photo sitting in that position. There was a window behind her, but I couldn't see anything as it was night. Her bed was made perfectly and there was a stack of neatly folded clothes on it. Her bedside table had a lamp and a book on it. *That must be what she's reading now,'* I thought, trying to read the cover.

'Do you normally drink red wine?' I asked her.

She swirled the wine around the glass and smelled it like she was at a wine tasting. Nina wafted the wine towards her nose. She took a small amount into her mouth and let the flavours wash over her tongue before swallowing.

'Wine hound! Oh, wine hound! Where is my spit bucket?' she said, with a mock stiff face and an attempted Royal accent, her head swivelling around, pretending to look for a waiter. 'I'll have to make a complaint to the waiter when she comes back. She's doing a great job of losing her tip. Terrible service.'

'Shouldn't they have brought you some cheese, caviar, and biscuits by now too?' I asked.

'Yes, truly horrendous service,' Nina said, tilting her head and looking down her nose at what I presumed was her bedroom door.

'Sorry, what was your question again? Oh yeah, it depends on who I'm with. If I'm with my family, I might have one glass of wine or a small rakija. If I'm with my best friend, Andjela, we drink whatever's cheapest or whatever we can get our hands on,' she said, still swirling her wine. It looked like she was trying to get the wine as close as she could to the top of her glass without spilling it all over her stunning dress. She looked enamoured with the task.

'This is only my first glass, that must be your fourth by how you buttoned your shirt,' Nina said, as she continued swirling her wine, getting dangerously close to the lip of the glass. She then put her glass down just in time to see me look at my shirt.

I had missed a button. I missed the second button as well, so it was wrong the entire way down. *How could I miss that? You are so stupid, Luka!'* I chastised myself, wanting to find a hole to crawl into and hide away. I felt embarrassed. I quickly undid my shirt to fix my buttons, beginning from the bottom.

'Woah, woah, woah. I don't know what kind of girl you think I am, but this is a first date, dude; keep your clothes on,' she said, as she took another drink of wine. From the smirk on her face, she was really enjoying my head being in a spin.

She was mercurial. She quoted SpongeBob while drinking wine, called me dude, and wasn't scared to tell me if something was wrong. She had all the qualities I would want in a best friend wrapped in the most beautiful woman I had ever seen. Nina was weird, interesting, and incredible. *How is this woman single? I need to find an engagement ring now, because I'm ready to wife her,'* I thought. Somehow that thought didn't scare me. *Do people know this quickly if they've found their human?'* I wondered.

Nina was so smooth, seizing any opportunity to make a joke, and if she didn't think I could be on her level, I would get left behind. 'Oh sorry! I got a text from my boss to say you ordered a skinny stripper. Have I come to the wrong place?'

'Yeah, sorry you're too late. The bachelorette party has finished. If I ordered one just for myself to watch while I drank red wine alone, I would need to look in the mirror and reevaluate my entire life,' Nina said, looking relieved that I could play along with her.

'Sorry ma'am. You will receive a full refund on Monday.'

'Do you normally drink wine?' Nina asked, as I completed rebuttoning my shirt. I pulled my shirt down at the bottom and closely examined it to make sure that I hadn't made another mistake.

'When I drink, it's normally wine. The only time I get rakija is when I'm sick and Nana gives it to me. Nana said her Serbian home medicine works better than a doctor's. Well, when Nana gave it to me,' I said, looking down at my hands as I finished my sentence. I tried to push down the pain I felt bubbling up inside at the thought of Nana's absence.

'I'm so sorry you and your family have gone through that. That you are going through it,' Nina said. She was no longer playing with her wine glass. She was looking at me with such focus, like I was the only thing that was important in this world. There was genuine care on her face with a softness that made me feel like I could tell her anything and it would be safe with her.

'It's crazy because things can change so quickly. Nana was always healthy. She didn't drive so she walked everywhere and stayed fit. One day when she was walking home from church, a car came quickly around the corner and ran over her feet, breaking both of them. After that it all went downhill rather quickly. She couldn't stay fit, and she had several small strokes, then a big one which is how it ended. I miss her so much,' I finished in a choked voice, trying to maintain my composure.

'She must have been really important to you. Were you close?' Nina asked. Her words were coated in care and kindness. Things like that are almost impossible to fake. The best people in the world are genuine, and she was completely genuine.

'Very close. She was the one that suggested that I start playing the guitar, and she was the only one that I played for. No one else even knew that I played the guitar outside my house, so I would visit her and play the songs I wrote. The first time I played for anyone aside from Nana was when I played at her funeral because in my mind, I was really playing for her. Playing for her for the last time,' I said, making sure to look Nina in the eye when I spoke. Focusing on Nina helped keep me strong.

'That's beautiful. I'd really love to hear you play. I know it won't be the same as going to see your nana and playing for her, but if you wanted to share that with me, I would feel honoured,' Nina said with a sweet smile.

'How did I get so lucky that you lowered your standards to go on a date with me? You are so far out of my league it's unbelievable,' I said with a small laugh, before taking another drink of wine. I said it as a joke with an element of my truth in it, but she didn't think it was funny at all. After putting my glass down, I looked at Nina. She looked angry.

'Don't ever put yourself down like that again. I could tell as soon as we started talking that you're a good person. The people who aren't in my league are mean, lying, and disingenuous people. If I thought even for a second that you were any of those things, then I wouldn't be here now. Why would you say something like that about yourself?' she asked.

Even though I felt bad immediately, like I just stepped on a puppy's foot and heard it yelp, I couldn't help but be impressed with her English skills as it wasn't her first language. 'I don't want to saddle you with my trauma too soon. Isn't this supposed to be a first date? Shouldn't we be talking about our favourite movies and musicians?' I asked, trying to deflect from the question.

'We can talk about whatever we want. It's our date, there are no rules. We can talk about whatever you're comfortable with.

I do want to get to know you. Everything about you. I want to know which movies you've watched a thousand times, that you put on every time you feel sick or sad. Songs that you listen to on repeat and each time you hear them, you fall more in love with them. I want to talk about things that make your eyes light up. Things that have hurt you. I want to know you, Luka. I feel as though if you share the things that have hurt you, then you take away their power. If you just keep them inside, then they will eat away at you. They will own you,' Nina said.

'I don't think those books are just for decoration,' I thought, blown away at how she was the most beautiful, and the most intelligent woman I had ever met. Her face made me say hello; her mind made me want to know her as deeply as you could know another human.

'I want to get to know everything about you too, but it's hard to talk about. I don't want you to lose respect for me. I don't want you to think I'm weak and not a man,' I said. It didn't feel like a first date. I felt a different level of familiarity with her; as if we had known each other for years. There was a feeling of nervousness, but at that point it was from the idea of opening up to someone. That I was even thinking about sharing with her showed a level of comfort I had never had with another person.

'I would never think that. Being open and vulnerable is real strength. It's hard to let someone in because if it goes badly, it hurts even more. This idea that a real man keeps his emotions bottled up and never shares anything is draconian. Would you feel more comfortable sharing something with me if I shared something painful first?'

'I would love if you shared something with me, but only if you're comfortable,' I replied, leaning forward in an attempt to get closer to her. I was craving to touch Nina, to hold her hand. To feel the warmth of her.

Nina proceeded to tell me about the night before, and how the creature at the party sexually assaulted her. I felt sick.

'That couldn't have been easy for you to tell me. Thanks for sharing. I have to be honest; I feel sick hearing that. I'm angry; I don't understand how someone can do that, drunk or not. I know we've only just met, but I know you didn't do anything to lead him on. Some people just don't have any respect. He's a crumb. I'm disgusted,' I said, and could feel the hatred boiling in my stomach. My hands were shaking. I didn't even know his name, but I already hated him more than I had ever hated someone before. I took another drink of wine, and Nina did the same.

'It was a bad night, but I want to focus on something good instead. Like being here with you,' Nina said, a sparkle in her eye.

'I want to share with you, but I don't really know where to start, Nina,' I said confused.

'I don't want to push you; I know it can be hard. How about I ask you a question instead? Why did your nana suggest that you start to play the guitar?' Nina asked. There was no judgement in her eyes, no frustration because I hadn't opened up to her yet. There was just patience and care. I wanted to tell her everything.

'Well, all through my teenage years I was bullied. I'm lucky to have a great family, and two amazing friends, James and Michael, but everyone else made my life miserable. James and Michael didn't go to secondary school with me, so I was alone at school. I spent six years on my own at lunch because I knew that if I interacted with anyone, they would abuse me. I was completely ostracised and to this day I don't know why. The only time it was physical was when I was held on the train so I couldn't get off at my stop. I just wanted to go home. I still don't get it. They would talk about how I looked, and that no girl would ever go near me. They would say no one liked me, and no one ever would, so I may as well just kill myself,' I said. If I recited this story to myself the emotion would overwhelm me, but not when telling Nina. She gave me a strength and courage that I had never had before. With every word I felt like a weight was lifting from my chest. The previous day I had felt the lightest I had in living memory, and as I let go of things I didn't know were still bothering me, I felt lighter still, like I was floating.

'I'm so sorry you had to experience that. Maybe it's just the school I go to, but everyone has friends at our school. Not everyone is friends, but no one is on their own. If someone is sitting on their own at lunch, someone will go and sit with them. I can't comprehend going out of my way to be cruel to someone else, let alone for no reason. That must have been so hard, and you clearly are a strong person for being able to get through that,' Nina said, a tear trickling down her right cheek. That was what empathy looked like. She felt my pain.

'Thanks for listening. It was a long time ago, but it's hard not to carry those things with you. It felt like there was an elephant sitting on my chest making it hard to breathe. If you're told enough times that no one likes you, then it's almost impossible not to believe it. You turn up to school every day being yourself, wanting to be yourself, but you're made to feel like there's something inherently wrong with you. That if no one likes you while you're being yourself, then you must be the problem. You're the common denominator. It starts to affect your other relationships. If I didn't get a quick reply from Michael or James, I would think it was because they didn't like me anymore, or I did something wrong, never that they might just be busy. You overthink everything and start to be cruel to yourself. You become one of your own bullies,' I finished, trying to breathe through my old pain that felt suddenly very raw.

'I bet you would get to the point that if someone said something nice, you thought they were just being polite, that they didn't really mean it. If someone insulted you though, then that was the truth, they weren't being mean, just honest. I know that I was never bullied, but I've spent a lot of time feeling anxious. I've spent a lot of time insulting myself. It's not always easy, but you have to remember that you spend a lot of time in your own head, so you have to make sure it's a nice place to be,' Nina said with a quivering voice.

'You're exactly right. The only person I ever confided in was Nana. I would go to her house and we would cry together. She promised that she wouldn't tell anyone what was happening, not even Mum. One day I went to visit her and she had bought me a guitar. She said I should start to play and write some songs, because it would be a great outlet for me to try and express how I was feeling. I shouldn't be bottling it up. So, I did, and I've been doing that ever since. I know I would never have gotten through that time if it wasn't for her,' I said, looking deeply into Nina's eyes that were pulling me in. I felt like she was sitting on my bed. She felt so close that I could touch her. Maybe I told her more than I should have, but once I started, I couldn't help but keep going. Getting something off your chest that you've been carrying around with you for so long was an amazing feeling. Nana was my safe place, and I could already feel that on our first date, Nina was going to be my new safe place.

'Is there any other adolescent trauma you want to get off your chest? We're on a roll here,' Nina said, a sparkling smile breaking across her face. It was easy with her. I thought I was going to have to try hard to impress Nina, but I could just be myself.

'Just one other thing I want to get out of the way now. When I was fourteen, I was walking and, wow this is harder than I thought. Okay, so I was walking at home, and didn't see the corner of the table. I bashed my little toe into the leg of the table. It hurt so badly that I wanted to take an axe to it but realised it couldn't feel the pain I felt. Ever since then I've not been able to look at a table without suffering a flashback to that day,' I said laughing, and she rolled her eyes.

'Yeah, ha-ha, very funny. That is the worst though. I think one day I will find out what hurts more, childbirth or stubbing my toe,' she said sarcastically. 'I feel like it'll be a coin flip, but at least childbirth has the positive of a baby at the end of it.' She turned her attention back to her wine, enamoured with the swirling deep red liquid in her half empty glass.

'Well, if we have children one day you can know that I've felt the same level of pain that you're experiencing when you give birth,' I said, taking another sip of wine. *If we have a baby? Seriously, Luka? Have you ever spoken to a human before?'* I thought in disbelief. I wanted to scream in frustration but needed to hold my composure.

'That's true, but if you bring that up during childbirth, you're risking a punch to *your* birth canal. I'm not a violent girl, but I want complete sympathy, empathy, and a lot of apologies for putting me in that position,' Nina said, batting her eyelids looking like an angel. I laughed. Her eyes looked like the kind that you could tell if she was smiling even when you couldn't see her mouth. The people with the most beautiful smiles are the people that smile with their eyes. Nina's eyes smile. She was a natural, effortless beauty.

'I'm probably getting ahead of myself bringing up children when I haven't even held your hand,' I said, feeling relieved that she hadn't freaked out at the idea of us making babies.

'Who knows? I never thought I'd meet someone online that I liked, but here we are. Never say never,' Nina said, shrugging. I gave an uncomfortable little smirk. There was a moment of silence, both of us feeling as though that topic had run its course, and it was time for our conversation to travel down a new path.

'So, how many dates do we need to have before you play a song for me?' Nina asked, raising her eyebrows and taking another drink of wine. Her glass was almost empty. She stared at it, as if imploring it to refill itself.

'Well, the real question is, am I able to play for you without you feeling uncomfortable? You know the feeling you have when people sing happy birthday to you? Having someone sing a song just for you could be even worse, especially if I'm terrible,' I said.

'Nope, it would never go badly. It will be amazing whenever you decide to play. You know I am drinking. There's a reason that the band comes on late at the pub. Music sounds better with a drink in your hand,' Nina said, smiling and swaying to the music that hadn't started yet.

'*I don't think it's possible to say no to that smile,*' I thought, glancing down at my guitar, resting just arms-length from me. Aleks spent the night at a friend's house, so I didn't have to worry about waking him in the next room.

'Well, I do have my guitar right here. I wrote a song only yesterday and would love to get some feedback on it, seeing as I can't play for Nana anymore,' I said, as I placed my laptop to the side and picked up my guitar. 'Drinking on an empty stomach always leads to some loose decision making, so hopefully this goes well.'

I tuned my guitar carefully and wondered why I had let her talk me into playing so easily. *If I couldn't say no to her asking me to play a song for her, how would I ever be able to say no to her when we go house hunting?*' I wondered, getting ahead of myself once again.

Nina laughed and shook her head. 'I have a cute Australian man who's going to play me a song he wrote, and I have a glass of red wine in my hand. This might be the best date anyone has ever had, cyber or not. It would be even better if my wine hound refilled my glass though.'

For some reason I wasn't nervous in the slightest. Even when I played a song in my room alone, I got a little edgy. I would have one ear on what I was playing, and one ear on the stairs listening for anyone coming. I was sat there with my guitar, looking into Nina's smiling eyes, and felt no nerves at all. I was completely in the moment. I felt at home. She didn't know then that the song I was going to play was about her. *'In about three minutes time I think she's going to figure that out, but I don't want anyone else to hear this song before she does,'* I thought.

I was walking, completely lost.
Sun blocked by the thick forest.
No idea where to turn next.
Or how to make the fall arrest.
Then by a chance encounter,
I struck gold and found you.
The path cleared before me,
The way back home was free.

I found my smile in your sparkling eyes.
I found my smile in your brilliant mind.
I found my smile in your angel light.
I found my smile when you said hi.

You struck me by surprise,
And broke the never-ending night.
To me a hard ten,
So here I am born again.
Beautiful colours in the sky.
My taste buds now alive.
The sound of children laughing.
The smell of flowers blooming.

I found my smile in your sparkling eyes.
I found my smile in your brilliant mind.
I found my smile in your angel light.
I found my smile when you said hi.

If it's gone it's not forever,
And you'll see things get better.
If you ask the question aloud,
What is lost can be found.

I found my smile in your sparkling eyes.
I found my smile in your brilliant mind.
I found my smile in your angel light.
I found my smile when you said hi.
I found my joy in your platinum smile.
I found my heart when yours found mine.
I found my life when our souls combined.
I found my smile when you said hi.

Nina was twirling her hair around her finger while she watched me sing, as if she didn't know she was doing it, but damn it was adorable. I didn't break eye contact with her for the entire song. I didn't want to look anywhere else. There could have been the Aurora Australis happening in my bedroom and I wouldn't have paid any attention to it. I knew Nina was special when I wrote the song, but looking into her eyes while playing it removed any doubt about the future I wanted. I could feel the lyrics in my soul as I sang to her. As much as I didn't want to take my eyes off her, she didn't take her eyes off me either. I didn't understand what I was feeling, I just knew that I was addicted to it.

As I finished the song I got hit by a feeling. I had heard of this phenomenon where your heart skips a beat. I thought that was just a figure of speech until then. I felt it. A moment where my entire body stopped, and my breathing and heartbeat paused. The only thing I could feel in that split second were butterflies exploding, bouncing off the walls of my stomach. *What is this sensation?' I* wondered, feeling both scared and excited. I couldn't explain it.

'Wow,' Nina said, a sparkle in her eye. 'Was that song for someone, or was it just a song?' It felt like a leading question. I just smiled and didn't say a word. I didn't have to say anything. She knew the answer from the way I smiled at her. I placed my guitar back on its stand just to the side of my bed.

'I loved it. The standard has been set. You have to sing for me on all our dates. What do you call it?' Nina asked.

'I found my smile,' I replied, going back to my glass of wine. My glass was looking sad, but I didn't need liquid courage anymore. I felt completely joyous.

'I hope you're going to start playing in front of people. You need to share your voice and tell these stories. You can't just tell them to me and your bedroom walls,' Nina said.

'Well, actually, on the weekend I'm playing my first gig. I'm nervous, but at the same time, I can't wait.'

'I'm sure you'll be amazing. I really want to see it. Is there any way I can watch it?' Nina asked.

'I'll ask Michael or James to do a live stream so you can watch. Knowing that you're watching will calm me down while I play. I'll be thinking of you, wishing I was looking out at your face,' I said, and still had that weird feeling in my chest. *I'm going to have to do an internet search after our date to see what this feeling is. Dr Internet will probably tell me that I have three weeks to live. Well, at least then I can still play the gig,'* I thought, remembering the last time I consulted internet with my symptoms. It said I had cervical polyps.

'Maybe you should get some Nina masks made for them to hand out at the door,' she said, and I laughed just as I was having the last of my wine. I was able to flush my sinuses and covered my keyboard in wine. If she thought I looked cool singing her a song, then I undid all that good work with one poorly timed drink. Getting through the date after the shirt incident without making a fool of myself again was too much to ask. 'I'm really shocked you have a box of tissues by your bed,' Nina said with a devilish grin, as she wiped the tears from her eyes laughing. I wiped up my mess with a wad of tissues.

'Yeah, I spill a lot of wine,' I replied, as I shot the tissues into the rubbish bin by my bed.

'I think seeing a room full of your face on different bodies might do more harm than good,' I said, wiping the last of the wine off the keyboard.

'Yeah, that might be a bit confusing for your body. So, when are you coming to the motherland to visit?' Nina asked. Her smile was spread widely across her face and her cheeks looked flushed. I hoped it was because she was enjoying our date, and not from the glass of wine she just finished. 'You can play a gig at the local bar here.'

'When's your birthday? Maybe if I'm worthy and get an invite to the social event of the year I'll have to come. If you allow an Australian to be on the very exclusive guestlist, I couldn't possibly miss it,' I said, placing my empty glass aside, leaving my hands to feel lost once again.

'It's August twenty-third. I'm sure we can find a way to squeeze you in. Everyone will want to talk to the Australian guy, so I may have some competition for your attention,' Nina said, giving me a half smile.

'I don't think anyone could be competition to you for my attention,' I said sincerely, turning Nina's half smile into a full smile. I had seen her twice in my life and was already addicted

to her. I could look at her smile every day for the rest of my life.
I already knew that I was falling hard for her, and I wasn't about
to stop myself.

'Okay I think you just broke the cheese meter with that and
it's a complete lie, but I absolutely love it. Maybe I need to go
into one of those beauty pageants so the world knows it instead
of just you,' Nina said, giving her hair a flick, standing up, and
doing the most exaggerated runway walk a person could do.

'I really like the way you walk,' I said, trying to pick my jaw
up off the floor. The way she moved was so graceful, like she
was floating an inch above the ground. Nina laughed and sat
back down much to my disappointment.

'It's getting late, so I better get to bed, and you should do
something constructive with your day,' Nina said. She smiled
but her smile didn't reach her eyes. There was a touch of sadness
in her eyes that our date had to come to an end.

'Yeah, you should get some rest, but let me tell you, time
can't be more constructively spent than being with you and
getting to know you. You should know that when I come to
visit, I can't wait to take you out to dinner. I can introduce
myself to your family, and after they go against their better
judgement to let you go, we can go to the nicest restaurant in
Požega. Or more likely, get a bottle of wine, find a place that
serves chicken nuggets, and eat them on a bench somewhere in
town,' I said, picturing in my mind how incredible it would be
just to sit next to her. To look across and see her face. To walk
down the street and be able to take hold of her hand would be a
dream.

'I think you just described my perfect date. Marry me,' Nina
said, and even though I knew she was joking, my insides did a
backflip.

'As long as we have chicken nuggets at the reception, I'm
ready. I want to see the ring before I say yes though,' I said, and

held up my hand as if waiting for Nina to place an engagement ring upon it.

'Will this do?' Nina asked, and pulled out a plastic ring with a hard, diamond shaped orange lolly atop.

'Oh, it's beautiful. Yes. A thousand times yes,' I said, fanning my face.

'You're so cute. Well, I've had a great time, Luka. Thanks for tonight. I hope we can have a second cyber date very soon,' Nina said, her smile returning to her eyes.

'I had so much fun, and I absolutely want to do this again. I'll text you,' I said as she waved goodbye. 'Oh Nina, wait. You almost forgot your flower,' and I pushed the white rose into the camera. I blew a kiss to Nina and waved goodbye.

'Aww, that flower is so beautiful. Thank you. See you soon, Luka,' Nina said, placing her hands over her heart. She blew a kiss back to me before hanging up the call.

The image of her blowing me a kiss seemed to linger on the screen. Her kiss moved through cyber space, covering the thousands of kilometres separating us to instantly touch my soul. I knew it wasn't a real kiss, but it made me feel like no kiss ever had before. That kiss was at that point, the best kiss of my life.

CHAPTER SEVEN
The Pairing

As I climbed into bed and pulled the covers over my shoulders after my date with Luka, I couldn't wipe the smile away. Even when I woke the next morning, I could feel the smile painted to my face. All thought of the incident with Marko had been knocked from my mind. You can't be in a dark place when you're radiating light. All I could think about was Luka. Any time I blinked I saw his beautiful blue eyes. I saw how his entire face would light up when he smiled. Seeing that face in my mind's eye sent a kaleidoscope of butterflies swirling around my stomach.

I rolled over to pick up my phone and saw a text from Luka. 'Good morning, sunshine,' it read. *How could my man be any more adorable? Well, he isn't my man, yet, but is it too early to want him to be my man?'* I wondered.

'Good Aussie evening. How was your day?' I replied immediately, looking for an accompanying selfie to send him. When nothing jumped out, I took several photos and scanned through them trying to find the perfect one. It needed to say I just woke up, but I'm not ugly. *Nope, ugly. Urgh, gross. Trying too hard. What am I doing with my eyes? Yep, that's the one,'* I finally decided. A gentle smile and soft eyes as I laid on the right side of my bed.

I laid in bed for the next hour exchanging texts with Luka. Replying so quickly to each other that I didn't even have time to get out of our chat thread. We talked about our families, sending photos of them to each other. Both close to our families, his mum sounded like the same woman as my mama. It must be the Serbian connection. His brother, the star athlete, and his sister, the smart mouth that would get her into, and out of trouble. His family was his entire world. I could feel that with every new thing I learned about him, I liked him even more. 'Why does he have to live so far away?' I groaned aloud to myself.

Finally, I decided that I needed to get up and try to accomplish something with my day aside from getting to know my future husband. I rolled out of bed and stumbled to the living room with my phone in hand. I had a mountain of homework that I needed to finish for Monday. Biology, Serbian, English, and psychology books were stacked on the floor of my room next to my desk. Class didn't start until two-pm Monday, so I would be able to work late. I worked best at night anyway. Plus, the later I stayed up, the longer I could talk to Luka.

'Good morning. So how was your date?' Mama asked, as I plonked myself on the couch unable to drag my eyes from my phone.

I took a moment to respond to her as I replied to another text from Luka. 'It was cool. I had fun,' I said, not even looking at her. I knew I was being rude, but for that moment, the portal to Australia in my hands was the most interesting thing in the world to me. If a murderer stormed into our house, I would be easy prey. *Hopefully, they'll have the courtesy to wait until I press send on this text to Luka before they kill me,*' I thought.

'That's it? It was cool? Honey, your smile is so big that I'm worried you're about to split the sides of your face open just to smile a little bit wider. Would you like to try again, and this time maybe try a little bit of honesty?' Mama said, putting down the pot that she was scouring in the sink.

'Okay, it was amazing. I had so much fun getting to know him. He's such a sweet an interesting man. Hopefully I can see him again really soon,' I said, finally taking my eyes off my phone to look at her. *It's been over a minute since Luka replied, what on earth could be so important?*' I thought in frustration.

'I'm glad you had a good time, but Nina, please make sure it doesn't interfere with your schoolwork. You're in your last year of high school, so you can't risk your future and possibly mess up getting into university. You've always got your work done before, but I don't want you to lose focus. You need to maintain your priorities,' Mama said. Education had always come first in our house. Nothing else could be done unless our schoolwork had been finished. Jovan routinely got into trouble for not telling Mama about his homework until late the night before it was due. Mama had started checking Jovan's bag every day after school to see what homework he had been given.

'Mama, please. I'm female. We have been designed to be able to multi-task. I think you should save that worry for when Jovan is seventeen. Or for tonight with Jovan,' I scoffed at her concerns. I spent a lot of time on my phone anyway. So instead of looking at memes I would text Luka, or text Luka memes. I just had to make sure that I had time for the things that were important to me. My family, school, Andjela, and fingers crossed, Luka.

'Well, then how are you going to utilise your God given multi-tasking skills today, Nina?' Mama asked, turning her attention back to the dirty pot in the sink. Mama would annihilate me in an arm-wrestling match. All that time scrubbing pots after her delectable meals had her strong without ever stepping foot into a gym.

'Andjela has tennis practice, so I thought I'd go into town to watch her train. I'll spend a little bit of time with her and then come back here to do my homework. I have a bit to get through, so I'll be locking myself in for most of the day to get it all done. I don't want to have to get up early and worry about it in the morning. Still worried about me losing focus?' I asked, now tearing my eyes from my phone after Luka finally had the decency to reply to my message.

'Just doing my job. When you come back from town, please make sure that you bring Jovan with you. He has schoolwork to do as well but won't tell me until after dinner. I found it in his bag, but he snuck out to play with his friends when I wasn't looking. I don't want to be doing homework at twenty-one tonight,' Mama said, finally finishing with the pot and putting it in the drying rack.

'I'm going to be back around lunch time, so you'll have plenty of time to torture him,' I said, opening my phone as Luka replied again. He was telling me more about the concert he was playing Saturday night. I couldn't wait to watch him. I loved how he didn't just sing; it was as if he was telling a story from his soul. He wasn't just singing the words; he needed whoever was listening to feel what he felt.

'I'm going to visit your grandparents now. I know we were all supposed to visit them, but I'll just go on my own. Please make sure you bring Jovan back. See you when I get home,' Mama said, and planted a kiss on my cheek before she walked through the door.

I walked to the tennis courts an hour later to find Andjela working on her serve. That meant she was almost finished her practice session. She had cones on each of the lines, one on the tee, and one on each sideline where it met the service line. Her coach Stefan watched intently for any corrections that could be made to Andjela's technique. Andjela looked so focused on getting better that I doubted she noticed I had taken a seat at courtside.

The news that she was playing in qualifying at the Australian major tournament had clearly taken her up to another level. I sat and watched for the rest of her session, being careful not to say a word, as I didn't want to distract her. It was serious business, and I needed to respect her craft as much as she did. She wanted to be remembered for her exploits on the court, and not be famous for how beautiful she was like many female tennis players before her. Growing up in a small town where people don't have a lot will motivate you to work your butt off. Motivate you to fulfil every little bit of your potential. Not so you can buy a bunch of pointless things, but so you know that your family will be provided for.

Stefan had been coaching her for five years. A small, portly man, balding beneath the hat he constantly wore. You would never see him wear anything other than a tracksuit. It remained unclear whether he had several of the same navy-blue tracksuits, or he would air them out each night at home when he went to bed. I always thought he had several of them because I assumed he slept in them too.

After a short conference with Stefan, Andjela bounced over and sat in the chair beside me. 'You looked great out there. Feeling confident?' I asked. I really wanted to tell her all about my date, but I felt like it would be rude to not talk about her first.

'Yeah, it's going well. I don't really care about that now though. All I want to talk about is your date. I'll grab my stuff and we'll go to the café. I want all the details.' I could feel the excitement in her voice. She sounded just as excited to hear about my date, as I was to tell her about it.

She put on her jacket, threw her bag over her shoulder and we walked from the courts as we both waved goodbye to Stefan. He waved back before returning to his notebook of tennis strategies and ideas.

We walked into our favourite café, our second home. It had two personalities - during the day a cute and relaxing café, but at night a wild nightclub. Almost everyone in Požega had their first date there, and it was the scene of Marko's party. The Sunshine Café. I loved and hated it for its two personalities. There were a dozen tables of differing sizes spread around the room, compared to Friday where there was an open dance floor. The platform which served as the VIP area during club nights, had four small two person tables and chairs. We headed straight to our favourite two-person table by the window. We loved sitting there and seeing the serene landscape of Požega. Before we even had the opportunity to sit down, the waiter came to take our order of two cappuccinos. We took off our jackets and sat down.

Our table overlooked the beautiful fields in town. Wheat and corn fields ran into the mountains which were turning from green to white as winter approached. Wood panelled walls surrounded us; it felt like being in a small mountain cabin. It felt homely. Andjela didn't waste any time and hit me immediately with the question that was on the tip of her tongue. 'Well, I'm waiting, Nina. Go on then, how was it?' She leaned in like I was about to tell her the meaning of life. The waiter returned and placed our cups in front of us. Accompanying our coffee was a glass of water each and a small biscuit. Andjela stirred her cup, while I poured one sugar into my coffee and stirred. It was only lukewarm, so it probably needed to sit for five minutes until I got the cold coffee that I liked.

I told her everything that happened during my date with Luka. Making sure to give her every bit of information that I could think of because I really wanted her analysis. Telling her about my date made me feel like I was on it once again. I told her about the way he smiled, his head tilt when he looked embarrassed. The way his eyes sparkled when he spoke about something that was exciting to him. I liked Luka more after telling Andjela about our date.

If there was something Andjela thought was concerning, then she would tell me with her never-ending, brutal honesty. 'You really like this guy, don't you? I mean you could be the Joker with how wide your smile is,' she said, hoping that the piercing gaze of her green eyes would get me to admit how I really felt.

'Yeah, I do. I shouldn't like him this much though, should I? I mean we've only spoken to each other twice. This can't be normal, can it?' I asked her, looking for some reassurance. It was making me anxious how much I liked him.

'If you're feeling it then how can it not be normal? Yeah, it's quick, but where's the rulebook on this? Please show me the rule that says you can't have intense feelings quickly for a person. You feel how you feel, and trying to fight it isn't healthy. Just enjoy the excitement, because it doesn't come along too often. This is exciting. Be excited. It's supposed to be fun. You deserve this. He sounds like a special guy. I mean, how long has it been since you felt like this?' Andjela asked, taking a sip of her coffee.

'I don't think I've ever felt like this. This feels different. I don't know. I can't explain it,' I told her, trying to recall all the previous occasions I had feelings for a guy.

She looked at me in complete shock. 'Never? Not for your ex? Never before?' she asked, and I shook my head.

'I don't ever remember feeling like this. I think about him and immediately feel butterflies. Barely five minutes goes past where I don't think about him. It's crazy. He is so special and different. Different to any man I've ever met before. He might be the first real man that I've met. My ex was only a boy. Luka is a man.' I wasn't sure if I should admit to the lie I told Luka. I looked through the window and watched a butterfly land on the windowsill. Its wings were turquoise and green. It sat peacefully, not moving a millimetre. *It is incredible how there can be so much beauty in something that's so small,'* I thought, serenely.

'I kind of did something bad though. I lied to him about something. I feel guilty,' I said, temperature testing my coffee. It was finally cold enough, so I started to drink, placing my attention on the cup to take the pressure off myself. If I was going to get Andjela's thoughts, then I needed to tell her everything, not just include the things that made me look good.

'What did you lie to him about?' Andjela asked, furrowing her brow.

'I told him that I'm eighteen,' I mumbled. I could see her look of disappointment reflected in the window, but I looked through that. I looked out of the window peering over the fields. I couldn't look at her. I was scared because I didn't want to hear how I had ruined things just as something beautiful was beginning.

'Why would you do that?' Andjela asked, sounding disappointed.

'He's twenty-two. Do you really believe that he would want to talk to me if he found out that I'm seventeen? He was so cute and looked at me with these angelic eyes, so I knew I had to keep speaking to him. If he knew I was only seventeen he wouldn't have spoken to me again. And I can't tell him now because he'll never talk to me again,' I finished, and I could feel my anxiety rising. My heart was racing, and my breathing was becoming shallow. My mind was spinning thinking about him blocking me because I lied. *What if I tell him and he hangs up on me? What if I hurt him? I don't want to let him down. How am I supposed to get out of this? I can't believe I've got myself into this situation,'* I thought, panic stricken.

'I mean you are right that he might not want to be with you if he found out that you're seventeen. You still shouldn't have lied to him. That's no way to begin a relationship,' Andjela said, opening her biscuit and dipping it into her coffee.

'What would you have done?' I asked, desperate for any way out where I wouldn't lose him.

'I would have been honest. I've met people online before and always been upfront with that stuff.'

'Well, I guess I'm just not as good a person as you are, Andjela,' I said, unable to hide my frustration any longer. *'Can't she just tell me how to get out of this?'* I thought, desperately.

'Don't get angry at me because you lied. It's not my fault,' Andjela snapped back. We sat in an uncomfortable silence for a few moments before Andjela finally broke it. 'So, when are you going to tell him the truth?' I didn't regret telling her about my lie, because it helped me decide on my path forward. I prided myself on telling the truth, but I didn't want to do anything to ruin how things were going with Luka.

'I can't tell him until I meet him in person. I want things to progress with him. I know this might sound crazy seeing as he lives so far away, but I can see a future with this man. He's special. I've never come across a person with such an unusual combination of beautiful characteristics. And he feels the same way about me. Well, at least I think he does. I want him to come to my eighteenth birthday and I'll tell him if he visits then. If he can't come to visit, then there really isn't a future so there's no point in telling him the truth and hurting his feelings,' I said. *If his feelings for me are strong enough, then he will be able to forgive me for lying to him,'* I hoped.

'I think you know that you did the wrong thing. What you do from here is completely up to you, but I won't sign off and say yeah, that was okay, because it wasn't.' Andjela wasn't lecturing me, wasn't speaking down to me. She was just telling me what she thought. You would think that someone who was as beautiful as her, always tried hard in school, and gifted athletically, would have some major character flaw to balance things out, but no, she was almost perfect. She could even throw a mean right hook, just ask Marko. Her only flaw was her singing voice, where she sounded like a six-year-old with a badly tuned violin.

'I will tell him. I just need to find the right time, and the right way. I know you're right; he deserves better than this. If this is going to be something, then I need to give it a chance. It doesn't have a chance if I lie to him. Urgh…. why do you always have to be right? You know it's really annoying, don't you?' I said, gently banging my head on the table in frustration.

'Try and stop loving me,' Andjela said, and she blew me a kiss. We both laughed and I felt my anxiety lift a little as I drained the last of my cold coffee. 'So, are you going to show me pictures, or am I going to have to stalk online?'

'I only have a handful, and no, I don't have any of his brother, you creeper,' I said, looking up from my phone knowingly. I opened my phone and handed it to her. I watched her swipe through the photos of Luka.

'Ahh, so he does have a brother then. Looks like your girl is going to have quite a bit of local support in her players box when she goes to Melbourne,' Andjela said, shimmying her shoulders back and forth. She was so ridiculous I couldn't help but laugh.

'I'm not sure what you're more excited for in Melbourne. The tournament or trying to score a date with an Australian basketball player,' I said, reaching across the table and grabbing my phone. She had gone past the Luka photos and was just snooping.

'His brother plays basketball? It just keeps getting better. Well just imagine if in ten years' time we'll be best friends married to Australian brothers. That's the dream, isn't it?' she asked, finishing the last of her coffee.

'Don't say that. I've had one date with Luka, and his brother Aleks doesn't even know you exist, yet we're married to them both? I don't need to think about that…but yes of course I've imagined it,' I said. *Good job, Nina, you've had one date with a man and you're already walking down the aisle in a white dress,* I thought.

'Oh Nina, his brother is a tall, athletic Australian. Not only am I married to him in my head, but I've also already named our three children. I think we'll have a girl and then twin boys. It would be nice if we spend time in both Serbia and Australia so we can have two summers a year. I think the kids will like that,' she said, staring dreamily through the window and we both laughed.

We left our money on the table with a tip, headed for the door and said our goodbyes. We shared most of the same classes so I knew we would talk later about our work for Monday's classes.

I went the long way home via the football pitch to pick up Jovan. He was running around with five of his friends playing football. I sat down and watched him enjoying playing with his friends. It was so peaceful and soothing to watch. There was still some bite in the sun sitting on the lush green lawn, but it got cold as soon as the sun disappeared behind a cloud. *'Look at him, he's so happy,'* I thought, smiling. I took a short video of Jovan playing and sent it to Luka. He hadn't replied to my last message, but he had probably just fallen asleep. *'I wish he had said goodnight though,'* I thought, looking at his smiling profile picture. I longed for him to be sitting beside me. We didn't have to be talking, but just to feel his presence. My imagination was taking hold, and I could almost feel him. I extended my hand a little before realising that he was asleep on the other side of the world.

After about fifteen minutes Jovan saw me and came sprinting over. His legs were moving too quickly for his body; he lost balance and fell face first onto the grass. He looked up to find me laughing in hysterics and joined in as he brushed himself off, walking the rest of the way. I gave him a big hug, and he kissed me on the cheek. 'Are you ready to go? Mama told me to get you on my way back home,' I said, putting him back down and trying to brush the grass stain from his cheek.

'Do I have to? I'm having fun. She's going to make me do homework,' Jovan said, giving me the very manipulative and effective puppy dog eye look. That look from Jovan had gotten him his way many times, and me in trouble too many times before. I was not looking for a repeat of that.

'You can't use that look every time you want something. Come on, we really do have to go,' I told him, rubbing his shoulder.

'I can try to use it every time. Okay, fine. I'll grab my jacket and tell my friends I'm leaving,' he said, and he ran off towards the boys still playing. He had learned his lesson from before, as he lowered his speed when he ran back to me, and we walked home together.

As we walked back in through the door, Jovan kicked his shoes off and I put mine neatly next to the rest of the family's. I placed Jovan's next to mine, and by the time I walked into the kitchen Jovan already had a plate full of food and was eating his first piece of chicken. 'I hope you do your schoolwork with the same enthusiasm that you eat lunch with,' Mama said to Jovan, who had to make the choice between firing back a snappy retort or finishing his mouthful of chicken like it was about to be stolen. He chose the chicken.

Milica was sitting at the table eating lunch in a very sophisticated manner, looking at her phone. I took my place at the table next to her. 'Nina isn't the only one that has a new boy in her life. Milica has herself a cute little boyfriend too,' Mama said, enjoying giving the gossip of the day.

'MAMA! He's not my boyfriend. We're just friends,' Milica shot back with indignation. Roses appeared in her cheeks, belying her point that she was just friends with the mystery boy.

'Well, why then, when I was spying on you through the front door, did I see him kiss you? Not on the cheek, but on the lips. You were still blushing when you got back to the house. Yes, just like that,' Mama said, pointing at Milica's burning red face. She took her place at the table, tearing at a piece of bread and chewing it while raising her perfectly sculpted eyebrows towards Milica.

Milica yelled in frustration and covered her face with her zip-up hoodie. The temptation was so strong for Jovan that he put down the chicken. He took his attention from his lunch for a moment to make a kissing face at Milica. 'Stop it!' Milica yelled at Jovan, after reappearing from underneath her hoodie.

'Wait, he kissed you? Was that your first kiss? Also, Mama, I've had one date with Luka, he's not my boyfriend...yet,' I said, making sure that I didn't let that little comment slide. Milica said nothing, but her silence said everything. 'Aww, your first kiss. That's so cute.' I leaned over and gave her a hug that she didn't return but didn't push me away either.

'So, what's his name?' Mama asked, looking very chuffed with her handiwork, cutting a piece of chicken and eating it. 'Jovan, slow down. You'll make yourself sick.' Milica looked like she wanted to keep it a secret for as long as she possibly could, and by that, I mean forever. The cat was out of the bag though.

'His name is Nikola. I didn't want anyone to know though,' she mumbled, continuing to pick at her lunch and placing her phone face down on the table.

'Is that why you kissed him in the secret driveway that no one ever goes down?' I asked, which caused Mama to burst out laughing. Milica didn't find it funny and looked on the verge of her head exploding. When Milica got mad, she bit. *I should probably lay off; I don't want to get a matching set of teeth marks in my right forearm to go along with the marks on my left arm from a few days ago,'* I thought.

'If you would like to have him over for dinner one night, then he is more than welcome. If you like him then he must be a special boy. I know I'd love to meet him. Now Jovan, finish up your lunch, we need to get your work done. Milica, when you finish daydreaming about kissing Nikola, you need to go and do yours as well. Nina, can you please clean up before starting your work? Thanks. Come on Jovan,' Mama said, grabbing Jovan's hand and dragging him to his room to study.

I spent the rest of the day studying; only stopping to refill my water bottle, eat and reply to Andjela who was drowning in work. Halfway through my biology work, my phone lit up. Assuming it was Andjela again, I left it sitting there. *I'll reply when I finish,'* I thought.

Around an hour later, almost finished with a very productive evening of study, my phone buzzed once more. I was positive it was Andjela again, so I grabbed my phone to respond to another question she had about the homework. I was wrong. It was Luka! He was awake! The message an hour ago was also from him. He texted, 'Your brother is so cute. He's loving life. I wonder if my family used to play on that ground.'

He followed up with another message saying, 'If you're not busy and aren't ready to go to bed, do you want to have a movie date?'

I threw down the pen that was still in my right hand and replied. 'Yes, I think they would have. I bet your grandpa played there with his friends. Your nana probably watched him play to check him out too haha.' I sent a second text immediately after the first. 'I would love to. Let me just finish my work and then we can watch one together. Can you pick? I need to use my brainpower for biology, not movie choices.'

I polished off the rest of my work as quickly as possible and put my books away. I texted Luka to say that I was ready for the movie, and he sent a link to my laptop. 'Give me ten minutes to get ready for bed, and then we can watch,' I replied, putting my phone down and getting up from my desk.

I bounced down the hall to the bathroom and completely skipped my usual nightly skincare routine. I scrubbed the day from my face and brushed my teeth and quickly applied moisturiser to my face. Everyone else was fast asleep, so I tiptoed back down the hall to my room and picked out a cute matching tracksuit. It was light blue and as comfortable as clothes could get, in the perfect combination of I'm not trying, but hopefully he thinks I look cute.

I opened the link that Luka had sent me and got into bed pulling my blanket up to my waist. 'I want to watch *The Bucket List'* with you; it's one of my favourites. I hope you like it too,' Luka's most recent text read. I video called Luka from my phone, and leant it against my laptop, so it was like we were really on a movie date.

His huge beaming smile greeted me immediately and my heart melted. He was wearing a navy-blue hoodie, which I wanted to steal, not only so I could wear it, but so I could wear his scent too. The hoodie brought out his blue eyes. I was entranced in them. I thought back to what Luka told me on our first date, and I didn't understand how a man that was so handsome, had such a radiating face, was incredibly kind and compassionate, could ever feel so badly about himself. There was a twinge in my stomach at the thought of other people making him feel like he wasn't enough. *I'm going to make sure that he always knows that he is special to me,'* I thought. You don't need everyone to think you're special, just a select few. If he couldn't see the best in himself, then I was going to see it for him.

'I love your smile, Luka. It makes me smile,' I said, as my hair wrapped itself around my finger.

'Thank you. You look beautiful. I'm really happy to see you. Are you ready?' he asked, and I nodded. My ex was never as openly sweet and kind to me. I could remember on one hand the number of times he paid me a compliment.

We watched the movie and didn't say a word to each other the entire time. I split my attention between the film, and watching Luka watch the movie. Occasionally we would lock eyes and smile. He must have been sneaking looks at me to watch my reaction to his favourite parts. I hoped that meant he liked me as much as I liked him.

I felt everything I could during the movie. I cried and I laughed. I felt happy and sad. The movie had left me feeling emotionally full. The only thing standing in between the date we had, and the night being perfect, was not being cuddled up next to Luka on the couch watching it together. *'One day Nina. It will happen one day,'* I thought, which sent a wave of butterflies cascading through my stomach.

'So, what do you think?' Luka asked, and I felt like it was important to him that I liked the movie. I was glad I didn't have to lie.

'I loved it. I'm disappointed in myself that I hadn't seen it before. It was such a beautiful story. I will say though, if my husband was terminal and he left me to run around the world with a man he just met, I would end him before the cancer did,' I said, and Luka burst out laughing.

'I need to make a little notebook and write down these things, so I don't get physically hurt,' he said, as he continued to chuckle.

'There's no huge list of secrets, just one really obvious thing. We come first, and you do things because you want to, not because you think I'll get mad. There's your list of secrets to women. You're welcome.' I hoped he got the hint, but maybe I was too subtle.

'What was your favourite part of the movie?' I asked.

'Well, I love when he writes kiss the most beautiful girl in the world on his list. And it seems like a lame man thing to write on a bucket list. But when he meets his granddaughter for the first time and kisses her, then crosses it off, that just hit me. It was so beautiful and pure. If that doesn't make your soul smile, then you're a sociopath,' he said.

'The only thing more beautiful than his smile is his heart,' I thought, my finger finding its way back to my hair. *'If I were next to him, I would kiss him right now. I want this man to be mine, and I want to be his girl.'*

'That might be the sweetest thing I've ever heard,' I said, feeling my heart quiver. Just when I thought the butterflies had gone to sleep, they woke up and seemed to have multiplied. *'Surely, he can't be real,'* I thought, in disbelief at how he made me feel.

'It's super late there and you have school tomorrow. I think you should go to sleep. I'm sorry if I've kept you up too late,' Luka said.

'No, you didn't. I've had the best time, and I don't want to go but you're right, I should probably get some rest. Can we talk tomorrow?' I asked, praying that he would be free.

'I would love to. Sleep well and I'll talk to you tomorrow, sunshine,' Luka said, and he blew me a kiss.

'Ljubim te,' I said, and returned his kiss goodnight, before I hung up on the video call.

Setting my alarm on my phone for midday, I put it on my charger and placed it on my bedside table. I closed my laptop and gently laid it on the floor just next to my bed. Rolling over I immediately fell asleep with dreams of Luka and I together.

I awoke the next morning and grabbed my phone to check if I had any messages from Luka. He had sent me a couple of photos of him and his dog. *'This is the content I need to wake up to every morning,'* I thought, smiling at how adorable they looked together. I stared at the photos for a few minutes, when suddenly I noticed the time; it was thirty minutes until class started. I checked my alarm to see why it didn't go off. I had it set for twelve-am, not pm. Classic Nina.

In Serbia we have two shifts for school. A morning, and afternoon shift of classes. That week I was on the afternoon shift.

I jumped out of bed and raced to the bathroom. I climbed into the shower and took my toothbrush with me. Efficiency was the key to getting to class on time. I normally liked to take long, scalding showers, but unfortunately that wasn't an option.

We would be put into groups for our biology assignment in my first class, and I couldn't get stuck with the slow guy again. That was the punishment from the professor for being late when we last had a group assignment. He wanted to contribute, God bless his soul, but if you collaborated instead of doing the entire assignment yourself, it was a one out of five grade waiting to happen.

I brushed my teeth with my right hand and soaped myself with my left. As soon as I finished brushing my teeth, I jumped out and wrapped myself in a towel while running to my room leaving a trail of water in my wake. I threw on a pair of jeans and a basic white t-shirt that was definitely coming back to my room with a stain on it. Whenever I rolled the dice on wearing white, I found a way to drop something on it. I shoved my books into my bag and headed for the door.

I was the only person home which answered the question of why Mama didn't wake me up. She worked all day on Monday at the kindergarten. I raced to the door trying not to slip on the trail of water I left, jammed my feet into my already tied shoes by the front door, picked up my jacket and began towards school. I took my bag off while I walked as quickly as I could and put my jacket on, throwing my bag back on my shoulder and breaking into a gallop. It was a twenty-minute walk to school, and I had fifteen minutes until class began. *'A quick walk once I get to the underpass should be enough to get me there on time,'* I thought, not wanting to undo the shower I just took seeing as I forgot to put on deodorant.

The weather had turned from the sunshine of the day before, to complete cloud cover as I continued my race to class. I hoped we hadn't seen the last of the sun for the year, because being in the Serbian mountains, what came next was fog and snow. I could deal with the snow, but the sub-zero temperatures were not my friend. I needed a warm climate, maybe an Australian climate.

I walked into the classroom with only a couple of minutes to spare and found Andjela sitting at the back of the biology laboratory keeping a seat for me. 'Thanks. How many thirsty guys did you have to keep out of this chair for me?' I asked, sitting down breathlessly, and taking my books from my bag.

'One or two, or maybe five. If you were two minutes later, you would have been stuck doing the assignment with Tomislav again. I heard for this assignment we get to pick our own partners though. Do I need to ask, or do we both already know?' Andjela asked.

'Oh gosh, that was a nightmare. Stupid question, of course we're doing it together,' I said. I looked around the laboratory and found where Marko was sitting. He was two rows ahead of me and three seats to the right. I felt disgust when I looked at him. I didn't feel disgusting anymore though, it was all directed at him. My anger and hurt had left me. Luka had helped take that pain and anger away. I was just disgusted with him as a human.

The professor started to read out the pairs for the assignment. 'Looks like you were wrong about picking our own partners,' I said, looking at Andjela with concern.

I had forgotten to text Luka back from the photos he had sent me overnight, so I grabbed my phone to quickly reply. 'You two are so cute. Can't wait for the three of us to take photos like that,' I texted, and tucked my phone away.

'Nina. Are you now completely with us, or would you like to text a few more people that are clearly more worthy of your time and attention than we are?' Professor Potelić asked loudly in front of the entire class.

'Sorry, Professor. It won't happen again,' I said, making strong eye contact with my notebook in front of me.

'Well, I did have you paired with Andjela, but I don't think you two will be able to focus on your work seeing as you two haven't stopped talking since you walked into my classroom,' Professor Potelić said. He peered down at his list and made some notes upon it. 'Hmm, yes, I think I need to make a change. Nina, I'm going to pair you with…. Marko instead. Maybe then you will be able to focus on just doing your work,' he said, and moved on reading the rest of the pairings.

Marko turned around to look at me and I felt like I had been kicked in the stomach. I began to pick at the skin on my fingertips as we made eye contact. I thought I had moved on because I didn't have to speak to him again. All that anger and hate that I thought had left my body returned immediately with a vengeance. I felt Andjela's conciliatory hand touch my arm. *Not him. Anyone but him. Give me Tomislav. I knew things were going too well for me with Luka. Something bad had to happen. And here it is,'* I thought, as Marko forced a smile before turning his attention back to the professor. I wanted to run from the room and cry.

CHAPTER EIGHT
The Gig

I was smitten. Absolutely, and unequivocally smitten with Nina. No thoughts entered my mind apart from Nina, the gig, and my dog Monty. Immediately after I kissed Nina goodbye on our first date, I walked downstairs into the kitchen to find Mum sitting at the table. Dad would be home from work soon, but Aleks and Maja wouldn't be back until later in the afternoon from school. They only had a couple of weeks left of classes before their summer holidays started.

'Good afternoon,' Mum said in some cutting-edge parent humour, as I walked into the kitchen at ten-thirty.

'Good morning,' I replied, as I opened the kitchen drawer and removed a bowl, before walking into the pantry to pour myself a bowl of cereal. I put the bowl in front of my usual spot at the table and added a glass of orange juice to the dietary equation.

'You must have slept well. It's not like you to sleep in. Are you okay?' she asked, not trying to hide her tone of concern for my bizarre behaviour.

'Yeah, I'm fine, Mum. I've just been on my computer for a couple of hours talking to a friend,' I said, failing miserably to suppress any kind of smile behind eating my cereal.

'A friend? Isn't it a bit early for James or Michael to be up?' Mum asked, her concern had shifted to suspicion.

'Not them, another friend. I have more than two friends. I have three now,' I said in a deadpan tone, focused intently on my cereal. I was trying to hold in the information that I could feel slowly slipping from my lips. I had never brought a girl home before, not that there had been anyone to bring home anyway. I had never even mentioned being interested in anyone.

'My family probably think I'm asexual,' I thought, taking a gulp of orange juice.

'That's nice, but why are you smiling? Something's going on that you're not telling me,' Mum said, putting her newspaper away to increase the pressure of her interrogation.

'Can't I just enjoy being in your company?' I asked, avoiding eye contact because I knew if I looked at her, my smile would get even wider.

'Oh, give me a break. I'm flattered that you are complimenting me in your lie, but when you smile you don't smile like this. This is a different smile. I've never seen you look like this before, so it must be something new that's happened. Did you meet a girl? A boy? It's okay, you can tell me anything,' she said, and I could see her brain filtering through all the information she had about me to figure out what could possibly be putting that special smile on my face.

'Well, James told me that the bar in the city wants me to play there this weekend. I'm happy about that and I'm trying to think about what songs I'm going to play,' I said, hoping that my answer would be good enough to end the questioning.

'That's amazing! Congratulations. I'm so proud of you,' she said, and jumped from her seat to wrap me in a mama bear hug and kissed me on the cheek. She took the cereal box and poured more into my bowl before retaking her seat and going back to reading her newspaper. She had a smile on her face as she continued to flick though the newspaper, humming a melody that sounded very similar to 'I found my smile'.

'I'm going to take Monty for a walk,' I said a few minutes later, as I put my bowl in the dishwasher. I opened the backdoor and went outside to see Monty. He bounced up to me like I had just returned from two years at war. Just as he had after Nana's funeral, he was matching my mood. He looked as happy as a dog could ever be.

We were deep into spring and the cherry plum tree in our backyard was in full production. The morning spring sun felt warm on my skin as I walked onto the grass, with Monty following as if I was carrying a shin bone. There was almost no wind, which was unusual for springtime by the Melbourne Bay. The temperature was in the mid-twenties. I could hear birds chirping, bees were collecting nectar from flowers all around the backyard, and there was not a cloud in the sky. It was a perfect spring day.

I clipped the lead to Monty's collar and we proceeded to walk through the side gate and into the street. Normally I would listen to music on a walk, but not that day. I didn't want to be taken away from what I was feeling. I had spent so much time being miserable in my life, that I wanted to enjoy every second with that euphoric feeling. Enjoy the moment, the sun on my skin, the company of my dog, and the thoughts of Nina that radiated through my mind and into my step. I wanted to be present. All these things flowed through my mind like sand through my hands. Not trying to hold onto any of them. They came and they went, enjoying each of them while they were with me.

We made our way down the street towards the water. Monty sniffed every tree, light pole, and traffic sign that we passed. Boy dogs, am I right? We reached the bay and walked along the path that ran next to the water. Gentle waves crashed against the rocks of the Williamstown shore. In times of stress I would sit there to listen to the soothing sounds of the water. It relaxed me, but I was feeling no stress. I was out of the negative mental prison I had been incarcerated in, and felt emotionally light, emotionally free.

The beach was approximately two hundred metres in front of us, so we continued along the path towards the sand. Monty's head was on a swivel, curiously looking at everything around him. Flies, people, and other dogs. People were looking at

Monty as they walked by like they had just walked by the Brad Pitt of dogs.

I wanted to sit on the sand and look out over the water. We continued along the path that was lined with palm trees, their branches not moving a millimetre. We passed the beach carpark and the small kiosk on our left where people were lined up for coffee and finally reached the beach. I stepped to my right off the path and was standing upon the Williamstown beach sand. People were laying on their towels, others running in the shallows with their dogs. Small children were digging in the sand making sandcastles as their parents read a book and feigned being impressed by their child's sand lump pretending to be a castle.

I took off my shoes and socks so I could feel the sand between my toes. We walked towards the water so Monty could play in the shallows. I looked to my left as we walked along the water and saw the park across the road. There were a couple of kindergarten aged children playing on the playground while their parents carefully watched over them. Beautiful big trees surrounded the park. Monty looked at the trees with longing, as if he wanted to spend all day sniffing and marking them.

We walked back about thirty metres from the water, and I sat down on the sand. Monty continued to sniff and explore around me as I looked across the water. It was so calm and serene. There was nothing as far as the eye could see, just the water meeting the horizon. I closed my eyes and breathed in the salty air to cleanse my sinuses. The smell of the beach was one of my favourite scents. *'I bet Nina smells better though,'* I thought, as her smiling eyes and flowing hair returned to my mind's eye. I hated to admit it, but I was obsessed with her. I didn't want to think about anyone else, about anything else. *The only thing that could make this better, is if she were sitting next to me on the sand. My arm around her shoulder, Monty exploring and sniffing, before settling beside us and resting his head on my leg,'* I dreamed. It was such a cliché, but it was one that I craved.

'Monty!' I called, and he came running towards me before sitting next to me. I pulled out my phone and took a couple of photos with him. I sent them to Nina saying, 'We wish you were here.' I missed her already. *'I can't wait for her to wake up so we can talk again. Can you miss someone that you've never met in person?'* I wondered, as Monty rolled over in front of me so I would pat his belly. Every day since meeting Nina I was feeling a new level of happiness. An emotion I had heard about but never experienced before. I was addicted to it.

Monty and I spent an hour sitting on the sand, looking over the water, just enjoying the spring day. Finally, I decided it was time we left, so I stood up and we walked off the beach beginning our short journey home.

I spent the rest of the day floating around the house trying to get a firm picture of what the weekend's gig would look like. I spent hours in my room thinking of different covers to play amongst my originals. If I wanted a regular spot, then I needed to get their attention. I needed to have them wanting to listen to what I had to say. The best way for them to care about my originals was to play songs they loved as well. I picked up my guitar and began working on a new song, wanting to be able to play as many of my own as I could.

Before I knew it, Dad's bellowing voice was reverberating around my room from downstairs, calling me to the kitchen for dinner. Mum had obviously asked him to get me, so instead of walking up the stairs to tell me, his energy conserving solution was to scream up the stairs.

I sat down at the table to find Aleks and Maja already seated. Mum divided up the lasagne amongst the five of us and Dad placed a plate on each of the placemats. Dad sat at the head of the table, Aleks and I next to each other with Mum across from me and Maja across from Aleks.

'So, how was work, dear?' Mum asked Dad, as we all started on our lasagne. Table manners were valued highly in our household, so any question was usually met with a delayed response due to the clearing of a mouthful of food.

'It was busy. We had a great day. Things don't look like they'll calm down any time soon so that's positive. Luka, I think you should start on Monday. Enjoy the rest of your week but be ready to go then. How's that sound, mate?' Dad asked in his classic, I'm asking you, but I'm really telling you fashion.

'Umm, yeah, that's fine. It's good timing because I'm playing at a bar this weekend. Gives me a chance to focus on that and then come in on Monday,' I said, glad that I could get that information out of the way in a conversational manner, rather than making some grand announcement.

'Well done,' said Dad in a, that's a complete waste of time but you do you, sort of way. The news didn't even register with Maja and Aleks. The lasagne was much more interesting to them, and to be fair, I couldn't blame them, it was incredible.

'He was so happy about it this morning he couldn't stop smiling while he was eating his breakfast. I think we should all go along and support Luka. We're all incredibly proud of you for having a go at this. Aren't we?' Mum asked the table, eyeballing everyone in turn, trying to impart her level of enthusiasm on the rest of our family. They all nodded not taking their eyes off their plates. If my goals were to be crushed, then they should be crushed because I sucked, not from her putting me off my ideal future and in turn, causing me to resent her. I was incredibly lucky to have her.

'Well, I think it will be at an eighteen and over bar, so Aleks and Maja won't be able to go,' I told everyone.

'I want to go to the bar. To support Luka of course. Do you really think they're going to card me if I try to get in?' Aleks asked. It was a good point; he was a towering figure and looked three years older than me even though he was four-and-a-half years younger.

'Yeah, just sneak us in. What if you have a panic attack on stage and I miss it? I can't hear about something like that from James. I need to be there to see it,' Maja said. She was always teasing for fun, but often didn't know where the line was, or when to pull back, which could cause big fights if someone was in the wrong mood. She was always ready with a joke in any situation, but if you got on her bad side, look out. It was like lighting dynamite.

'And it better not be too late. I don't want to be getting to bed at some ridiculous hour like ten-thirty,' Dad said. Clearly the genuine support began and ended with my mother.

'None of you have to come. James and Michael will go with me, so it'll be fine. Don't worry about it. If I get to play again, and if it's at a less ridiculous hour, Dad might join you to watch, Mum,' I said, not attempting to hide my disappointment in their attitudes. I didn't need them to be standing in front of the stage with pom-poms, but even the slightest bit of encouragement would have been terrific to hear. *How am I to believe in myself if these three don't?* I thought, moodily poking at my lasagne.

'I think we all need to be more supportive of Luka doing this. We saw him at Nana's funeral, and we can all agree he was amazing. He's going to be just as amazing this weekend. You go and do your thing this time, sweetie, if that's what you want, but you better believe that we'll all be there to see you soon. Won't we?' Mum said sternly to Dad, who nodded with a look of fear on his face, and his mouth full of lasagne. I got the feeling they would be having a conversation later about encouraging their children.

'Mum, we know Luka is good. That's why we're teasing him. If he becomes a famous musician and gets a big head, then that's our fault for not making fun of him enough. We're doing it because we care,' Maja said.

'Well, maybe he needs a little less of that kind of caring, Maja,' Mum said.

'I think that's the nicest thing you've ever said to me,' I said to Maja.

'Yeah, well don't get used to it. So, who were you talking to this morning? I heard a girl's voice coming from your room. Did you sneak one in last night?' Maja asked, doing her best to start drama and enjoy watching the chaos unfold in front of her eyes.

'What!?' Mum, Dad, and Aleks all exclaimed in unison.

'What are you talking about Maja?' I asked, trying to stop my body from giving away my lie. My acted indignation was futile though. I could feel the heat rising in my face, and a smile fighting its way through my deadpan expression. *If my performance on the weekend is this bad, then it will be a one show career for me,*' I thought, hating my sister for the public outing.

'You know exactly what I'm talking about. Look at him. He's blushing. Who is she? Don't let him try and tell you she's just a friend either, Mum, because I heard him tell her that he thinks she's really beautiful,' Maja said, ending in a bad impression of my voice, unable to hide the joy of revealing the juicy gossip to the rest of the family.

That fresh revelation grabbed Dad's attention a lot more than hearing about me singing on the weekend. I couldn't see a roadmap out of the situation that retained my secret. I didn't want to keep it a secret for long, I just wasn't ready to tell my family. Nevertheless, it had been taken out of my hands, so I just had to tell the truth.

'Well, I met a girl online. Her name's Nina,' I mumbled in a voice barely above a whisper. I felt uncomfortable, but I wasn't sure why. I should have been shouting from the rooftops that this smart, kind, beautiful woman was in my life. *I was comfortable telling James and Michael, so why wasn't I comfortable telling my family? Was it that I wanted my friends approval, or was it just because they always talked about those things with me?'* I wondered, feeling ashamed of how uncomfortable I felt. I normally tried to keep things close to my chest, I felt uncomfortable revealing feelings of any kind, but if Nina was to be the important part of my life that I felt she would be, then I should be telling my family about her sooner rather than later.

'I asked you this morning why you were smiling, why didn't you tell me about her then?' Mum asked, putting down her fork.

'I don't know. Maybe I thought that you might judge me for meeting someone online,' I said, pushing the food around on my plate. My cheeks felt so hot that you could have fried an egg on them.

'Luka, I'm disappointed in you. Do you not know me better than that? You know I wouldn't judge you because of how you met someone,' Mum said, shaking her head in disappointment.

'I know you wouldn't, but these three would,' I said, raising my head to gesture towards Dad, Aleks, and Maja.

'I'm not going to judge you until I see her. Do you have a photo?' Aleks asked, causing Maja to burst into laughter.

'Oh Aleks, grow up. She's obviously gorgeous if my handsome son likes her,' said Mum. Maja keeled over in hysterics, which set off a chain reaction. Aleks joined in as he looked at the tears of laughter streaming from my sister's eyes.

'Maja, enough,' Dad said, as he tried with all his might to keep a straight face. I knew laughter was contagious, but that didn't make it feel any better.

'Come on. Even you two don't really believe that do you?' Maja asked, struggling to get the words out between fits of laughter.

'Is this more of you caring, Maja?' Mum asked. Maja shook her head, wiping away her tears and trying to get her laughter under control. 'Okay then. You either be nice to your brother or you leave,' Mum continued, with a reproachful look at my brother and sister. 'Ignore these two. Just talk to me. What's she like, Luka?' Mum had turned her complete attention to me. I knew they were joking, but I felt a twist in my stomach hearing my siblings laugh at how ugly I looked.

'She's smart, funny, and caring, Mum. I'm so lucky I got to meet her,' I said, as I pulled out my phone and opened our conversation thread. Nina had seen the photos that I had sent her but hadn't replied. Every interaction, every thought I had about Nina, had been positive before I saw that. I knew it was silly, but I felt like I had been punched in the chest. It shouldn't have bothered me, but I felt rejected, like I wasn't worthy of a reply. *She has her own life, with her own demands on her time, and maybe she just got busy. Maybe her phone died when she saw them. Maybe she just doesn't like you anymore, Luka. Maja is right, you ugly loser. Stop it. Stop it now!* I thought, hoping that I was hiding the hurt from my face. I wanted to stop the thoughts before they became a full-on self-loathing spiral, but once the horse had bolted, it was hard to get it back in the barn. I wanted to disappear. I felt three centimetres tall.

I closed our chat but could still see in my mind the word read under the photo of Monty and I together. I found a photo of Nina and handed my phone to Aleks. 'Not to be rude, but are you sure this is her? It is the internet, so have you thought that you could be getting catfished?' Aleks asked.

'Show me,' Maja said in a whiny voice, having finally recovered from her laughing fit, and Aleks passed her my phone.

'Yeah, this is definitely a catfish. I was joking before, you're not ugly, but this girl is way out of your league. It's probably a fat guy.' Aleks and Dad laughed together as Mum peered over Maja's shoulder.

'Nina and I have video chatted so that is her. It's not a fat guy,' I said, snapping at Maja. I could feel an anger bubbling inside me. If one more thing was said like that, I was going to explode. If my photo hadn't been left on read, would I have been able to handle that comment better? Maybe. The joy I had felt all day had been drained from my body, and was replaced with an anxiety and the rising voice of a bully in the back of my mind.

'You never know, technology can do some incredible things,' Maja said, placing my phone on the table, returning her attention to her plate.

'Mum, you'll never believe where she lives. Požega,' I said, deciding that the best course of action was to ignore Maja and Aleks.

'Like Požega, Serbia, Požega?' Mum asked in disbelief, as she snatched my phone from the table to have a closer look at Nina. As Mum always did, she began to scroll through the photos in my phone, looking for more of Nina and whatever else she might find interesting. 'Oh, this is a nice one Luka. Can you send it to me?' Mum asked, showing me the photo I took with Monty earlier that day at the beach.

'I will. Do we have any relatives still there, Mum?' I asked, extending my hand to ask for my phone back.

'Nana's brother still lives there. We spoke when she passed away, but he wasn't healthy enough to make the trip for her funeral. I'll have to ask him if he knows her family. Nana would be beaming that you've met a nice Serbian girl. She sounds fantastic, Luka. I'm happy for you,' Mum said with a soft smile, and finally returned my phone to me.

'Let me say first that I'm happy you've met someone. That's great, mate. I just want you to have a think about how this is going to work though. Think about how you can have a future with someone that lives so far away. You don't need to answer me now, or ever. I can tell you that a woman with Požega roots is someone special, but the distance is something you need to think about. Now, am I going to get to see her, or is that picture just for everyone else?' Dad asked, and I opened my phone again and showed him a picture of Nina.

'How old is she?' Aleks asked.

'Eighteen. She's in her last year of school, and then she's going to the University of Belgrade in September,' I said, before finishing the last of my lasagne.

'If she has any hot friends let me know,' Aleks said, as he got up from the table leaving his dirty plate on his placemat. He left the kitchen and headed for his room. I assumed to play video games; school wasn't a priority for him.

'She looks older than eighteen. I would have guessed in her twenties. Well, you can't do much better than a Serbian woman,' Dad said, placing his hand on Mum's hand and smiling at her. 'Okay everyone, I'm going to bed. Love you all. See you tomorrow.' He stood up, kissed Mum, and left the kitchen for bed, his dirty plate remaining on his placemat. Having to get up at midnight for work, he always ate dinner with us and then went immediately to bed.

I stood up and took the plates to the sink, making sure to rinse them with hot water before putting them in the dishwasher. Mum and Maja were beginning their nightly ritual of arguing about homework. 'But you don't push Aleks about his homework all the time. Why do you just pick on me?' Maja asked, the volume in her voice rising with each syllable. Mum had to constantly push Maja to do her work. She would try and get away with everything that she could. You never knew if Maja was arguing for fun, or because she was upset until it was too late. She had the Balkan fire.

I heard my phone buzz on the table, so I placed the last dish in the dishwasher and picked up my phone. 'Oh, you two are so cute,' Nina replied.

'I was being stupid. Of course, she likes me. I'm not sure why, but she does,' I thought, closing my eyes. I breathed a big sigh of relief that I felt all the way to my toes. The argument between Maja and Mum, and the bully in the back of my head were muffled as I focused on replying to Nina.

'When the three of us take a photo together it will definitely be my wallpaper,' I replied. The anxiety elephant that frequented my chest in my times of stress had gone to look for food.

'Maja, he has a fully paid college scholarship already. When we get you into university, then I'll relax,' Mum shot back at Maja. If Maja put as much effort into doing her work, as she put into not doing it, she would have been top of her class.

I walked out of the kitchen and headed for my room to leave the two of them to continue their battle that would leave no winners. I was sure if it really kicked off, I would be able to hear it from my room upstairs at the opposite end of the house to the kitchen.

Walking into my room, I picked up my notepad and pen to continue working on the half-written song from earlier in the day. I put together a second verse to go along with the first verse and chorus that I had already written. I was happy with my chord progression, and then turned my attention to the bridge, but I couldn't manage to keep my mind completely focused on the task at hand. My mind was being drawn to something else, a trip to Požega. It would be her nineteenth birthday in August, and I had every intention of being there for it.

The temptation was too much to bear. I put down my guitar and notebook and turned my attention to my laptop. I looked at every airline that flew to Europe, playing with the dates to get the best deal possible, so the trip would agree with my sad little bank account. I knew I was crazy for looking into it, but the idea of flying to see Nina sent waves of anticipation and another feeling through my body. It wasn't excitement, it was something deeper than that. It was like I could see my life in front of me, and all I had to do was reach out and take it.

I thought about whether I should surprise her or tell her I was coming. Surprising Nina on her birthday would be something special. It would be unbelievable if I could pull it off. I had probably watched too many movies though, but the scene played out in my mind. I saw the look of shock and joy on her face, and it felt like I was living it. It was happening to me right then. I felt euphoric dreaming about seeing her for the first time. About hugging her for the first time. That would be a memorable birthday present. Clearly Nina had given me a confidence boost because I was thinking of myself as the gift.

It felt like an eternity away, but the nine months would go by in the blink of an eye. *'I just hope she isn't sick of me by then. Wow, that newly found confidence disappeared quickly,'* I thought, shaking my head with a grin, and I continued to scroll through flights to Belgrade.

I routinely checked my phone throughout the rest of the night to see if Nina had replied. She hadn't. *'She was at school, so she wouldn't be able to text,'* I thought. 'People get busy and can't always be on their phones, Luka. They have lives,' I said out loud, to try and silence the bully who was once again trying to find his voice.

I finally shut my computer off and put my phone away. I needed to rest my brain because it had worked itself to exhaustion. *'I'll make sure I walk Monty to the beach again tomorrow. It's not possible to feel anxious there,'* I thought, as I closed my eyes and peacefully drifted off to sleep.

It was the day of my first gig, and a million different scenarios were playing on a loop in my mind. I tried to tell myself that the feeling in my chest was excitement, that everything would go how I planned, but there was that little voice. That bully in the back of my mind telling me all the different ways things could go wrong. The bully said the feeling in my chest was nervousness, not excitement. My body couldn't decide if I was nervous or excited. Every time I thought about it my heart began racing, but a smile always broke across my face. It was good to feel that excitement, it showed that I cared. I needed to keep my nerves under control, and use the excitement to create energy on stage, not let nerves paralyse me. *This is excitement, not nerves,*' I reminded myself repeatedly, trying to shut out the other voice in my head.

I wanted Nina there to keep me calm and relaxed. She wasn't though. *'She wasn't at the funeral either and I performed well there,'* I thought. I was trying to talk myself into being confident that the gig would go well. That I didn't need anyone there, I just needed myself and my guitar. That I was enough.

Throughout the day I tried to fill in the time as well as I could. I was able to finish the song I was working on earlier in the week and added it to my set list. I spent time going over every other song I was playing until my fingers hurt and the songs were seared into my mind.

I plodded around the house trying not to watch the clock, yet finding my eyes constantly drawn to it. The clock felt as though it was going at half speed. *'God, why did you have to pick today of all days to mess with the rotation of the earth? Couldn't you have kept this experiment for tomorrow?'* I thought frustratedly, unable to stop myself from once again looking at the time to discover only one minute had passed.

Mum noticed how edgy I was and asked, 'What would you like for dinner? I know it's a big night for you so you can have your pick.'

'I'm not sure. Umm, we haven't had chops for a while. Maybe we could have them if that's okay with you?' I asked hopefully. I needed to start spending time in the kitchen with Mum to find out how she managed to harness heaven, and channel it onto a plate every time she cooked. We were not worthy of her on this earth.

'I've been eavesdropping on what you've been playing. You sound amazing, and I'm not just saying that as your mother, Luka. Are you sure you don't want Dad and I to come tonight?' Mum asked. I wanted her there and knew she would love to come, but it would be tough for Dad. Working nights was torture on your body clock, and he had been doing it for forty-five years. In two days, I would get a taste of how difficult it was.

'It's okay. James and Michael are coming with me so that will be enough. I'd love for you to come another time though. You can all come and see me,' I said, really hoping that she wasn't offended. I would hate for her to think that I didn't want her there. She was incredibly supportive of everything Aleks, Maja, and I did. She was born to be a mother.

'As long as you have someone there to support you, and you're not going to be doing it alone. Being able to look out at the crowd and see a couple of friendly faces will help. Can I do anything to help?' Mum asked. She looked concerned, I assumed that was just part of being a mother.

Mum was a teacher before she had children, so maybe she could help me. 'Well, there is one thing. Being a teacher, you're used to being in front of groups of people. I don't think there's much difference between being in front of children, and drunk adults. How did you get comfortable being in front of a group of people?' I asked, sitting down at the table.

'I never would have thought to draw a comparison between being a primary school teacher and being a musician, but somehow you've done it,' Mum said, a surprised look on her face as she took a seat in Dad's spot at the table.

'Well, what I always tried to focus on was commanding the room, and a big part of that is being the most interesting thing in the room. It's a bit like if you're training a puppy. If you aren't interesting when training a puppy, then the puppy will look at the bird flying around, or the stick on the ground. If you can hold their attention though, then you have them in the palm of your hand. You must demand their attention. You do that by being interesting. If you aren't interesting, then the audience will drift into a conversation with their friend, get another drink, go to the bathroom, or leave. You must demand their attention by being great. And Luka, I've heard you. You are really talented, and I know in my soul you will be great tonight,' Mum said, not breaking eye contact with me the entire time. No wonder schools continued to call her to fill in for sick teachers.

'What if I'm not interesting? What if they find a bird or a stick more interesting?' I asked.

'You are entering a world of no doubt. You can't go up there and think to yourself, "Do they really want to hear what I have to say?" It's a bar, people go there to spend time with their friends, meet new people, and have some music in the background. That's what it will be like at the start. I guarantee you though, Luka, sweetie, by the time you're playing your last song, all eyes will be on you. No matter what bird or stick is around. Don't be afraid of being great,' Mum said, standing up and giving me a kiss on the forehead.

'Where are you going?' I asked, turning as she started to walk from the kitchen.

'I have to go and get your chops,' she replied from halfway down the hall, as she continued through the front door.

'That was amazing, Mum, thanks,' I said, as I stood up and started clearing the empty plates. Whenever I felt nervous or anxious, I felt like it relieved some of the tension from my body to keep busy. Even if it was something as simple as putting the dirty dishes into the dishwasher. Maja and Aleks had left their dishes on the table as per usual.

I was grateful that I hadn't dropped any dinner on my chinos or black t-shirt and be forced to change. It had taken long enough to come up with that simple ensemble.

My phone buzzed in my back pocket, so I pulled it out and looked at it. A text from Michael read, 'James and I will be there in five minutes.' My heart began to race. I was another step closer to walking on stage.

'I'm glad you enjoyed it. What time are you heading off?' Mum asked, as I increased my urgency in taking the plates from the table.

'James and Michael will be here to pick me up in a few minutes,' I said, as I got to the last plate that was lying in front of my father. I scraped the scraps into the food bin before I placed the last dish into the dishwasher and closed it. I scanned the bench and table to see if there was anything more I could do. Active time meant less time thinking about what lay ahead of me.

'Thanks, mate. Luka, just so you know, I do really want to go tonight. I'm sorry if you thought I didn't care when you told us the news the other night. I was tired and had another big day coming up. You're talented, and we're proud of you for taking this chance. Take care of things tonight but know that we'll be there in spirit. I can't wait to see you play,' Dad said. He didn't say encouraging and heartfelt things like that often, but he had a great sense of the moment. Picking his spot to great effect. It was relaxing to know that he was on my side, even though I knew Mum told him he needed to be more supportive.

'Thanks, Dad.' I squeezed his shoulder gently as I walked behind him. 'I better go,' I said reluctantly, then kissed Mum on the cheek and walked quickly from the kitchen.

My guitar was already sitting by the front door, so I picked it up and left the house. James and Michael were sitting in James' car waiting outside the front of the house. I put my guitar in the boot and jumped into the rear passenger seat.

'How are you feeling, superstar?' James asked, putting his foot down and accelerating down the street.

'I'm alright. I think I'll feel a lot better once I'm all set up there and start to play the first song. Hopefully it all goes smoothly,' I exhaled, and I could feel my anxiety elephant return to my chest. My right leg bounced on the ball of my foot as James took a right-hand turn at the end of the street. Michael didn't say a word, he just looked over his shoulder and tapped me on the knee reassuringly.

We drove over the West Gate bridge towards the city. The city lights were turning on as night fell. Even though I was playing in a bar where nobody knew who I was, it felt like I was playing a huge concert because it was in the heart of the city and not a suburban pub.

I felt my phone explode in my pocket, but I resisted the temptation to look at it. I wanted to focus on the lights. The elephant had settled on my chest, and I wanted to try anything that could alleviate the pressure he was putting on my breathing. I tried deep breathing, in through my nose, and out through my mouth, but he wasn't going anywhere. My right leg began bouncing again.

'So, how are things going with that girl you met online? Nina?' Michael asked. There was a nervous energy in the car so

I felt grateful to talk about something that could take my mind temporarily off the gig. I wasn't feeling excited, I was feeling nervous, and it was growing as we drew nearer to the venue.

'It's going well. We had a movie date earlier in the week and we talk a lot. I feel happier than I can remember since I met her,' I said, unable to keep the smile from my face. 'I don't think I'll have to see the psych anymore.'

'Why?' Michael asked, turning around to look at me.

'I feel good. If I'm feeling good then I don't really see the point,' I said shrugging. Michael continued to look at me.

'Are you sure that's healthy?' Michael asked.

'What do you mean?'

'Well, I just think you shouldn't base your attitude to your mental health on feeling good for a few days after just meeting someone from the other side of the world online,' Michael said softly.

'I'm already looking at flights to go and visit her for her birthday in August, so I'd rather save my money for that.' Michael turned back around to face the road, deciding to leave the subject alone for the moment. 'It sucks she can't be there tonight, but she wants to watch, so if one of you two could hold my phone up during a video call for her to be able to watch then that would be great,' I said at an express pace without taking a breath. They exchanged looks as if to ask, should you tell him, or should I?

'Umm, isn't knowing someone only a week a bit soon to be planning flights to go and see them in Europe? Don't get me wrong, I'm happy for you and glad you like her so much that you're already thinking about that, but don't get too ahead of yourself, mate,' James said, looking at me in the rear-view mirror.

'James is right, Luka. Just take your time. You don't need to rush things like this. If you like each other that much, then that stuff will happen organically. There is a reason food is better out of a wood fire oven than a microwave. Heat things up too quickly then they will fall off quickly too,' Michael said, turning in his seat to face me again. They both had a lot more experience in these matters than I did, but I felt like they were talking down to me.

'I'm not their little brother,' I thought, feeling frustrated.

'I'm not buying a ticket. I was just having a look at it. Do you really think I'm so insane that I'd buy a ticket already?' I asked sharply, swivelling my head from one to the other. I tried to lean forward but my seatbelt held me back. My leg began to bounce faster.

'No, but we just want you to be careful. Just enjoy getting to know her and take things slowly. She lives in Serbia, so how well can you really know her?' James asked.

I could feel the frustration turn to annoyance. *We're on our way to my first gig, and they have to ride me about this now? Couldn't they just ask me about her and then talk about footy? They wouldn't be talking like this if I met her in a bar,'* I thought, feeling a flash of anger as they ganged up on me. I needed to keep calm, or else it could ruin the night.

'How well can you know someone if you meet them in a bar? If people want to hide who they truly are, then they can do it no matter how you're interacting with them. You just have to try your best to see if they're being genuine or not, and I know Nina is genuine.' The exasperated words gushed from my mouth coated in frustration. I needed to calm myself down. *They're just trying to help,'* I thought repeatedly, as I closed my eyes for a moment to try and relax.

'I'm sorry Luka. We love you. We just don't want to see you get hurt,' Michael said quietly.

'Look, I don't know what's going to happen, and I appreciate you guys looking out for me, but she is real, and our feelings are real. I'm going to get hurt, that's part of any relationship whether you break up or get married, but what matters is that I do what feels right, when it feels right. That's what matters to me,' I said defiantly to end the discussion.

I knew they were trying to look out for me, but I didn't need that in that moment. I spent enough time being the negative influence on myself, I needed them to be the positive influence on me.

Fifteen minutes later we walked into the bar named, 'One Note'. As soon as I crossed the threshold, I stood and took a moment to look at my surroundings, to look at the kind of people that were already there. There were booths lining the walls where people were eating dinner. A large bar made of mahogany was directly in front as I walked through the door. There were pictures of famous musicians plastered all over the walls. *Surely, they weren't people that had played there, they were way too famous to have played in a bar in Melbourne,'* I thought. There was a small stage against the wall on the left-hand side of the bar, and a large dance floor in front of it. The microphone and amplifier were already set up for me to just hook in and play.

'Come on, I'll introduce you to the owner,' James said, clapping his hand on my shoulder, and we headed towards the office. A steady stream of people were arriving, but there was still some time for us to kill before I needed to go on stage, so the bar would probably be at capacity by the time I began. My heart quickened its pace, so I shifted my focus to following James. Watching James work his way through the growing crowd and following his every step, trying not to hit people with my guitar. I followed James through the kitchen, and down a hallway. We stopped outside a door that read 'Manager'. James knocked loudly and the voice that crept through the door said, 'Come in'.

'Hi Sam, I want to introduce you to Luka and our friend Michael,' James said. I smiled and extended my quivering hand to shake Sam's as he took his attention from the laptop he was working on and stood up.

'Hopefully, my hands are more stable when I begin playing,' I thought, looking down at my shaking hand. Sam was a short and thin man with shoulder length brown hair and round glasses. He wore a suit without a tie and his jacket hung on a coat hanger just over his left shoulder on a rack.

'Great to meet you guys. Luka, I'm really excited to have you play here tonight. I was complaining to James about the people I've had here lately, so when he sent me the video of you playing, I couldn't have you here fast enough. I'm so sorry for your loss by the way. Awful thing to happen. How are you feeling? Nervous? Excited?' Sam squeaked in a high-pitched voice. His body language looked nervous; he looked to be carrying a lot of pressure. I could tell his bar meant a lot to him.

'All of the above. I'm keen to get started though,' I said with a nervous laugh, as I gently placed the guitar case I held in my right hand on the ground.

'I love it when people are nervous. The last person I had playing here regularly was cool and calm all the time. It looked like he didn't care, and it showed the second he started playing. He didn't have a connection with the audience. I felt a connection with you while I was watching the video and that's why I wanted you here. This was my father's bar and I've been running it since he passed away. I need people to care and I'm glad to see you do,' Sam said, dragging his left leg as he walked around his desk and sat on the front of it. He was pulling at his sleeves, as if trying to pull them off. His body kept moving in short, sharp motions, like he was trying to shoo fruit flies from landing on him.

'Luka's going to be amazing, Sam. I saw the same video that you saw, and I was blown away. I wish he told us sooner that he could sing like that,' Michael said.

'Yeah, we could have used it to pick up a lot of girls,' James joked with a wide grin, and Sam laughed.

'Well, there's always tonight isn't there? Let me take you out to the stage and you can get yourself set up,' Sam said, gesturing to the door and leading us from his office. Just as I was about to pick up my guitar, my phone vibrated in my back pocket.

'I'd wish you luck, but I know you don't need it. I heard you playing in your room and they're lucky to have you,' Maja's text read.

There was also a text from Aleks. 'I'm trying to sneak out to come.' It was followed with, 'Mum busted me, she's really mad. Good luck though!' I laughed imagining Mum wanting to yell at Aleks but not doing it in case she woke up Dad.

'Hey, I know you're probably at the bar but just texting good luck doesn't feel enough for your big night. Call me before you start if you have time. I miss you.' I miss you. Those three little words had a kaleidoscope of butterflies chase the elephant from my chest. I stared at those three words and smiled, glad that no one was in the room anymore to see me looking at my phone like that.

To feel the support from Maja and Aleks meant a lot to me. Those three words though… Nina made me momentarily forget about the gig. The only thing that felt important to me was seeing her face. *I miss you too, Nina,'* I thought, my eyes closed, imagining that she was standing next to me. I wanted to reach out and hold her hand, because then I knew everything would be okay.

'Thanks,' I replied to Maja and Aleks, making an incredible number of spelling errors for that one basic six letter word. My hands were so sweaty that I was worried I wouldn't be able to properly grip my guitar.

'Hey, are you okay?' Michael asked, sticking his head back into the office.

'Yeah, I'll be there in a second,' I said, looking up from my phone halfway through replying to Nina. 'I'll call you soon. I hope you're free to watch. I miss you too.' I put my phone in my back right pocket, picked up my guitar and walked out of the office to catch up with Michael, James, and Sam.

We walked into the bar and the crowd had grown. The demographic was a huge mix of people. A mix of ages, races, and genders. It would be hard to play to everyone's taste so I could only do one thing – be myself.

'Obviously, this is where you'll be playing Luka. Set up here and if you need anything just yell out,' Sam shouted in his squeak over the noise of the mulling bar, as he encouragingly tapped me on the arm and hobbled back to his office.

'We're going to hang out by the bar, do you need anything?' James asked. I shook my head, and they bounced off to order a drink.

After getting set up and comfortable on stage, I put my guitar down and headed for Sam's office. I knocked on the open door and Sam looked over the laptop that he was working on. 'Sorry to bother you, but is there a quiet room that I can make a phone call in?' I asked, and I could feel my voice shake.

'Two doors down on the left is a dressing room. No one will be in there so the room's all yours,' he said smiling, and pointing down the hallway. I nodded to him in gratitude and left for the dressing room.

I hurried down the hall to the room he indicated. The quicker I got to the room, the sooner I would be able to call Nina, and I didn't want to lose a second of seeing her face. I closed the door behind me with my heart pounding, not sure whether it was for the excitement of seeing Nina, or the nerves of the upcoming gig.

I took a seat on a bench opposite the door. Opening the conversation thread with Nina, I attempted to press the video call button, but my shaking hand missed and pressed the back button. On the second attempt I successfully pressed the video call icon. With each ring the anticipation built inside me. The butterflies were hovering, suspended in my chest and stomach as I held my breath, waiting to see the word connecting on my phone. I counted out the rings of my phone as the video call waited for her to answer. 'Seven… Eight… Nine… Come on, answer…,' I urged the phone. Finally, the word I was waiting for appeared. Nina answered and her smile radiated through the phone. The butterflies sprung back into life and started dancing at the sight of her. I wondered if my heart would ever stop pausing for a moment when I saw her smile at me.

'Hey, I was worried you weren't going to answer for a second there,' I said, smiling back at her.

'Well, I thought it would be a bit weird if I answered on the first ring, so I let it go for a little bit. I don't want you to think I'm too keen. Are you at the bar now?' Nina asked. She wore a light blue hoodie. Her hood was up, and her hair fell over her right shoulder. Sun was pouring through the window behind her and showed some natural highlights in her flowing brown hair that I hadn't noticed before.

'Okay then, Draganić, play your games. Yeah, I'm just in the dressing room waiting for it to be time. I really hope you can stick around and watch me,' I said.

'I wouldn't miss it for the world. I really need it after the week I've had. It's been a bit of a nightmare,' Nina said, and her expression turned from joyful to sombre.

'What's wrong?' I asked, with a concerned look, wondering why she hadn't told me about anything being wrong when we spoke during the week.

Nina proceeded to tell me how she had been paired with Marko for her biology assignment. 'You have to get it changed. You can't work with that scumbag. You're going to change it aren't you? Tell me you're going to get out of it,' I protested, feeling my rage for Marko begin to bubble inside me again.

'Luka, calm down. Yes, it's awful that I have to work with him. I hate it. I've thought about it, and I'm not going to get a new partner.'

'What? Why?' I asked in disbelief.

'I think it's the best thing for me to be able to get completely over it. I need to not be affected by it. I want to move on, and… and remove the power that night has over me,' Nina said, with tears starting to well in her brown eyes with flecks of green.

'You don't need to be so brave, Nina. Please don't put yourself through the ordeal of having to re-live it every day. Your mama can go to the school and get them to change it,' I pleaded desperately. Being so far away I felt completely powerless to help her.

'Luka, stop it,' Nina said forcefully, and the tears started to flow. Seeing her cry shattered my heart into a million pieces. With every fibre of my being, I held down the tears that were so desperate to escape me at seeing her cry. I needed to be strong for her.

'Do you really think I don't re-live it every day anyway? I don't want it to fester inside me and ruin other things in my life. What if I don't deal with it and I can't explore what this could be between us? I can't have that. So please, just trust me and let me deal with it in my own way.' Nina wiped the tears from her cheek that I longed to wipe from her myself.

'I'm sorry. I just don't want to see you hurting like this. I trust you, but whenever you need to complain about him, I'm your man. I think I'll start an exercise book on insults about him so when you kick off, I can jump right in,' I said, trying to get her to smile. She laughed and wiped away another silent tear with her sleeve. The tracks of her dried tears remained, stained to her smiling cheeks.

'You're my man all the time, not just then,' Nina said, with a sniff and a smile.

I felt like I had been hit by a lightning bolt. *She just said I'm her man. Did she mean that she wants me to be her boyfriend, or was it just a throwaway line that doesn't mean anything? Here comes overthinking Luka again. Thanks for coming but you're not welcome here tonight.'* I shook my head to try and rattle the thoughts from my mind.

'Can I at least see what this guy looks like?' I asked. I wasn't sure why I wanted to see him. The sensible part of my mind was telling me it was pointless, but I was with Nina, and the sensible part was easily drowned out by the emotional part of my brain. The part that wanted to be able to direct my feelings of hatred towards a face.

'Fine,' Nina said. Her screen paused for a few seconds and then a picture was messaged to my phone. I opened it quickly, feeling nervous for a reason I wasn't sure of, but I was very aware of the sensation. He looked like a man's man. A real alpha. Looks can be deceiving though, because an alpha doesn't treat women like that. His eyes looked cold and dead. He had a dangerous face. Rage bubbled inside me, and I deleted the picture before I let that anger consume me. I needed to settle and relax before my show. Doing that would be easy, all I had to do was return to Nina's radiant face and I would feel everything bad in the universe melt away from my being.

'So, enough about that, how are you feeling about tonight? I can't wait to see you play. I even dressed up for the occasion. Look.' Nina slowly undid the zip on her hoodie to reveal a tight, white long-sleeved shirt. Then panned the camera down to show her shirt tucked into her sweatpants pulled up to her navel. Even when she was trying to be silly, she looked beautiful. I laughed at her immaculate white shirt tucked into her faded navy sweatpants, that if they were any higher, she could use as a bra.

Whether she was dressed for a wedding or in sweats having just rolled out of bed, she would always look exquisite to me.

'You look like sunshine,' I said, which brought back to life her radiating smile and her finger involuntarily found its way to twirl her hair. 'I'm feeling a bit strange now. It's only just hit me in the last few minutes, that even though I didn't want to admit it, most of the day I was scared, as in all I could think about was what could go wrong. I kept trying to silence that voice in my head that was telling me what would go wrong, but I'm not thinking about that anymore. I see you smiling at me and I'm just excited, I'm confident, I'm happy. I just wish Nana was here to see me play too.'

'You know she's watching you tonight. I'm sure she felt so lucky being the first crowd to your concerts and would never miss your first public show,' Nina said.

'She's my guardian angel. When she was here, and now that she's passed. She always looked out for me, protected me when she was here, and she's protecting me again now. I feel like she saw how hurt I was at her passing, and because I didn't have her here anymore, she sent you into my life. I don't believe for a second that meeting you is a coincidence, Nina. Nana brought us together,' I said, and I could see another tear fall from Nina's left eye. Not a sad tear, it was a happy tear. When it came to matters of the heart, I didn't believe in coincidences, Nina was sent to me. I could feel it in my heart, in my soul, I wanted Nina to be my girlfriend. James and Michael would try and talk me out of it because it was too soon, but I didn't care, it was what I wanted.

'Luka, what are you doing to me? I'm a mess,' she said, giggling and pointing at her happy tears falling down her cheeks. 'I think we were meant to meet as well, and I know that in the blink of an eye we'll be hugging each other. Whether it's at Melbourne airport, or Požega bus station. I know it's going to happen. This feels special.' She left her happy tear to depart her face, falling from her chin in its own time, as if she wanted it to stay as long as possible.

'Luka, there you are. We've been looking all over for you. They announced that you're going on in five minutes,' James said excitedly, as he and Michael bustled into the room each trying not to spill any of the beer they were holding.

'Guys, I'm glad you're here. I want you to meet someone,' I said, beckoning them nearer. They walked over quickly and squatted beside me. 'This is Nina.'

'You're right, Luka. She's way out of your league,' James said, and Nina laughed.

'Great to meet you, Nina. Make sure you look after our boy,' Michael said, waving to her.

'And you two please do the same until I can get there. One of you needs to hold the phone up so I can watch him play. Who has the steadiest hand? Actually, maybe the better question is, who's had less to drink?' Nina joked, peering at their glasses.

'I think it's pretty even, but Michael will do a better job,' James said, clinking his glass with Michael's hard enough to spill beer on Michael's lap, and then skulled the rest of his drink. Michael stared daggers at James as he tried to dry off his pants. 'Well, at least you have dark pants on,' James joked, but Michael didn't see the funny side at all.

'Give me the phone Luka, come on, it's time to go,' Michael said. I handed my phone to Michael, stood up and walked to the door.

'Hey Luka, go and show them just how special you are,' Nina said. All the anxiety I had been feeling left me. I felt a perfect balance between calmness, and excitement. I smiled and blew Nina a kiss. Taking a deep breath, I walked from the room with Michael and James following me, like a boxer walking to the ring being followed by his entourage.

I stepped onto the stage and hung my guitar over my shoulder. I looked down in front and saw James and Michael smiling up at me with my phone in Michael's hand. Michael pressed a button on the screen and turned the phone around. I saw Nina beaming at me and waving, while seeing myself on stage in the corner of the phone screen. It made my soul do a summersault seeing the woman of my dreams there in the front row to support me. I waved back at her before Michael turned the phone back around and pressed the screen once more to return the phone camera to the stage. I took a deep breath and brought my attention back to my performance.

I felt at peace. I could feel it was where I belonged. *The best thing for me to play first is the new song I wrote this week. There's no better way to introduce myself and tell them who I am,* 'I thought, staring down at my guitar.

'Hi everyone. My name's Luka, and it's my first night playing here,' I said, without the slightest trepidation in my voice. I felt confident. My guitar laid perfectly still against my chest.

'Yeah, Luka! Wooooo!' Michael and James screamed from right in front. I thought I heard Nina as well, but that could have been my hopeful imagination. There were approximately thirty people focused on me, but the rest of the bar were milling around and doing their own thing. They were focused on birds and sticks. Just before I hit the first chord, I thought of what Mum said to me. *Be the most interesting thing in the room.*

I've read of this thing,
That makes people sing.
They lose all reason,
Find magic to believe in.
I thought love a story,
Lies told through history,
Cause emotion so strong,
Could never come along.

I could lie and say you're not on my mind.
In my soul there's no kaleidoscope of butterflies.
I could lie, that your lips don't belong with mine,
But I won't lie. I can't lie.

No matter the distance,
Our hearts beat as one.
We gaze at the same moon,
We dance around the same sun.
When you find a soul,
So pure and true,
I knew nothing of love,
Until my heart was held by you.

I could lie and say you're not on my mind.
In my soul there's no kaleidoscope of butterflies.
I could lie, that your lips don't belong with mine,
But I won't lie. I can't lie.

They can say I'm insane,
Completely sick, wrong in the brain,
But when I saw your eyes smile,
There was only one I wanted to be mine.

I could lie and say you're not on my mind,
In my soul there's no kaleidoscope of butterflies.
I could lie, that your lips don't belong with mine,
But I won't lie. I can't lie
I can't lie

'Thank you,' I said, smiling as the bar applauded loudly. All birds and sticks were forgotten. There were no loud conversations, or people looking to find a seat. Every eye in the bar, including the staff was on me. I felt a power in my fingers as the adrenaline ran through my body.

An hour later the adrenaline was still coursing through my veins as I put down my guitar and walked from the stage. *This is the second best feeling I've experienced today, and it's about to be the third because I'm going to do it now,'* I determinedly thought.

'That was amazing, Luka. You were incredible,' Michael said, as he and James hugged me. Michael was still holding my phone, so Nina was getting a great view of the back of my head.

'You did exactly what Nina told you to do, you showed them all how special you are. That's husband material right there Nina, he's already following instructions well,' James yelled into my phone. I couldn't see Nina, but I could hear her laugh. We all laughed excitedly as we walked towards Sam's office.

'I'll be back in a minute,' I said to the guys, taking my phone and I headed for the dressing room.

'My phone's about to die, so I'm going to say what I need to quickly,' I said to Nina, taking the same seat I had before the gig.

'Before you say anything I just want to say that I'm proud of you. I can't wait to watch you in person,' Nina said, her eyes smiling at me.

'I couldn't have done it without you.' I just looked at her for a moment, wanting to take in the expression on her face. I took a screenshot of my phone, to make her my screensaver.

'I don't know how to say this other than to just say it.' I looked down and saw my heart beating through my shirt. *'Come on, Luka, you can do it,'* I encouraged myself. 'I know it's fast, but I don't want to be with anyone else, Nina. You're special to me, and I feel the most me I can be when I talk to you. You bring the best out of me. I don't want to waste another second of you not being my girlfriend. So, I'm just going to ask, will you be my girlfriend?'

Nina put her hand over her mouth, and her smiling eyes widened in shock. She didn't say anything, she stared at me for a moment. 'Nina? Are you still there? Did you freeze?'

Nina nodded and then smiled as she took her hand away from her mouth. 'Thank you for sharing tonight with me. I'm over the moon I got to be a part of it. Luka, you're the man I've been searching for. I would love to be your girlfriend.' Nina's hand returned to cover her mouth, but her eyes continued to smile at me.

We blew each other a kiss, our first as boyfriend and girlfriend. My phone battery read one percent. 'I'll text you when I get home,' I said just in time, because as we waved goodbye, my phone fell dead.

I can't believe it. I have a girlfriend,' I thought in shock. I sat there for a moment, letting the feeling of being in a relationship with the woman of my dreams wash over me. After a few minutes, I stood up and returned to the bar to find James and Michael to tell them the incredible news.

CHAPTER NINE
The Assignment

As Luka's handsome face disappeared from my phone, I stood staring into space for a minute trying to comprehend how my life had changed in the last week. I had gone from walking home from a party having just been assaulted, and trying to recover mentally from a cheating ex, to having a boyfriend in Australia. *'Have I completely lost my mind?'* I wondered. If I had, then I was okay with it because I couldn't stop smiling. Luka was perfect to me. Luka was perfect for me. Well, apart from living so far away which was quite rude of him, but we could work on that in good time. I felt euphoric.

I needed to give Andjela the news, so I broke myself out of my love haze and called her, taking a seat on my desk. 'Hey, what's up?' Andjela asked the moment she picked up. I could hear the wind in the background, so I knew she was outside.

'Not too much. Are you busy now? Can you hang out for a bit?' I asked, as I stood up and walked to my closet. *This might be perfect for a spring night out in Williamstown, but it really isn't going to do the trick in Požega on the verge of winter,'* I thought, looking at a cute green dress. The warm weather had left us for the southern hemisphere and wouldn't return until around April.

'I'm just in town having a coffee with Mama. She's going to head home after this, so do you want to meet me in the town centre?'

I laid on my bed to try and pull my blue high waisted jeans on. That was really a three-step process. I needed to make sure they were sitting on my ankles properly and then get them over my butt. Lastly was where my poor upper body strength hurt me, buttoning them. With my phone sitting on my chest on loudspeaker, I used all my effort for buttoning.

'Are you okay? You sound like you're struggling there,' Andjela said, but I couldn't respond immediately because buttoning my jeans was taking every ounce of strength I had.

'Yeah, just doing up my jeans. Perfect. I'll take a taxi and should be there in like fifteen. See you then,' I panted. The effort from buttoning my jeans told me that I needed to start working out. I grabbed a black knitted jumper from my closet and slipped it over my head, before standing in front of my mirror and examining myself. I took a selfie in the mirror and sent it to Luka. *If he doesn't hype me up, then maybe he isn't as perfect as I think he is,* I joked to myself, before collecting my phone and walking from the room.

Walking into the kitchen I found Mama reading a book and Milica sitting on the couch looking at her phone. 'Hey Mama, I'm going into town to meet Andjela. Do you need me to get anything?' I asked as I booked a taxi on my phone. I probably could have walked, but it was cold out and I wanted to tell Andjela my news as soon as possible.

'No, I've got everything I need already. You can take your sister with you though. She's been sitting on her phone for the last hour,' Mama said, looking over at Milica reproachfully, who didn't even twitch at the mention of her name. Milica was normally good company, so I didn't have a problem bringing her along.

I might be able to get some more information about Nikola if she comes, I thought.

'Milica! Come on!' I yelled to get my sister's attention. 'The taxi's going to be here in a minute.' I kissed Mama goodbye and gestured for Milica to follow me from the kitchen. I slipped my shoes on, grabbed my bag and jacket, and walked through the door closely followed by Milica. We cut through the vacant lot that lay next to our house to get to the street where we found our taxi waiting.

'To the centre?' our driver asked as Milica closed the door behind her. The taxi smelled of ćevapi and old man. I didn't have to look far to find the root cause of the smell, as the taxi driver looked to be mid-seventies and was holding ćevapi in his left hand. He used just his right hand to steer towards town.

'Thank you,' I said, and within five minutes he stopped next to the centre of Požega. There was a large fountain in the middle of Trg Slobode that only operated during summer. You could always find small children and dogs running through it on hot days. Encircling the town centre were benches, backed by trellises. Creeper plants covered the trellis which would bloom beautifully during spring and summer. The trellis gave shade to the benches encircling the fountain. Lying beyond that were many different shops and cafés, one of which had a waiting Andjela shivering out the front.

Milica and I walked towards Andjela who saw us, and greeted us with a big smile, hugging and kissing Milica, then myself. 'How are you?' Andjela asked, as we began to walk around the shops circling the heart of Požega.

I was so excited to tell her my news I forgot to ask her how she was doing. The words just flew out of my mouth at the speed of light. 'I'm good. Actually no, I'm amazing. Luka had his concert which I watched, and it finished just a little while ago. After he came off stage he went into a quiet room and asked if I wanted to be his girlfriend. Luka and I are in a relationship,' I said without taking a breath. I was so giddy that my voice had raised about four octaves. Several dogs barked. Andjela and Milica stopped in their tracks; I walked a few metres past them before I realised and turned to face them.

'Woah, woah, woah. Hang on a minute. Didn't you two just meet for the first time a week ago? And he's in Australia. And he doesn't know how old you really are. Don't you think there are some things you need to solve before committing to a relationship?' Andjela asked.   The sun had just fallen below the buildings, causing the already low temperature to plummet even further.

Milica didn't seem too perturbed by the revelation.   She smiled and asked, 'Oh, can I please meet him next time you talk? I want to hear the Australian accent.'   I nodded my head and smiled, patting her on the shoulder, and she gave a little jump of excitement before turning to look in the window of my favourite book shop that stood behind us. Milica walked inside so Andjela and I followed her.

Milica walked ahead through the aisles browsing while Andjela and I stood next to a display of old looking notebooks near the entrance. 'Seriously Nina, I'm sure he's a great guy but what are you doing? I get you really like him and everything but are you sure this is a good idea? After what happened with your ex and that human pimple Marko, are you really in the best place to be jumping into a relationship?' Andjela asked in a voice barely above a whisper so the sales assistant wouldn't overhear.

'I know all of that and yes it might be impulsive, but it does feel right. I might not be completely over those things, but I won't let those things take someone special from my life,' I said, looking over my shoulder to see if the sales assistant was within earshot. The short woman with rounded shoulders had shuffled down an aisle to put away several books.

'I'm not saying never, I'm just saying wait,' Andjela replied.

'So, Luka can meet someone else? There can be a million reasons not to do something like this, to hold off and think about it until it feels like a bad idea, but I only need one reason to do it.   I want to,' I whispered, as I picked up a leather-bound notebook and ran my hands over the spine. *I love notebooks. I think I'm due for a new pretty one,'* I thought. A beautiful butterfly clasp held its covers closed. I put it to my nose and took in the smell of leather and fresh paper. The air just after it rains, freshly cut grass, a new notebook, or a man you love. Those are my favourite smells.

'You must feel really strongly about this if you've jumped in so quickly. I don't want to tell you that you're wrong, because it's not my job to tell you how to feel. Just make sure that you look after yourself because you're taking a big risk and I don't want to see you get your heart broken again,' Andjela said in a hushed voice, as the sales assistant returned to the register. Andjela picked up a book herself and read the blurb.

'Aren't you risking your heart in every significant relationship you have?' I walked towards the counter to pay for my notebook before Andjela could answer. Milica was on the floor reading a book, so I beckoned her to leave with us. We walked back into the street and strolled through town window shopping and chatting. No sooner had the grilling about Milica's 'friend,' Nikola began, did we see a boy walk out of a supermarket causing Milica to gasp and jump behind me.

'What are you doing?' I asked over my shoulder laughing. Her eyes darted to the boy who was now walking in our direction but didn't seem to have seen Milica. 'Is that him? Is that Nikola?' Milica gave a scared nod as she held onto my jacket to ensure she was hidden.

Andjela had never been backwards in coming forwards, so she turned and yelled to him, 'Hey Nikola, come here.' He walked over sheepishly with a confused look on his face as to why he was being summoned by the local tennis celebrity. Already as tall as me at only thirteen years old, he was skinny, had long awkward limbs and brown eyes. His messy brown hair was unusual for a boy in Požega, as most had a number one or two razor cut. As soon as he realised who was hiding behind me, he gave an uncomfortable smile as if he would rather be anywhere else.

'Hi Milica,' he mumbled, staring at his feet. I hopped to my right to stop Milica from hiding behind me. It was both the most adorable and most awkward interaction I had seen between a boy and a girl.

'I hope I'm a little bit more charismatic than this when Luka visits,' I thought, shaking my head.

'Hi,' Milica responded. She seemed to be equally interested in her shoes and closely examined the little scuff mark on the end of her black chucks.

'We'll just pop into this shop for a minute, but don't go anywhere Milica. We'll be back in a few minutes,' Andjela said, dragging me into the nearest shop.

'Nice to meet you,' I said to Nikola, as Andjela dragged me into the shop. I fixed my elongated sleeve that Andjela used to pull me away from the two young love birds and turned my attention to the store she had pulled me into. A men's clothing shop, which had everything from large winter down jackets, to underwear. *Maybe I should try and find a present for my new boyfriend. After all, Christmas isn't too far away,'* I thought.

'Urgh, that was physically painful to watch, we needed to get out of there for a few minutes,' Andjela groaned, beginning to look at the clothes on the rack. 'It's so much easier for men to dress. Look at all these basic things that men look good in, while we have so many complicated options. Think of how much time you would save if your only decision was what colour hoodie you would wear that day. I'm jealous.'

'The secret is not caring what other people think. Just wear what you want. I think if you had a sumo suit on you would manage to look good in it,' I said, following Andjela, and hoping that something would strike me as a good gift for Luka.

'I hope Luka's brother flirts with me as well as you do, baby,' Andjela said, winking at me and blowing me a kiss. 'Hmm, I don't have a boyfriend, but that doesn't mean I can't have boyfriend clothes, does it? I think I should buy a couple of baggy hoodies and sweatpants. What do you think?' Andjela asked, putting on a hoodie and walking the aisle like a runway model. She stopped at the end of the aisle, posed for a couple of guys standing outside the shop who were looking through the window. She waved to them and then jogged back to me laughing.

'I think if you wear that around Aleks you'll have someone's hoodie to steal in no time.'

'Okay, so his brother has a name. Aleks… yeah… I can work with that,' she wondered aloud, staring into space.

'Don't act for one second like you haven't already stalked his brother online,' I said, looking sideways at her. She gave me a coy smile and shrugged playfully.

'I want to buy something for Luka. Christmas is coming up and I want to get him a present. Not just a random present but something a girlfriend would give,' I said thinking aloud, turning to look through more clothes on the rack.

'Well, I think you are a bit far away to give a gift that a girlfriend would give… but hey, look at these. I'm sure he'd love a pair of these,' Andjela said, holding a pair of red Santa jocks in front of herself to show off her modelling skills again.

'You know what? That's not a bad idea.'

'Dude, I was joking.' I took the jocks from Andjela as she stared at me in shock.

'No, seriously. I think this would be something fun to give him and it's Christmas themed too. Have they got a small? From the pictures I've seen he looks like he has a skinny butt,' I said, rifling through the rack of Santa jocks until I found a pair sized small and took them. Andjela and I walked to the register and paid for our items before leaving the shop to find Milica standing outside staring at her phone.

'Ready to go?' I asked Milica as she looked up at the two of us with our bags in hand. She nodded as we went left and continued walking along the street. Turning right into Kralja Petra Street, we continued along and came across a bakery. 'Are you two hungry?' I asked, as Andjela pushed me out of the way to rush inside.

'I think that means no,' Milica said sarcastically.

'Where did Nikola disappear to?' I asked.

'His mama called and said she needed him home.'

Milica and I followed Andjela inside to find her already biting into a piece of pizza. Milica carefully browsed through the selection of cakes, sandwiches, and pizza, before deciding on a piece of chocolate cake. I bought a sandwich and lemon drink for myself and paid for Milica's cake, before joining Andjela in the booth that she had already claimed. We took a seat opposite Andjela just as she finished her first piece of pizza.

The bell above the door rang so I turned my attention towards it to see who was entering the bakery. Marko shuffled inside, wearing a white hoodie and a pair of skinny blue jeans. He took a quick glance in our booth's direction and dropped his keys. He stood for a moment before picking them up and deciding to walk to the counter and place an order.

My heart was beating through my chest the moment I saw him. I began to pick at the skin on the end of my fingers. *Is he going to come over and talk to me before he leaves? We do need to talk about our assignment, but I was praying for a meteor to hit the biology lab, so I didn't have to do the assignment. Or alternatively, it could just hit him on the way home. Not a massive meteor, just about the same size as the one that knocked out the dinosaurs should do the trick, directly on his head,'* I thought.

The woman behind the counter handed Marko a loaf of bread and his change, before he turned towards the door. He hesitated once again, before deciding to veer off course, and in a moment of sudden courage, walked towards our booth. My heart felt like it was about to shatter my rib cage and land on the table. I continued to pick at my fingers until Andjela reached under the table and placed her hand on mine. Marko and I hadn't been that physically close since the night in the bar, and I didn't know if I was ready to be, but I didn't have a choice if I wanted to get over it. *'I refuse to be a victim,'* I shouted resolutely on repeat in my head.

'Hey Nina, Andjela. Is this your sister, Nina?' Marko quietly asked with a quiver in his voice. Milica stared at him, and Andjela gave him a rude hand gesture while I took a mouthful of my lemon drink with the ice clattering together.

'What are you doing here? What do you want Marko? I'm trying to spend some time with Andjela and my sister. Can this wait?' I asked, trying to keep my voice strong. I stared directly into his eyes. My heart continued its desperate attempt at escape, but I wasn't going to let that show in my voice. There was a sense of relief that the first words had been spoken between us. I was grateful that it happened by accidentally seeing him, rather than having to dread an organised meeting. I felt an urge to begin picking at my fingers again, but I resisted. Andjela's hands were on the table, clenched in fists, knuckles white, intently watching Marko to see what he would do next.

'Mama asked me to come and get some bread for her. I'm sorry for interrupting, but I just thought…' Marko began before being cut-off by Andjela.

'Then don't say anything more and leave,' Andjela said through gritted teeth, making sure to use the same finger from her previous gesture to point at the door.

'I just wanted to organise a time for us to meet up to start the assignment. I have some ideas already about what we can do,' he said with the nervous quiver in his voice becoming more pronounced with each syllable that left his lips. Sweat was starting to develop on his brow, and he held the bread to his chest as if he were a small child holding on to a soft toy after waking from a nightmare, standing at the foot of his parents' bed.

'Yeah, we should just get it done with as soon as we can. Can you meet in the library after school Monday?' I suggested, praying that it was the end of the first interaction between us.

'Perfect. See you Monday,' he squeaked, before turning as quickly as possible and heading for the door with his bread still clutched to his chest.

That's going to be perfect for crumbed chicken if he keeps holding it like that,' I thought, looking at the squashed bag.

'Try not to grope anyone on the way home,' Andjela yelled after Marko as he walked away, loudly enough for everyone in the bakery to hear. He paused momentarily, as if considering coming back to the table, before restarting his journey towards the door and back home.

'Are you okay? I love the plan to agree to meet him and then just not show up. It's brilliant!' Andjela said, her jaw relaxing and her white knuckled, balled up fists falling limp on the table. I could feel the sweat building up in my armpits, and I was grateful I had three layers on to hide the fact that my antiperspirant had failed me.

'I'm okay, just relieved that's over. I'm going to meet him though. We need to do this assignment, and hopefully it's relatively pain free so we can move on with our lives,' I said, scrunching up the packaging of my food and sinking back into the booth.

'Okay then. Hopefully pain free and grope free too,' Andjela said, balling up her wrapper and shooting it into the bin. 'Kobe.'

Walking out of the bakery Milica and I said goodbye to Andjela before finding a taxi back home. Night had completely fallen over Požega, so the only light was the one in the entrance hall window as we walked through the front door. Milica kicked off her shoes and walked quickly into the living room. I heard a squeal from Milica as I was in the middle of taking off my shoes. Panicked, I tore them from my feet and ran into the living room to find the cause of the scream. There he was, standing in the middle of the living room, his long arms wrapped around my sister who he had picked up in his embrace. His face was hidden in her neck, so I could only see the top of his shiny bald head, but I knew exactly who that bald head belonged to.

'Tata!' I shouted and sprinted the three steps separating us before hugging him and Milica at once. He put Milica down and the three of us held our hug for what felt like forever. 'I missed you so much. When did you get home? I didn't think you were coming home for another few months.'

We finally let go of our hug and Tata said, 'Oh I missed you too. There's a delay in the project that I'm working on which won't be fixed for a couple of weeks. So, I thought it was a good chance to come back and see you guys before I have to go back to work.'

I stood back and looked at him in the flesh for the first time in six months. He had been in Montenegro working on a building project. There wasn't much construction work in our city, so he had to look beyond for work. He had been travelling for work my entire life. I had no idea how Mama handled being away from her husband for so long.

'I'm so happy you're home, Tata. Why didn't tell us you were coming?' I joyfully asked him, as Tata sat at the table and lit a cigarette to enjoy with his glass of rakija.

'Your mama and I wanted to surprise you. I think the biggest shock is that she managed to keep it a secret for two days. I left the day after I found out I'd be able to sneak away for a couple of weeks. So, what's been happening? How is it going with your boyfriend, Nina? What's his name?' Tata asked, taking a drag of his cigarette. Clearly Mama hadn't been keeping him in the loop.

'The boy you're talking about doesn't have a name, we broke up. I actually found a man that is a bajillion times better than him. You will love him; he lives in Australia, but his grandparents came from Požega. I think he's going to visit for my birthday,' I replied, as he had another drag of his cigarette before taking a sip of rakija.

'I will love him if he doesn't take my daughter away from me. Make sure he knows that it is customary when an Australian boy is dating a Serbian girl, the boy must bring the father of the Serbian girl ten beers,' Tata said, finishing the last of his rakija and sitting back in his chair with a cheeky grin on his face, cigarette hanging from his mouth and holding up ten fingers.

'Tata, do you really think he's stupid enough to believe that's a real thing? If I tell him that then he will actually bring you ten beers because he's so nice. I can't tell him that,' I said laughing with Milica, who was staring at our father as if in awe of him. She couldn't have been in awe more if Jesus was in the room.

'I can be a trendsetter. I can trend on the Twittster. Make sure you tell him that it needs to be one bottle of ten different Australian beers. An Australian beer smorgasbord if you will. I don't want my palate to get bored.' I shook my head laughing and walked out of the kitchen towards my room to put away my present for Luka and my new notebook. Mama was in my room putting the last of my freshly cleaned clothes in a neatly folded pile on my bed.

'Hey honey, nice surprise for you. I bet you didn't expect that,' she said, as she picked up the empty basket and tucked it under her arm. 'What did you buy today?'

'I had no idea he was coming. Oh, these? Just a couple of presents. One for me, and one for Luka,' I said, pulling out the notebook first and handing it to Mama.

'Oh Nina, it's gorgeous. I hope you're going to write in this one compared to all the empty notebooks you have sitting on your shelf. What did you buy for Luka?' Mama asked, trying to peek inside the other bag. I took out the red Santa jocks and held them up to cover my face.

Mama took them from me and shook her head looking at them. 'So, you two are already in a place where you're buying underwear for each other?' Mama was trying not to laugh looking at them.

'Apparently I am anyway,' I said with a wry smile and burning cheeks, taking the jocks back from her and hiding them away in the top drawer of my desk. I put the notebook on my top shelf along with my others. I normally didn't want to desecrate my beautiful books by writing in them, but I thought that would be my Luka book. *I'll write about our future adventures together in there one day,'* I thought, trying to hide a smile.

'Dinner will be ready in about twenty minutes. Jovan should be back from football practice soon,' Mama said, as she walked from my room with the laundry basket.

Our family sat at the table and enjoyed each other's company for the first time in six months. The five of us so seldom got to spend time together as a family, that it always felt special when we did. When I was younger, I used to resent Tata for being away all the time and thought he should have tried harder to find work in town so we could all be together. I still wanted him to do that, but I understood better that he was sacrificing for us every day. He was spending all his time away from his family so we could enjoy our lives; so, our lives could be better. That he wanted to be with us instead of being away working. I hadn't once taken for granted my time with my father though. *I just wish I had my tata with me more often than I do. We all do,'* I thought.

I walked out of class on Monday and went straight to the library with a purpose, with a strength, with conviction. Don't they say to face your fears? Remove their power over you. Go to the top of the mountain, hold a spider, do the assignment with the guy that drunkenly groped you. 'I have the power. I have the power,' I said aloud to myself, as I approached the door of the library.

The weather had turned quickly in Požega. Two weeks ago, we had warm days, but the days were getting shorter, getting colder, and the freezing wind was piercing through my winter jacket.

Walking into the almost abandoned library I saw Marko immediately. He was sitting inside one of the study rooms that lined the left side of the library. I was glad it had a glass door because if it were completely private, I would have turned around and walked straight out. The moment I saw Marko I felt like the elephant Luka spoke about took a seat on my chest, causing me to take short, sharp breaths. It was just a baby elephant for now, but I knew the pressure would grow as soon as I was alone with Marko.

Andjela had been texting me all day, imploring me not to show up. She was sure there was a way for me to get out of having that human vermin as my partner. Marko looked as though he was wearing a shirt two sizes too small, as his large arms and shoulders looked as though they were about to rip it apart.

'Hey,' I said strongly, making sure to make eye contact. I took off my backpack, sat down, and placed my bag on my lap so I could take my books out. I brought my ugliest notebook for the assignment. I was not going to waste a pretty one on something associated with Marko. I placed it and my biology textbook on the table waiting for him to break the silence.

'Hi, do you want me to take your jacket? They've really got the heat pumping in here,' Marko said as he stood up and extended his large right hand towards me. Well, I thought it was his right, I had always struggled with my rights and lefts.

I'm not sure how he can say it's warm with those nipples sticking through his shirt. I thought free the nipple was a feminist movement,' I thought.

'No,' I said shortly, forcing as much distaste as I could into my stare. *'Three layers of clothing and my backpack aren't enough of a barrier between the two of us. I don't want to be here. I want to be in Williamstown with Luka, or home with my family and Luka, or in Damascus with Luka, instead of here. Oh gosh, why aren't you here with me, Luka?'* I groaned longingly to myself. I missed him so much. *'How can you miss someone that you've never met in person?'* I wondered.

He was wearing the same cologne that he was that night. It cut through me like an Antarctic wind. My breathing shortened even more, and my heart started racing. I felt clammy. I began picking at my fingers underneath the desk, hiding my anxiety from Marko. I felt as though the elephant was growing by the second as I sat there looking at him. I could feel those big hands grabbing at me once again. *'Get off me,'* I protested in my mind. I closed my eyes for a moment and pictured Luka. Those eyes and euphoric smile tattooed on my mind. My breathing and heartrate slowed back to normal. The enormous elephant shrunk to the size of a baby. *'Okay, I can work now,'* I reassured myself, and opened my eyes. No one was there to get me through it; I had to navigate it on my own.

'We have a week to finish this assignment, so I think we'll need to meet a few times to finish. There are four sections, so if we take two each to research, then we can do the writing of it together. What do you think?' he suggested in an upbeat and positive voice, trying to overpower the undeniable tension in the room.

'He's such a waste of a hot guy,' I thought, not trying to hide the look of disgust on my face. 'Why don't we just take two sections each, write them on our own and then put them together at the end? That way we don't have to meet at all, we can just do it by email.' With every passing moment I was regretting my decision more and more to face my fear. My anxiety was growing again. The room was closing in on me. *Luka's eyes, Luka's eyes, Luka's eyes,'* I repeated to myself to stop the elephant from increasing the pressure on my chest again.

'Can we talk about it and put it behind us?' Marko asked. The thing I least wanted to talk about, but needed to talk about most, was on the table. I felt like I was standing outside the death chamber, waiting to be strapped to the electric chair. Every sense I had was on fire, my throat was constricting, my nerves were so high that I could feel my entire body tingling. The room continued to close in on me so I couldn't move, and Luka's face was fading from my mind so I couldn't relax. There was only one way to relieve the pressure.

'By 'it', do you mean the whole, sexually assaulting me in front of almost everyone we know and then saying I asked for it? That 'it'?' I asked aggressively, as I clung to my bag. *The second I leave here I'm calling Luka. I need him. I need my boyfriend,'* I thought, craving a hug from Luka. I put my hands onto my knees, squeezing them so I would stop picking at my fingertips.

'I can't ever ask you to forgive me. I don't think I can ever forgive myself for what I did to you. I feel sick to my stomach every time I look at you. Every time I think about what I did I feel like my insides are twisting. I can't sleep; I can't eat. Somebody told my mama about it, and she told me that she was ashamed of me. I...' he trailed off and I could see his body trembling.

I could feel the elephant leave my body and be replaced with anger. Anger at myself because I was sitting there feeling sorry for him. For Marko! He sexually assaulted me, and I felt sorry for him. *'No, I won't. Stop it, Nina,'* I screamed in my own head.

'Am I supposed to feel sorry for you?' I spat. 'It's so awful that Marko hasn't been able to eat the protein he needs for his pumped-up body because he invaded me at a party. Yeah, we were never best friends, but I thought you at least respected me. You clearly picked this room so you could talk to me about this. I wouldn't be surprised if you asked Professor Potelić to put us in a group together so you could get me alone.' My voice was raising uncontrollably with every word that left my lips. I was determined not to cry. *'I won't let him see me cry,'* I thought resolutely. My tears were reserved for people that I loved.

We sat in silence, and I made sure not to look at him. A game of chicken was happening to see who would break the silence first. I wanted it to be over. I'd had enough of the saga, and I wanted to move on with my life.

I reluctantly made eye contact with Marko, and in a voice barely above a whisper I said, 'I forgive you.' I felt the walls push back; I could breathe again. A calmness fell over me and my entire body relaxed. The subconscious urge to pick at my fingers dissipated. I could feel the anger and anxiety float away into the atmosphere. The elephant on my chest stood up and walked away into the African plains.

'Really?' he asked gratefully, and I could see his shoulders relax. The pen that was spinning in his hand fell to the table.

'I'm not saying what you did was okay. I'm not even forgiving you for your benefit. This is for me. I don't want to be affected by this. I don't want to be having a friendly conversation with a guy in a bar and be worried the entire time that he's going to grab me. I don't want to be angry anymore. I don't want to be constantly worried if I'm leading someone on just by being nice to them or smiling at them. I just want my peace,' I said with a steely resolve in my voice. The effect of forgiving Marko gave me a levity, the feeling that I had only recently felt when I was talking with Luka.

'Thank you. I know it won't mean anything to you, but I owe it to you and everybody around me that I show you I'm not a bad person. That I did a bad thing and that will never happen again,' he said softly, extending his large hand to shake mine. The thought of touching him as a way of putting him touching me behind us seemed ironic, but I gave him my hand. His hand engulfed mine in a firm yet gentle shake then released my hand. 'Maybe we could even be friends?'

I gave him the clearest look of 'don't push it' that my face could muster. 'Can we just do some work?' I asked, keen to move on, and placed my bag on the floor.

Walking from the library an hour later I felt emotionally drained. While the biggest issue in my life had been resolved, I felt like I needed to nestle into an hour-long hug from my boyfriend. The last issue to tackle was being on the other side of the world from my Luka. 'One problem at a time Nina,' I said aloud to myself, as I almost bounced past the bus station. Taking my phone out of my right back pocket, I called Luka hoping he was awake.

As I placed my phone to my ear, I heard a sleepy and deep voice groan, 'Good morning, sunshine.'

I'm going to have to call him in the Australian morning more often because I could get used to this hot morning voice,' I thought. His morning voice was so cute I felt a tingle in my stomach. If I woke up next to him and he spoke in that voice, I wouldn't be able to stop myself from putting kisses all over his face.

'Hey, did I wake you?' I asked feeling sorry that I did, but happy I was talking to my man.

'Yeah, but you're worth being woken up for. I used to always keep my phone on silent when I slept, but I haven't since we met in case you called. I think I'm addicted to talking to you,' Luka said, stifling a big yawn. He always said the perfect thing to make me feel special. Even with the rapidly dropping temperature of the Požega night, I could feel my cheeks burning.

'I won't keep you long so you can get some more rest. I'm walking home from the library and was thinking about you, so I thought I'd call. I just wanted to hear your voice. My boyfriend's voice.' I smiled widely at being able to call Luka my boyfriend. I was wrong thinking that forgiving Marko gave me the same light feeling as talking to Luka. Luka didn't make me feel light; Luka made me feel euphoric.

'I love hearing you call me that. Tell me about your day. How was school?' he yawned again. His voice was waking up.

'Maybe I should let him go back to sleep and wake him up again to hear more of that super cute, sleepy Australian accent,' I thought jokingly.

'Just had school, so that wasn't interesting. Life will get a bit chaotic in January when I have my first lot of exams. Before then it's just assignments. I had my first meeting with Marko today,' I reeled off casually as if it were nothing interesting like the rest of school. I prayed Luka wouldn't make a big deal out of it. My prayer wasn't answered.

'Just hearing that name makes me sick. That he's been in the same room as you and I haven't just isn't fair. How was it?' he grumbled. It felt like he was torn between asking out of polite obligation because the topic of Marko disgusted him, and also, he was interested in how it went out of care for my well-being. Luka hated Marko more than I did. He was in no rush to forgive.

'It went as well as I could have hoped. It's all behind us now and I just want to move on. It's done. It's over. We'll do this assignment, be mature about it, and then go our separate ways. I don't want to talk about that anymore though, when there are a million other things we can talk about.'

'Okay, I just want you to be safe.'

'I know. Can we talk about something more interesting? That stuff's boring me. Have I told you that my best friend is going to be in Melbourne in January for the major tennis tournament? She's playing in qualifying and said she really wants to meet you,' I said, grateful we were finished talking about Marko. I walked under the underpass, being careful to avoid the puddles in the potholes. I was glad that it was dark, so I didn't have to worry about saying hello to every neighbour as I walked by their house. I increased my cadence as the temperature felt like it was dropping every minute, trying to get to the fire in my living room as quickly as possible.

'That's incredible. I go every year. How have you not told me about this before?' I could hear the ruffling of a blanket and a grunt of effort to signify he was getting up.

'Because I'm telling you now,' I said with as much sass as I could muster.

'Well, make sure you tell me when she's playing because I want to go. I'd love to meet her. She can take your Christmas present back to you,' Luka said with a muffled voice meaning he was putting on a shirt.

'I'll send you a photo of us together. She's really pretty so please don't fall in love with her,' I joked.

'You're ridiculous,' he said dismissively.

I quickly scanned my photos to find one where I looked okay, so Andjela wasn't completely overshadowing me. I walked down the street, around the corner from my house, as I continued to scan my photos. My neighbour was taking some wood inside from the pile stacked on the side of his house. Finally, I found one of Andjela and I with makeup on, heading to a party.

'Wow,' he exclaimed, and my heart sank a little.

I know she's stunning, but I don't really want to hear my boyfriend slobbering all over my best friend,' I thought, feeling a little sad. I was emotional from my meeting with Marko, so it didn't take much to upset me.

'Yeah, I know, I told you she's pretty,' I mumbled, trying not to let a hot jealous streak come out of me.

'No, it's not that. You look so beautiful. I'm glad you can't see the look on my face or else you would think I'm a creep. You're the most beautiful woman I've ever seen. Remind me again why you talk to me?' Luka asked, and I laughed feeling about as stupid as a person could. My ex always talked about how beautiful Andjela was, but I couldn't act like Luka was him.

I can't let my baggage from past relationships ruin Luka for me. He is different and I'm lucky to have him,' I scalded myself.

'Stop it…. Hmm okay, now say more cute things,' I said, and he burst out laughing. No man had ever made me feel that pretty, that wanted, that special. 'Andjela saw photos of your brother and wants to meet him too. She thinks he's cute.'

'That's funny because Aleks asked if you have any hot friends. I'll make sure to bring Andjela over for dinner to meet him. I can't believe I'm going to meet your best friend in person. This is insane.' His voice was bouncing at the prospect of meeting Andjela.

Walking down the driveway towards my house I could see the light behind the door. I felt torn between walking slower so I could continue to talk to Luka or running towards the refuge of the warm living room.

'It will be crazy to see you two together. I can't wrap my brain around it. Well, I'm at my front door, I can hear Mama and Tata, ahh, let's call it discussing something loudly,' I said, deciding that the refuge of the fire was too much to pass up. I may have made a different decision if he was still speaking with his sleepy voice though.

'You mean arguing. Wait. Your tata is back? That's incredible. I thought he was working in Montenegro for another few months. Why didn't you tell me he was coming back? You don't tell me anything!' he exclaimed, sounding as excited as I was when I saw Tata in the kitchen.

'I didn't know he was coming until I walked into the house and saw him a couple of days ago. He's just here for two weeks, but it's amazing having him back. I was able to tell him all about you, and he's really excited to meet you. He wants you to know that in Serbian culture, it's customary to bring the father ten different Australian beers. He's crazy, you'll love him,' I said, laughing and starting to take off my shoes before going through the door.

'I'm sure I'll manage to fit them in my bag. I can't let down my girlfriend's tata the first time I meet him,' Luka said, and the Luka butterflies in my stomach awoke with a force I hadn't felt before. Something as simple as hearing him call me his girlfriend made me feel a joy I had never experienced. I couldn't even imagine what it was going to feel like when he wrapped his arms around me. My freezing fingers found their way to my hair and began to twirl it around my fingers. 'Get inside and get warm. I'll talk to you tomorrow. Say hi to your family for me.'

'Talk soon,' I replied, opening the door, and jumping inside the warm house, only to be greeted by Mama and Tata yelling at each other. They're not fighting, that was just how they spoke to each other. I was already regretting saying goodbye to Luka, the hypothermia would have been worth it. The warmth of my house washed over me the moment I closed the door, spreading to my freezing and numbing fingers.

'Hi,' Tata said, as I kissed him and Mama hello before sitting on the couch next to Jovan. He didn't even flinch when I put my arm around him. Milica was sitting at the table while Tata helped Mama take dinner from the bench to the table. That's why I hated having Tata away so often. Being able to sit around the table, as a family, and eat dinner together. Making fun of each other and laughing. I had a new boyfriend; I had resolved things with Marko, and I was with my family. I felt happy.

A week later I walked back into the library to put the finishing touches on my assignment with Marko. The entire assignment had been as painless as I could have hoped. Even though I said we could do it all by email, in the end it was best to meet in person a few times to make sure we were on the right track. He went out of his way to make sure we had fun while working together, constantly making fun of himself and sneaking a different snack into our library room each time we met. I wondered what he had brought as I approached our study room for the final time. The assignment was critical to my final grade; I couldn't afford to do poorly if I wanted to study biology at university. It had taken up almost all my non class time, so I hadn't been able to talk with Luka much that week. He always said that school came first, that needed to be my priority, but I could tell he was getting upset that we hadn't been able to talk as much. I was upset about it too.

'Hey, how are you?' I asked, walking into the room with a smile, and placing my bag on the floor, taking a seat. I pulled my book out and placed it on the table, opening it to where I had finished my section of the assignment. We were there to review our work and then either Marko or I would put the final assignment together.

'Great, thanks, how are you?' Marko said, smiling with his big, white teeth, as he reached into his bag. I waited with bated breath as he teasingly rummaged around, only to pull from it a notebook and pen. He placed them on the table and laughed at the look of disappointment on my face.

'I'm good but it does depend a little on what you've brought for us today,' I said, craning my neck, trying to get a peek inside his bag. Marko smirked, reaching inside his bag again and he pulled out a packet of Eurocrem. Half white and half brown, cocoa and hazelnut flavoured chocolate. 'Oh my gosh. Yesss. This is my absolute favourite. How did you know?' I took the Eurocrem from him and stared lovingly at the red and white packaging.

'I took a shot,' he chuckled. I tore the packaging open like a leopard in a tree tearing into an antelope carcass. Breaking off a big piece, I gently placed the packet onto the table and savoured the Eurocrem, lounging back in my chair with my eyes closed. Eating Eurocrem made me feel like I was lying on a sunbed by the water in the Maldives. Pure paradise for my tastebuds. 'So, are you ready to start, or do you need a minute?'

I held up my hand for a moment while I enjoyed my Eurocrem, before opening my eyes and falling back to reality. 'Oh yeah, we have an assignment to finish. I knew I didn't just come to eat. So, I'm assuming you've finished your sections too. Why don't we read each other's work and see if we can make any improvements?' I suggested. Marko nodded and we exchanged books, taking the next twenty minutes to read each other's work.

Marko's work was amazing. He was so intelligent I felt like I was reading the work of the professor, not of a student. I snuck the occasional look at him to see if I could tell if he was impressed with my work or not by the look on his face. Marko had a steeled look of concentration, giving away nothing as to his thoughts on my work. *Why do I care what he thinks?'* I wondered.

My phone started to vibrate on the table; it was Luka. I declined the call and turned my attention back to reading through Marko's section of the assignment. 'That was a pretty emphatic rejection. Who was that?' Marko asked, his eyes focused intently on reading.

'Oh that? Umm, just my boyfriend. I'll talk to him later,' I said nervously. It was weird that we had spent so much time alone together and I hadn't mentioned I had a boyfriend. *Why do I feel nervous telling him I have a boyfriend?*' I thought, feeling slightly ashamed. I shouldn't have been hiding that from anyone, especially Marko.

'Oh, I didn't know you have a boyfriend. I bet you probably haven't settled for one of us from school. He would have to be somewhere else like Belgrade, or America,' Marko said, turning the page of my notebook nonchalantly.

'What is that supposed to mean?' I snapped, dropping his notebook on the table. *Is it a compliment or an insult? Is he saying that I'm stuck up? Or that I'm such a nice person I'll give someone a chance from anywhere, if they are respectful,*' I pondered. I felt both chuffed and annoyed at the same time. Even I was confused by my emotions. We females are complex creatures. Both emotions swirled around me, waiting for his response.

'Well, your last boyfriend was from Čačak, and even though literally every guy in school has a crush on you, I don't think you've ever looked at any of them twice. You're super talented, and I know your talents will take you a long way from this town. So, it only makes sense that you'd be interested in men that match your worldly talents. I bet he's older too, isn't he?' Marko asked, finally looking up from the notebook. My mouth was slightly open, silently gazing at him. I didn't know how to respond.

When I finally found my voice I said, 'Well, actually he's from Australia, and yes he is older.' Marko suppressed a snort of laughter. 'Are you saying that I think I'm too good for the people at school? I don't think that at all,' I protested incredulously. I folded my arms in defiance, and he set my ugly notebook upon the table.

'I don't think that at all. I assumed he's older because I think you're very mature; too mature for the dumb stuff seventeen-year-old boys do. Why wouldn't you want to be with an Australian guy? He's from a faraway land which must sound interesting and exciting. All I know is that he's a really lucky guy to have such a special girlfriend, and I hope he knows that,' Marko said, picking up my notebook to finish reading the assignment.

What does he really mean?' I wondered, sitting aghast.

I heard Marko put my book down as I turned the page to find only a paragraph left to read. Finishing Marko's work, I put down the book and said, 'I think what you've written is amazing. You haven't just answered the question, but you've written it almost as a story, like I was excited to know what you would say next.' There was a reverence in how I said it. I felt my respect for his gift grow through reading his work. It wasn't the first time we had worked together; his knowledge was always great, but his writing had improved significantly.

'I'm glad you liked it. You've ticked every single box you had to from the criteria. The detail in what you've written is brilliant. I'm in the same class as you and I felt like you were teaching me about biology. It's fantastic,' Marko said, smiling at me. I felt uncomfortable with him complimenting me, like my mind had forgotten what happened but my body hadn't. I began to pick at my fingers, placing them on my lap so he wouldn't see.

'Thanks,' I whispered, feeling slightly flush, picking up my water bottle and having a deep drink from it to give my hands something to do. I could feel his brown eyes staring into me. I ran my hands over my water bottle, waiting for him to stop staring, and speak again. ·I glanced up and saw that he was putting his book in his bag, so it could have just been my imagination.

'So, do you want me to type up the final report?' What he wrote was so brilliant I felt like I needed to type it to carry my weight. My phone rang again. It was Luka. Again. I rejected the call and texted him, 'I'm in the library, I'll call you when I finish….'

'No, please let me do it. You've been a star to do this assignment with me. I assumed you would get the pairing changed, but I'm glad you didn't. I've really loved doing this assignment with you. I wouldn't want to do it with anyone else,' Marko said.

I looked up and saw that he was staring at me this time. I felt a nervousness come over me. Not that I felt uncomfortable, but I wasn't sure what his look meant. *Was he flirting with me, or was he just being nice?'* I wondered. Those deep brown eyes were looking through mine, causing my heartrate to elevate. *'Go down heartrate, your heart is only allowed to do that for Luka. Or cardio,'* I urged myself.

'I'm glad I did it with you too. I was able to get past all the anger and sadness I had and put it behind me. Thanks for being a great partner and letting me see that you really are a good guy, that you just made a mistake,' I said. Over that week I had got to know the real Marko, not the one that was just a guy in my class, or the one drunkenly groping me in a bar.

I took a photocopy of my part of the assignment and gave him the pages. We walked together from the library. Standing in front of the library he turned to me and said, 'I hope we can be friends now.' He looked sheepish, like a little boy nervous to ask his mama for Eurocrem from the supermarket.

'Yeah. Yeah, I would like that,' I said, looking up into his smiling face.

I was about to begin my walk home, but something held me to that spot for a moment. In that moment, Marko took a step forward and hugged me tightly. *'Push him off,'* a voice inside my head screamed, but I didn't. I did something that I could never explain to myself. I put my arms around Marko and hugged him back. He had a new cologne on; its citrus scent pleasantly rushed over me. His muscles felt as hard and strong as he looked, with my hands feeling his large lats.

'Why am I doing this? And why am I liking it so much?'

CHAPTER TEN
The Australian Major Tournament

Nina and I had been together for two months and it had been the best two months of my life. Life had been chaotic working for Dad, playing at One Note, and having my relationship with Nina, but I wouldn't have changed a thing. Everything in my life was better, and it was all because of Nina. My family didn't even recognise the person in their house because I may have actually, possibly, looked happy. That's because I was. I thought that how I felt before was just how life was, that maybe I was too sensitive, and the suffering of life got to me more than others. That when I didn't feel miserable that was what happiness felt like. Yet out of nowhere, I met the most incredible woman, and she taught me how real happiness looked and felt.

My time with Nina felt surreal, it felt like I was immersing myself in someone else's story. *'When I meet Andjela that will change,'* I thought, still not able to comprehend that I would soon meet my girlfriend's best friend. That would be my physical connection with Nina until I flew there for her birthday.

I was sitting on my bed on a hot January night, waiting for Nina to video call me. Andjela was about to leave Belgrade, heading for Melbourne to play in the Australian tennis major tournament. Nina said they would call from the airport. I had seen on social media that Andjela was at the airport, so I was expecting the call at any moment.

I should have been asleep. You know someone is special when you sacrifice sleep to talk to them. Lying in bed I struggled to keep my eyes open as the time went past nine and still no call. My eyelids felt weighted as I struggled to hold them open, the thought of talking to Nina the only thing keeping me awake. I had my lamp on hoping the light would keep me from drifting off into a short sleep before waking at midnight for work.

My phone started to loudly ring on my chest, giving me the kind of fright that Maja would give me when she turned off the lights and jumped out from behind a door. After a couple of deep breaths to get my composure back from the shock, I answered the phone to be greeted by two beaming smiles.

'Hey, how are you two?' I asked, suddenly wide awake with a shot of adrenaline coursing through my veins. *Is this what happens to everyone when they answer the phone and see their girlfriend?'* I wondered.

'Hey, I'm great. So excited and envious. I wish I was coming too. I've heard Melbourne's a cool city. Oh, and I hear there's a guy there that owes me a date,' Nina said, smirking. Andjela shook her head and looked extremely uncomfortable.

'Yeah, I hear the Hemsworth boys are back in town and waiting to take you to dinner.'

'Wow, I was meaning you, but a Hemsworth? I could get on board with that.'

'Great, the other one is excited,' I joked, poking my tongue at Nina.

'Can you two save your weird and awkward flirting for after I've left for my flight, please?' Andjela asked, twitching uncomfortably.

'Sorry. How are you feeling about your trip, Andjela?' I asked. I had been rude relegating Andjela to play third wheel in the conversation.

'I can't wait to get there. It's going to be amazing to play in a tournament I've watched on TV for so long. Plus, it's snowing here, so I'm excited to get a tan on my pale skin. I'm so pale I can camouflage in the snow.' Andjela looked positively giddy. She looked as though she was bouncing, but that may just have been Nina's shaking hand.

'What she's most excited for is Aleks though,' Nina whispered, as if Andjela couldn't hear.

'Hey! I'm most excited for the tournament,' Andjela said in fake outrage. 'Aleks is number two on the list,' and they broke into a fit of giggles. Even though Andjela was talking, I couldn't take my eyes off Nina. The joy on her face was infectious. I felt her happiness spread through my body like a hot chocolate on a winter day.

'I know you'll be there, but is Aleks going to be there with you to cheer her on?' Nina asked, causing Andjela to give her a playful smack on the arm.

'If he isn't then I'm going to file for divorce. I've packed my cutest tennis outfits,' Andjela said, flicking her hair over her shoulder.

'He said he'll come if you get into the main draw. The last girl he dated made it to the main draw, so he doesn't want to go backwards,' I joked, as Nina laughed, and Andjela looked jokingly offended.

'This boy has way too much attitude for my liking, so we need to get that under control. At least I know he isn't a simp though, I don't think there's anything less attractive than that,' Andjela said, excitement radiating through her words. The kind of excitement that only comes when you are about to begin an adventure.

'I'll let you find out for yourself what he's like if he manages to score a date with you. How long until you need to go through customs? It's getting pretty close to your flight, isn't it?' I asked, looking at the time on my phone. I should have been worried about getting some sleep, but I didn't care if I didn't get a second of sleep. I just wanted to keep talking to Nina.

'You should probably go through in about ten minutes to be safe. The last thing you want is to be waiting in line at passport control watching the time and stressing that you might miss your flight,' Nina said, and Andjela nodded checking her own watch. 'Make sure you take care of her when she's there. It's your city so anything that happens to her is your fault.'

'Even if she loses?'

'Especially if she loses. That just means you weren't cheering hard enough,' Nina said, unable to keep a smile from her glowing face.

'Thanks, Andjela's tata. I'll do the best I can, but if a murderer comes at us, then all bets are off.'

'We'll just push a stranger towards the murderer. That's what I've done every other time that's happened,' Andjela said, absentmindedly looking at her watch again.

'Was the murderer's name Marko?' I asked, causing Andjela to put her hand over her face to cover her laughter, and Nina to roll her eyes.

'He's more of an attack from behind kind of guy,' Andjela said, looking sideways at Nina. She looked frustrated, like she wanted to say something, but decided to hold her tongue.

'Mum has already invited you for dinner. She's super excited to have you come over. I think it will be extra special because you're from Požega. That's where her parents grew up. I can't believe that we've never been before,' I rambled, completely forgetting that Andjela had a flight to catch. Unable to pick up the social cues that almost all other people would notice. The looks on Nina and Andjela's faces were of growing anxiety at the closing deadline. Sometimes I just needed someone to tell me to shut up.

'She should be excited, Andjela is her future daughter in law,' Nina said, as Andjela checked her watch again not listening to Nina. I could see the line for passport control beginning to grow. People were rushing to line up, which was noticed by both Nina and Andjela. 'Anyway, she really needs to go now, her coach has already gone through to the gate, and the departure board says her flight to Doha is boarding now. Text me when you get to work okay?'

'Of course.'

'I can't wait to get there and meet you. I've never been on a flight this long. Five hours to Doha and then fourteen to Melbourne is a lot. They better have some good food or else I'm going to go PMS on people,' Andjela said, and I could see them starting to walk towards customs.

'Have a safe trip and I'll see you soon. Sunshine, I'll text you at work. Just think, the next time you're at the airport it might be to meet me,' I said, and her look of anxiousness at Andjela being late turned to one of joy at the prospect of seeing me walk through the doors of Belgrade airport.

'What!? You're not going to meet me when I come home?' Andjela exclaimed, turning to look at Nina with a look of shock.

'It's so far away. Don't worry about that. You have to go now! Bye, Luka,' Nina said, giving me a kiss, and the most beautiful woman in the world and her best friend Andjela disappeared from my screen.

It didn't feel real that the person who was closer to Nina than anyone was coming to my city, and I was going to meet her. The excitement was too much. *'She's actually on her way,'* I thought in disbelief, a smile spreading on my face from ear to ear. *'If I'm this excited to meet her best friend, what will it feel like to meet Nina?'* I wondered, the smile on my face trying to spread wider. I couldn't even imagine what it would feel like to see her for the first time. To hug her for the first time. The thought of it was too much to bear. *'We're only in January, but it's going to happen this year. I'm going to make it happen,'* I thought determinedly.

I was wide awake and couldn't stop thinking of those perfect brown eyes with flecks of green. Her smile, her flowing brown hair, her freckles were tattooed on my mind's eye. I grabbed my phone and started to scroll through the photos Nina had sent me. Photos of her just waking up, photos of her about to go to class, dressed up to go to a party, of her on a video chat with me. With every passing second my feelings for Nina grew stronger. *'I've never been in love before, but this has to be what falling in love feels like, doesn't it?'* I asked myself, trying to comprehend my feelings. I felt completely weightless, yet like I had the strongest bullet proof vest on as well, because nothing could touch me. That I could see a beautiful woman walking down the street and she may as well be an eighty-year-old man, because she wasn't Nina. She was my woman, and I was her guy.

I scrolled to my favourite photo of Nina. A black and white close-up of her face smiling. The top of her white shirt was visible, her thin and elegant neck was framed by her brown hair which cascaded down over her shoulders. Part of her hair slightly covered the right half of her face. Her joy was infectious. I closed my eyes and imagined myself lying next to Nina on freshly mown grass under a tree. A light breeze offset the warmth of the sun that broke through the branches, hitting our skin. I put my arm around Nina, and she pushed her body into mine, rolling her leg across. Without even making a conscious decision to, I said aloud, 'I'm in love with you, Nina.'

Three days later I walked through the gates of Melbourne Park, into Garden Square at a speed just short of a run. Andjela was the first match of the day on Court Eighteen, playing against Millie Wilson of England. Wilson was ranked one hundred and fifteenth in the world compared to Andjela's ranking of three hundred and eight. On paper, Andjela didn't have a chance, but matches aren't played on paper.

It was a warm, thirty-two-degree cloudless day. The temperature was expected to rise to forty by the mid-afternoon, so Andjela was lucky she was playing first. In a few days the grounds would be bursting with people from all over the world, but during qualifying, there were only a handful of employees, and a couple of tennis fanatics there. I had been attending the Australian Open ever since I was five. Mum started taking me to watch some of our favourites like Andre Agassi and Pat Rafter. Some of my best memories of my childhood were packing a lunch and going to the tennis with Mum, yet I had never been as excited to watch tennis as I was to watch Andjela.

Rod Laver Arena looked down at Melbourne Park from its dais high above the rest of the precinct, with Show Court Three and Margaret Court Arena both lying on my right as I walked in and Show Court Two tucked behind them. Power walking through Garden Square, I veered to my left towards Show Court Eighteen. Without lowering my speed, I glanced at my phone and saw ten fifty-eight staring up at me, pushing me to break into a run towards the court. I didn't want to miss a second of the experience, not even Andjela walking onto court. *'It could be the birth of a tennis legend,'* I thought, as if that had anything to do with my excitement. I felt like I was about to see Nina for the first time.

Thankfully there was barely anyone in the grounds, so I was able to sprint unimpeded towards the court without having to worry about navigating my way through fifty-thousand people. I arrived right on eleven o'clock and took a seat near the baseline opposite, and to the left of the umpire's chair. There were ten people there to watch the match. Six people chatting away sitting diagonally to me who were part of Wilson's party, three people with a Serbian flag, and a man sitting alone behind one of the empty players chairs, who I assumed to be Andjela's coach. He was wearing a cap and a full navy-blue tracksuit. *'He must not know how to check the weather app on his phone,'* I thought, shaking my head in disbelief. There's sun smart, and then there's heatstroke dumb.

The umpire walked onto the court, placing her bag underneath her chair, and then stood at the net waiting for the players to arrive. Following her were the ball kids and lines people taking their positions around the court. I craned my neck and could see two women walking towards the courts with tennis bags on their backs surrounded by security. The first was a relatively short woman who had a stout, strong frame. She walked through the gate with her hood up and visor protruding from it. Pulling off her hood she revealed a thin face completely out of tune with her body. Sunken, shadowy eyes with a pointed nose and pursed lips.

Standing head and shoulders above walking behind her was Andjela. Wearing a light blue dress with white shoes, her blonde hair in a tight ponytail falling all the way to the small of her back. Andjela walked onto court with her shoulders back and head held high. If I had to bet on who would win based on body language, then it looked like a quick kill for Andjela. She paused for a split second, having caught someone out of the corner of her eye, on the opposite side of the court. Me. Andjela's head sprung back to life, meeting my smile with one of her own. Her piercing green eyes were noticeable even from the opposite side of the court, glimmering in the sun. She looked like she was made of silk from the elegant way she moved, almost like she had wings to float above the court. Andjela took her seat on the left-hand side of the umpire and withdrew a racquet from her bag.

Both players walked to the net to meet the umpire and receive their instructions which they would have heard a million times before. The umpire tossed the coin high into the summer sky before letting it fall to the court and gesturing to Andjela who said she would serve. Wilson picked the side opposite to me and both women jogged to the baseline, each accepting a ball from the baseline ball kid.

Andjela's ranking was a lie. As soon as they started to warm up Andjela looked like she was a class above. Wilson was struggling with the weight, depth, and power of the ball that Andjela was hitting, and it was only the warm-up. Most of the shots from Wilson were getting left mid court and Andjela almost looked bored, just wishing the match would start so she could punish each of those pedestrian shots.

Five minutes later they were ready to play. Andjela set up ready to serve, as Wilson swayed from side to side, focused on returning Andjela's first serve of the match. 'Players ready? Play,' said the umpire. Andjela threw the ball high into the Melbourne sky and hit a rocket down the middle for a huge ace. Wilson didn't even have time to put a racquet out, all she could do was helplessly watch it fly by and walk to the other side, hoping the second point of the match went better. Andjela looked in my direction and winked, smiling. I did what her opponent couldn't do, I returned what she served and smiled back while applauding.

I took out my phone and filmed Andjela tossing the ball up and crushing another huge serve past her helpless opponent and sent the video to Nina. I got an immediate reply, 'She's so good. I can see you there on my computer.'

'Amazing start. I'd wave but I don't want to look like I'm insane just waving to thin air.' With a thirty-love lead in her first game, Andjela hit her next serve just wide of the forehand line. Her second serve was sent to her opponents forehand also, but this time just touching the line, getting a meek return from Wilson, and Andjela was quick as a cat to the ball at mid court, eyes wide in anticipation, spanking the winner behind Wilson as she tried to cover the open court. At forty-love Andjela hit a wide serve which Wilson sent high into the air. Andjela ran in and treated the ball with almost as much contempt as she had for Marko, smashing the ball into the court and over the back fence to close the first game. She looked in my direction with a fist pump as I rose to my feet applauding her almost perfect opening to the match.

Andjela's height, timing, and long levers helped her to strike the ball with enormous power. Her anticipation combined with speed around the court meant she was able to read the play incredibly well, getting to the ball early, leaving lots of time to balance herself and place her shots where she wanted with power. *'As soon as she plays a full schedule, she'll be a top thirty player within twelve months,'* I thought, in complete awe of her talent. It was hard to believe she was ranked as only the number three junior girls' player; she looked like a generational talent.

Andjela led five-one in the first set with a set point on her serve. Wilson had worked her way into the match and had pushed several games to deuce, but Andjela's power and athleticism were too much. Her high ball toss disappeared into the sun, before she pounded a serve right down the middle for her eighth ace of the match to clinch the first set. 'Idemo!' Andjela shouted in my direction, as I stood cheering for her.

'Game, and first set Marjanović,' the umpire announced, and I continued to cheer and applaud until Andjela sat down in her chair. Placing a towel over her head, she closed her eyes and spent the break drinking water and performing deep breathing to relax herself and reset for the second set.

'Time.'

Andjela took a bite of the banana sitting on the small table to her right, picked up her racquet and ran out to return serve for the beginning of the second set.

The second set was a back-and-forth affair. Wilson found her groove and even though Andjela had an enormous power advantage, she became erratic with her groundstrokes. She was starting to press, trying to force the issue and end points prematurely. Andjela's emotions were in step with her groundstrokes, as she began to lose focus, she became frustrated, which culminated in a warning for breaking her racquet. The second set wound its way to a tiebreak and, with the score tied at five-all, and Andjela having one point to come on her serve.

Serving to the deuce court, Andjela struck her first serve fractionally wide. On her second serve, the biggest serve of her life, she laid it all on the line; all or nothing. Her biggest serve of the match with a bomb down the middle at one hundred and eighty-nine km/h in an outrageously risky shot finding the edge of the line to bring up match point. Andjela let out a war cry of self-encouragement as the umpire announced, 'six-five, Marjanović.' The Serbian fans were jumping up and down screaming. I shouted towards Andjela, both fists clenched, urging her to finish the match, 'Come on. One more point. You've got this.'

Wilson prepared herself to serve. Andjela had a look of laser focus as she swayed from side to side ready to close out the match. Wilson served to Andjela's backhand, and they exchanged groundstrokes in one of the longest rallies of the match. Andjela looked oddly tentative for the first time in the match, looking like Wilson in the warm-up, not wanting to make any mistakes. Andjela played a short slice backhand that brought Wilson to the net. Leaving a lollipop forehand volley at midcourt, Andjela's eyes widened with excitement as she rushed forward. Setting her feet, she had the line, and cross-court pass available, or the lob. Taking option four, Andjela hit a full-blooded forehand straight at Wilson standing at the net, striking her in the shoulder.

My phone buzzed as soon as Andjela put her hands up in celebration, not bothering to give an insincere apology. 'She did it! I'm so proud of her,' Nina texted immediately.

Andjela was screaming in excitement, jumping up and down with a clenched fist. Wilson walked off the court without shaking hands, and Andjela looked like she hadn't even noticed.

'I'll be here for all her matches. She's my favourite player. Get your butt here to watch her next game with me,' I replied to Nina.

'On my way to the airport. You better be there to pick me up.' Shaking hands with the umpire, Andjela threw her racquet down on her bag, picked up her broken one and ran over to where I was sitting.

'Hey, thanks so much for coming,' Andjela said, pulling me in for a sweaty hug with the fence in between us. Letting go I stood back and looked at her, trying to comprehend who was in front of me. I felt Nina's presence standing with us.

'I wouldn't have missed it for the world. Congratulations, that was amazing,' I said, smiling. Still caught up in the excitement of her victory, my brain was struggling to process that I was face to face with Andjela.

'Thanks for your support. I couldn't let myself lose with you here. Take out your phone, let's take a photo and send it to Nina.' We both smiled widely at the camera taking a selfie together, which I sent immediately to Nina.

'Here. Just a small thank you for coming,' Andjela said, handing me the broken racquet. I smiled and looked down at the decimated frame, broken in three places. 'Sorry, it's a bit used.'

'Thanks. It's okay, I have some tape at home. You'll have to sign it for me. So, is there any chance you have a bit of time later to hang out?' I asked, spinning the racquet nervously in my hand.

'Yeah, just let me do my recovery work and have a shower first. Can you meet me in Garden Square in about an hour?'

Andjela asked, starting to back away from the fence. Wilson departed the court behind Andjela with her head hanging.

'Perfect. I'll see you there,' I said, as Andjela turned and walked back to her bag.

'Aww this photo is adorable. My two favourites. I'm so sad I'm not there with you two. It's two-am, I better get some sleep,' Nina texted.

'Sleep well, sunshine,' I replied, and began walking towards Garden Square.

A touch over an hour later I was sitting at a table waiting in the sweltering Melbourne sun for Andjela. I felt a tap on my shoulder and turned around to see Andjela smiling at me. She wore a white t-shirt and short navy-blue shorts with slides. I jumped up and we hugged each other. The water bottle in her hand bouncing off the back of my head.

When we hugged after her match it didn't hit me, but it did the second time. I was hugging someone that had hugged Nina. In my mind, I was really touching Nina. We broke apart and I noticed we stood eye to eye. I thought she would be taller than me. We both took a seat and sat in silence for a moment with neither of us knowing what to say.

Andjela broke the awkward silence, 'Sorry, I don't have much time, but I had to come. This is so crazy. I can't believe that I'm meeting my best friend's boyfriend before she does. I hope she doesn't hate me.'

'The entire relationship has been a huge whirlwind for me. Meeting you today makes everything feel so much more real. More tangible. I'm trying to wrap my head around what's happening, but it feels beyond me at times,' I said, laughing uncomfortably. My hands were shaking so I put them on my knees hiding them below the table. Andjela would be telling Nina everything she noticed about me, so I needed to impress her like I would if I was on a date with Nina.

'How are you finding the long-distance relationship? It can't be easy for you,' Andjela asked, taking a large swig from her water bottle.

'It's not, but it's so much better than not being with her. I'm happier than I was before we met. I've never connected with another person like I have with her. I'm lucky that our paths crossed. She's special.' I was surprised at my candour to a person I was just meeting.

'She's seemed really at peace since she met you. I think you bring a real calmness to her that she hasn't had before. Her brain is normally working at a million miles an hour until it shuts down and she pushes everything and everyone away, but your presence has brought clarity to her. Slowed her mind down and allowed her to focus on what's important. Her friends, her family, school, and you. I've seen her with boys before, but I've never seen her like this. You treat her like a man should. You're special to her.' I thought that I was special to her; I wanted to believe I was special to her, but to hear it from someone that saw Nina everyday quietened the bully in my head that told me I wasn't.

I didn't know what to say. I looked down at my hands in my lap, trying to count how many lines there were on the back of my fingers. 'I can't wait to come and see her. I already have a countdown clock on my phone to her nineteenth birthday,' I said, my eyes lifting from my hands to meet Andjela's and lighting up. My voice rose an octave at the prospect of finally meeting Nina. Meeting Andjela just made me more excited to be with my girlfriend. I felt a step closer.

'Yeah, will be cool,' Andjela mumbled, shifting her weight in her chair.

'You must be a year younger than Nina if you're still playing juniors,' I said.

'Yeah, I am,' Andjela said, not looking at me, but looking up at Rod Laver Arena that was sitting quietly on my right.

'I can't wait to play there. I'm going to win this tournament one day. Obviously, my future husband Aleks is going to be in the player's box cheering me on,' Andjela said, in a tone of half-serious, half-joking. She had changed the subject quickly.

'I'll do my best to help with one of those. You two would have talented kids,' I said, the sound of my voice bringing her dreamy gaze back on me.

'I think I just felt my uterus flutter,' Andjela said, and we both burst out laughing. 'So, when am I going to meet this fine specimen, you call a brother? Nina can't be the only one with an Australian man.'

'I told you that you're invited for dinner. Pick your night. Mum would love to meet you.'

'I'd love to come. I'm going to win my next match, so why don't I come after I win my third on Thursday and qualify for the main draw? That gives your mum time to get ready for a guest, and Aleks time to wash his nicest shirt.' I felt like Andjela would be a lot of work in a relationship, but when she met the right person, it would be relationship goals.

'Let's do it. I'm sure Aleks will definitely not ask Mum to wash and iron that shirt for him,' I said, as Andjela's phone vibrated. She looked at the message and immediately looked flustered.

'I have to go, but let me give you my number,' Andjela said, taking my phone and entering her information. 'It was amazing to meet you. I'll see you Thursday,' Andjela said smiling. We stood up and exchanged three kisses on the cheek before she ran off towards the players' area.

Andjela won her second qualifying match with ease, six-three, six-one. She was more controlled the entire match, unlike her first, where her consistency dropped away in the second set. She looked too good to have to qualify for a major tournament.

Her final qualifying match was a back-and-forth affair. Andjela was down five-one in the first set and fought all the way back to claim it in a tiebreaker. The second set was the polar opposite, with Andjela jumping to a four-one lead before being pegged back to four-all. Andjela then put her foot down to close the match out six-four, and gain entry to the main draw of the Australian major tournament.

'So, what time are we expecting her to get here?' Mum asked, as she pulled a freshly cooked pan of burek from the oven. I set the table making sure to place Andjela and Aleks next to each other.

'She texted me a couple of minutes ago saying she was about to leave. So, I'm guessing about thirty minutes. Do you need any more help, Mum?' I asked, putting down the last of the dining utensils. Earlier in the day I printed the photo of Nina and I on our first video chat and got it framed. Our first photo together. It was Nina's Christmas present, and I wanted Andjela to take it back to her.

'I think I'm all good. I'll call you down when she gets here,' Mum said, placing the pan back in the oven to keep it warm.

I rushed from the kitchen and up the stairs to my bedroom, grabbing tape and wrapping paper on the way. The framed photo was sitting on my bed. I picked the photo up and ran my fingers over Nina's smiling face. I missed her. We texted every day, yet as soon as she went to sleep, I missed her. I could feel a longing in my chest for her, just to be in her presence. Oh damn, how I missed her.

She was smiling at me. *Is she awake yet? Is she thinking about me or dreaming about me? Does she think about me as much as I think about her?'* I wondered, as I gazed upon the photo.

I grabbed a pen and my music notebook and began to write. Not a song, but a poem. A poem for Nina. I felt like she was home to me. Even though I had never been in her physical presence, she was my home. *'Home isn't a place, it's a feeling,'* I thought, with my pen hovering above the blank page. I wrote furiously, my pen flying across the page.

I am home.
Thinking of your eyes and hair a perfect brown,
Your immaculate voice my soothing sound,
Even when you're not around.
I am home.
When I see you smile,
Remembering my mind's lies,
Desperately craving to hold sunshine.
I am home.
When I see your name on my phone,
Knowing I am not alone,
Dreams of giving you that sparkling stone.
With you, I am home.

I tore the paper from my book, folded it, and placed it on top of the framed photo of Nina and me. The internet told me that girls always hijack their boyfriend's hoodies, so I thought I should send one of mine to her. Finding my favourite grey hoodie in a pile on my bedroom floor, I folded it and placed the photo and poem on top of it.

Unfurling the blue wrapping paper, I placed the photo, hoodie, and poem on top. I slid the scissors through the paper like a hot knife through butter in a beautiful moment of pure satisfaction. Struggling to wrap Nina's gift with all my might, sticking tape to the gifts and myself, using more tape and paper than anyone ever should. The wrapping was completely asymmetrical and far from a Santa's elf level wrapping job. I was just happy I had managed to cover all the gifts with paper, and it wouldn't come off due to it looking like it was held together with shrink wrap.

The doorbell rang and it could only have been one person. I walked immediately from my room and stuck my head in next door to see if Aleks was ready. 'That'll be Andjela. Nice shirt. Are you wearing cologne?' I asked, turning my nose up at the overpowering aroma. Aleks was wearing a dark blue shirt and tan chinos. He had put in a lot more effort than I had with my blue jeans and plain white t-shirt.

'Thanks, Mum ironed it for me. Yeah, I bought it from the chemist today, I wanted to make a good impression. Do you think she'll like it?' Aleks asked, walking towards me, but I held my hand up to halt his progress.

'If she likes being punched in the face by a smell she will. She can probably smell it from outside the front door.'

'I was just wanting to put on a little bit, but I dropped it all over my hands. Then I put some on my neck because that's where the pulse points are, and it makes the scent last longer.'

'Aleks, if you accidentally drop too much on your hands and wrists, then why would you need it to last longer? Put it on a pulse point and it will last for a month. Who taught you about pulse points anyway?'

'The internet obviously. What do I do? She's here, help me, Luka,' Aleks said, with a panic stricken look on his face.

'Go and have a quick shower. There's so much it won't all go, but it might dilute to the point where it's the proper amount. I can't believe you're so nervous.' I shook my head laughing, unable to believe how unsure of himself he was.

'Well, she's really hot. Okay, I'll have a quick shower. That way I can make a late entrance as well.'

'You're not a girl getting taken to prom at the end of the movie. Just hurry up and shower. I'll see you down there in a few minutes,' I said, holding my nose as the aroma became too much to bear.

Aleks grabbed his, what I assumed was still wet towel off the floor of his bedroom and raced into the bathroom. The second most confident person I knew behind James had been reduced to a quivering, nervous mess at the prospect of meeting a woman he had never spoken to before. *What witchcraft do these women have that they can turn us into a puddle of our normal selves?'* I thought. Shaking my head, I walked down the stairs and into the kitchen where I found Mum, Dad, Maja, and Andjela all sitting around the table.

'Thanks for taking the time to join us, mate,' Dad said, rocking back casually in his chair, and taking a sip of his wine.

'Sorry, was just wrapping a present for Andjela to give to Nina. How are you feeling after the win?' I asked, sitting down at my usual spot around the table.

'I still can't believe that I'm going to be playing in the main draw. I always thought I could do it, but you can't really know until you do it,' Andjela said, adjusting the shoulder on her dress. A white sundress with daisies on it falling to halfway down her thighs. If Aleks was nervous before he saw her, then I had no idea how he was going to be able to string a sentence together when he arrived.

'When do you find out who you play first?' Mum asked, with all eyes on Andjela, like she was in a post-match press conference.

'It should be any minute now. I thought I would have heard already, but my coach said he would send me a message when he finds out.' Andjela looked at her phone and then placed it face down on the table.

'We'll all be watching. A girl from Požega on the biggest stage, it will mean a lot to everyone back home. It's special you're here,' Mum said. Mum treated any person that came into our house like her own child. You better not do wrong by one of her real or adopted children because she will breathe fire if you do.

'That's right. I've been so focused on my matches I forgot that you guys come from Požega. It's incredible how the universe works. I'm just grateful you invited me for dinner. It's not easy just sitting in a hotel room on your own all the time. The only person I eat with is my coach, and I'm really sick of watching him chew with his mouth open.'

'Did you hear that, Dad? She's sitting directly opposite you so try not to give her prime viewing of your teeth doing their finest work,' Maja said, never missing an opportunity to take a shot. I didn't even try to stifle a laugh because it was in all our interest that he listened to her. Sitting next to him for my entire life meant I had been hit by way too much food. I loved pasta but there was an element of fear that started to course through me when Mum announced that it was on the table.

The screech of the door opening announced Aleks' arrival. He walked into the kitchen with his mouth hanging open slightly with a stiff jaw, trying to stop himself from smiling. He was looking everywhere except at Andjela. Aleks took the empty seat on my right as Dad said to him, 'Aleks, this is Andjela. She's a friend of Nina,' gesturing towards Andjela, who nodded in acknowledgment of his arrival. Her eyes widened as they scanned his considerable height.

'Hi, nice to meet you,' Aleks said in a quivering voice, making strong eye contact which Andjela met, and they shook hands. A fuse had been lit. It was palpable.

'That's a well ironed shirt; did you do that yourself?' Andjela asked. Aleks answered her question with a wry smile not wanting to get caught in a lie. His cologne was still strong, but a definite improvement on what it was like upstairs. I hoped for his sake that Maja didn't pick it up and run with it or else dinner could go sideways. Andjela leaned slightly to her left towards Aleks, with her nostrils flared in search of the scent she had noticed.

'So then, is everyone ready for burek?' Dad asked the room, mercifully taking the focus off Aleks and Andjela. It was beginning to get uncomfortable.

'Yes, please!' said Andjela.

'Andjela, I knew you would like burek so hopefully it holds up well to Serbian standards. I know it won't be as good as your mama's, but it's my mother's recipe so you're still eating Požega burek,' Mum said, beginning to serve it onto a plate and handing it to Dad.

'Luka told me that we were having burek. When I was in important moments in today's match, I started to think about this meal which helped me relax. Burek won me the match. When I win the tournament, you will get a special thank you in my speech. You and the burek. Thank you,' Andjela said, as Dad placed the first plate with a large serving in front of Andjela.

'I don't think anyone has ever said that after a tennis match before. Maybe I should try that during an exam,' Maja said, as Dad placed the second plate in front of my sister.

'If it calms you down then you should think about it when you're on the verge of getting into a fight with one of your teachers. I could do without the anxiety every time I see the school number on my phone wondering who you opened your mouth to this time,' Mum said, as Dad put the final plate in front of his own seat and sat down.

'Or we could have emergency burek here and start to throw it at her when she gets angry with one of us,' I said, as Andjela, Maja and Aleks had their utensils in their hands ready to tear into dinner.

'Before these three destroy their plate I want to say a big thank you to Andjela for coming to share a meal with us. Any person that is special to Luka is special to us, and we're extremely fortunate to have you here tonight. Now go and kick some butt in the Open and bring that trophy home. Živeli!' Dad announced, and everyone clinked their glasses before tucking into their dinner.

We all dived into our dinner apart from Mum, who watched the table tensely for a moment to make sure we were enjoying it. Paying particular attention to Andjela. 'Oh, wow Mrs Robertson, this is…. it's just…. I have no words. I feel like I'm home.'

Mum's face lit up and her shoulders relaxed at getting the reaction she wanted. 'I'm glad you like it. There's plenty more there if you want seconds. Help yourself.'

Andjela's phone buzzed. She picked it up and gave a half grunt, half laugh, before putting it back face down on the table, returning to her plate. 'Found out who I'm playing,' she said, as she broke off some burek with her fork.

Utensils clattered as they hit plates, and we all stopped eating to look at Andjela. Waiting with bated breath, we all stared silently at Andjela for her to announce who it was. Her dramatic pause caused Maja to burst out, 'Out with-it woman. Who are you playing?'

'Oh, you wouldn't have heard of her. Her name is Sofija Nowitzki. I'm on Rod Laver Arena Monday night,' Andjela casually said, continuing to work away at her burek with a huge smile on her face.

'Sofija Nowitzki? She's a legend. How many slams has she won now? Eighteen?' I asked, slightly bemused at the smile spread across Andjela's face.

'Nineteen actually,' Andjela replied, continuing to smile.

'Shouldn't you be upset you got that draw? I mean, you could have been playing another qualifier ranked three hundred in the world but no, you're going against one of the greatest ever. That's awful,' Maja said, with a look of utter bewilderment.

'It's brilliant,' said Aleks before Andjela could answer. 'I don't want to speak for you, but I feel like you're not playing tennis to make money. You're playing for greatness. What better way to start your career than beating one of the greatest players ever on one of the most iconic courts in the world?'

'Exactly. I'm seventeen years old. If I want to win major tournaments and be the number one player in the world, then I need to test myself against the absolute best that there is. I need to find out where the holes in my game are and fix them. There's no better way to do that than testing my game against a living legend. I can't wait.'

'We'll be screaming at our television cheering for you,' Mum said, almost bouncing in her chair with excitement.

'Oh no you won't,' Andjela scoffed at Mum. 'You five will be in my player's box. I have twelve seats in there and the only person here with me is my coach. I need you there.'

'Honestly, I would have been offended if I wasn't invited after being there for all your other matches. Wasn't worried about these jokers,' I said, gesturing to the rest of my family and laughing. 'You know the rest of the crowd will be against you right?'

'That's the best. When you have the entire crowd against you, and you get to break all their hearts. I played in the under eighteen world championships against Turkey in Istanbul. I hit a shot at the buzzer to beat them, and the collective groan of fifteen thousand hearts breaking at once is the best sound I've heard in my life,' Aleks said, turning his torso completely to face Andjela. Andjela looked back at him like it was the sexiest thing anyone had ever said.

This must be how athletes flirt,' I thought.

'You know what? On Monday night, I'm going to make news all around the world. The seventeen-year-old from a small Serbian town that beat Sofija Nowitzki on centre court at the Australian major. And my legend was born,' Andjela said, with a smirk, extending her arms outward.

We enjoyed the rest of our night laughing, and hearing stories from the old country. Standing by the door, Mum and Andjela continued to chat while the rest of us stood there being uncomfortably polite, not knowing if we could just walk away, or had to stand there until Andjela left.

'The next trip we take is to Požega. Did you hear that, John? I haven't been since we left. I'm not going anywhere else before we go there,' Mum said, while I could see Dad suppress a yawn and look at his watch begging her to allow him to go to sleep.

'If things work out between Luka and Nina then you might have a wedding to go to there,' Andjela joked, winking at me, causing Maja and Dad to laugh. I definitely hadn't thought about what it would be like to be standing at the altar in a tuxedo, watching Nina walk down the aisle in a white dress. I would be crazy to think about anything like that.

'I better call a taxi and get some rest. A big couple of days coming up.'

'Don't be silly. Luka, drive Andjela back to her hotel,' Mum said, grabbing my keys and throwing them to me.

'No worries. Let me just grab one thing,' I said, remembering Nina's gift was sitting on my bed.

'Your car kind of smells. What is that?' Andjela said, turning her nose up and sniffing like a drug dog in the airport as soon as we got into my red sedan.

'Monty and I like to go on adventures together. You're sitting in his seat. Don't worry, I won't tell him.'

'It's a shame Aleks isn't here. His cologne would easily overpower the dog smell,' Andjela said with a deadpan expression, buckling her seatbelt and lowering the window.

'So, you could smell it!' I laughed, as I began to drive. I explained to Andjela Aleks' ordeal with the cologne.

'I appreciate the effort. He had a nice shirt on and tried to smell good. I can train him though. The most underrated quality in someone is effort; in anything. It's so attractive to see someone really give it everything they have. Acting like you don't care is the fastest way to gain indifference.'

'I couldn't agree more. Effort shows that you care. I want to show you something before we go back to the hotel.' I drove down Ferguson Street, and as we got closer to the end of the road, the city lights appeared on the other side of the bay.

'Wow, that's stunning' Andjela said, her pupils dilated as I parked the car. We got out and sat on a bench to look across at the city lit up over the water. You need to look at things from a distance to really appreciate how beautiful they are. The buildings stood high above with their reflection bouncing off the water that was filled with yachts of all sizes. 'Nina wanted me to give this to you. She said she's sorry she can't give it to you in person, but Merry Christmas.' Reaching into her bag, Andjela pulled out a small soft present wrapped in red paper.

I stared down at the package and ran my hand over the paper. Meeting Andjela made everything sink in, but having something tangible to keep, something from Nina was different. Something that every time I looked at it, I would think of her. I could feel her in the present. *'She touched this paper,'* I thought, imagining her hand on mine. I wanted to press it to my lips so I could kiss her hand, but Andjela was watching me, and I didn't want her to see how weird I could be, so I placed it on my lap. 'I have something for her as well,' I choked slightly on my words. I quickly walked to the car and grabbed the present for Nina before handing the gift to Andjela.

'I hope you two know what you're doing,' Andjela said after a prolonged silence of soaking in the beautiful city.

'I'm in love with her, Andjela. It might seem stupid to you because we haven't met in person, but I know what I'm feeling. While everyone else might think it isn't real, if I'm feeling like this, then how can it not be real?'

'Have you told her yet?'

'No, I want to tell her face to face. I want to be able to hold her hand and look into her eyes when I tell her.'

'I hope you two make it. I haven't known you for long but you're the perfect man for her. I can tell right away if someone is genuine, it's my superpower. So many guys have tried to manipulate and lie to be with her and kept doing it once they got her. I can see you're different. You're what she needs.' Andjela put her hand on my arm.

I felt determined. *The distance and time apart won't ruin what we have. I won't let it. We won't let it. It'll make us stronger,'* I thought.

'Can you give one more thing to Nina for me?'

'Of course. What is it?' Andjela asked, turning to face me.

I took Andjela's hand and kissed the back of it. Andjela looked at me knowingly, placing her hand on my shoulder. Without saying another word, we stood up and walked back to the car.

When I got home from taking Andjela to the hotel, I got into bed and called Nina. Laying on my side I propped my phone up against my spare pillow and waited for her to answer. Two months in, and my heart still raced with the anticipation of seeing her. Every time seeing her face was like the first time. I wasn't sure if the video paused or my brain paused, because for a moment everything stopped. '…talking to Andjela. I wish I was at dinner with you guys. How are you?' I laughed to myself realising that the connection glitched. Nina was wearing a yellow hoodie and had some toothpaste on her face, yet no woman had ever looked so beautiful.

'I'm tired but it was so cool getting to spend some time with her. It was such a bizarre feeling being with someone in person that's so close to you. All it did was get me even more excited to meet you,' I whispered, not wanting to wake up Aleks in the next room.

'It feels like it was a step closer for us. I can't even explain how it made me feel to see a photo of you two together. I don't even have the words in Serbian to explain it.'

'And yet I completely understand what you mean and how you're feeling. It was surreal. The entire time I was looking at her I was thinking about you, like I was with you. It made my feelings even stronger for you and I'm desperate to get there as soon as I can. I just hope you can wait for me.'

'It's funny that you're worried about that when I'm worried you'll find a beautiful Australian girl, forgetting all about me.'

'As far as I'm concerned there are no other women. I don't want anyone else. I want you. Only you. You're my sunshine.' Her right hand rose to her face, and she wound her hair around her right index finger absentmindedly.

'I don't want anyone else either. I've never met a person that can articulate how they feel as well as you do. Every boy I've met acts like he doesn't care, like he's too cool to have feelings or emotions because they think it's weak. They're wrong. Being raw, honest, and real with people is strong. I love that you're not afraid to be vulnerable with me. You're one of the only real people I've ever known.'

I craved her to be next to me. To be able to hold her while we slept was the type of magic I was looking for. *'This is what people must mean when they talk about soulmates,'* I thought.

'Thank you for thinking I'm worthy of being a part of your life,' I said, with a pained smile on my face. Nina looked as though she understood how I felt, and that she was hurting by not being next to me.

'You don't ever need to thank me for that. Just make sure you're here soon so I can hug you. We can do this. We just need to do it together,' Nina said, laying back on her bed. She picked up a pillow and held it to her chest with her free hand.

'We will. Andjela gave me something,' I said, holding up the present.

'Oh yeah, she gave it to you. I almost forgot about that. I can see your eyes drooping and while it's really cute, I want to see you open it before you fall asleep on me.' I tore open the paper and pulled out a pair of red jocks with Santa's face on them. I burst out laughing and Nina laughed with me. 'I hope you like them.'

'You're so cute. These are the best,' I said, holding them up next to my face and smiling. Santa's smile and my own were side by side.

'I have the most adorable boyfriend. That screenshot is definitely going in our photo album one day.'

'I'll make sure I'm wearing them when we meet. Now I get to carry you around with me whenever I wear them.'

'Yeah, on your butt,' Nina said, and we both continued to laugh.

'I should go to sleep. It's really late here.'

'Yeah, get some sleep. Text me tomorrow.'

'I will. Oh Nina, you have some toothpaste on your face,' I said laughing, as she held her phone closer to have a look. She picked up a ball and fake threw it at me with the colour rising in her cheeks, looking embarrassed and laughing.

I waved and blew a kiss. Nina returned my kiss and hung up the phone. I rolled over and held my spare pillow tightly, imagining that I was holding Nina falling asleep. It was the only way I wanted to sleep for the rest of my life.

'How good is this?' Dad asked rhetorically, taking a spot in the front row, sitting next to Andjela's coach. 'Hi, I'm John. We're friends of Andjela.' I didn't think Coach Stefan spoke any English because he shook Dad's hand and nodded politely at the rest of us before turning back to stare at the court.

The stands filled quickly over the next ten minutes until there was barely a spare seat in the arena. There was a buzz of anticipation in the air, an excited energy that's unique to big sporting events. I had been to the tennis at Melbourne Park for years and I had never felt an energy like it in the first round. It was incredible.

'I was listening to the radio earlier and they said the session's sold out. They're saying it's because it could be Nowitzki's last appearance in Melbourne, and because she's playing the next big star,' Aleks said.

I opened my phone to the newspaper website and on the homepage the headline read, 'I'm up next!' with a picture of Andjela pumping her fist in one of her qualifying matches. *She can do this,* I thought, excitedly.

The public address announcer walked onto Rod Laver Arena and welcomed the crowd, causing a hush to come over the arena, with all eyes turned towards the players' entrance. 'Good evening, and welcome to night one of the Australian Open at Melbourne Park. Introducing to you first, one of the brightest young stars in women's tennis. She is just seventeen years old from Požega, Serbia. Making her first of many appearances on our historic court, please give a warm Melbourne welcome to, Andjela Marjanović.' There was strong applause around the arena with loud pockets of Serbian fans in the stands making their presence felt. We all applauded loudly except for Stefan, who was still in his seat with a stoic expression. Andjela had a look of steely focus as she glided onto the court. Her blonde ponytail gently bouncing on the back of her light blue dress. Giving a polite wave and smile to the crowd as the cameraman approached her, spinning to ensure she waved to the entire crowd, taking in the atmosphere. If she was playing anyone else her smile would have been enough to win the hearts of the crowd, but not against a legend like Sofija. She glided towards her seat, setting her bag down and carefully selecting her racquet.

'Now introducing to you the living legend, seven-time Australian major champion, and nineteen-time singles grand slam tournament winner. From Frankfurt, Germany, please welcome, Sofija Nowitzki.'

The crowd exploded as Sofija walked from the players' entrance and waved to the packed stadium. Mum began to politely applaud before Maja smacked her on the arm and sternly asked, 'Why are you clapping for her? She's the enemy.'

Andjela was on the court doing some shuttle runs to rid herself of the nervous energy that must have been flowing through her body. Sofija took her time and eventually joined Andjela and the chair umpire at the net. The umpire flipped the coin, and after indicating that Andjela won the toss, she elected to serve first, then both players ran to their respective baselines to begin their warm-up.

Andjela stood at the baseline ready to serve. There was a constant murmur of excited noise encouraging both players. The crowd was ready for a great match on the first night of the tournament. The anticipation was electric. I wondered how

Nina was feeling watching at home. I took out my phone to record Andjela's first point on Rod Laver Arena. Scanning the crowd with my phone as the umpire said, 'Play,' causing a hush to descend over the crowd. I focused my phone on Andjela. Throwing the ball high into the balmy summer night, with every muscle fibre contracting, Andjela thundered a serve down the middle. Releasing a bellowing scream, 'Come on!' as she stared directly at Sofija at the other end pumping her fist. Andjela wasn't out there to make friends or have a moral victory. She wasn't scared of the stage or the moment. She knew she was exactly where she belonged.

My family and I, and the Serbs in the crowd erupted with applause, while the rest of the crowd were in shock at the audacity of the young upstart and clapped politely. They didn't seem sure of the in-your-face attitude of Andjela.

Sofija seemed stunned at the all-out attack of Andjela. Not often in her career had she been challenged before the fourth round, and here she was in round one being hit off the court by a seventeen-year-old from a small mountainside Serbian town. Analysing her body language and little shakes of the head, Nowitzki seemed confused, in a state of deep thought trying to figure out what was happening. Andjela couldn't miss a shot, she was on fire, and nothing Sofija did was working. Serving at eighty percent first-serve for the set, the returns Sofija was able to get into court were swiftly put away. Andjela jumped out to a three-love lead in ten minutes.

After the change of ends, Sofija settled as she held serve, getting on the board and taking the set to three-one. Andjela held her serve with ease to take a four-one lead. A long Sofija service game followed; it had six deuce scores before it was advantage Marjanović. Sofija gifted the break with a double fault. Andjela was one service hold away from taking the first set.

Exchanging points, the game reached forty-thirty. There was a murmur in the crowd. Noise of collective disbelief at what they were witnessing. Andjela stepped up to serve on set point. 'Quiet please. Players are ready. Quiet please,' the umpire pleaded with the crowd, as Andjela continued to bounce the ball focused on only that ball. Nothing else in the world existed apart from that tennis ball. I was sitting on the edge of my seat, elbows leaning on the railing in front of me, nervously bouncing my right leg.

'Come on Andjela, you've got this,' Aleks whispered from the row behind, urging her on. That high ball toss soared above the court once again, and Andjela coiled her long legs, before powering up to meet it at the highest point. She pounded the ball into the backhand corner of Sofija who could only get the end of her racquet to the ball which flew into the stands. Andjela turned to us screaming and pumping her fist. The crowd erupted in applause as we stood in her players' box yelling words of encouragement. Stefan didn't move; he almost looked bored by the entire experience.

My phone buzzed with a text from Nina. 'I can't believe what I'm seeing! We're all watching on TV here losing our voices screaming. She can really do it!' Nina sent me a video of her entire family watching set point and yelling in celebration as Andjela clinched the first set.

'I feel like I'm more nervous than she is. She can do it, but Sofija won't go down without a fight,' I replied.

The first point of the second set was where it all went wrong. Sofija and Andjela exchange forehands until an angled shot from Sofija sent Andjela sprinting wide. A blood curdling scream was released from Andjela, sending a shiver of horror down my spine. Andjela fell in a heap crying and clutching at her ankle. The entire crowd gasped and stood trying to see what was wrong with the young star. Training staff, the chair umpire, and Sofija all ran to her aid. We all stood with our hands over our mouths feeling sick from the pain that Andjela must have been feeling as she writhed in agony on the floor of Rod Laver Arena. Stefan had not moved since we took our seats, but with the energy of a twenty-year-old he leapt out of his seat and sprinted up the stairs for the locker room. Just like that, Andjela's first Australian major tournament was over.

CHAPTER ELEVEN
The Head Vs. Heart

'You're back!' I exclaimed, as Andjela hobbled through the front door of my house on crutches. 'You said you weren't going to be home until Thursday. I was planning to surprise you at the airport.' I embraced Andjela, being careful not to knock her off balance.

'Well, I wanted to surprise you. Looks like I won,' Andjela said, struggling her way to the couch, putting her crutches and bag down next to her.

'So that's why you didn't reply to my text. Where are the rest of your things?' I asked, as Andjela hobbled past me.

'Yeah, it's tough to reply to a text at thirty-five thousand feet. Stefan dropped me here then took my bags to my parents. I'll get a taxi home from here.'

'Do you want something to drink?' I asked, as I walked over to the kettle waiting by the sink.

'Do you have a cup of fire handy? It's fifty degrees colder here than it was in Melbourne when I left.'

'Sorry, I just finished the last of it. You'll have to settle for a coffee.' Andjela nodded and I began to make our coffees. 'Look at the tan you've got. Another thing for me to be jealous about. I'm not jealous of that ankle though. How is it?' I asked, turning back to Andjela as I waited for the water to boil. I winced looking down at the tightly bandaged ankle.

'It's some fun colours. It's okay, just some ligament damage. I keep asking myself, if it didn't happen, would I have won? I'll just have to beat her next time I guess,' Andjela said, leaning back on the couch and exhaling loudly.

'I know you would have beaten her. You were dominating. Tell me about the entire trip though. What was it like?' I asked, handing Andjela a mug and taking a seat next to her on the couch with my legs crossed like a primary school student sitting on the floor staring at their teacher. I held my cup tightly in both hands facing Andjela, hoping the coffee would warm my entire body. It was minus ten outside and it had been snowing for days. Our entire town was white, completely frozen in the heart of winter.

'It was the most amazing experience of my life. Playing in front of that crowd, knowing people all around the world were watching me play. I can't even put it into words. I'm addicted to that feeling. I think I proved something to myself too. That my dream of being the best player in the world isn't a dream, it's a goal.'

'I so desperately wanted to be there to watch you. I wanted to be able to cheer you on from the player's box. Those flights are just so expensive,' I said with a pained smile, just imagining what it would be like to watch my best friend play in a grand slam tournament, and to feel that energy in the air.

'Getting a holiday visa for Australia is a nightmare for us Serbians too,' Andjela said, sympathetically.

'Well, it sounds like it was even better than you dreamed it would be.'

'It was hard to imagine what it would feel like to be out on that court in front of all those people. I knew they didn't want me to win, but they were still appreciating the show. I'm just disappointed I couldn't finish the job. Hopefully I'll be fit for Federation Cup in May. If we win, then we could be playing against Australia in the next round, and it would be there. This time I'm getting myself an actual date with Aleks.'

'I couldn't wait for you to get back to hear all about the Robertson family. How was it!?' I leaned forward in anticipation, unable to wait any longer to ask about Luka's family. I wanted to hear every detail.

'They're the sweetest family. John and Milena are really welcoming. Within five minutes I felt like I was part of their family. Maja has no filter. It was tough not to laugh at some of the things she said. That Aleks…. he was so nervous right from the start, it was adorable. His voice shaking when he said anything around me. His height though, wow, that's what dreams are made of. I can tell he really understands what I'm trying to do in tennis because he has similar goals himself in basketball. We've been texting non-stop since I was there for dinner.' Andjela had a sip of coffee as I stared at her waiting to hear about the other member of the family. She just sat in silence looking through the window, watching the snow gently fall.

'And?' I implored her to continue.

'And what?' Andjela said, putting her coffee down because it was still too hot, looking as if she had no idea what I was talking about.

'Luka!' I shouted.

'Oh yeah, that guy,' she said, rolling her eyes sarcastically, enjoying toying with my emotions.

'We hung out a couple of times and I can see why you like him so much. He's the perfect man for you. He cares so much about you that he barely wanted to talk about anything apart from you. It wasn't just what he said either, it was written all over his face when he spoke. Here, this is yours.' Andjela reached inside her bag and pulled out a gift wrapped in blue paper and almost completely covered in tape. I giggled at the cute effort he put in to wrapping.

I stared down at the gift. It felt like there was an energy flowing from the gift to my hands. It felt different to other gifts I had received. It felt like love. *Luka was thinking about me when he wrapped this for me,'* I thought, as the butterflies sprung to life in the deep recesses of my body. It was the first time I was touching something Luka had touched, and maybe that was the energy I felt holding it. *'I'm touching Luka,'* I thought, as the butterflies continued to bounce around my stomach. I tried to keep my composure and not get emotional in front of Andjela, but it was taking all my strength to do so. Putting the gift down on the bench, I turned my attention back to Andjela who was again trialling the temperature of her coffee. 'He is special. Through my phone I can feel that he's special. He's different. He's real. Just the way he looks at me, when I see those eyes, my heart just melts.'

'Well, when you meet him in person, you're really in trouble, dude. When I walked onto that court and saw him sitting there, that was the first thing I noticed. His eyes. I almost stopped for a moment. There's a calmness in them. You don't have a chance when you meet him if his eyes already make you feel like that on video chat,' Andjela said, raising her eyebrows as she took a sip of her coffee.

'In trouble? Andjela, I'm in love with him. How much more trouble could I really get into?' Her mouth opened wide as I casually dropped that atomic bomb on her. She stopped dead with her cup halfway to her lips, as if time had ceased. I peeked over at the analogue clock to check if time had in fact stopped, only to be met with the seconds hand ticking away. 'What?' I asked.

'Have you told him that?' Andjela asked, springing back to life, lowering her cup to rest on her lap.

'Tell him first? What a ridiculous thing to say.' We both laughed before I dropped my head slightly as I felt the disappointment from my joke. Luka had been so strong and raw sharing his inner most emotions and struggles with me, yet I was holding onto my true feelings for him. 'It's a big deal saying that, and while I know I feel it, I want to be sure he feels the same as me or else I'll scare him away. I'm not trying to be out on that island alone,' I said, shrugging.

'I know I don't know him like you do, I just get this feeling that you're perfect for him too. Don't ask me why, it's just the vibe I get.'

'Every day since we met, I've wanted to go there and see him. At least now I know I'm not getting catfished by an eighty-year-old man.'

'That wouldn't be ideal, but I think he'd be a cute old guy, and at least he'd have some good stories,' Andjela said, taking a gulp of her coffee.

I rolled my eyes giving a half smile and said, 'So you would trade Aleks in for an eighty-year-old man?'

'No, I think I'll keep my hot, young Australian basketballer thanks.'

'All the boys at your welcome home party next week are going to be disappointed. They're probably all going to fight over who gets to buy you the first drink,' I said, grabbing the gift again and holding it on my lap. I wanted to feel Luka close to me, and that was the best I could do. There was a part of me that wanted her to leave so I could see what was inside the wrapping.

'I'm an elite athlete, Nina. I don't drink alcohol anymore. Only water…. And maybe vodka on special occasions. And the occasional rakija, but that's not really drinking.' I burst into laughter as Andjela looked over her cup at me and catching the contagious laughter, snorted coffee all down her shirt.

'I know you like coffee but wearing it is a bit much. I'll take a photo of you and send it to Aleks,' I said, reaching for my phone and taking a picture. Andjela posed with her cup and pouting lips, never missing a chance for a photo opportunity.

'He will see me much messier when I'm having his babies. Well, I need to go, my parents will be wondering why I came and saw you before them. I'll see you at the party tomorrow night?' Andjela asked, struggling to pick up her crutches and stand up.

'It's Friday next week, not tomorrow,' I said, furrowing my brow in confusion.

'It was but I texted a few people at school to tell them I'm back, so it got moved to tomorrow. I didn't text you because it would have ruined the surprise.' I picked up Andjela's bag and helped her put it on, before walking to the door together. 'Oh, I nearly forgot. Before I go, kiss my hand,' Andjela said, holding her right hand up high, standing just inside the front door.

Although I was confused, I obeyed her and kissed her hand. 'Why did you want me to kiss your hand, your Highness?' I asked laughing.

'Luka kissed my hand and asked me to give it to you. See you tomorrow,' Andjela said, and hugged me before departing my house into the freezing cold. It took me a minute to close the door behind her. I didn't even notice her getting into the taxi. I stood for a moment and touched my lips staring into space, imagining how it would feel to finally have Luka's lips on mine.

I rushed back inside to pick up the gift and took it to my room, and even though I was home alone, closed the door behind me. Sitting on my bed I felt my heart pounding in my chest. Carefully navigating the copious amount of tape, trying not to rip the paper, I pulled out a silver framed photo, and I could feel my soul smile in unison with my mouth. There he was, smiling at me in a video chat. I remembered that moment; it was the first photo we took together. I knew in that moment he was going to be special to me, but I didn't think I was about to fall in love with him. I hugged the photo tightly to my chest, then kissed Luka in the photo, before I placed it delicately on my bedside table.

There was more inside the wrapping. Next, I pulled out a grey hoodie. I searched for a tag but couldn't find one. It wasn't a new hoodie; it was a used one. It was Luka's. I looked over at the photo Luka sent to see it was the hoodie he wore when we first met. I lifted it to my nose and for the first time I could smell Luka. I could smell the man I loved. There are moments where you can physically feel yourself falling deeper in love with someone, and that was one of them. I pulled the hoodie over my head and wrapped myself in Luka, committing his scent to my memory so I could smell him long after the scent was washed away. For the first time combining his scent with mine. In the last five minutes I had kissed where Luka kissed and worn something that had been against his bare skin. I tried to imagine what it would be like to be in his arms, to feel his lips gently against mine. The thoughts were all consuming. 'Never have I wanted something more than I want my man right now. I just want him here with me. I need Luka here with me,' I said aloud to my empty room, closing my eyes and letting his scent consume me. I loved him and missed him so much it hurt.

Ever so slightly sticking out from the wrapping paper was a folded sheet of paper. I had almost missed it. Picking it up and unfolding it, I found a handwritten poem entitled 'I am home'. My hand covered my mouth, and my breath started to shorten. My hand moved from my mouth to my hair as I read the poem. Taking that sharp hard breath to try and stop the tears from coming. I could feel his old pain in it, and that I had been able to help take that away. Always thinking that a home was a place with walls and a roof, but my man had shown me I was wrong. Home is a feeling; home can be a person.

I snatched my phone up from my bedside table and quickly texted Luka, 'Thank you for the greatest gift I've ever received. We are home now.' With tears streaming down my cheeks, I held the poem close to my chest, against my beating heart, and I said aloud, 'I love you Luka.' There was another feeling that struck me also as I basked in Luka's gifts; for the first time I felt scared.

Ever since I opened Luka's present, I had felt scared. Scared of my feelings. Scared of the intensity of my feelings. I was head over heels, absolutely and unequivocally in love with a man that lived on the other side of the world. I didn't know what to do. I felt a yearning to be with him every second of the day, but him visiting for my birthday seemed like a lifetime away. Not being able to be with him every day was hurting, and it only seemed to be getting worse.

There were two notifications on my phone. 'Where are you?' Andjela had texted, as I checked my winter jacket at the door of The Sunshine Café for her welcome home party. I wore waist high khaki green pants with strapped high heels and a white halter top. The other text was from Luka, 'Good morning, sunshine'. I didn't go into the texting app because I didn't want Luka to think I was ignoring him. I didn't want to leave him on read. I knew I should have replied, but I wanted to forget about how much I was hurting for just one night. *'Am I bad person for wanting that?'* I wondered. I didn't want to talk to him; it was too much for me to handle. Immediately I began my search for Andjela.

'Hey, what took you so long?' Andjela asked, when I found her at the back of the bar, propping herself up on her crutches, standing with some of our friends. We hugged and kissed three times on alternating cheeks.

'Sorry, I got held up doing some things at home,' I fibbed to her. In reality, I was sitting in my room reading the poem from Luka over and over, while wearing our hoodie. I thought I had been in love when I was with my ex, or the guy from that movie I saw a couple of summers ago, but with how I was feeling about Luka, I knew Luka was my first real love. Although, the more I fell in love with Luka, the more my fear rose. It was consuming me; I couldn't breathe.

'I'm so happy you're here. I missed hanging out with you. Hey everyone, Nina's here,' Andjela shouted to no one in particular, but everyone within ear shot turned and screamed a greeting to me. 'I think I saw Marko around here somewhere. I'm not sure who invited him, but if he starts to bother you just let me know,' Andjela said, tapping one of her crutches on the floor threateningly.

'He won't bother me. We talked everything out and we're okay now. I let all that go,' I replied, getting very close so she could hear me over the pounding music. The music was overpowering, so much so that I knew my ears would be ringing when I left. I didn't like going to bars, but Andjela did, and I found that if people around me were having fun, then I fed off that energy. After making myself so emotional about Luka, I needed a night out. I needed a night to forget about everything and enjoy being with my friends.

'Well, okay then,' Andjela said, giving me a sceptical look. She didn't need to know that we had begun developing a friendship. I hated disappointing her, and I just couldn't deal with that. 'So, what was the present?'

'There was a beautiful, framed photo of Luka and me. He put in a hoodie of his, and he wrote me the most beautiful poem as well. The ink is a little bit smeared from my tears,' I said with a chuckle. I covered my face feeling slightly embarrassed.

'Aww, you two are adorable,' Andjela said, taking a drink.

'Thanks,' I said, keen to change the subject to take my mind off Luka. Andjela was staring at her phone smiling and texting furiously. 'I'm going to get a drink; do you want me to get you anything while you text Aleks back?'

'Just a water please,' Andjela said, still smiling at her phone. I turned and walked towards the bar, trying to fight through the sea of people. The residual body heat of the packed Sunshine Café had me starting to sweat. Finally, I reached the bar and ordered a water for Andjela and a vodka lemonade for myself.

The next couple of hours were filled with dancing and singing with school friends while I continued back and forth from the bar for drink four, five, six, seven, and then who really cares about counting after that? With every drink I had, I felt less worried about my fear surrounding my feelings. I cared less about why I didn't want to talk to the man I was in love with. Every time I came back from the bar, another friend had left, until I was left dancing with only my drink for company. There were people around me, but they were just faceless shapes, as I worked on drink number who knows. Alcohol made my mind blank; I was just listening to the music that was blaring around the bar.

'Are you okay?' I heard Andjela yell into my ear. I couldn't see her, but I recognised her voice.

'Andjela! I love you. Where have you been all night?' I yelled, slurring my words. Pulling her into a big hug, I accidentally spilled some of my drink on her and myself. She barely kept her balance on her crutches.

'I've been looking for you. You're really drunk, Nina. I'm going to take you home. Let's go,' Andjela said, trying to grab my wrist, but I pulled it away. Her tone was one of worry. I narrowed my eyes and focused them on her face and saw the concerned look in her eyes. 'Your mama will be really upset, and Luka is worried about you. He texted me asking if you're okay?'

'I feel amazing. So, so, good. Don't worry about them, let's just have fun. Dance with me Andjela. Come on,' I implored her, trying to put my glass on a bench, but I dropped it. I watched the lights in the bar dance off it as it fell to the floor smashing into tiny pieces, lying on the floor like a thousand different disco balls. Not caring at all about the glass, I grabbed

Andjela's hands even though she was resting her body weight on her crutches, I tried to get her to dance with me. Putting weight on her injured ankle she squealed in pain and pulled her hands away from me quickly like she had grabbed an electric fence.

'I'm so sorry, are you okay?' I asked, trying to hold Andjela up, shocked into lucidity. Ten seconds before I felt amazing, but after hurting my best friend I felt like human garbage. The negative thoughts about my contradictory feelings for Luka came flooding in also, to create a cocktail of misery. *What the hell is wrong with me? I'm hurting my best friend because I'm so drunk. And Luka. I love him so much but how long can I handle being away from him? Am I stopping him from meeting someone there? Am I being selfish holding onto him? Do I really deserve either of them?'* I wondered, feeling shame spreading to every part of my body.

'Nina, stop it. You're drunk and you need to go home,' Andjela shouted at me.

My phone started to ring. Pulling it out I strained my eyes to find Luka's name on my phone. He had texted me five times and there was one missed call. I quickly rejected the call. 'Leave me alone!' I screamed aloud at my phone, resisting the urge to throw it, and putting it back in my pocket.

'Aren't you going to text him why you can't talk?'

'I just don't feel like talking to him now, okay? He should understand that and realise I'll talk to him when I want to instead of being a pest and blowing up my phone. I just want to enjoy my night. Is that okay with you?'

'He's going to think you're ignoring him, and that he did something wrong. He'll be feeling terrible all-day stewing about it,' Andjela shouted over the music, putting a caring hand on my shoulder.

'And? Why do you care if I do or not? You think just because you met my boyfriend you know him better than me? Huh?' I snapped, causing her hand to recoil like a black mamba just attempted to strike her. The first time it was for self-preservation, this time she recoiled with a look of disgust on her face, like she didn't know who she was looking at anymore. Without saying another word, I walked towards the bar.

'I don't even deserve them. Look at what I do to the people I love. They're better off without me,' I thought, not even wanting to be with myself.

Once I reached the bar, I ordered a glass of rakija. I knew I was going to regret mixing alcohol in the morning, but I deserved that pain. The waiter placed the glass in front of me and I drank it like a shot. As I placed the glass down, I felt a large hand on the small of my back and saw Marko appear.

'Hey, I've been looking for you. You look great,' Marko said, making sure that he got close to my ear to say this before kissing me on the cheek. I smiled and tried to drink from my empty rakija glass. 'Can I buy you another drink?'

It felt like the hardest thing in the world to stand upright so I turned my back on the bar and leant against it. 'Go try that one on one of these other girls, I have a boyfriend.' Marko stood close to me, and while I could see his arm against mine, I couldn't feel it. I knew I should take a step away, but that seemed to be beyond my drunken body's capability in that moment. My nails picked at the skin on the ends of my fingers, no longer having an empty glass to play with nervously.

'What's wrong?' Marko asked, standing in front of me, leaning in unnecessarily closely to speak. I could feel his hot breath on my ear and neck with his citrus cologne wafting into my nostrils.

There was a tingly feeling in my stomach that horrified me. *'I have a boyfriend, I should only get feelings like this for Luka,'* I thought, ashamed of how my body was reacting. I closed my eyes and leaned closer to him so that he could feel my body press against his, pretending just for a moment that I was pressed against

Luka. *'I want to be going home to bed with Luka, but he's in Australia,'* I thought sadly.

'What's wrong....' I whispered into Marko's ear as he leaned down to me, '....is that you're not Luka!' I screamed at the top of my lungs. I found some strength deep in my being and pushed my way past Marko towards the exit. I collected my jacket and rushed through the door, putting as much space between myself and people as possible.

Snow was falling outside and while I could see there were people singing at the tops of their lungs in the street, I could barely hear a sound apart from the ringing in my ears from the music. Not an animal, not a tree rustling, or even a breath of wind. I put my jacket on and walked towards home. I might not have understood how to deal with being in love with a man that lived so far away from me, but I would never cheat on him. I couldn't deal with doing something like that to the man I loved, especially when I understood exactly how much that kind of betrayal hurt. I breathed the cold night air in deeply, hoping it would cleanse my body from the alcohol and misery as I continued towards home.

Passing the empty bus stop I halted in my tracks and stared for a moment, before changing course towards it. I took a seat on one of the empty flat pine benches painted green and leant back against the brick wall. As I closed my eyes, tears began to fall. I watched in my imagination what it would be like to be waiting there, watching each bus stop and wondering if that was the one. My heart thumping against my ribs, wondering if Luka was about to walk off the bus. The anticipation rising with each bus that stopped and left without delivering my man. A mangled sense of excitement and nervousness, hoping he would like me in person. My eyes darted up and down the bus, convincing myself over and over that I saw him, until the disappointment hit when I realised it wasn't him. Until finally the right bus stopped. Trying to look through the windows to find him standing up, head slightly down as to not hit it on the roof as he walked towards the door. While I watched the door hoping it was really him, I would see him appear finally. His brown hair, handsome face, and those perfect blue eyes, my gosh those eyes, walked down the steps, and we met each other's gaze. The look on his face was unforgettable. Luka's face lit up with a look of unbridled joy, reflecting perfectly how I felt when he saw me waiting for him. I stood up and ran to him, jumping into his arms. His heart was beating against my chest, against my heart, and I knew he was feeling exactly how I felt. That it was the most special moment of our lives. I opened my eyes half expecting to see Luka standing there, alas, I was alone with my fantasy, tears streaming down my cheeks.

My hand found its way to my hair and began to spin it around my finger, feeling a love stronger than I had ever felt before rise in my soul. Even stronger than I felt when I read his poem. Every day I fell deeper in love with him, and it hurt more not to have him by my side.

I pulled out my phone and texted Luka. 'I'm sorry. I'll call you when I wake up. Please don't worry.' I stood up, and for the second time walked towards home. I scrolled through my photo file entitled 'Luka', looking for my favourite photo of him. Andjela took it when they met in Melbourne. Wearing a white t-shirt and a long sleeve blue checker shirt unbuttoned, he was looking at something away from Andjela and smiling. The sunlight making his eyes look pale blue. I hoped he was thinking about me in that moment to bring out that smile. To bring out that sparkle in his eyes. I set it as my wallpaper so that every time I opened my phone, I could see his smile. I could see the face that made me happier than any other.

Before I even opened my eyes the pain hit me. My head was pounding, I felt nauseous, and my mouth was drier than the Sahara desert in July. My eyes cracked open the slightest amount and looked to my bedside table in search of water. Either I made a great investment in my future before going to sleep and put a full water bottle next to my bed, or Mama left it there for me. Whichever it was, I was eternally grateful. Not even having the strength to lift myself up, I consumed the entire contents of the bottle laying on my side. I spilled water down the side of my face and onto my sheets, but I didn't care, that was the price I was willing to pay for nature's greatest treasure, water.

I laid on my back and somehow found the strength to raise my hands to my temples and rub them. I tried to remember everything that happened the night before. Things were hazy, but I remembered having feelings so intense for Luka that I didn't even want to talk to him. I needed to talk to Luka and Andjela, but I was in no state to have a conversation. It was going to be a day filled with self-pity because I knew that no one else would have any for me. Those conversations would have to wait.

Reaching for my phone, I picked it up and saw a text from Luka reading, 'I hope you're okay. Text me when you have some time.' Even though I said I would call him when I woke up, I just couldn't face talking yet. Or breathing. Or existing.

'I'm okay, just really hungover. I'm too sick to talk today but I'll call you later. Hope you had a good day,' I replied, and put my phone down wanting no part of it.

I forced myself to sit up. That was a mistake because the thin air that I found raising myself to those great heights caused me to feel even more nauseous. Closing my eyes and taking deep breaths, I tried to regain my composure. In through my nose for a three count, paused, and then out through my mouth for a six count.

My phone buzzed. I begrudgingly picked it up expecting to see a reply from Luka, only to find a text from Marko. 'Hope you got home safely last night. I'm planning on going for a burger in an hour, do you want to meet me for one?' If I wasn't feeling so sick, I would go and meet my friend, yes, my friend, but just the thought of food was disgusting to me. *We are friends now. Just friends,'* I told myself, confused by that tingling sensation in my stomach the previous night.

'Thanks for the offer but I'm feeling sick,' I replied, putting my phone face down and closing my eyes to continue the raging pity party I was throwing.

My phone buzzed again immediately. I thought it had to be Luka this time, but no, once again it was Marko. 'I'm sorry you're sick. I'll see you at school tomorrow. Hope you feel better xx.'

'Two kisses? Is that one on each cheek? Or are those more intimate kisses?' I wondered, totally confused by his motives. My mind flashed back to the night before when we were standing at the bar. *I think he was trying to kiss me, but I can't be sure. No, he couldn't have been. It was just loud in there and he needed to get close to me so I could hear him. Plus, we're just friends. I'm sure I just misread things last night because I was so drunk,'* I thought. After screaming at him I wasn't sure why he wanted to see me at all.

Tired of having my thoughts rattle around my head without being counterbalanced by a sane person, I decided to get up. My clothes from the night before were lying on my bedroom floor so I kicked them out of my path, only having the energy for the shortest route possible, and headed for the kitchen. Walking down the hall I prayed Mama wasn't there because I didn't think I could look anyone in the eye, especially someone that wasn't hungover.

'Good morning booze Queen,' Mama said, as she sprayed air freshener around the kitchen.

'What's good about it? What are you doing?' I asked confusedly, as I plodded on to the couch and curled into the foetal position.

'You drank so much last night that it seeped through your pores when you came home and now all I can smell is alcohol. Here, have this,' Mama said, as she handed me a cup of lukewarm coffee and some plain bread. 'Look Nina, I want you to have fun with your friends and I don't mind you having a couple of drinks at a party, but last night was way over the top. Nina, you're seventeen. I need you to be safe and have your wits about you which you can't do if you drink so much. Why did you get so drunk? Is everything okay?' Mama asked, looking very worried with her hand on her hip and the other tightly clinging to the air freshener can.

'I know and I'm sorry Mama. Believe me, I'm sorry,' I said, as I nibbled the bread. Each time I had to raise and lower my jaw it took more energy than I thought I had. *I should just go back to bed and hope that I don't wake up for three days,'* I thought, closing my eyes. 'I was just in my head a bit too much about Luka and needed time to switch off from that. I just got carried away. It won't happen again. I promise.'

'Don't make a promise you can't keep, because getting that drunk will definitely happen again, so let's not begin lying to each other. Relationships are hard Nina, so if you want to talk about it, you know where to find me,' Mama said, kissing me on the head before spraying air freshener in my direction and walking from the room.

I took a sip of my perfectly warm coffee and a more adventurous bite of my bread before smacking my hand to my forehead. Andjela! It was her special night, and not only did I barely spend any time with her, but I snapped at her as well. Picking up my phone I quickly composed a text message to her. 'Hey Andjela, I'm really sorry for how I acted last night. I was feeling emotional about Luka, and I didn't handle it well. I didn't mean to snap at you, and I hope you forgive me. See you at school tomorrow. Love you.'

Laying my phone on my stomach, I closed my eyes and took another bite of my bread. My phone vibrated, so I picked it up and saw the name I wanted to see appear on my phone. Luka. 'I wish I was there to look after you. Hope we can talk tomorrow.' I replied with a kiss emoji and slowly finished off my hangover meal.

I was on early shift classes for the upcoming week, so I was thankful to be hangover free when I walked into school early Monday morning. Wearing jeans and my blue winter coat, I took my hood down as I walked through the school's doors and began my search for Andjela. I was trying to find her before my first class because I needed to clear the air, especially seeing as she left my last text on read. Looking carefully down the hallway it was hard to tell any people apart as almost everyone had a coat on, and half the people had their hoods up. I turned right and headed towards the maths room, our first class of the day, hoping to find her outside the classroom.

As soon as I turned the corner, I didn't find Andjela, I found Marko. He was leaning against the wall looking like he was waiting for someone, with his left hand hidden from sight. His blue jacket unzipped, and he hadn't shaved for a few days. The stubble looked good on him. I tried to quickly turn around, but he saw me before I could escape. 'Hey, I was hoping to run into you,' Marko said, turning his body to face me still holding his left hand behind his back.

'You're probably mad at me too. I made Andjela and my boyfriend mad, Mama was disappointed with me, so why not go for a clean sweep and have you angry as well. Have you seen

Andjela? I'm looking for her,' I said, my head on a swivel looking for any sign of movement. I was early for class so not many people were heading for their class yet. Marko and I were alone in the hallway.

'I think I saw her outside the library a few minutes ago,' Marko said. I turned to leave but he put his strong right hand on my arm to stop me. I felt a little tingle in my stomach, that was probably because I hadn't eaten much since before the party. Yes, that's all it was. 'Nina wait, I'm not mad at you. No way. I could never be mad at you. You said you were sick, so I got you this to say I hope you're feeling better.'

Marko pulled his left arm from behind his back and revealed a flower. A red rose. Marko handed it to me and kissed me on the cheek. Not a quick kiss, he lingered there with his warm soft lips pressed to my cheek. I stood there frozen, staring at the immaculate red rose in my hand, my brain feeling like radio static. 'Wow. Umm, I don't know what to say. Thank you, I guess,' I stuttered, still not looking at him.

'That rose is nowhere close to as beautiful as you. I hope you have a good day,' Marko whispered smiling, and he walked past me, taking one more glance at me before rounding the corner.

That was weird. Friends don't normally do those things, do they?' I asked myself, trying to cling to the hope that he saw me just as a friend. Shaking my head, I made my way directly to the library. Andjela was sitting on a chair across from the library door with her headphones in, staring into space. 'Hey, can we talk?' I asked, taking a seat next to her before she could say no. Her crutches were leaning against the seat beside her, their rubber bases covered in dirty snow.

'Sure,' Andjela said indifferently, removing her headphones and putting them into her coat pocket. She had a resting bitch face that would scare away almost anyone as she continued to stare into space. I felt like I was performing neurosurgery. That I needed to craft my words perfectly, or it could lead to disaster.

'Do both of your headphone's work? I don't remember the last time I had a pair where both worked,' I said, trying to diffuse the tension.

'They're new,' Andjela said coldly.

'Not a great start, but at least she hasn't punched me yet,' I thought, wracking my brain for what to say next.

'They're really cute. Where did you get them?'

'Australia. It helps when you get ninety thousand Australian dollars for losing in the first round.'

'This approach isn't going to work. I need to take the band-aid approach and just rip it off,' I thought, steeling myself for the blowback I was about to feel.

'Look Andjela, I'm really sorry. I ruined your night. I should have been hanging out with you and hearing more about Australia. It's not an excuse, but I was overwhelmed about Luka and didn't know how to handle how I was feeling. How I am feeling....' I trailed off, unable to find the right words.

'I'm not mad about that. It's okay, we all have times where we don't know what our brains are doing. The reason I was upset was that I was worried about you, and you snapped at me. I was just trying to help you and make sure you were safe because you were so drunk. We look out for each other, and you made me feel like a bad person for trying to look after you,' Andjela said, turning to face me. My hands were held together, clinging to the rose sitting between my knees.

'I wasn't thinking straight. I wasn't me. Can you forgive me?' I asked, looking up at her face.

'I said I was mad, Nina. You were forgiven as soon as you texted me. I just wanted to make you sweat a bit,' Andjela said, playfully pushing me. 'Who gave you the flower?'

'Ah, no one. Just some random gave it to me when I came in this morning,' I said, panicking for a good answer. I couldn't have her know that Marko gave it to me. I had forgiven Marko, but Andjela never would.

'I wish one day I can be as cute as you, so boys just hand me flowers for existing,' Andjela said, laughing.

'Dude, boys will give you cars just for existing.'

'Maybe if I go to the right parts of the world. So why are you confused about Luka? I thought everything was going well,' Andjela asked.

'I don't know. I guess when you got back everything became more real. I think when we first started dating, I just got caught up in the idea, but it can't be an idea forever. When I saw you with him it all sank in. He isn't an idea, he's a man. My man. With a huge heart and I don't want to hurt him. I love him so much more than before you left and it's scaring me. I'm feeling things I've never felt before and all for a man that lives twenty-four hours on a plane away. That was running through my head, it is running through my head constantly, and I just needed some distance from it all,' I said solemnly, looking down at the ground.

'It sounds like you don't want to be with him anymore,' Andjela said softly, as if we were in the library.

'I do want to be with him. More than anything. I just don't know if I'm strong enough for this kind of relationship,' I admitted, finally saying the thing I was afraid to voice aloud.

'Look Nina, I'm on your side. Yes, I don't want you to string him along because I don't think it's fair, but most of all I want you to be happy. I joke about being sisters-in-law, but you'll always be my sister no matter what. You've picked the hardest kind of relationship; it's going to be a lot of longing and suffering. And if you're not planning on moving there, or him moving here, then it cannot work. I guess you just have one question to answer,' Andjela said, putting her hand on my wrist.

'What's that?'

'Is he your soulmate?'

'It's not fair. Why can't he live next door?' I thought, frustratedly. 'Urgh why does it have to be so hard?' I groaned, leaning back looking at the ceiling.

'Isn't that how you want your man,' Andjela said winking, and I rolled my eyes with a smirk. 'Look, if it were easy, you wouldn't want him. Having to fight for him every day is part of the experience. You have to wake up every day and choose him, because in the end you believe he'll be worth it. Come on, we need to get to class. Let's go to lunch after though, my treat. We can chat about why Tomislav is wearing shorts in the middle of winter again. That boy's insane.' Andjela gestured to a guy walking past in running shorts. I stood up and offered my hand to help her to her feet, then picked up her bag and put it on my back. Andjela collected her crutches and together we made our way back to the maths classroom to be tortured for the next fifty minutes.

Two days passed and I still hadn't spoken properly to Luka. Finally, having found some time not dominated by school, I kicked off my shoes as I walked into my house after the early shift. No one was home so I laid down on the couch for a moment and stared at the ceiling. *It's late in Australia, but I'll see if he's up,'* I thought, as I pulled out my phone and began texting Luka.

'Hey, I just got home from class. Do you have some time to hang out?' I texted.

I dropped my phone onto my stomach and closed my eyes, exhausted from another mentally draining day of classes. The falling snow made everything feel like a greater effort, especially waking up at six am to get to school.

My phone vibrated on my stomach, so I opened my eyes to read the message. 'Hi, I'm in bed but yeah, I'm keen. Call me when you're ready,' Luka replied.

Sitting up on the couch I pressed the call button and waited for Luka to answer. I felt nervous calling, unsure how he would be after what happened on the weekend.

'Hi,' I said enthusiastically, feeling a swarm of nerves and excitement. His hair looked scruffy and eyes slightly droopy.

'Hey, how are you?' Luka asked, then coughed to clear his throat.

'Cold and tired. Did I wake you up?' I asked.

'Yeah,' Luka said sleepily, running his hands through his scruffy hair.

Why is it so attractive to see a guy run his hands through his hair?' I wondered.

'Oh, I'm so sorry, Luka. Go back to sleep, we can talk another time.'

'No, I want to hang out with you. I can just sleep in, well I can try,' he said laughing, rubbing his eyes.

'I'm sorry I'm keeping you up. It's been too long since we've hung out and talked.'

'Yeah, I wanted to call you, but I didn't want to be annoying seeing as I was such a pain on the weekend. I just wanted to leave it to you to reach out to me.' I wondered how long it would take for us to begin talking about the elephant in the room, but I didn't have to wait long. It was a relief we could get onto it immediately.

'I'm sorry I had you feeling so worried about me, I didn't mean to stress you,' I said quietly. He looked sad, and a deep shame washed over me, a guilt for putting that look on his face. I couldn't bear to look into those hurt eyes for longer than a moment, the pain was sharp in my chest. I had to look away.

'I'm sorry I was such a pest. I don't know why I kept trying to contact you. I kept telling myself, leave her alone, she'll reply when she can. Then all of a sudden, I'd call or text again. I was more upset with myself than you.'

'It wasn't a Luka thing. I would have ignored my own mother. I just wasn't feeling good and needed a break from everything for a bit. I'm sorry. I should have just replied and been honest with you,' I said remorsefully, chancing a look into his blue eyes. He didn't look sad anymore, he looked peaceful talking to me, as if a weight had been taken off his shoulders.

'Can I ask what you weren't feeling good about?'

'It's just hard,' I said with a forced smile.

'What is?' Luka asked, leaning forward slightly.

'This isn't an easy relationship, Luka. I guess some days are just easier than others.'

'So, it was a Luka thing? What do you mean? Did I do something wrong?' Luka asked, concern spreading across his face.

'Kind of a Luka thing, I guess. I just mean that I want to be with you every day, but you're in Australia. It just hurts being away from you. Isn't it hard for you?' I asked, desperately craving him to be with me on the couch. I was growing weary of the screen.

'Of course it is, but I would rather struggle and be with you than be with anyone else. I guess I just feel like the struggle and the hurt now is all going to be worth it when we meet,' Luka said, smiling with just his eyes.

'What about after that though? Don't you ever worry about what will happen after we meet? You'll go home and I'll still be here. What will be different?' I asked, begging him to say something reassuring. I could feel myself beginning to stress about what might or might not happen. I needed answers from the one person that could relate with what I was going through.

'I just think we'll work that out when we get to that point. All I know is that the bad pales in comparison to the good. I'm not sure of much, but what I am sure of, is that every day is better because you are in my life. Everything bad that happens isn't as bad, and everything good that happens is better,' Luka said. He knew the exact right thing to say but just having words wasn't enough anymore. It felt right when I was with him, I just wasn't with him enough. I didn't want to let him go; I just wasn't sure how much longer I could hold on.

'Really?' I wanted to hear him say more beautiful things, but I couldn't shake that it was feeling less and less practical. I understood perfectly how he was able to write such angelic lyrics, he said what I needed to hear, but what I really needed to hear was that he was on his way.

'Yes, really. I didn't understand how heavy I felt until I met you. You make me feel light, Nina. All the bad things I used to say to myself, I rarely say anymore. I don't believe that voice now. I believe your voice. You're my girl. You're my sunshine,' Luka said. My heart melted. I felt butterflies dancing in my soul hearing him call me his girl.

'And you're my man,' I replied. He had a beaming smile on his face. I felt like my cheeks were about to split from the smile Luka brought out in me. I felt euphoric at looking into his smiling eyes, but the question of how still lingered in my clouded mind.

'Is this a date? Because if it is, I feel very underdressed,' Luka said, looking down at his creased blue t-shirt. He must not have liked the trajectory of the conversation and changed the subject.

'Of course, it's a date. Why don't you have a tie on? I love seeing a man in a tie,' I said, looking at Luka flirtatiously, giving in to his topic change. I was emotionally drained and needed to talk about something fun.

'Good point,' Luka said. He must have put his phone down because his camera was pointed at the cream ceiling.

'What are you doing?' I asked.

'Wait a second,' he replied distantly.

Moments later, the camera moved and was back on Luka's handsome face. He had put a red and navy-blue tie on, looking at me with a cheeky smile. 'Wow! It doesn't get any better than that,' I said laughing, blowing a chef's kiss.

'I aim to please. I think I've done a good job on this, if I don't say so myself,' Luka said, slightly adjusting his tie, so it sat perfectly below his Adams apple.

'You look very handsome,' I said, trying to get my giggles under control. I took a screenshot of us both smiling, wanting to hold onto a moment of joy together.

We talked deep into the Williamstown night. I disregarded the pile of homework I had because I didn't want to see his face disappear from my phone. As it approached two-am in Williamstown, I watched Luka's heavy eyelids droop, I took mercy on him and told him to go to sleep. I didn't want Luka to go, but I hoped there would be many more opportunities to talk. *'Perhaps, even a lifetime? Just keep fighting, Nina,'* I thought stubbornly.

As we cyber-kissed goodbye, I opened my phone and looked upon the screenshot I took earlier. Staring down at our smiling faces I felt both happiness and misery swirl inside me like the warm, humid air meeting the cold, dry air to form a tornado. My head was spinning, unsure which was the stronger emotion.

The joy I felt at talking with my boyfriend was fighting with the misery of wanting to go to sleep with him but not being able to. I craved to have his chest pressed into my back, with his arms wrapped around my body, our fingers intertwined. I loved him more each day and there was no possible way that my love for him was not going to continue to grow every minute. I just knew that the pain would continue to grow alongside it.

'I would give anything to wake up next to him and feel his gentle breath on my neck as he continued to sleep. Feel his chest rise and fall. To feel his heartbeat against my back,' I thought dreamily, craving him more deeply than I imagined I could crave someone.

I had just spoken to Luka, yet I missed him. Missing him didn't seem to be enough to properly describe it though. There is a Serbian poet named Laza Kostić and he has a beautiful poem called Santa Maria Della Salute. He didn't think a word in existence was strong enough to describe missing a woman, so he created one. Beznjenica. Without-her-ness. So, maybe the word I'm looking for is there. Beznjeganica. Without-him-ness. I felt like he was a part of me and that I could never fully be me until I was in his arms. He had so quickly become a part of me it was scary. I missed his presence so much my stomach hurt, even though I had never truly experienced being with him. I didn't need to have been in his physical presence to miss him. I may not have known how he walked when he was excited, or if he yelled or got quiet when he was upset. I did know his heart though, and that was the most important thing to me.

There were four long years of university in front of me, and I wasn't sure how I would handle not being able to wake up with Luka every day for those four years. I loved him so much I was hurting, and I didn't know how to make the pain go away, in a way that didn't end in both our hearts broken.

Over the next four months my feelings continued to grow, alongside my fear, and I had no answer for how to deal with any of it. My feelings would become so intense that the only way to deal with the pain was to avoid Luka all together. *Was I hurting him by doing that?'* I wondered. That he would call, and I would ignore it, lying in bed paralysed by not having him with me. I was at breaking point and had no immediate practical solution that had a happy ending. Not once had Luka been angry at me for being distant. He would only ask if I was okay. I didn't deserve someone as pure as him. He didn't deserve to be treated how I was treating him.

I had dragged myself from bed, thinking that the sunshine could alleviate my pain, even if it was a temporary solution. I was desperate for anything that would take my pain away just for a moment. I focused hard on the maths book in front of me, trying to push all thoughts of anything else from my mind. It was the end of May, and I sat just beyond the shade of the sycamore tree that held a chirping bird searching for a mate. Mama's garden was blooming with bees pollinating the flowers, before returning to their hive.

I opened my phone to find a picture of Luka smiling up at me. For a split second I smiled back at him, forgetting he wasn't beside me, before a stabbing pain shot through my chest. 'Why aren't you here?' I cried aloud at the picture. I began texting Andjela to ensure I hadn't missed any of the recommended revision work when my phone began to ring. It was Luka.

The pain quickly turned to anger. *Why am I annoyed seeing him call me?'* I wondered, aggravated at everything, including myself and the chirping bird. I felt angry at myself that I was trying to avoid my problem rather than deal with it. *'He deserves better than this,'* I thought shamefully. Luka had called me the last three days and I hadn't answered. Rubbing my eyes and exhaling, I answered the call. 'Hey,' I said coldly, but that didn't seem to dampen his enthusiasm.

'Hey, I was thinking about you, so I thought I'd give you a call. We haven't spoken for a couple of days, how are you?' Luka asked, with a fake bounce in his voice, though I noticed there was a quiver. He was nervous. He was either hoping by being positive it would rub off on me, or he was too scared to ask the question he desperately wanted to ask.

'I'm fine. Just studying,' I replied monotonously, very aware that I hadn't asked how he was. *'Maybe if I don't give him anything he will realise that I don't want to talk,'* I thought. My anger at him and myself was rising. I was mad at him for not taking a hint that I would talk to him when I was ready, and me because if Andjela was treating her boyfriend like this, I would tell her it wasn't okay.

'How's your day going? What are you up to?' he asked, trying to engage me, but with each question he asked I became angrier.

'Why is he pushing me when he knows I don't want to talk? Can't he read my signs? Does he have no social skills at all?' I thought, my anger at the world bubbling inside me.

'Fine. Already told you, studying.' My heart and head were in a war. My heart was full of feelings for Luka, a kind of love that I hadn't felt before, but my head had no interest in having any kind of conversation with him. *'How is this even possible?'* I wondered frustratedly.

'Are you okay?' Luka asked with trepidation, trying to mount the courage to question why I had been blowing him off.

'Yep,' I said shortly, and the phone went silent as he waited for me to add to that answer. I didn't. *'Why is he acting like everything is fine? Does he even care that he's not with me? Obviously, he isn't in love with me like I am with him,'* I thought painfully.

'Well… umm… I should let you get back to your study. Sorry for interrupting. I'll talk to you tomorrow. Hopefully….' Luka said with the sound of fear and trepidation turning to a tone of sadness. He knew something was wrong, and while I knew I was treating him badly, all I wanted to do was get away from him.

'Okay. Bye,' I said, and hung up the phone before he could say goodbye to me.

I put my phone down on the table and stared into the distance. I wasn't sure how long I sat in silence for, but I had an overwhelming feeling of sadness wash over me. I was beginning to feel misty, struggling to keep my tears at bay. I felt like I had punched myself in the stomach. That I treated my boyfriend, a man that I was so desperately in love with, and who would do anything for me, like that. He would be stressing until we spoke again, which could be days, about what he did wrong and wondering why I was upset with him. He did nothing wrong. He was perfect, as always, apart from one big thing. He wasn't with me.

Andjela was in Belgrade winning a round of Fed Cup with Team Serbia, so I didn't have her to talk to about it. I had been stewing for days and felt like I was a hair away from a complete breakdown. My heart was on the verge of shattering.

Mama's car appeared from around the corner at the end of the driveway and crawled to a halt next to where I sat. She got out of the car and walked over to sit across from me, seeing it written all over my face that I was hanging on by a thread. Before even saying hello, she asked the question I didn't want to be asked, because I knew I would answer it completely honestly. 'What's wrong?' No one will ever know you how your mama knows you.

Suddenly, the tears started to flow. I tried to fight them. I tried to keep them inside, but they were like a hiccup, they were coming, and there was no stopping them. The tears were streaming down my face, my nose was beginning to run, yet I made no effort to wipe them away. My loud cries from the pain I was feeling in my heart, from in my soul caused Mama to jump up and sit next to me, pulling me close to her. 'Luka,' I struggled to say, wailing, as she held me tightly and I put my head on her chest.

'Shhhh, it's okay honey,' Mama whispered soothingly, trying to stop my heaving breaths and streaming tears. 'What happened?' I hadn't cried in my mother's arms for years. Not even when I found out my ex cheated on me. I had never cried like that before. I had never hurt like that before.

'I don't know what to do. My boyfriend is on the other side of the world. I'm so confused.'

'Confused in what way?' Mama asked in the same soothing tone, not loosening her grip at all. If anything, holding me tighter.

'How am I so in love with a man yet have no interest in talking to him? I just got off the phone with Luka and all he wanted to do was talk about me, talk about how I was, how my day was, and I barely said two words to him. He can tell something's wrong, and he probably thinks I don't like him anymore, but it's the opposite, Mama. I'm in love with him. It just hurts so much.' The words were like my tears, once they began there was no way to stop them, and I didn't want to stop them. I was finally talking about what had been bothering me for months. I needed to get it all off my chest.

'Maybe you're trying to protect yourself. Your heart has gone out on a huge limb to fall in love with this boy before your brain had time to comprehend what it involved. To contemplate what it really meant,' Mama said, stroking my hair with her left hand, while her right arm was still wrapped tightly around me.

'What do you mean, Mama?' I sobbed, struggling to get the sentence out between my bursts of tears, loud sniffs, and shallow breaths.

'I go through it with your father. I'm in love with him, yet I barely get to spend any time with him. It means waking up every day with the man you love not there next to you. It means that when all you want is to sit quietly next to him, having his arm around you, that the best you can do is send a hug emoji to him.

It means it just gets harder and harder until that day comes,' Mama whispered soothingly, continuing to stroke my hair.

'What day is that?' I asked, my breath becoming slightly more under control, but the tears were still flowing.

'When you either decide it's too hard, and you can't do it anymore, or the day when you finally get to hold him in your arms. Let me tell you honey; holding your soulmate is one of the greatest feelings you will ever have.' I looked up into my mother's eyes and saw she was smiling with a glint of a tear in her eye. Mama made me realise how self-centred I was, to never once ask her how she was feeling with Tata so far away. That maybe someone else could understand how I was feeling; that she could even help me through it. No, I could only think about myself. Shame began dancing with the sadness.

'How do you handle being away from Tata,' I asked, sniffing loudly.

'It's hard, but I realised a long time ago that we are a team. That while it hurts, that's better than having anyone else on my team. It hurts him just as much as it hurts me, but that pain is temporary. Our love isn't though, that is infinite,' Mama said. I looked up at her and she forced a smile at me through her twinkling eyes.

'I was looking for an easy answer. You're supposed to tell me what to do, not spell out my problem more articulately than I could,' I sniffed, forcing a laugh through my tears which had finally stopped flowing.

'I can't tell you what to do. It's your life and they're your feelings, so you have to decide. I'm here to give you as much information as I can, and if I've spelt out a problem you didn't understand, at least now you can answer it. So, what do you think you will do?'

'I don't know,' I said honestly, closing my eyes and taking a deep breath before exhaling loudly.

Mama kissed me on the forehead and said, 'Come on, I'll make you a cup of tea.'

I laid in bed all night without a wink of sleep. All I could think about was Luka, and the distance I so desperately craved not to be there. *'I don't want to be with another man, but how can I truly be with a man that lives in Williamstown, when I live in Požega? I'm only seventeen, so how can I commit my future to a man when I can't even hold his hand? I want to know how he walks, how he brushes his teeth, how he sneezes. What does he do when he's nervous, happy, or sad? What does he look like when he sleeps, and is he a cuddly or solo sleeper? How does he hug hello and how does he hug goodbye? How will he kiss me good morning, and how will he kiss me goodnight?'* I wondered painfully.

I closed my eyes and imagined what it would be like to walk down the street with our fingers intertwined. To walk so closely to him that I felt his arm on mine. Our arms swaying as we walked, my hand grazing his leg. I groaned out loud longing just to be able to touch his face, to look into the most beautiful eyes I had ever seen.

My anxiety grew through the night, and my frustration at his physical absence turned to anger. The beautiful dancing kaleidoscope of butterflies in my chest had been squashed by that enormous elephant falling asleep on my chest. I knew that any attempt to rouse that elephant, to get him to move would be futile. The butterflies were gone, and the elephant was there to stay. 'It's not fair,' I screamed into my pillow, pounding my fist into my mattress. *'Why can't he live next door to me?'* I thought furiously. I felt itchy, irritated, the anger burning in my chest. I picked up my cuddle pillow that I always imagined was Luka and threw it hard against the wall. I got out of bed to pick it up and noticed his hoodie hanging over the back of my chair. I tossed my pillow back onto my bed and put on his hoodie, our hoodie, the hoodie that had long lost his scent, but lived long in my memory, before laying back down in bed.

Picking up my phone I opened my Luka file. My happy file. I looked through all the different photos I had of him — screenshots, or photos sent just to me that weren't on social media. I stopped on a video he took with Monty at the beach. They were sitting on the sand, happiness radiating from them both, smiling at the camera. 'Good morning, sunshine. I've had so many great days since I've met you, but I know a perfect day doesn't exist until you're sitting here with us. Are you excited to meet her, Monty?' Luka turned the camera towards his dog. Monty looked up at him with complete adoration, his tongue hanging out. 'Me too, buddy. We'll be together soon, sunshine.' Luka blew me a kiss and the video ended.

A tear rolled down my cheek as I watched the video on a loop. I must have watched it for twenty minutes before I cried aloud, 'I'm so sorry, Luka.'

'Yes, we might be together soon, but how soon? And for how long before he leaves me for Williamstown? This hurts too much. I'm not strong enough,' I thought, feeling desperately incomplete.

I was in my house, but I couldn't be at home until I was with Luka.

As the sun finally rose, I decided that I needed to talk to Luka. Really talk with him. 'We need to talk,' I texted Luka, and hoped that he didn't hate me so much that he would ignore me like I had been ignoring him.

CHAPTER TWELVE
The Decision

Nina had seemed a little distant and hadn't been returning my calls as often as usual, but I tried to not overthink about it. I felt a little sting, like a needle for a flu shot if my call wasn't returned, but I brushed it away. *'She's just busy studying,'* I would tell myself. Trying to shake the nagging question in my mind of why she didn't answer my call that morning, I felt a wave of relief when I saw her name appear on my phone while I readied myself for bed. I could only imagine how difficult it would have been to sleep, wondering what I had done wrong, if she hadn't called. The bully in the back of my mind who had been silenced for so long was beginning to find his voice.

'So has she told you when she's coming home?' I asked Nina, as I paced up and down the upstairs hallway from my room to the door that led onto the balcony overlooking the backyard. Some of the most exquisite sunsets you could find were to be seen from that balcony.

'She said she'll be back on Thursday, so we have a big party planned for her next Friday. I can't wait to see her; I've missed her a lot. I'm going to Belgrade to surprise her at the airport,' Nina said, and I could hear the kettle boiling on the other end of the phone.

'Aleks saw her a few days ago. He went to visit her at the hotel before she checked out. He told me she was going to Sydney for a few days before heading home,' I lied. I knew Andjela was on her way to Požega. *'She landed in Belgrade three hours ago so she should be there very soon. Nina's going to be so surprised — I can't wait to hear all about it,'* I thought, checking the time on my phone.

I heard a loud knock on the door in the background. 'Can we talk later? Someone's at the door.'

'Sure. Have a good day and we'll talk later,' I said, hoping it was Andjela. She said that her first stop was going to be Nina's house. The phone fell dead, and I went back to preparing myself for bed.

I laid in bed waiting. *'Chill psycho,'* I told myself, checking my phone for the fifth time to see if Nina had opened her present. I wondered what I would give Nina for her birthday. I had spent every good idea I had on her Christmas present, so I was going to have to get creative for what I took when I visited.

There were three loud bangs on my wall that startled me from my silly worry. I was impressed at some of the things I managed to stress about. 'Luka, come and look at this,' Aleks yelled through the wall.

Begrudgingly I got out of bed and walked into his room. 'You could have walked into my room, or used the word please, but no. You had to pick the most asinine way of getting my attention. What is it?' I asked, scowling at him, adjusting the creased shirt I had just pulled on.

'Asinine? Luka, you need to stop reading the dictionary and start reading normal books. Well, I wanted to show you this,' Aleks said, turning his phone around and showing me a photo. Nina was sitting with her feet on the couch facing Andjela and lying on her lap was the wrapped gift that I gave to Andjela for Nina. Nina was staring down at the gift, mouth slightly ajar.

'It's crazy that Andjela was just here and now she's back in Požega. When did you get this?' I asked, trying to read the time on the clock hanging above the stove in the picture, but the hands were too blurry.

'Well, I only just saw it, but Andjela sent it to me about ten minutes ago. She just texted again to say that she's home now. We'll have a video chat in the morning if I don't wake up too late,' Aleks said, taking back his phone and tossing it onto his bed.

'She better be staying up late because I don't think I've seen you before midday on a Saturday when you didn't have basketball, in years. So, I guess you'll be talking tomorrow night,' I said, turning and heading for the door.

'What can I say? She's worth losing sleep over,' Aleks said, sitting at his desk, putting his headphones on, and turning back to his computer.

I got back into bed and put my phone down. Trying not to get in my own head and go into full Luka-mode, by convincing myself that something was happening when it wasn't, it was just my mind being cruel. When that happened, it was best just to go to sleep. I was tired and that was when my thoughts got away from me by creating situations. *When I wake up there will be a missed call from Nina and we'll talk then,'* I thought, trying to beat the bully in my head with positivity.

Five minutes later my phone began vibrating. Reaching for it in frustration at forgetting to put it on silent, I saw a text from Nina. She had opened the present and loved it. There would be no need for caffeine tomorrow morning. Making someone you love happy worked much more effectively. I just wished that I could have given it to her in person. *Next time I will,'* I thought, as determined as ever to get to Požega in August. I implored the clock to tick faster, the calendar to race by more quickly. There would never be a need for her to give me a present, because seeing her smile was the only present I would ever need.

Responding quickly, I texted, 'I'm glad you love it. I'll call you tomorrow.' I laid my head back on my pillow and fell asleep, smiling the entire night.

The sun was yet to rise when my eyes opened Sunday morning. Immediately my hand sprung for my phone which was waiting for me on my bedside table. The only notification was an alert email saying that prices for flights to Serbia had increased. I texted Nina and closed my eyes again, my ears alert for the sound of my vibrating phone. The urge to hear her voice was increasing in my chest, that texting her wasn't enough. I needed to feel close to Nina, and the only way to feel connected to her was to hear her voice. I hit the call button and sat the phone on my chest, waiting for her to answer. Even though Nina had been inconsistent with answering my calls, I felt sure she would answer, after all, I did tell her I would call. After what felt like an eternity the phone fell silent. *'It's okay, she'll call me back,'* I thought, trying to talk it into existence, quieting the rousing bully in the back of my mind.

Rolling from my left to my right side, I couldn't get comfortable. I felt restless, weight increasing on my chest with each passing moment that I didn't get a reply. *'Get up and do something. Take Monty for a walk. Stop focusing on it,'* I told myself, but I couldn't move. I felt as if I was trapped in bed by my growing anxiety as the elephant sat on my chest, and the volume of the bully's voice in the back of my mind grew steadily louder. *'She's not going to call you back. She doesn't want to talk to you,'* he said, relishing in my growing anxiety and misery.

'Shut up!' I screamed in my head at the bully. *'No, she just can't talk on the phone now, or maybe she's been away from her phone and is back to it now. Yeah, that must be it. I'll text her and ask how her day's been.'* After sending the text I laid my phone on my bedside table and rolled away from it, hoping that out of sight would be out of mind.

I was wrong. Staring at the back of my eyelids for what felt like hours waiting for a reply. The elephant on my chest growing, constricting my breathing to short, sharp breaths. I hadn't felt so anxious and overwhelmed since the night before I met Nina. It was a place I thought I had left behind, but it was waiting for me the entire time.

'Did I remember to put my phone on vibrate or ring? Maybe she called and I missed it,' I wondered. Spinning rapidly back to my phone, I checked and saw that I had. Nina just hadn't replied.

My phone vibrated loudly and this time at an even greater speed I snatched my phone up to see what I hoped to be a text from Nina. Disappointment washed over me, and my bully cackled with laughter as I read an email entitled, 'The best getaway's this winter'. In an act of revenge, I immediately unsubscribed to the weekly travel emails. *That'll show them for getting my text hopes up,'* I thought, putting my phone down in frustration.

I shook my head, trying to rid my mind of the cruel thoughts that were circulating my being. I was unable to lay still, yet the idea of removing myself from bed and seeing the sun was an impossible prospect. *Why is she ignoring me? Did I do something wrong? Maybe Andjela said something about me that made Nina rethink me as her boyfriend,'* I stressed, feeling those thoughts bouncing off the inside of my skull. *'She would reply to a good-looking guy. She would reply to an interesting guy. You're an ugly loser and you know it,'* the bully said, and I could almost see a sneer on his non-existent face as he spat those words at me.

I craved her presence. Hearing her voice was only a stay of execution. I needed to be laying with her, to be sitting next to her. Anything, I didn't care, as long as I was within arm's reach of her. It was eating away at me, and the more deeply in love I fell with her, the more I craved it. *You knew it was too good to be true. It was only a matter of time before she came to her senses and realised, you're not good enough for her,'* I told myself, giving in to the taunts of the bully.

My anxiety was at boiling point. I couldn't take it anymore. I needed a release. The only way I knew how to achieve just a moment of respite was to act. 'Is everything okay?' I texted Nina and felt my anxiety drop a level. Even if the contact was only one way, it was still contact with the woman I was in love with.

I laid there nailed to my bed, staring at the clock, which sat one metre from my face, watching the time slowly tick past. If you want time to stand still either do a plank or wait for a text, because it will work every time. I was starting to get restless again. Turning over, and then again, and then again. I felt tingly, like there were ants running over my entire body. I tried to scratch but it was an itch much deeper than my skin. Even the Egyptian cotton sheets were annoying as they got caught under my leg, so I ripped them out in anger.

Just leave her alone Luka. She's either busy, asleep, or doesn't want to talk to you. It's okay. Get up and do something,' I calmly thought to myself, taking several deep breaths, trying to get the elephant to leave me alone.

Without even realising it I was putting my phone down again. *'Oh no, what did I just do?'* I panicked; all serene thought having disappeared from my mind. I looked at my phone and saw that I had texted Nina again. 'Sup.'

'Enough is enough,' I thought. I couldn't continue to lay there playing those silly games all day. It was time to get up. *'This is beyond embarrassing, Luka,'* I told myself, feeling ashamed. Ripping the covers off, I picked up a shirt from the pile of clothes on my floor. I had no idea if it was clean or dirty, at that point in my mind it was both, before taking my phone and heading downstairs. I should have left my phone on my bed. No one was awake yet, so I went straight to the backyard. I placed my phone on the outdoor table and sat on the back veranda where the late autumn sun was rising. Monty extricated

himself from his kennel, bringing a toy with him for a morning tug of war.

It was one-am in Požega, and I didn't know if I should feel worried or upset that she wasn't replying or be mad at myself for being pushy. I felt all three. It surely wasn't a good sign that my girlfriend wasn't replying. It was my first relationship, so I wasn't sure what I was supposed to do next.

I felt helpless. All I wanted to do was hold my girlfriend, but seeing as I couldn't do that, I would settle for a conversation, or even just a text message. I was madly in love with this woman, yet I couldn't even get an acknowledgement of my existence from her. I was craving the smallest bit of attention, and I didn't know how else to get it. It wasn't just one elephant; it was two elephants crushing every bit of positivity in my body. There was no fighting the bully anymore, he had spread to every part of my body like a cancer.

I knew I shouldn't look at my phone, but I couldn't help it, the temptation was too much. It's as if my phone was speaking to me, telling me to look at it and ignore the morning before me. Giving in easily, I began to look through social media. There Nina was, posting videos of herself in a bar. I could hear her singing so obviously there wasn't anything wrong, she just didn't want to talk to me. She looked like she was having a great time. Andjela had posted Nina too, dancing on her own in the middle of the dancefloor. I was hurt. She was just ignoring me, and I didn't know why. There was a time where I thought she would do anything to talk to me, and at that moment, I didn't know if she even liked me anymore.

What if Andjela had said something awful about me when she saw Nina? That could have turned her off and led her to ignore me,' I wondered, as Monty checked the perimeter of our backyard. I searched my swirling mind for any kind of explanation, no matter how ridiculous it seemed.

'I could send Andjela a message and see if Nina is okay. That would be okay, wouldn't it?' I wondered.

'Hey, I haven't heard back from Nina for a while, so I'm getting worried. Is she okay?' I texted Andjela.

I didn't want to get angry with her, I needed to at least appear as if I had my composure, even though that horse had bolted long ago. And if she was drifting away from me, getting angry would only push her further away. A concerned approach was the best one to take, so I made one final attempt at texting Nina. *'I'm starting to worry. Are you okay?'*

As soon as I pressed send on the message to Nina, I received a reply from Andjela. To receive any message felt like finding water after being in the desert for a week. 'I think so, she's just very drunk. I'll check on her for you.'

'Thank you,' I replied immediately, and put my phone down. I was exhausted. Emotionally drained. I had only walked about fifty metres but the mental strain I had put on myself had me ready for a nap and it wasn't even ten o'clock.

If she was really drunk, then Nina probably hadn't even realised that I wanted to talk to her. That I could feel her drifting from me and all I wanted was to be close to her. I couldn't stop myself. *'What are you doing? This is psychotic,'* I thought, as my finger, as if having a mind of its own called Nina again. On only the second ring my call was rejected. I buried my head in my hands and silently screamed, feeling like I had just been stabbed in the chest. The two elephants had turned to an entire bachelor herd, making it increasingly difficult to breathe. Monty sauntered over to me with his tug rope and offered it to me. I began to pull on it, but I could see on his face that he knew my mind was a million miles away.

'Is it so hard to just text and say I'm busy, we'll talk tomorrow? Tell me to go away, or that I suck, and you hate me. Anything is better than being ignored,' I angrily thought.

I was mad. I needed to punch something, break something. Anything to vent the anger, frustration, and helplessness from my body. I was mad at her for not replying and mad at myself for being so pushy. *Why can't I just relax and let her text me when she's ready? Do I really want to make her feel so guilty she feels obliged to talk to me? Nina should talk to me because she wants to, not because she feels guilty. Urgh, I hate my brain sometimes. Maybe the harder I push, the more she'll pull away. Calling and texting all those times? Really, Luka? You couldn't just send one and understand that she'll reply when she can? This isn't normal behaviour; I need to see my psych again,'* I thought, my brain was in a complete tailspin.

I didn't know who to be mad at. I felt anger, embarrassment, shame, and frustration, in a huge concoction of emotions that had me unsure what to do or even where I wanted to look. I stared towards the sky, the cherry plum tree, and Monty in turn, but nothing seemed to be able to hold my focus. I just wanted to scream, to let something out upon the world.

I sat on the veranda and watched Monty chase birds out of the yard. In his life things weren't right unless there were no birds around. Clearly, they were evil and needed to be rid from this world, and by this world, his yard. My phone vibrated again. I wasn't sure if I had the emotional strength after whipping myself into such a frenzy to even see what the notification was. *'If it's another damn email, I'm going to throw my phone over the fence,'* I thought, heaving myself up and slowly dragging my empty body towards my phone. I didn't allow the voice in my mind to even say the name Nina. I didn't deserve to have hope. I had made a fool of myself.

It was Nina. The moment I saw her name on my phone all my anger and anxiety melted away. I was like a drug addict, desperate for a hit and when I finally got it, I was free of all that was bad in my world.

She apologised for not replying and assured me that we would talk in the morning. The elephants of anxiety that were sitting on my chest, preventing me from breathing finally got up and moved on with their day. All the negative thoughts that were circling around my head ran away, giving me some desperately needed mental respite.

Now that my anxiety and anger had left me, I was left with one overwhelming emotion. Shame. To think that Nina didn't like me anymore, or that Andjela said something bad about meeting me, was awful. *These people care about me and like me, I need to stop always creating the worst-case scenario in my head,'* I scalded myself. It was no way to have a healthy life or a healthy relationship. Those are the things that would push her away and end our relationship, which I couldn't bear to happen.

Over the next four months the same dance happened multiple times, each time sending me into a spiral of self-doubt and self-loathing to be followed by shame and embarrassment. Each time creating an anxiety stronger and more intense than the time before. At least I hadn't bombarded her with texts or calls again though. Personal growth, right? Trying not to push Nina away, I didn't get angry or ask her why she was ignoring me. I just kept moving along like a donkey ploughing a field. I was afraid that if I confronted her and it turned into a big fight then she would break up with me. That was the last thing I wanted. I had never been in love with someone before and was worried that I wouldn't find it again. All I was focused on was making it to her birthday. Everything would be fine as soon as we met each other in person. *Just keep focused on August twenty-three,'* I told myself repeatedly.

It had been three days since speaking to Nina and my anxiety was at fever pitch. The cruel bully in my head telling me I wasn't good enough; I wasn't smart enough; I was boring; I was ugly. That she had probably found someone superior to me in every conceivable way, and they would laugh together about how she could ever have been with a loser like me. The bully always seemed to be loudest at night.

The days were getting shorter in Williamstown with winter fast approaching. The sun had completely fallen as the evening arrived late in May. I was sitting on the couch not watching the show about UFO's that was playing on the television. I felt restless; unable focus or even think about anything apart from how distant Nina had become, as if I was becoming a stranger instead of her boyfriend. I felt at a loss, unsure what to do. I reached for my phone and for the fourth day in a row called Nina. Hoping, desperately hoping, that she wanted to talk to me, or would at least tell me what was wrong.

Every time I had called Nina before that day, I had been excited, but not that time. I told myself it didn't matter; she wasn't going to pick up anyway. The anxiety coursing through my body at the prospect of what was waiting for me on the other end of the phone, was beyond my conscious control. I pictured the look on Nina's face as she looked at her phone and saw my name pop up. I could see Nina having a great time, laughing with her friends and then rolling her eyes at my incoming call, shoulders slumped at the prospect of me trying to talk to her again.

The phone went silent for a moment, and I assumed the call had rung out, so I removed it from my ear when I heard Nina's voice. My heart did a little cartwheel before my brain could communicate to it that her voice was cold, distant, and uninterested. When I asked how she was all I got was a short answer, and she didn't ask me how I was in return. *'Is she busy or does she just not care?'* I wondered. It felt like she had answered the phone out of obligation, not because she wanted to talk to me. My heart sank.

I tried to be upbeat and enthusiastic in the hope that she would feed off that, but it was no use. Nina sounded as if she had no interest in talking to me, and with each word she said, that point was hammered into my heart again and again. There was no use continuing to force her into the conversation. She said goodbye and before I could say the same, she had hung up the phone.

I sat there in silence staring at the wall, completely confused as to how we got to that point. I wished there was a moment that I could put my finger on, something that happened that I could point to and say, that's where things turned. Ever since Andjela returned from the Australia, Nina's attitude had changed towards me, but that had to be a coincidence. *'I guess sometimes a person just changes their mind,'* I thought, heartbroken. For the first time, August twenty-three seemed like a pipedream, and not an inevitable reality.

My phone vibrated, breaking the silence, and I picked it up to see if it was a text with an explanation, or even a nugget of information as to why Nina was so cold towards me. Instead of Nina, it was a text from Michael. 'Hey, I'm working at the café. It's dead here so come hangout if you're not doing anything.'

Even though the prospect of wallowing in self-pity seemed appealing, I opted for the alternative. I immediately picked up my phone and headed for the door. I didn't even tell Mum that I was leaving. I heard her in the middle of another British real estate show, just in case she decided to invest in property on the outskirts of London. 'Property prices in London are astronomical. You're much better buying just outside and commuting in,' I could hear the host tell a British house hunter. I collected my wallet and keys, jumped in my car, and drove straight to the café. I blasted music as loudly as I could handle and sang at the top of my voice. If I sang loudly enough maybe it would drown out the cruel voice that I could feel waking in my mind. The bully was like a shark smelling blood in the water.

The café was a five-minute drive, so I just managed to belt out a rendition of Chasing Cars and finish as I parked directly in front of the café and walked in with my hood up. 'Hey Luka. I texted James as well so he should be here soon,' Michael said, looking up from his phone. He was leaning on the counter with his palm planted firmly to his jaw but stood up straight to welcome me. He was wearing an apron over his white shirt and blue jeans. It was a bar style café with a high bench counter and stools which was where I took my seat.

'What's wrong?' Michael asked, furrowing his brow in concern as I sat down.

I had always said to myself that I was able to hide my emotions well, but apparently everyone that knew me could tell how I was feeling just by looking at me. *Clearly, I've been lying to myself, like I was lying to myself when I said Nina liked me. Shut up, Luka. SHUT UP!'* I roared in my head, trying to silence the returning bully's voice.

'It's nothing major. Just feeling a bit flat. Business is clearly booming I see,' I said glumly, turning around and looking at the empty café.

'You've been here on weekends, and it's packed. I'm not sure why we stay open this late on weeknights. Feels like money down the toilet paying me to stand here and swipe away on a dating app,' Michael said smirking, and placing his phone face down on the counter. 'Do you want a drink?'

'Yeah, please. Get any matches?' I said and removed my hood.

'A couple but nothing that has me thinking I've got a Nina in my life. How are you two going anyway?' Michael asked, as he placed a coffee in front of me and poured some bourbon into it. 'There you go, a happy coffee.'

'Thanks. We're going how James goes on a Sunday morning. Looks dead, and feels dead, even though you know he's alive. Speak of the devil,' I said, as the door opened, and James walked in with his famous smile that caused his eyes to squint.

'Hey guys, how are we? What are we talking about?' James asked the empty café, as he dropped himself into the seat next to me and slapped me on the shoulder. 'Geez Luka, you look rough. What's wrong?'

'I asked him how things were going with Nina, and he compared them to you on a Sunday morning,' Michael said, pursing his lips together trying not to laugh at the imagery.

'Mate, surely things can't be that bad. What makes you say that?' James asked, turning his chair to face me with a look of deep concern on his face, as Michael poured him a happy coffee.

'She ignored my calls for the last three days. So, I called her again just before I came here. She answered this time, but everything she said was in an Antarctic cold tone as if I was a telemarketer. I have no idea what I did wrong but clearly, she isn't feeling it like she was,' I lamented, taking a sip of my coffee before tapping the cup looking at Michael to encourage him to put a little more happy in my cup.

'So, nothing stands out to you for even a possibility as to why her attitude has changed towards you?' Michael asked, pouring more bourbon into mine and James' cups.

'I mean, I've been wracking my brain for ages. I can barely think about anything else apart from it and I can't pinpoint anything. Maybe I'm too pushy sometimes? That would be about it,' I said in an exasperated tone, shrugging my shoulders. 'Maybe she just doesn't like me anymore.'

'I'm sure that's not the case, mate. From everything you've said she's super keen on you. Aleks is talking to her best friend so surely he would have said something if she didn't like you anymore. There's another possibility and I hate to ask the question, but I will. Do you think she's met someone else? I know how hard it's been for you being so far away from her, so I'm sure it's just as difficult for her. Maybe it's too hard for her and she broke,' James posed delicately. One of the reasons I loved James was he would always voice the thing that was hardest to say. I loved Michael too, but sometimes he was too worried about hurting my feelings. Sometimes the kindest thing to do is to hurt someone's feelings.

'Sure, it's a possibility. That's probably the one thing that I'm trying not to ask myself, because the thought of her with someone else hurts too much to think about,' I said, feeling a stabbing pain inside me, and taking an extra-large drink from my cup.

'Didn't you say that her last boyfriend cheated on her? I'm sure she wouldn't do that to Luka if she's been through it herself,' Michael said, turning towards James.

'I don't think she would from everything Luka's said about her. I'm not saying she would be cheating on him; I'm just saying maybe there's someone that's caught her eye. There might be someone she has feelings for but wouldn't do anything with because she's still with our boy. Social media shows so much that people don't pay attention to. Maybe she's liking all of a certain guy's photos. Is there a guy commenting on her posts? Do you ever see posts from her with the same guy hanging around? I mean you wouldn't even notice if you weren't looking for it,' James said, leaning forward on his stool.

'To be honest with you I wouldn't want to know if she met another guy. You're right, James, I'm sure there are other guys sniffing around because she is awesome. Maybe the whole distance thing is too much for her. I don't know. I just want to know if she's done with me or not. If she is then just tell me, and if not, then things need to change because I'm not okay with this,' I said, looking down at my cup. I leaned forward against the counter with my hands on my head and rubbed my eyes as James and Michael exchanged looks before turning to me.

'Luka, how long has this been going on for?' Michael asked delicately.

'I told you, three days.'

'No, he means how long has she been acting differently than she was at the beginning,' James asked, sensing I wasn't being completely forthright.

'Four months,' I mumbled.

'Four months!?' Michael and James exclaimed together. I nodded shamefully.

'Look, mate, I love you but that's ridiculous,' James said, shaking his head.

'I just thought if I could ride it out until her birthday then it would be okay when I got to spend some time with her in person,' I replied, unable to make eye-contact with either of them.

'And you're okay being a bitch until then?' James asked, goading me to fire up.

'Come on, James,' Michael whispered.

'No. It's not right. How are you supposed to have a relationship with someone if you're not being honest with them? Stand up for yourself. I don't know what you've done with Luka, but this isn't him,' James said, not breaking eye contact. James watched me silently, unsure how I would respond.

I sat silently, going over in my head what James had just said. 'You're right,' I said, finally breaking the silence. 'I guess I'm just scared is all.'

'I get that, but you can't keep putting yourself through this,' James said, placing his hand on my shoulder.

'So, what are you going to do?' Michael asked carefully.

'I guess there's only really one thing I can do. Ask her.'

'You're right, it's the only thing you can do. You can't keep living in a world wondering where things sit. You two need to work it out because you both deserve that. It'll either bring you closer together, or it'll break you. Either way, you have to know,' James said, patting me on the shoulder and Michael nodded in agreement.

I didn't get any sleep that night. I tossed and turned all night thinking about Nina. All the possibilities about what was wrong were racing through my head and I couldn't find a way to stop them. I couldn't slow them down or relax my mind to give myself some peace to fall asleep. I didn't need the bully to speak; my own voice was already telling me that she was going to leave me.

With each passing hour the pressure on my chest became more intense. The elephant continued to grow until it felt like my chest was about to cave in. I loved those majestic creatures, so I wasn't sure why they were picking me out to cause me distress.

There had to be something wrong, because Nina wasn't being the same person to me that she was when we met. She wasn't firing texts back immediately. She wasn't making time for us to have cyber dates because she was always too busy. I used to get random phone calls from her just because she wanted to hear my voice. The call to tell me about something that happened that day that made her smile, or something that upset her. All of that had stopped. Every call between us came from me, and most of those went unacknowledged.

The clock hit five in the morning, and the same thoughts continued to run on a loop in my head. My cruel mental bully joined my own voice, getting louder and louder. You're not smart enough. You're not interesting enough. You're not kind enough. You're not good looking enough. You are not good enough. I was paralysed by those thoughts and could feel them crushing my will to fight. *'She's found someone else, or she just doesn't like me anymore. Or both,'* I thought, feeling defeated.

I wanted to get up and do something, anything to break the cycle my mind was in, but I was paralysed by the conversation I needed to have. The conversation that could have me lose the woman I was in love with, without ever being able to hold her; without ever being able to kiss her.

I reached for my phone and opened social media. The first thing I saw was her face. Nina was smiling in a selfie posted just fifteen minutes before. We weren't talking, and she was happy. A silent tear ran down my cheek and fell to my pillow. I said out loud in something barely above a whisper. 'Luka, you are a loser.'

I knew I needed to have the talk with Nina, but I wasn't quite ready. I wasn't ready to have her breakup with me yet. My day was spent laying on the couch staring through the screen of different shows on the television. I felt like a zombie, that even though I was physically present, there was nothing behind my eyes. I even felt too tired to overthink and stress. I was completely drained.

My family drifted through the house during the day, but the most communication I could muster was a cursory wave and grunt in their direction. Mum tried to sit down and talk to me about what was bothering me, but I didn't feel ready to talk to her about everything that was happening. I was just biding my time before I could go to bed. For in my sleep, I wouldn't have to feel the pain and impending doom of my fledgling relationship. That's if I was even able to sleep. I hoped that being awake for two days straight would be enough to send me into a dreamless sleep. One devoid of the face that I was so head over heels in love with, but the one that didn't reciprocate those feelings. Finally, I decided that I needed to go to bed and prayed that my brain would take mercy and allow me to sleep.

I shuffled into my room, unable to lift my feet off the ground, desperate for my bed and some peaceful sleep. I sat on my bed and with all my might, lifted my right foot and removed my sock. Tossing it onto the floor, I felt my phone vibrate in my pocket. Being so desperate for sleep, I considered not looking at it, as I doubted I had the energy to even delete the email for the music store newsletter that I was sure the notification was about.

Begrudgingly I opened my phone to rid it of the cluttering email. It wasn't an email though. 'Hey Luka, are you busy? We need to talk.' It was Nina.

The four words that send a shiver down the spine of every person on the planet. We need to talk. *Did she have something specific in mind, or she just thinks we need to talk in general?'* I wondered, staring at the text. Rather than sitting and pondering what Nina wanted, I chose to take the path less travelled for me, the path of discovery rather than crippling overthinking.

'Sounds good. Call me when you're free,' I replied, and almost as soon as I pressed send, Nina was video calling me.

The final reserves of energy my body possessed was a small amount of adrenaline which my adrenal glands released through my body. My body was aware of how critical the conversation would be and kicked into 'fight-or-flight' mode. All signs of weariness dissipated, and my focus was intent on my phone screen.

There was a feeling of impending doom as I watched the phone ring, staring at it and wondering what was waiting for me on the other end. People don't say we need to talk unless it's bad news. Otherwise, she would have said 'I want to talk,' and sent it with a sweet emoji. I pressed answer, ready to face what was coming my way. I felt a steely resolve to finally ask Nina what was wrong. Whether I was ready or not, the time had arrived.

'Hey,' I said, unable to muster anything more than a grimace.

'Hey, are you alright?' Nina asked with a concerned look. She was wearing the hoodie I sent her, and even though it was the same face that I loved, that face didn't look at me with those sparkling eyes like before. Nina looked sad. There were bags under her eyes, and they looked bloodshot. Before she called, I felt numb, but seeing that sadness in her brown eyes with flecks of green, I fell to an even greater depth of despair. The same voice, deep inside me that said the morning I met Nina, that she would be special to me, was telling me what I didn't want to accept. That the end was near.

'I'm okay. I just didn't get much sleep last night,' I said, trying to muster an upbeat tone, but it didn't come. My voice came out monotonous and hurt, I sounded heartsick. I felt like I was imprisoned in the guillotine, waiting for the blade to drop.

'Yeah, me either,' Nina replied. Our conversation for the first time felt awkward and uncomfortable. As if we both had a million things to say, but no one knew how to open the floodgates.

I didn't know how to start because I was scared that if I did say what I was feeling, it would be the thing that caused her to let go of the blade. There was no other way though, the best way was to just ask straight out. 'I know you said that we needed to talk, but I need to ask you something because it's been weighing me down for a while. What's wrong?' I asked, my voice racing at the speed of Usain Bolt breaking the one hundred metre world record in Berlin. The question had been at the tip of my tongue and the tips of my fingers for too long. Before I even received an answer, I felt some of the pressure come off my chest as I had put the question into the universe. I had done the hardest part, I had started.

'What do you mean? Nina asked quietly, her face dropping slightly.

I could feel the frustration prickle inside me at her question; anger on the verge of spilling out. *What do I mean? Please don't act like this is all in my head,* I thought hotly. There was no backing away. I had to say everything on my mind and get some answers.

'Don't do that, Nina,' I whispered in an exasperated tone.

'Don't do what?'

'Do not do that. You know exactly what I mean.' The floodgates were open, and I felt everything that I had wanted to say for the past few months coming out. 'You never call me anymore, and when I call you, most of the time you ignore me. If you do happen to answer, you sound like you'd rather be in the middle of a war zone than on the phone with me. I feel like you couldn't be less interested, like my presence in your life bores you as if I'm an obligation you want to get away from. There are times when I wonder if you even like me as a person at all anymore. And this is all while I'm liking you more and more. So again, what's wrong?' I had to hold my composure to stop my voice from raising to a shout. I didn't care that Aleks could probably hear me in the next room and was texting Andjela about what was happening. I didn't care about anything in that moment aside from getting answers. My hands were shaking; I looked down at my chest to see my heart beating through my shirt. I was scared but determined. I feared her answer, but I needed it. More than I feared her answer, I feared not having an answer. I was tired of living that way.

There was a look of shock on Nina's face, like she had just been slapped. She sat in silence trying to figure out how to respond to the question. 'I don't know. I'm very confused,' Nina whispered, refusing to make eye contact with me.

'Confused? Confused in what way?' The conversation I had been dreading had caused my heart to shift from beating out of my chest to beating in my throat. It was constricting my breathing, yet I knew the only path to peace was to forge ahead. I found my courage to have the conversation I was terrified to tackle. To ask the questions that I had been too scared to ask and finally get some answers. Even if it meant getting my heart broken.

'I've just been having a tough time, and I don't know what to do,' Nina said, finding her voice, but still looking everywhere apart from at me.

'I'm your boyfriend, if you're having a tough time then why don't you talk to me about it?' I asked, still pushing for her to tell me what was really going through her mind. She was holding something back and I needed to know what. 'Can you at least look at me?' I asked, desperate for our eyes to connect, unsure of how many times it would happen again.

'Because I'm having a tough time about you,' Nina said exasperated, finally looking me in the eye. She pulled her hood down to have her plaited hair fall from the hood and over her shoulder, reaching her navel. There was a twinkle in her eye, but it wasn't the radiant one of joy that caused butterflies to dance in my soul. It was the twinkle of a breaking heart, holding back tears from streaking down her porcelain cheeks.

My heart sank. Sure, it could have been that she was busy at school or had something else going on in her life that was pulling her attention away from our relationship, but it wasn't that at all. It was purely about us. While I thought I knew what the answer was going to be, it hurt to finally hear it, my worst fear confirmed.

'In what way?' I asked, swallowing my lips. Even though I didn't want the answer, I needed to hear it.

'You're my boyfriend. You're the best boyfriend I've ever had, but you're there, and I'm here. That doesn't look like it's going to change any time soon. I can't keep doing this. I desperately want to walk down the street with you, holding hands on our way to a dinner date all dressed up,' Nina said, her voice began to quiver and the faucet in her eyes was turned on. The tears streaked down her cheeks like the left and right were racing. Frustration radiated through my body because all I wanted to do was hold her, console her with my body, but I was stuck in Williamstown on my phone. I would have given anything to reach through my screen and hold her, even just for a moment. I was letting her down, and I didn't know what else I could do apart from sit there and listen helplessly; completely powerless.

'I want to text you to hang out, and we just sit in silence wearing lazy clothes cuddled up watching a movie. I want to sneak out in the middle of the night to your house and sleep in your arms. I want to wake up and just lay there watching you sleep, but I can't. I want to kiss you, to hold you, to just look into those eyes, but I can't. And every day since we've met, every damn day I've wanted it more. I crave it. Not like I crave food when I'm hungry. Like I can feel my soul crying for you. I'm crying because I know you're my soulmate. So, the pressure just builds and builds and builds, but there's no release. I just can't put myself through being with someone that I can't truly be with. Even if I know he is my soulmate.' The tears now were flowing more heavily, but Nina made no attempt to wipe them away.

Nina had given up on me. She had given up on us. What I had dreaded hearing, but felt like was coming, had finally arrived. I was lost for words. I didn't know if I should fight for us or just say okay and hang up. *Is there anything I can say to change her mind? Is there something I can do to make it better?'* I thought desperately, searching the deepest recesses of my mind for the magic words that would make it all better.

'How can you say I'm your soulmate but say we can't be together? I just want to make things better. To be like they were.

Obviously, you don't feel as strongly for me as I feel for you, if you're giving up on us. Does this just not mean enough to you if you're not going to fight?' I whispered, feeling my composure slip away.

If she loved me like I loved her, then surely, she would wait for me. *'I can't believe she wants it to end,'* I thought, even my internal voice quivered. I couldn't look at her because I knew if I did, I would break down. I hadn't slept, and I was emotionally on edge before we started talking. Seeing Nina cry was pushing me even closer to the edge. I could feel my grip slipping. Before I wanted to reach through the screen and hug her, that was now a desperate need to lunge through my phone and hold her and never let her go.

'Are you even listening to me? I'm in love with you, you idiot' Nina yelled at me, her twinkling eyes almost popping from her head.

'Did I just hear what I think I heard? Did Nina just say she's in love with me?' I asked myself in disbelief. I was speechless. My mouth was like a goldfish's, just opening and closing with no sound coming out.

'I wake up every day and the first thing I see before I even open my eyes are your eyes. Every day I'm more in love with you than I was the day before, and every day it breaks my heart a little more to be away from you.' I couldn't hold them back anymore; the tears began to fall from my eyes to match her tears. We sat there, staring into each other's tear-filled eyes, neither knowing what to say next. My body felt like it was going to burst. I never knew I had such a capacity to feel so intensely. From the tips of my toes to the ends of my brown hair, I could feel it. To love someone so much and to hurt so deeply. My soul was broken, and everything was pouring out. I was suffocating in my own emotions.

'You're in love with me? You never told me that before. Why didn't you tell me that before now?' I stuttered, finally finding my lost voice.

'Before Andjela went to Melbourne it almost felt like we were an idea. The most beautiful idea ever conceived, but still an idea. That I would meet a man from Australia, and I would fall in love with him. It was like a book. If you date the person that's in your biology class, then that isn't anything extraordinary, because of course you would meet being in the same class. To meet a man from the other side of the world and fall in love, that must be destiny, mustn't it? This is the type of love story they make into a movie, and I was watching it playing in my mind. Then Andjela came back, and I kissed where you kissed, I wore what you wore, and I had your heart on a piece of paper. It wasn't an idea anymore, it felt so real. Seeing you in photos with Andjela, I felt like I was there, that you're a real man that I can touch. I desperately crave the day when we finally touch, but that day is still nowhere in sight, and my heart can't handle it anymore.' Nina's tears had not stopped and neither had mine. I could feel another piece breaking off my heart with every word she said. I couldn't believe it was happening before we got to meet in person. Life just isn't fair.

It was time to either quit or fight back. There would be no other time. I needed to fight or else I didn't deserve her. 'Don't do this, Nina. Don't do it. Don't give up on me. Please don't give up on us. We will see each other soon. I promise. You are my sunshine,' I urged her, trying to stay on the right side of begging. I needed her to see it would be worth the wait; she just needed to fight a little longer. Hold on a little longer.

'I'm sorry, Luka. We can't sit here and waste the best parts of our lives waiting for each other when we can be out meeting other people. To feel love in person with someone that we won't if we're still attached to each other. We'll meet people that can give us what we can't give each other. I'll never have another soulmate, but at least I could have someone with me,' Nina said, finally wiping the tears streaming down her face away with the sleeve of our hoodie. There were no more tears after those, she had cried her final tear for me.

'I don't want to meet anyone else. I don't want to be with anyone else. I only want you,' I frustratedly said, wanting to scream so she would see that I was right. I wanted to grab her shoulders and shake some sense into her. There was no use though. Nina looked resolute. She had made her decision. I mirrored Nina by wiping away my own tears that were making a trail down my cheeks to my chest. Fresh tears traced the previously travelled path, no matter how many times I tried to dry my eyes.

'I'm sorry. I love you, Luka. Goodbye,' Nina said. Before I could say another word, she hung up the phone. I was left standing in the middle of my bedroom, the place we had our first date, missing a sock, with my phone still held in front of my face. The tears hadn't slowed down, they only increased in ferocity, blurring my vision. I didn't know if I would ever see her again. Nina was gone. My heart and soul were broken beyond repair.

CHAPTER THIRTEEN
The Spiral

I pressed the hang up button and watched the tear-stained face of Luka turn to black. My right hand, which was clasping my phone, dropped to my side as I stood there staring into space for what felt like an eternity. I tried to push my brain to have some thought, any coherent thought at all but nothing happened. I felt like I had ripped my heart out of my own chest and stomped on it.

My body was numb from the pain, like I had gone into shock over what just happened. I didn't even know how I did it, to say goodbye to the most beautiful man I had ever known. I thought there would be a release of the pressure that I had felt building in me, a release of all the anxiety I had been experiencing. There wasn't. A bolt of pain shot through my entire body. The numbness had gone. All I felt was pain and a crushing sadness.

I couldn't move my feet; it was like they were nailed to the floorboards. My brain started to tick back to life, and my first thought was to call Luka. To undo it all, because the pain that I felt at not physically being with my boyfriend, was nothing compared to what I felt after the breakup. Like a ripple in the water compared to a tidal wave. If I felt that devastated already then it had to be a mistake. I opened my phone to call him, but I stopped. I couldn't do it. I didn't know what was stopping me, but I couldn't call him back and see those eyes.

Still standing in my room I didn't know where I should go. *Do I go into the living room and surround myself with people? Or do I head to bed, close the blinds and door, blocking out all sunshine? I was his sunshine,'* I thought, groaning with the pain of my broken soul radiating throughout my body. Even the thought of seeing sunshine made me feel sick. I closed the door and climbed into bed, pulling the covers over myself. Still with our hoodie on, I laid there just staring into the darkness, hoping the pain would go away soon.

I wasn't sure how long I laid in bed before Mama came to check on me. There was a clock on my bedside table, but I couldn't see the time. My eyes were open but all they could see was Luka. The way his nose moved up slightly when he smiled, and those eyes. Gosh, I missed those eyes.

The door cracked open letting light into my room for the first time since I imprisoned myself. I saw the outline of a figure in my peripheral vision, blurring my image of Luka. I felt like I was getting stabbed in the chest again watching those eyes fade before me. 'Honey, it's four in the afternoon. Why are you still in bed? Are you sick?' Mama whispered, walking towards me and crouching next to my head.

'No,' I mumbled, as Mama started to gently stroke my hair.

'Well, if you're not sick then what's wrong?' she asked in a soothing tone, trying to coax out of me what was causing me to bunker myself in bed.

'I can't talk about it,' I said, my voice catching like something was stuck in my throat. My mouth wasn't even opening to talk, as if I was a ventriloquist. I wanted to turn over so my back would be facing her, but I didn't want to hurt Mama just because I was in so much pain. It felt perpetual, engulfing me completely with no respite from the crushing pain in sight.

'If you tell me what's wrong then we don't have to talk about it. I just want to know if I can do anything to help with what's bothering you so much,' Mama said, continuing to stroke my hair. It felt both nice and annoying at the same time.

'Okay, but I don't want to talk about it. I'll tell you, then I just want some space to feel how I'm feeling. Okay?' I looked into her kind, loving eyes wishing they would hold the answer to stop the pain. I wondered what it would feel like to see your child in that state. It must be tearing her apart as well, but she wasn't showing it. I couldn't believe the strength of my mama.

'Deal.'

'Luka and I broke up.' My mother hugged me, and I began to sob. Hearing the words aloud took me to a place even lower. The pain inside me pouring from my tear ducts, with no way of stopping them. My tears soaking Mama's blue shirt, but she just held me tighter, kissing me on the forehead.

'I'm so sorry, honey.'

'The distance was too much. I thought I did the right thing but if I did, why does it hurt so much? He's going to find a beautiful Australian girl, have lots of kids, and I'll never get to see him again. I'll never get to talk to him again. The man of my dreams is gone just like that, before I even got to hold his hand,' I whaled, struggling to get my words out between my pained cries. I thought I didn't want to talk about it, but I needed to try. Anything to get the pain to stop. The elephant wasn't sitting on my chest, he was jumping up and down, killing every butterfly that ever fluttered in my soul.

'I know you're hurting now, but with each passing day you will feel a little bit better until you feel back to your normal self. Each day you will think about him a little less and a little less. Then a day will come where you don't think about him at all. I'm sorry it happened, but it will be okay. I promise,' Mama whispered in my ear, continuing to stroke my hair. She kissed me on the forehead, stood up and walked to the door. She turned to look at me and said, 'You know where to find me if you need me.' Mama closed the door gently behind her and left me with my broken heart.

Those words from Mama were supposed to be comforting, but they just hurt me even more. The idea that a day would come where I didn't think about Luka was a nightmare. That a day would come when I thought about him, yet I would have no emotional response at all, because he no longer held a place in my heart was unimaginable. *'Why does he have to be so far away? Life really isn't fair,'* I thought despairingly, clinging to my Luka pillow.

People think that the person that initiates the breakup just skips into the next part of their life, happily moving on. That is a lie. I thought it would be best for both of us to be with someone we could see every day. To have a real relationship. This thought though, that what we had wasn't a real relationship just because of the distance, pained my soul. Nothing had ever felt more real in my entire life. It was hard to believe that choosing heartbreak was the right path forward, but I had to give it a chance. I could not bear the pain of being apart from my soulmate for a moment longer.

I hoped Luka wasn't hurting more than me. Love alone was not enough to have a successful, long-lasting relationship. You need so much more. I needed so much more. The Beatles were wrong.

Mama must have told Jovan and Milica to stay clear of my room for the rest of the day because I could hear them moving around the living room, but no one came in to see me. I didn't eat the entire day and just had a small amount of water that was sitting on my bedside table. I had no interest in eating. Even though I had been in darkness all day, I could feel the spring sun set outside. I fell asleep shortly after, completely exhausted from breaking my own heart.

I dreamt deeply that night. The type of dream that felt so real that when you wake up you feel like it just happened. It was filled with Luka and I together. Images of us walking down the street towards the beach in Williamstown hand in hand, lying next to each other on our towels, running through the water splashing each other. He chased me through the water, catching me and pulled me in close to his body. I could feel his wet skin on mine in the sun. We kissed deeply as I pushed my body more firmly into his to be as close as I could to him, yet it wasn't enough. I craved to be closer.

The image faded and I was left with a lingering momentary feeling of euphoria before the cold, hard reality hit me that I was lying alone in my bed in Požega. The euphoric feeling was replaced by a polar opposite feeling of devastation. As I stared up at the ceiling, I could feel my heart shatter again. How could my heart ever recover from shattering repeatedly?

I picked up my phone and opened the text thread with Luka. He was online. The word online disappeared and was replaced by typing. Devastation was replaced by hope. My heart started to beat so rapidly it felt like it would leave me with bruised ribs. *'What is he texting?'* I wondered. It had only been a day and I missed him so much. A part of me was missing and I couldn't be me until he was part of my existence again. We had only met six months earlier, yet I had forgotten what life was like before Luka. I sat up in bed anticipating his text, but I was left waiting. I continued to stare at my phone, but it never came. Typing returned to online, which in turn became offline. The moment of excited nervous hopefulness was replaced with all-encompassing despair. I laid back down and turned my phone off, throwing it in my bedside drawer and slamming it shut.

'Jovan! Leave her alone!' I heard Mama yell, as my bedroom door opened, and Jovan tiptoed into my room with a big smile on his face.

'Nina, are you awake? Guess what?' Jovan asked in a whisper, as he moved slowly towards my bed, and kissed me on the cheek. He was in his football practice uniform, covered in dirt.

'What?' I sleepily groaned, pulling him down towards me and giving him a big hug. He was like my teddy bear and gave me hugs like no other human could. I didn't care that I was getting covered in dirt, it was just nice to have my baby brother with me.

'I scored three goals at practice and coach is going to let me play striker this week. Are you going to come and watch me? It's our last game of the season,' he said excitedly, still in a hushed voice.

'Of course, I will. I wouldn't dream of missing it,' I replied, kissing him on the cheek and letting him go.

'Great. Please make sure you shower before you come though. You smell,' Jovan said, holding his nose and playfully wafting away the smell before running out of my room. I smiled and smelt myself. I couldn't smell anything, so he was probably right. That small visit from Jovan helped me feel slightly better though. Even if it was just for a moment, he did make me smile.

A few hours later, with the covers pulled over my head, I heard my door open again, but this time it was Milica. At least I think it was a few hours, it could have been days later for all I knew. I had stopped concerning myself with trivial things like time. 'Hey Nina, I have a date soon and I was wondering if you could braid my hair for me?' Milica asked timidly, tentatively walking towards my bed as if I was a rabid animal. I peered over the top of the blankets to see she had on an adorable grass green dress with a matching headband.

I pulled the blanket down to my waist and looked in her direction, then sat up. 'I wouldn't trust Mama with it either. Sit down,' I said, patting the side of the bed. Milica broke into a huge smile and skipped the last couple of steps before sitting down on the edge of my bed. 'So, do you want a French braid or a Dutch braid?' I asked, running my fingers through her hair.

'French, please,' Milica responded, sitting with perfect posture waiting for me to begin. I picked up a comb and ran it through her hair, removing a couple of small knots causing her to squeal, before separating it into three sections, and leaving a curtain of hair below. Her hair was beautifully brown, shiny, and naturally straight, the kind of hair that you see in ads. It was a shade lighter than mine and looked like it glowed when she was out in the sun.

I began intertwining her hair slowly, weaving the hair from the outside, over the top of the middle, adding a small amount of hair from her curtain of hair on each pass.

'So how is it going with Nikola?' I asked, as I continued to therapeutically braid my sisters' hair.

'Pretty good. We're going to get a milkshake and see a movie. He always holds my hand during the movie. It's very sweet even if his hands do get a bit sweaty,' Milica said, as I got to the bottom of her braid.

'You two are adorable. I'm sure I'll see you two together around the pool this summer,' I said, tying the braid together at the bottom. 'There you go. Happy?'

Milica stood up and walked over to the mirror on my cupboard to examine my work. Turning around and looking over her shoulder to see how she looked from behind. She faced me smiling and nodded enthusiastically. 'Thanks, Nina. You're the best,' Milica exclaimed beaming, running to me and giving me a hug. 'I'm really sorry you're not still with Luka. If you need to, you can talk to me.'

'You're welcome. Have a nice time on your date,' I said, forcing a smile to my little sister as she gave me a pained smile in return. I could see she felt sorry for me and asking me to do her hair was her attempt to help me feel better. It did while she was with me, but as soon as she left, the misery at losing the love of my life returned.

I don't know how long I spent in my room without even thinking about leaving. Mama brought in food and water three times a day and took it almost untouched each time. It felt like days passing, and that meant I must have been missing important classes. There was only around a month left in the school year which meant big assignments and exams. My last weeks in high school before going to university. Well, I wouldn't be going to university if I didn't maintain the grades I was achieving throughout the school year, but I couldn't care less. I knew it was important, but it didn't feel important.

I heard muffled voices from the living room that sounded like Mama and Andjela talking. Moments later Andjela came bursting through the door and walked straight to my window tearing open the blinds. A jet of sunlight came streaming through the window, answering my query of whether it was day or night. 'Come on, let's go,' Andjela shouted, opening my closet, and rifling through my clothes.

'Why are you here? Let's go where? And no,' I grumbled, burying my face in my pillow to protect my sensitive eyes from the sun. Andjela pulled out a plain white shirt and a pair of denim shorts, throwing them onto my bed.

'Oh yes you are. You haven't replied to my texts all week, so I had to come. Come on, we're just going for a drink. You need to get out. And before you ask, your mama told me,' Andjela said, holding a hand up to thwart my indignation. 'She had to tell me. You missed a week of school. Tata is a doctor, so your mama got him to write you a medical certificate for the week, but you need to come back to school. Hurry up and shower, this room smells disgusting and I'm quite sure that's your fault,' Andjela said, turning her nose up at the smell as she ripped my blanket off me, and I continued to cling to my Luka pillow.

'Fine. I'll have a shower now and then we can go for a little bit. Then I'm coming right back here. I need to shave my legs if I'm going to wear those shorts though,' I groaned, pushing myself up into a sitting position. Andjela took my phone from my drawer and put it on the charger.

'Whatever you have to do, Sasquatch. Now move your butt,' Andjela demanded, she took a seat at my desk and opened my biology notebook to read my notes. 'I'll be right here waiting.'

Forty-five minutes later after I had thoroughly scrubbed myself, washed my hair, and shaved my legs, Andjela and I left my house and walked to the nearest café. It was a tiny café that only had room for two small tables inside, and two outside. Andjela took a seat at one of the outside tables and I followed her lead sitting across from her. The sun was greeting my skin for the first time in a week, so I made sure I left my sunglasses on to stop the glare. With every fibre of my being, I wanted to be back in bed. I didn't want to have to talk through my heartache with Andjela, who was just starting her romance with Luka's brother.

The café owner approached our table with a big smile and took our order before returning inside to prepare our drinks. Andjela ordered a warm coffee, and I ordered a lemon water. 'Do you want to start or should I?' Andjela asked, placing her sunglasses on the table as she was in the shade. I knew the vitamin D was good for me, but I didn't want to feel better. For breaking my own heart and Luka's, I deserved to be hurting.

'I don't even want to talk so it feels like it should be you,' I replied monotonously, looking up at the clouds slowly drifting across the sky.

'I want to say I'm sorry. I don't think I was supportive enough of your relationship. I underestimated how in love you were with Luka. I've never seen you this miserable before,' Andjela said, trying to get me to look at her, but those clouds were just so interesting. You don't notice them moving unless you sit there and really watch them.

'I'd never truly been in love before,' I said, dragging my attention away from the clouds as the café owner returned with our drinks.

'Are you feeling any better at all?' Andjela asked, as she added sugar to her coffee.

'Somehow, I feel worse. The first day I felt awful, but it didn't feel real. Like I was in an alternate universe or something. Every morning we were together I woke up to a good morning text, so I woke up the next morning to check my phone for his message. Nothing. Then I was waiting for him to send me a meme, or a photo of Monty, or ask me how I am, or a big text saying he wants me back, but nothing. Urgh, I miss him so much,' I groaned, putting my head down on the table.

'Would it have made a difference if he had done any of those things?' Andjela asked, as I raised my head to see her watching me as she stirred her coffee again.

'No. Maybe. I don't know. My brain says I did the right thing but also how could I have done the right thing if I still feel like this? It's been a week and it's not getting better at all. I even told him that I'm in love with him. It was the first time I said it,' I admitted, stirring my lemon water to make sure the lemon was evenly distributed around the glass.

'Wow. What did he say?' Andjela asked, open mouthed in shock.

'Well, he didn't say it back. All he said was 'why didn't you tell me before?' Maybe he didn't care about me as much as I cared about him. As much as I care about him. Obviously, he isn't in love with me like I am with him or else he would have said I love you too,' I said shrugging, and drinking from my glass of lemon water.

'He may not have said it, but I met that man, so trust me when I say this. He loves you, Nina. The look on his face when we were talking about you, it completely lit up. I think that was the first time I've looked at someone's face and been able to see love.'

'Then why didn't he tell me? Why didn't he fight for me instead of letting me get away?' I asked, the anger rising in my voice. 'He barely put up a fight, he didn't even put up an argument or say he's coming to visit me. Nothing. He just gave this meek little 'don't do this,' line,' I said angrily.

'That's not fair. You told him you didn't want to be with him anymore. So, what was he supposed to do? Tell you things to convince you to stay? He knows you well enough that you didn't just come to this decision on a whim. You thought about it for a long time. In his mind, trying to hold you down to be in a relationship you didn't want to be in wasn't right. If you wanted to go, then he would let you go. I get that you're hurting, but you're not angry at him, you're angry at yourself. Lashing out at Luka won't make you feel better.' Andjela's impassioned voice shot right through my chest and her glare bore directly into my soul. She seemed genuinely angry at me for saying that. I knew I was wrong; I was just upset.

'You're right,' I whispered, looking down at my hands in shame. 'I wasn't strong enough to last. I just wish it wasn't like this. When you told me about the site you said you never gave out your information to people because you didn't want to be in a long-distance relationship, but you're basically in one now. Why did you change your mind?' If I could understand how she changed her mind, then maybe I could get some perspective as to whether I could make it work with Luka in the future.

'I don't know what to say. I'm obsessed with Aleks. We video chat every day, even if it's just for a minute. I'm going to be in Melbourne in a few weeks for Fed Cup, so I'll see him then. I'm going to stay at their house for a couple of weeks after the tie. I know in the future I'll be travelling for tennis a lot and he'll be away from home for basketball. I just realised I'd rather spend less time with him, than more time with someone else. Quality over quantity,' Andjela said, taking a large mouthful of coffee, then placing her cup down.

'You're going to stay with their family!? This is huge! Why didn't you tell me?' I asked, grateful to have something to feel good about.

'I did. You just didn't look at your phone,' Andjela said with a smirk. 'I saw Luka the other day.'

'You saw Luka? How was he? Did he say anything about me?' I asked in an attempted casual tone, stirring my water but shifting my body weight nervously.

'Yeah, he looked okay. It was just a quick hello and then he left to go somewhere.'

He looked okay? Is he over our breakup already?' I wondered sadly. Images of Luka looking happy with another woman floated through my mind, looking like he had completely forgotten who I was. I placed a hand on my stomach to try and dull the sharp pain that shot through me. *'It's all my fault,'* I thought, trying to maintain my composure, but I could feel it slipping.

We sat in silence for a few minutes while we finished our drinks before I broke the silence. I couldn't handle talking about Luka anymore, I needed to change the subject. I had said everything that my soul could handle on that subject for the day. Just showering and leaving the house felt like a major win. 'So, how's school been?'

'Starting to get a bit intense with everything that's going on. You'll have plenty to catch up on, so you better get that butt into gear today. I collected what you needed to do each day and dropped it off to your house, so your mama has everything.'

'At least I'll have plenty to distract myself with,' I said, standing up and pushing my chair back in to the table. 'I'll start on it when I get home. Thanks for bringing my work home and dragging me out. I love you.' I stepped forward and embraced Andjela. Andjela stayed in our hug, waiting for me to be the one to break it.

'I love you too. You should be twice as grateful to me. Marko tried to get your work from biology to bring it to you, but I told the professor I had other work to bring over, so he gave it to me,' Andjela said, shaking her head at the audacity of Marko. We put our money on the table and began the walk home.

Over the next few days, I managed to get to school and back on track with my studies. Andjela was at my house every morning to wake me up because I wanted nothing more than to return to my dreams where Luka and I were together. If it wasn't for Andjela, I may have thrown away everything I had worked so hard for through my entire school life. The hurt hadn't gone away, but the realisation that I couldn't let it ruin my future had set in.

Saturday arrived, and even though I had a mountain of study to do, I told Jovan I would be there for his game, so I wasn't going miss it. It was the only thing I was looking forward to. It was still morning, but I could feel that a warm day was waiting for us, there was a real bite in the sun already. I walked to the pitch five minutes before kick-off and began to look for my family. Mama and Milica brought Jovan to the pitch an hour earlier so he could warm-up with his teammates.

'Oh Nina, I just called you to see how far away you were,' Mama said sounding stressed, walking up to me and kissing me on the cheek. 'The game is about to start, and Jovan was getting nervous that you wouldn't make it in time.'

I looked onto the pitch and saw Jovan taking his position. He looked adorable in his little uniform. Royal blue shirt, shorts, and socks, with his fluorescent orange boots. He had let his hair grow so he could style it, his hair in a perfect part on the left side of his head with just the right amount of gel. He had the flair to be a striker, I just hoped he scored a goal.

As the game began, Jovan was looking around the crowd full of families watching, trying to find me instead of paying attention to the ball that was three metres away from him. His coach was screaming to get his attention. 'Jovan, the ball!'

Finally, he found me and gave me a big wave which I returned, trying to stop myself from laughing. I had to turn away before bursting into laughter at my baby brother jubilantly waving at me while the football game happened around him. *'He is too cute to be real,'* I thought, trying to regain my composure before turning back to watch the game. The innocence of all those kids running around playing made my heart smile. It was the first time I had felt that inside me since Luka and I broke up.

There were four pitches in the precinct with all different ages playing. As the second half of Jovan's game began, I looked towards the pitch behind where Jovan was playing. The under-twenty team had started, and I could see several of my classmates on the field, including Marko. I pulled my attention quickly back to Jovan, wanting to keep my mind joyful.

He had improved significantly since we played our family game. Paying attention to where his teammates were and how to move through the pitch. He didn't just look at the goals as soon as he got the ball, he calculated the best path to goal, whether that be for himself or his teammate. He was playing well and doing it with a smile which made me feel present and happy.

Halfway through the second half Jovan timed a run perfectly and his teammate passed him the ball to put him one-on-one with the goalkeeper. Mama, Milica, and I were jumping up and down screaming. 'Go Jovan! Go!' The goalkeeper had his feet nailed to the goal line when a boy from the opposition brought

Jovan down from behind to give Jovan's team a penalty and earn himself a red card.

'He's never scored a goal in a match before. Do you think they'll let him take the penalty?' Mama asked, looking towards me. I shrugged my shoulders, like Mama, I was hopeful the coach would let him take it. After all, he was the one that got fouled.

The referee placed the ball down on the penalty spot with Jovan there ready to take the kick, when one of his teammates walked over and pointed to himself. *Is this kid really going to take my brother's penalty off him?'* I thought furiously, as if I had just seen someone steal his sandwich. I felt like running onto the pitch and pushing the kid over. The last time I was that upset at a child was when Jovan took my school notebook and drew pictures in it.

Jovan shook his head to say no and both boys looked over to the coach. The coach screamed loud enough for those on the furthest pitch to hear. 'Jovan!' The other boy walked away disappointed, and I smiled as my brother stepped back from the ball to prepare for his shot. Mama took hold of both Milica and I as the referee blew his whistle. Jovan stared intently at the ball in front of him like he was trying to solve a math problem. He turned his gaze up to face the goalkeeper who was shifting his weigh right to left. The goalkeeper seemed to be shifting his weight harder to his left though. *'He's diving left, kick to your left, Jovan,'* I implored him telepathically. He slowly began his approach. I held my breath, praying that he had noticed the goalkeeper's movement and kick hard left. The goalkeeper dived to his left but had guessed the wrong way. Jovan had powered the ball into the open goal, causing the net to bulge. He ran to the corner screaming, tearing his top off and swinging it around his head in celebration as his team chased him jubilantly. Jumping all over him, there was now a pile of children on the ground next to the corner flag. They were in the lead one-nil. Mama was screaming at the top of her lungs hugging both Milica and me. We wanted to cheer, but our airways had been cut off.

Twenty minutes later the referee blew his whistle to end the game with Jovan's goal being the difference. All his teammates came and congratulated him for the goal, and his coach gave him a huge hug with a smile spread from ear to ear. Jovan came rushing over to us after shaking hands with the dejected looking opposition. 'Well done, Jovan. That was amazing. You were super. I'm so proud of you,' Mama said, dragging him in for a rib breaking hug.

'You were amazing,' I said, pulling him away from Mama and giving him my own bear hug, feeling his back crack.

If his smile was any bigger you would have been able to see it from behind him. 'Best on pitch,' Milica shouted, taking her turn to hug him. We all had his sweat on us.

'Thanks. Is it okay if I go with my team to get pizza now? Everyone is going,' Jovan said, looking hopefully up at Mama.

'Of course. Here's some money. Have a good time,' Mama said, pulling some money from her purse and handing it to him. He turned and sprinted towards the rest of his team standing on the pitch. 'You two ready to go?' Milica responded with a nod to Mama.

Getting out and watching Jovan play had put me in a great mood. I was not ready to go home yet though. I was scared to go home and be alone with my thoughts, even if my head was going to be buried in a book. 'Some friends are playing just over there, so I think I'll go and watch the end of the game before coming home,' I said to Mama. She kissed me on the cheek and walked towards home with Milica.

I walked to the pitch behind where Jovan played and stood by the fence. *I'm going to watch my classmates,'* I told myself, even though I knew exactly who I was watching. Marko had let his hair grow the past few months. His mane of brown hair was falling in his eyes as he ran around the pitch shouting instructions towards teammates from defence. He was having to run his hands through his hair to clear it from his face.

I stood watching the rest of the game. It ended with a three-two win to Požega. The team huddled in the centre of the pitch and as Marko was walking towards the rest of his team, he took his shirt off. He was very lean and muscular with his sweaty eight-pack glistening in the sun. His body looked like it had been edited for a magazine. I was trying not to stare but it was impossible not to, I just hoped he didn't notice. Staring open mouthed at him while he talked to the rest of the team, he looked in my direction. Busted. I was embarrassed he caught me staring and could feel the heat rising in my face. I looked down and smiled at my feet. I was hoping to watch and escape unnoticed, I guess I could scratch secret agent from my list of potential careers. *'I need to get out of here. Now,'* I thought, a panicked voice ringing in my ear.

Turning to walk away, I headed toward the exit. 'Nina. Nina!' I heard a familiar voice shout from behind me. I couldn't ignore it and run away; I had to turn around. I turned and saw Marko running towards me smiling broadly with his shirt tucked into his shorts. His pecs bounced each time his foot struck the ground.

'Suck on your cheeks, Nina. Don't let your jaw drop. He's just your friend remember. Your enormous, glistening friend...' My thoughts were getting away from me, and I needed to escape.

'Hey, where are you going so quickly?' Marko panted, standing in front of me, sweat dripping from his chiselled physique.

'How was it possible for an eighteen-year-old to have that body?' I wondered, trying to maintain eye contact.

'Heading home to study. Why?' I said in the coldest voice I could muster, feeling my focus on his eyes waning. It felt like my right eye was on his face and my left eye refused to come off his body.

'I just found it interesting that you came to watch me play after your brother's game finished is all,' he said, his smile turning into a smirk as he ran that large right hand through his hair.

'I didn't come to watch you. There are a bunch of people playing from school. I just wasn't ready to go home, and study is all.'

'So, you're not going to hang out for a bit?' Marko asked, taking a small step forward.

'I have a lot of study to catch up on. I was unwell so I missed a lot of classes,' I replied, taking an equally small step back. My right eye betrayed me and joined my left eye to look upon his body. He must have noticed because he bit his lip to stop his face from breaking into a smile. I snapped myself out of it and demanded both eyes return to his face.

'I'm sorry you weren't feeling good. I will admit, I did wonder why you didn't reply to any texts. I was going to ask if you wanted to get something to eat once I'm done here, but that's cool if you're busy.'

'Yeah, my phone was off. Sorry, I have too much to do now.' Marko looked at the ground a little disappointed. I hated disappointing people. He nodded in acceptance and turned to walk away. 'Maybe tomorrow night?' I blurted out, and he spun back around. Marko beamed. 'I'm not promising, but if I finish my work early enough, we can go and get a burger if you want.'

'That would be great,' he said excitedly, his smile spreading wider across his face. 'My treat.'

'No. This isn't a date, so I'll pay for myself, thanks. I need to go home, but I'll text you tomorrow and let you know either way.'

'Perfect,' Marko said softly. He took one large step, then kissed me softly on the cheek before turning and running back to his team. I raised my hand to wipe the sweat from my face, only for my hand to stop as I touched the spot Marko kissed. I stood with my hand on my cheek as I watched him run back to his team, wondering if going to dinner with him would be a good idea or not. Even if he was just a friend.

I wanted no distractions over the weekend, so I turned my phone off and put it in my bedside drawer. No social media, no friends, no internet, and hopefully no thoughts of Luka. Well at least the odd Luka free hour, or minute. I made sure to tell Andjela that my phone was off and if she needed me to text Mama. I locked myself in my room once again, this time to focus on schoolwork and not cocooning myself in blankets because I had let the love of my life go.

It's remarkable how much you can get done when you're not looking at your phone every thirty seconds because you're so addicted to it that you pick it up out of habit. Closing an app, then reopening it twelve seconds later for no reason at all. No, I wasn't missing out by not checking my phone, I was missing out by checking my phone.

On a piece of paper that I stuck to the wall in front of my desk, I made a list of things that I needed to finish by the end of the weekend. One by one I ticked them off. Ranging from revising content from earlier in the school year, to completing projects that I missed submitting while I was lying in bed heartsick. I couldn't believe how lucky I was to have Andjela watching my back.

Sunday evening arrived, and I had ticked off the last thing on my weekend study list. It was an essay about microclimates and how they affect fruit and vegetable production. I printed the essay and put it in my school bag to submit in class the next morning.

I had been cooped up in my room since returning from Jovan's game and felt like I needed to get out. Taking my phone from my drawer, I turned it on and as I did, it felt like it was exploding in my hand. Multiple notifications came at once, but I had no interest in sifting through them all. Dialling Andjela's number, I paced around my room waiting for her to pick up. 'Hey, what's up?' Andjela said in an exasperated tone.

'You sound stressed. What's wrong?' I asked, continuing to pace around my room.

'There's just so much work to do and I'm missing out on tennis training. I just want to get out and train, but I promised Mama and Tata that I would finish school. There's so much to do, and I have Fed Cup coming up in Melbourne soon too. It's all just too much,' she said, speaking at a speed that rivalled a horse racing commentator.

'First of all, just take a few deep breaths and relax. I won't let you quit like you wouldn't let me throw it all away. Do you want to me to come around and help you?' I asked, trying to balance myself on the line in the carpet.

'I think I'll be okay, but thanks for offering. I just need to focus,' Andjela exhaled. She sounded like she just needed to vent.

'Well, if you need me, I'm here. When do you go to Australia?'

'The day after the last exam. I had to get them to condense my exam timetable so I could go. I know you didn't call to hear me complain though. What's up?' Andjela's voice was slowing down to her normal cadence.

'I was just calling to see if you wanted to hang out for a couple of hours. Go and get some dinner together, but you have too much on your plate,' I said, trying to cover the disappointment in my voice.

'I'm sorry. I really want to but I'm going to be up until two trying to get all this done. Can we do something after class tomorrow?'

'I'd love that. I'll let you get back to kicking that schoolwork's butt.'

'I think it's kicking my butt. Thanks for always being here for me. I'll see you tomorrow,' Andjela said, and the phone went dead before I could reply.

Continuing to trace the same path around my room, I tapped my phone to my hand and looked at the ceiling trying to think of someone I actually wanted to see. That list was short at the best of times, but even shorter after the events of last week. I told Marko if I finished my work we could hang out. The question was, was it a good idea?

Marko hadn't texted me since I saw him after his game which was strange. I thought he would have been on me to hang out, but nothing. *What's the worst that could happen?* I thought.

'Hey, I've finished all my work. Still up for getting that burger?' I texted Marko. I continued to pace around my room to work off some of my built-up energy until Marko responded.

After a couple of minutes, I received a reply. 'Sounds great. Meet me at the place on Kralja Petra in twenty minutes.'

I didn't want him to think for one second that it was a date so I thought it would be best to dress down as much as possible. The night was cool, so a hoodie and tracksuit pants were the perfect combination. I absentmindedly grabbed the first thing I saw, throwing on the grey hoodie lying on my bed and put on a pair of navy tracksuit pants. Putting my hair into a casual low ponytail, I headed for the door.

'I'm heading out to meet a friend for dinner. Is that okay?' I asked Mama, sticking my head into the living room.

'Have a good time,' Mama said, lifting her head from the schoolwork she was helping Jovan with.

'Nina! Don't go. Save me!' Jovan implored me, reaching his hand out towards me.

'Sorry, you have to do it. Bye.' I waved to them and withdrew my head from the living room.

Standing next to the door while putting my shoes on, I saw myself in the mirror. Without even realising, I had put on Luka's hoodie. Our hoodie. It felt like my heart had stopped. Even though I had worn it a lot and Luka's scent had been washed from it, I could still smell him in my memories. I couldn't wear it out and not think about him. I needed to change. Jogging back down the hall to my room and pulling off the hoodie as I went, I opened my closet and hid it at the bottom. I snatched my yellow hoodie off its hangar, dragged it over my head, and walked back to the door collecting my keys and wallet as I walked into the spring evening.

As I approached the restaurant, I started to feel disappointed in myself. I felt dirty. Even though I was crystal clear with Marko and myself that it wasn't a date, I felt like I was cheating on Luka. *How can I feel like I'm cheating on him when it isn't a date, and I'm single now?* I wondered, confused at my feelings.

With each step closer to the restaurant, I felt worse and worse. I wondered how Luka would feel if he knew I was going to dinner with a guy so soon after breaking up? And not just any guy; Marko. He would probably say go and do what makes you happy, and that he hopes I have a good time even though it would be killing him inside. I hated myself for doing it. Even though Luka had no idea, I felt like I was hurting him. *Am I bad person for doing this?* I wondered.

I was standing at the door of the restaurant and could see Marko sitting at a table waiting for me. My legs had gone dead. I couldn't move them forwards or backwards. They had carried me from my bedroom to the door of the restaurant, but it felt like they couldn't carry me those final steps through the door and to the table.

My legs finally coming to life, I turned from the restaurant and started to walk back the way I came before my phone started vibrating in my pocket. Stopping to see who was calling, I saw it was Marko. 'Hey,' I said trying to sound as casual as possible. I could hear my heart beating. I could feel the sweat running down my sides. Once again there I was, completely confused about how I was feeling and had no idea what to do. I knew whatever I did was going to hurt someone.

'Is everything okay? I've been waiting a while so just wanted to check that you're still coming,' Marko said, and I could hear a tone of nervousness in his voice. He almost sounded scared that I was standing him up. All the self-confidence from the football pitch gone. I didn't respond for a moment, turning to look back towards the restaurant and even in that moment, I wasn't sure what I was going to do. What was the right thing to do? I either hurt Marko who was sitting there waiting for me, or feel like I was hurting Luka, even though he couldn't possibly know what I was doing. I was tired of hurting people.

'Okay, come on Nina. You're going to go and have a nice conversation with a friend and have dinner. You can do that,' I told myself.

'Sorry, Marko. I'm just running late. I'm walking to the door now. I'll see you in one minute.'

'Awesome. See you in a minute,' his voice perked up and the quiver disappeared.

I walked through the door and Marko bounced up immediately to greet me with a beaming smile. He gave me a big, strong hug so I could feel his abs against my body. Wrapping my arms around his large torso, I felt how firm his lats were and couldn't help but think of the image of him running towards me yesterday with that sweaty, glistening body. We separated and took a seat beside each other. He wore blue jeans, a white hoodie, and a black down vest. He was smiling at me but there was something missing from it. I couldn't quite put my finger on what though.

'I was worried you weren't going to come,' Marko said.

'It seemed silly for him to be nervous for dinner with a friend,' I thought hypocritically, as I began picking at my fingers. Maybe my resting bitch face had him feeling a little edgy. I tried to soften it and smile at him, hoping it came across as a genuine smile.

'Sorry for worrying you. I was just running a bit late. You know what girls are like when they go out. Making sure that their clothes and makeup are just right. This is a process; it doesn't just happen,' I said sarcastically, gesturing down at my hoodie and tracksuit pants.

'You do look amazing,' Marko said, tilting his head slightly, running his hand through his hair and giving me a half smile.

'Okay, that was really cute. It's super attractive when he runs his hand through his hair like that,' I thought. He knew what he was doing, that wasn't an accident.

'Yes, who doesn't love the, "I just woke up and I'm going to lay on the couch all day eating chips" look?' I said, pretending to brush crumbs from my hoodie.

'You would be stunning in whatever you wore.' That coy smile returned to his face causing me to start picking my fingers again.

'Stop it. I said this isn't a date and it isn't, so stop with the flirting. Understand?' I brandished an admonishing finger at him, unable to keep a straight face.

'Who's flirting? I'm just being honest with you. I know it's not a date which you made perfectly clear yesterday. You better not have forgotten your money or else you'll be left to try and talk your way out of your half of the bill,' Marko said laughing.

'Yeah, I'm sure you would let me suffer like that.' I was starting to relax, laugh, and have a good time with Marko. All the guilt and anguish I was feeling before I walked through the door was gone. My heart rate was at a healthy level and the sweat beads I could feel racing each other to the waistband of my pants had finally stopped. My hands, which remained hidden under the table, had stopped picking at the tips of my fingers.

The waitress came over to take our order. My appetite had returned so I ordered a chicken and bacon burger with fries, while Marko ordered a barbeque cheeseburger also with fries. It didn't take long before our meals were in front of us, and we were diving into our food.

'So, you're feeling better? Did you have the flu or something?' Marko asked, taking a large bite from his burger. He ate his chips in between mouthfuls of burger. He took large bites, but his mouth remained closed, and I couldn't hear him chew. He had even placed a serviette on his lap.

'It's not a date. It's not a date,' I reminded myself repeatedly. 'Not really. I wasn't sick. I broke up with my boyfriend, so I was having a hard time with that. I just needed some time to process that away from everyone. I didn't care about anything else for a week. It just didn't feel important.' I wasn't sure why I was being so candid with him, the words just seemed to spill from my mouth even though I didn't want them to. 'I just realised I couldn't lay in bed miserable for the rest of my life. That the world keeps moving and the best way to feel better is to get myself back into normal life. Well, that's what Andjela told me anyway.'

'I'm sorry to hear that. If you don't mind me asking, why did you break up?' Marko asked, finishing the last of his burger. He may have said he was sorry for my news but the look on his face said he felt anything but sad for me being single again. There was a sparkle in his eye when he said it.

'That's what was missing from his smile,' I thought. 'Distance. I didn't want to, but the path to a future with him was too murky. Too many maybes. Yes, we could visit each other and that would be okay for a while but then what? Would he move here? Would I move there? Would neither of us want to move? By that time, we could've wasted five years of our lives when we could've been developing other relationships. It just sucks. I wish I lived there. All this would be so much easier,' I said, putting my hands to my face and rubbing my weary eyes, before placing my hands back on the table.

Suddenly I felt exhausted, like it was going to be hard for me to walk home. Maybe it was all the study and the emotion of the last couple of weeks catching up with me. Whatever it was, my body was running on fumes. I just wanted to crawl into bed with my cuddle pillow.

'I'm sorry you've had to go through that. Whether you're the one to call things off or on the receiving end, it still hurts. You may wish you lived there but I'm glad you're here,' Marko said softly, extending his hand and placing it on mine. He wrapped his large and strong hand around mine. His touch was friendly and inviting. I hated when people touched me, but that felt nice. His touch felt warm, and I was glad he was holding my hand. I turned my hand, so my palm faced upwards and grasped his hand back. I looked up and met his gaze. We smiled at each other and for a moment, I felt scared. My breathing stopped and an anticipation built inside me. In the silence I felt like he was going to lean in and try to kiss me. I found myself wanting it, wishing he would lean in and go for it. That sick feeling in my stomach like I was cheating returned with a vengeance, tying my insides in knots. *'I can't do it. Not so soon,'* I thought, angry at myself for wanting that kiss.

He didn't lean in though. He stayed where he was and then withdrew his hand to finish the rest of his fries. My breathing eased as the moment passed. I felt conflicted about that moment. Both excited and disloyal. The boy that every girl in school apart from Andjela wanted, looked like he wanted me, yet the end of my relationship felt so raw. While I wanted to kiss him, I shouldn't have wanted it. If I felt like I was cheating on Luka by turning up, I was fearful of how my mind would react if I kissed Marko.

I finished my meal and we each paid for our food. We walked to the door, and Marko opened it for me, allowing me to pass through first. That was another tick for him proving he was a gentleman, and that he had changed since his birthday party.

I stopped just outside the restaurant and turned around to find him closing the door. Marko stopped a metre away from me and smiled. 'I had a really nice time with you, Nina.'

'Yeah, me too. Thanks for suggesting it. I definitely needed to get out and it was nice spending some time with you outside of school,' I said, making sure to break eye contact every few seconds to not create another moment like when he held my hand.

'Do you want me to walk you home?' Marko asked, slipping his hands into the pockets of his vest.

'No, thank you. It's sweet of you to offer but I'll be okay. I enjoy walking on my own. It's good to use the time to think.'

'What do you need to think about?' Marko asked, curiously furrowing his brow.

'Everything. Goodnight, Marko.'

'Goodnight, Nina.' I turned and walked home in the cool evening thinking about school, Luka, and Marko.

CHAPTER FOURTEEN
The Do I Or Don't I?

There was a crushing, hopeless despair inside me that I had never felt before. A sadness so deep that I didn't know if it would ever leave me. I remembered something Dr Martin Luther King Jr said about accepting that disappointment will come, but you should never surrender hope. In that moment though, I was completely and utterly hopeless. To be fair, I thought Nina would never leave me – and she managed to dump me, so maybe hopelessness could abandon me too.

Nina had occupied my mind constantly since the November morning she first appeared to me on my dad's computer screen. If there was a waking hour that passed without her sweet smile floating through my thoughts since our meeting, I couldn't recall it. Even though it had only been about six months of my life, it felt bigger than just a normal relationship – it felt like *the* relationship. Our connection would continue to grow and be a cornerstone in each other's lives forever. That Nina would be my wife, and we would have a family together. Instead, my heart felt shattered. The worst part? I didn't know if I would ever see her or talk to her again. I had lost my best friend.

I climbed into bed physically and emotionally exhausted. My brain had been whirling at a million km/hr for days and needed about a month's rest, but that wouldn't be happening. The clock had ticked past ten and I had to be up in a couple of hours for work.

'Luka. Come on. Time to get up,' Dad said, as the light blasted through my eye lids. It felt like the moment my head hit the pillow I was being woken for work. Before I could open my eyes and bring them into focus, Dad had already walked from my room. I turned my head to look at the time and the clock read twelve-seventeen-am. I grudgingly pulled myself up and stared at the wall for a moment while I felt my brain turn itself on, even if it was only at half power.

Within ten minutes I had brushed my teeth, dressed, and sat myself in the front seat of Dad's car as we headed towards the Melbourne fruit and vegetable wholesale market. I'm the fourth generation in my family to work in the market, and it sometimes felt like I was destined to take over the family business, no matter how badly I wanted to be a musician. Things don't always work the way you plan them, just look at what happened a few hours earlier with Nina.

'I hope you got some rest, mate, it's going to be a busy night,' Dad said, as the radio host talked about the dysfunction of the Melbourne Demons forward line.

'…there just seems to be a lack of connection between the midfield and the forwards,' the radio host said.

'It mustn't be that hard to be a radio footy analyst. I could've come up with something that in depth. Tell me how they fix it, idiot!' Dad yelled, looking at the radio while giving his feedback as if his voice travelled directly to the headset the radio host was wearing.

'Hmm,' I grunted, just to acknowledge that I heard him. In a weird way, going to work was good for me because it would keep my mind busy. Otherwise, I would have woken at four-am, unable to sleep the rest of the night, unable to stop thinking about Nina.

'When do you next have uni?' Dad asked, trying to force any kind of conversation to stop himself yelling at the radio again.

'Today. I pretty much have to go as soon as I get home from work. Just enough time to grab my bag and have a shower.' I was staring out the window and the city appeared lit up ahead of us as we approached the market.

'Geez, mate. Maybe you shouldn't go today. You won't be able to concentrate after being at work all night,' Dad said concerned.

'It's just a few classes in the morning. I'll be home by lunchtime.' I knew Dad could tell something was wrong. If it was Mum in the car, she would be asking me what was wrong and trying to force me to tell her what was bothering me. Dad's approach was that we would talk generally, and if I felt like telling him then he was there to listen. I needed that approach because I didn't want to tell anyone yet. I wasn't ready.

Walking into the market there were forklifts with pallets of stock and motorised scooters flying all over the place. Trucks driving in the gates to deliver fruit and vegetables from all around Australia. There was a distinctive smell of a mixture of every one of those fruits and vegetables combined to create a brand-new scent. Somehow it was the same smell as my brother's bedroom. Winter was quickly approaching so I had on a shirt, hoodie, and jacket, praying that would be enough to stave off hypothermia.

'Morning,' said every person that walked by Dad and me, as we returned in kind and walked into his store. Artfully they always dropped the 'Good' at the beginning because how could it be a good morning going to work at that unholy hour? Several of the staff were already there, including my uncles, Dad's brothers, who were the other salesmen, as Dad put down his things and placed his orders for the morning on the wall. Huge pallets of strawberries, avocados, blueberries, passionfruit, lemons, limes, and other fresh fruits sat in stainless steel racking around the store. We weren't late, but the market was already in full flow.

'Here Luka, start this one. Make sure you use a plain pallet. I've been trying to get pallets off this guy for six months. Pick out the worst one you can find,' Dad said, handing me a delivery slip. I stacked twenty trays of strawberries and five trays of blueberries onto the most broken, dilapidated pallet I could find. I wrapped it in an industrial plastic wrap, then forced the pallet jack under the broken planks, before dragging it to the back of the store. That was where the forklift driver would pick it up and deliver it to the customer's warehouse or parking bay.

I spent the next seven hours putting together different orders. Always focusing tremendously hard on the ticket and what was in front of my eyes to try and avoid any thought of Nina, or her perfect flowing brown hair, the way her eyes twinkled when she smiled, or how when you really get her laughing her body started to flop around like a fish on land. No, I wouldn't think about any of that because I had the delivery slip to focus on.

The morning was full of people yelling at each other. Customers and Dad negotiating over price, or guys on the sales floor trying to work out where things were. 'Hey Luka, who is the pallet of avocados for out the back?' the grizzly looking forklift driver asked, as he walked inside the store. He was hunched over and dragging his feet, unable to clear them off the ground so the toes of his shoes were completely worn through. The dishevelled look of his beard matched his shoes and clothes that looked like they hadn't been washed for three weeks.

'Umm, I think it's for Fruit Haven,' I responded, trying to think. I was almost positive it was, but being asked the question had me doubting it.

'I saw you take it out the back so you should know. If you put something out the bloody back, then you bloody better know who it's for and put a bloody label on it. Is it really that hard!?' he yelled in a scratchy voice that sounded like he smoked a packet of cigarettes a day for the last thirty years.

'Hey! Dad asked me to take it out the back and that was all. I think it's for Fruit Haven, but I'm not sure. If you have a problem, then take it up with the boss instead of going off at me!' I snapped back at him. With my lack of sleep, it was not the time to be talking to me like that. Oh, and losing the love of my life hadn't helped my mood either.

He grumbled inaudibly shuffling past me and asked Dad the same question, but in a much more pleasant tone. I guess that was the difference in respect for the man that paid him, and the guy that turned up twice a week to pack orders.

It was close to seven by the time the sun showed any genuine sign of life. After another ninety minutes of packing orders and cleaning up the store, work on the sales floor was finished. I followed Dad and my uncles as they left the store and headed upstairs to the office.

'Good morning,' I said, forcing a smile to the office manager as she greeted me with a wave. I was running on fumes, and even though my university classes weren't demanding, the prospect of doing anything but sitting was excruciating. I dropped myself into the chair at what I had claimed as my desk, the only vacant one in the middle of the office and pulled out my phone to check the time. I was greeted by Nina's beautiful face as my wallpaper. A stabbing sensation hit me in the chest, but I didn't have the heart to change it yet. If I changed it, then it would really feel like it was over.

'I'm going to order from the café. Would you like something for breakfast, Luka?' the office manager Linda asked, as she held a pen hovering above a notepad in anticipation for what I had to say. Linda was nudging sixty, wore jeans and a floral shirt. Her grey hair was parted in the centre and fell to her shoulders. Linda's glasses sat on the end of her nose as she peered over the top of them with her grey eyes, waiting for me to make a decision.

'Can I get a chicken and avocado wrap please?' I asked. My appetite was almost zero, but I needed to force myself to eat something to keep me going for a little bit longer.

Thirty minutes later I walked through the front door of home and headed straight for the bathroom. I quickly showered to wash the market off me, brushed my teeth, and grabbed my bag before heading back out the door to uni. The semester was nearing the end and exams were fast approaching.

I walked into the lecture theatre that had a capacity of seven hundred, finding myself a seat in the back corner. I sat down and every fibre of my being was screaming the same question, 'why are you here!?' I was so tired that I was purely running on adrenaline. The energy the wrap gave me ran out about three minutes after I finished it. I didn't want to disappoint Mum by not finishing school, so I pulled out my notebook and placed it on the desk in front of me, lying to myself that I was going to take notes.

Students slowly made their way into the theatre and took their seats before the lecturer began. I was there in body but mentally I was a million kilometres away. My mind was only thinking about Nina. I tried to think about elephants, or the plight of the snow leopard to distract myself as the lecture had no interest to me. Those thoughts gained no traction in my mind. A creature rarer than those had centre stage.

As the lecturer began his spiel about how to prepare an exercise program for hypertrophy, I opened my phone and entered my conversation thread with Nina. I scrolled back to the first text and read through as much of our conversation as I could in the forty-five-minute lecture. Not taking in one word that the lecturer was babbling about, my mind was transported back to the time of those texts. I remembered where I was when they were sent, how I felt when Nina texted me, knowing that the most beautiful soul I had ever met was thinking about me.

A kaleidoscope of butterflies danced in my soul, making me feel momentarily jubilant.

A mixture of joy, love, and a stab of heartache coursed through my body as I read them, remembering how happy I was. Even though I was still head over heels in love with her, that barring a miracle, I wouldn't ever get to meet Nina. To kiss her. To hold her. Our eyes would never truly meet.

When I finally looked up, I saw I was the only person left in the lecture theatre. I stood up and made my way to my next class. All I wanted to do was talk to her. I wanted to know how she was feeling, and what she did that day.

I went back to our conversation thread and saw online written under her name. My heart sprung to life, beating like I was reaching the end of the beep test. It felt like we had run into each other at the supermarket. I typed out, 'Hey, how are you?' My finger moved to the send button but paused just above it. My heart was screaming, *'Send! Press send! Do it now you coward! She's right there. Do it!'* My brain was whispering something else though. My brain said gently, *'She broke up with you, so why would she want to talk to you? She didn't say she wanted to stay friends, so she doesn't want to hear from you.'* I erased the message and opened her contact information. I needed to remind myself that she didn't want to hear from me. I changed her name in my phone from Sunshine, to Leave Her Alone.

I walked off stage on Saturday night from playing in my regular spot. I walked back to the dressing room that I had planted my flag in, the room that I asked Nina to be my girlfriend and put my guitar away. I laid on the floor and stared at the ceiling for a couple of minutes in complete silence. It didn't feel as good to play without Nina in my life. My songs didn't have the same meaning. They were missing something. The joy.

The door opened with Michael and James entering the room, each taking a seat on a plastic chair that was sitting against the wall opposite to where I was lying. 'Are you alright? You seem a bit flat,' James said, drinking a mouthful of his beer.

'What gave it away? The part where I'm lying on the floor staring at the ceiling?' I replied monotonously, continuing to stare.

'Well, we had an inkling something was wrong while you were playing because you looked miserable up there. This sort of confirms it though,' James said, gesturing to me lying on the floor. 'Did something happen with Nina?' He crouched down and placed his almost empty beer on the floor.

'Nothing major, she just dumped me. So yeah, that happened,' I said, rubbing my face with both hands and letting out a groan as I rolled onto my stomach and screamed silently into the dirty floor.

'What! Nooo!' Michael and James yelled in unison, as they got up and sat next to me. I pulled myself up and leaned against the wall so all three of us were sitting next to each other.

I told them the entire story of the breakup. They listened intently, barely moving a muscle. 'She told you she loves you?' Michael whispered, as if we were at a golf tournament, his mouth hanging slightly open.

'Yeah. It's funny. All that time where I thought she was losing interest in me, and it couldn't have been further from the truth. She was falling more and more in love with me, so she was hurting more and more. I don't like her solution to her pain, but there's nothing much I can do about it,' I said, shrugging my shoulders in resignation.

'Rubbish. If you want her back, then there's lots you can do about it. You can call her and fight for her. You can get on a plane tomorrow and fly to Serbia,' Michael suggested. 'There's always something you can do. It's just a matter of whether you want to do it and should you do it.'

'No. She thought long and hard about it and that's her conclusion. I need to respect her terrible decision. She doesn't want to be with me anymore. I just hope I don't have to see a picture of her with another guy. The thought of her being with someone else makes me sick to my stomach,' I groaned, and I began to feel both nauseous and disgustingly ugly at the thought.

'If she goes on a date with someone then there's nothing you can do about it, mate. She's single now, and so are you,' James said, tipping his glass in my direction and winking.

'I know, and I want her to be happy. It would just be nice if she waited a little bit to be happy without me again,' I said, painfully chuckling.

'Okay, so here's what we're going to do,' James announced, standing up as if he was giving the inspirational halftime speech in a sport movie. 'Lock your stuff in Sam's office. We're going bar hopping. Let's go.'

The next three hours were spent running from one bar to the next in the city, until we finally settled on a rooftop bar on Swanston Street. 'Hey, that girl has hair like Nina,' I slurred to Michael and James loud enough for her to hear me. She gave me a judgmental sideways look and kept moving.

'You shouldn't be looking for a girl that looks like Nina. Firstly, it's weird, and secondly, girls don't want to be compared to your ex. You should be looking for a girl that looks the opposite of Nina,' James said in my ear, wrapping his arm around my shoulder to scan the bar.

'You mean ugly?' I asked, looking up at James. Michael sniggered.

'That's not exactly what I mean. Just find a girl you think is pretty and talk to her. You're full of liquid courage now so that should be easy. What about her?' James asked, nodding towards a pretty, blonde girl sitting at a table with two friends.

'Okay. Follow my lead guys,' I said, shaking off James' arm and walking towards their table. I could feel James and Michael following and stopped just behind me when I stumbled to the girls table. The three girls broke off from their conversation and all looked at me, waiting for me to say something. 'Hi, I just got dumped and you look nothing like my ex, so I'd like to talk to you,' I said, trying to keep myself from slurring and struggling to maintain my footing.

'Smooth, mate,' James whispered in my ear, and patted me on the butt encouragingly. I turned with a thumbs up and a smile to Michael, to which he dropped his head embarrassed.

The two friends burst out laughing while the pretty blonde girl continued to look at me, as if examining me for a moment. 'Well, why don't you join me then?' she asked, moving over slightly on the bench where she was sitting and tapped the space next to her.

'I think I'm in,' I whispered back to James. Well, I thought it was a whisper. It's difficult to tell when you have had so much to drink.

'My name's Tayla, what's yours?' Tayla asked, as she extended a hand to shake mine in the very condensed space we had. My vision was blurred so the main thing I noticed about Tayla was her blonde hair. It was difficult to see anything else.

'I'm Luka. Nice to meet you,' I said, shaking her hand. 'So, what do you do when you're not letting weird guys talk to you in bars?' Michael and James took a seat next to the friends of Tayla and began talking to them.

'I'm a beauty therapist and study Law as well. What do you do when you're not coming onto girls in a bar by telling them you just got dumped?'

'Oh, very impressive. Beauty therapist huh? I think you've finished your therapy. I'm trying to flirt, in case you were wondering,' I said, not caring anymore if I slurred. She started laughing at what might be the stupidest thing a guy has ever said to a girl. 'I go to uni, work part time for my dad, and I sing in a bar near here. I played a bit earlier tonight in a place called One Note.'

'Oh my gosh. That was you? We've seen you play. We were there a few weeks ago and thought you were amazing. I wanted to see you play again but just haven't managed to get back there yet,' Tayla said excitedly. She turned to face me, and I was able to completely focus on her face. Tayla had plump cheeks, a small nose, huge blue possum eyes and big white teeth. She wore skinny black jeans, a tight white shirt, and a black leather jacket.

Why do girls like tight clothes so much? It must be difficult to breathe, I thought, leaning back to obviously check her out. She was somehow tanned which was unusual for May and had a very cheeky look.

'You should definitely come back. It'll be nice to see a friendly face there that's much prettier than these two,' I said, gesturing to Michael and James who were deep in conversation with Tayla's friends.

'I think they call that flirting too, Luka,' Tayla said, and she placed her hand on my arm. 'I'm going to get a drink, what are you drinking?' Tayla stood up and gestured towards the bar.

'I've been drinking bourbon so would like to be loyal to that. Shouldn't I be the one buying you the drink?' I asked, looking up into her blue eyes that were accentuated by her winged eyeliner.

'I buy you a drink, and then you buy me dinner,' Tayla said, with a cute half smile. 'Plus, I don't think the barman would serve you. It's actually quite extraordinary they let you in. It must be those eyes.' Tayla turned and walked towards the bar, lightly running her hand against my neck which brought a tingle to my stomach.

'It may be the alcohol lying to me, but I think she just asked me on a date,' I thought.

'Thanks,' I said, as Tayla handed me a drink and took her seat next to me.

'So, why did your girlfriend break up with you?' Tayla asked, edging closer to me on the seat so that her thigh touched my knee.

'She lives in Serbia, and I don't. It became too hard for her,' I said, trying to sound aloof. Talking about Nina was the last thing I wanted to do. The longer I could go without really talking about her, the longer I could hold onto the fading idea that we were still together. With each day that picture drifted a little further away.

'Long distance relationships are really hard. I used to have a boyfriend in London. I surprised him once by just turning up on his doorstep unannounced for his birthday. Cute, right?' I nodded, entranced by her story. Her voice pulled me in closer; I leaned in until her lips were barely a few centimetres from my ear. Tayla continued, 'Nope, big mistake. A girl answered the door in just a hoodie. The hoodie that I sent over to him for Christmas. So yeah, he came to the door, and I yelled at him. Then she yelled at him. I actually stayed with that girl for a couple of days until I could get a flight back to Melbourne. He turned up to hers the next day saying how I meant nothing to him, and he only wanted her, which he had also texted me earlier that day. He was surprised when I walked out of the bedroom. I'm still friends with her so it wasn't a complete loss,' Tayla said, finishing the last of her white wine and placing the glass delicately on the table.

'That's awful. I'm so sorry you had to go through that. I have to say though, that's an incredible story,' I said, looking Tayla in the eye.

'It's okay. Good things happen; bad things happen. It's called life. Those eyes are definitely a good thing, they're gorgeous,' Tayla whispered in my ear. She was so close to me that I could smell her rose scented perfume and coconut skin. I should have been feeling excited that such a pretty girl was so close to me, but I wasn't. Saying that about my eyes just made me feel like I had been kicked in the stomach.

Nina loves my eyes,' I thought, and I immediately tried to drag my thoughts from Nina, back to Tayla. I looked away for a moment and when I turned my head back, Tayla had manoeuvred her face so that her mouth moved from my ear to my lips. There was a pause as if she were waiting for me to move my lips that last centimetre, but I didn't, I was stuck. Tayla grew tired of waiting and removed the last bit of space between us and tenderly kissed me. She placed a hand on my neck, and I kissed her back, moving my hand to the curve in her waist. Her hand felt soft on my neck. *'She probably moisturises. Focus, Luka! Focus!'* I thought. I pulled back from her with my mind torn between two worlds. The world where I was still in love with Nina, and the world where a gorgeous girl was kissing me.

'Hopefully, that helps you forget about your ex,' Tayla whispered in my ear, and I could feel her hot breath on my ear and neck. The elephant was back sitting on my chest, pushing all the oxygen from my lungs, and wasn't letting me take any in. My lungs weren't working, and my legs were beginning to shake. I needed to get out of there. Right away.

'Umm, I need to go to the bathroom,' I said, standing up and heading to the stairs that led to both the bathroom and the exit. Instead of turning right into the bathroom, I turned left and ran down the stairs towards the exit with the speed and agility of someone not twelve drinks deep.

When I got into the street, I sucked in deep breaths of the cool night, and watched the fog leave my mouth as I breathed out. I texted the group chat with James and Michael. 'I'm outside. I need to go home.'

Two minutes later James and Michael came running from the exit, swivelling their heads quickly trying to locate me, and found me sitting on the gutter with my head between my knees. They sat on either side of me. 'You kissed her and then ran out of there. What's wrong?' Michael asked, turning his head to try and see the look on my face.

I picked my head up and leaned back on my hands. 'I know I was really rude for bailing like that, but I needed to get out of there,' I said, trying to get my breathing under control.

'Why? Mate, she kissed you. You should have gotten her number,' James said incredulously.

'I don't care. I feel disgusting. I feel like I just cheated on Nina. I'm so head over heels in love with her and I'm not with her anymore. I know it sounds dumb because she broke up with me, but I was living in this kind of alternate reality. This place where I hadn't moved on to anyone else or kissed anyone else which meant that in a way, I was still with her. Now that I've kissed someone it feels like it puts a full stop on our relationship, and I'm not ready for that,' I said, hanging my head and I felt the tears falling from my eyes, hitting the road between my feet.

James and Michael didn't say a word. They each put an arm around me and let me have a moment of silence. They said the perfect thing.

'Come on. Let's go home,' Michael said after a minute or so. James hailed down a taxi and we travelled back to Michael's house where James and I slept in the spare beds.

A couple of days later when my hangover had finally passed, I walked upstairs when I heard a familiar voice coming from Aleks' room. I looked inside and saw Aleks sitting at his computer with Andjela on the screen. 'Luka! Come here!' Andjela exclaimed, as she saw me peaking in to see who the familiar voice was.

I walked into Aleks' room and crouched down so that Andjela could see me. 'How are you? How are things back home?' I asked Andjela. It was my first contact with Požega since Nina and I broke up.

'It's okay. Things are stressful with school, tennis, and that other thing...' she said trailing off. She looked annoyed at herself for bringing up the Nina situation even though she didn't mention her name.

'I can imagine things are going crazy for you with school coming to an end and Fed Cup soon. Are you excited to play?' I asked, ignoring the topic of the breakup.

'Ask her about Nina,' I told myself. I tried to ignore that voice in my head.

'I'm just trying to get through to the end of school now and then focus on tennis. I'm still training but I can't wait to get out there and see you guys again. It's the number one thing keeping me going,' Andjela said with a big smile on her face.

'I'm excited to see you as well. How long are you here for?'

'Actually, she's going to stay here for a couple of weeks after the Cup tie. We were just talking about it when you came in. I'm going to ask Mum and Dad about it when we finish talking,' Aleks said.

'That's awesome. It will be great to have you back. I know Mum will be happy having another Požega woman in the house.' Andjela had an examining smile on her face, as if looking to see if I was happy for her to come back or just saying it to be polite.

Maybe it was an unhealthy thought, but I couldn't wait to have that Nina connection back. 'Things seem to be going really well with you two,' I said, looking from Aleks to Andjela.

'Why aren't you asking about Nina? I know you want to ask her,' that voice said more loudly.

'So far so good. Hopefully, it goes well when I visit and then we can go from there. We're taking baby steps though,' Andjela said, and I could see Aleks smile at his feet. He looked extremely uncomfortable.

'Well, I hope Aleks here has been working on cologne portion control,' I said, slapping a hand on his shoulder causing Andjela to laugh.

'Aww, don't make fun of him. At least he was trying,' Andjela said, trying to suppress her laughter.

'It's a bit hard to say that while you're laughing,' Aleks said, looking from me to Andjela.

I could feel that both Andjela and I were avoiding the topic, and it was building a level of anxiety in my chest. I needed to release that pressure and there was only one way to do it. 'So, I'm just going to address the elephant in the room, how is she?' I asked Andjela, and I could feel the temperature in the room drop as my knees began to shake.

'If you want me to lie then I'll say she's good, but if you want me to be honest, she's really struggling. How are you doing?' Andjela asked, leaning forward in her chair. I felt like a bad person for thinking it, but I was relieved that I wasn't the only one that was struggling.

'I don't know. Just getting through, I guess. I'm sorry she's not going well. I think about texting her sometimes, just to say hi. By sometimes, I mean about every twenty seconds,' I said chuckling painfully.

'If you want to then you should do it. Maybe you two could be friends? It would be sad if you two weren't in each other's lives because I know how much you care for one another.' I could see Aleks shifting uncomfortably in his chair, as if he didn't know if he should be listening to our conversation.

'I better let you two get back to your date. It was good seeing you, Andjela.' I lowered my head to whisper in Aleks' ear. 'Please don't tell Mum or Dad that Nina and I broke up.' Aleks nodded.

'I'll see you soon, Luka,' Andjela said as she waved goodbye. I waved back to her and walked from the room.

I tried to fake a positive mood, and I thought it was working well. No one seemed to have picked up on the fact that I had my heart stomped on in the last few days. When I couldn't fake it anymore, I would take Monty to the upstairs living room and let him sit on my lap and patted him while I watched television. If it got unbearable, then I would take him for a walk to the beach. The crashing waves and endless water soothed my anxiety.

Every person in my family had a unique sound to their step as they walked up the stairs. I could hear the unmistakable quiet steps of my mother as she gradually made her way upstairs. They didn't sound like the steps of a woman coming to get something, they sounded like the steps of a woman that had something on her mind and needed to talk.

'Luka,' Mum said, turning right from the stairs and immediately found herself in the living room. Monty raised his head to see who it was that had disturbed his slumber, before putting his head back down with a huff and returning to sleep. I continued to give him long stroking pats on his ribcage and could feel his heartbeat slow as he returned to dreams of a new shinbone.

'Can you turn that off? I need to talk to you,' Mum said, gesturing towards the television. I put the television on mute and sat up, turning my attention to her as she sat down on the couch, and looked straight at me.

Why does she look so worried? Something must be wrong,' I thought as Mum analysed me for a moment.

'What's wrong?' I asked, feeling perplexed as to what could have caused Mum to get me to turn my attention from a show on deep sea fishing.

'I was going to ask you the same thing. You seem miserable, and I'd like to know what's wrong. I'm worried about you,' Mum said with a stare that felt like she was mining into my soul. As it turned out, I hadn't been fooling my family like I thought I was, and Mum would be the one who would be able to tell if something was wrong. I had lived with these people my entire life, so as it turned out, at least one of them was able to see through my forced smile and fake enthusiastic tone.

'I'm fine. I've got no idea what you're talking about,' I lied, trying to continue the charade. Mum wasn't buying the protest; she leaned forward on the couch as if she was the lead detective getting close to breaking the suspect she was interrogating. I just hoped that she didn't mention the name that could send me over the edge. Nina.

'Luka, stop it. Yeah, your words and tone are the same as they've been since you met Nina, but your energy isn't. I'm your mother. I know when something's wrong. I feel like you're hurting, and I can't sit by and watch. So please tell me what's wrong. Is everything okay with you and Nina?'

She said it. Twice. I hated lying to her, but the hardest person to tell that you're hurting is your own mother. The saint of a woman had done everything she could to give me a happy life, and it felt like I was insulting her if I said I was back to my old miserable self again. That everything she had done for me wasn't enough for my happiness.

'Okay, fine. I'm not okay. I'm absolutely miserable, and I have no interest in talking about it. The less I talk about what's wrong, the less real it feels. I know that's insane, but I need to hold onto it for a little longer,' I said, trying to maintain my composure, but I could feel my tenuous grip on it slipping.

Mum didn't need me to say more than that, she knew from that what had happened. To be fair, it didn't take her elite investigative skills to come to the correct conclusion.

'Maybe you need to start seeing the psychologist again. Other people will affect your mood day-to-day, but you can't let someone affect your long-term sense of self-worth. I'm worried you're basing your entire self-esteem around whether you're with Nina or not. These things are hard, and they hurt. Even the ones that work in the end. It's…' Mum said before I cut her off.

'Mum, please. I don't want to be rude to you, but I don't want to talk about it. I just want to sit here with my dog and watch some guys catch fish. Can you please let me do that?' I asked, as I felt a mix of frustration, anger, and sadness swirl inside my chest.

Before Mum had the chance to respond, there was the sound of another person making their way up the stairs. There was a quick step at the bottom, and they seemed to be skipping stairs. *That's Maja,'* I thought.

Both Mum and I fell silent as we waited for Maja to complete her ascent and appear at the top of the stairs. 'Hey. Luka, are you able to help me with my maths? I have an exam in a few days,' Maja said sheepishly. She had never asked me to help her with her homework before, so she must have really needed it.

'What are you struggling most with?' I asked, grateful for the perfectly timed interruption. I glanced up and thought, *Thanks, Nana'.*

'Trigonometry is the main thing. It won't take long. I just need someone to explain it to me. My teacher is awful. Can you help me?' Maja asked, not moving from the top of the stairs, looking over the banister.

'The teacher did an awful job, or you weren't paying attention?' Mum asked Maja, turning to face my sister.

'Why do you always take the teacher's side? You never take my side,' Maja said, her voice rising in volume and anger.

'No worries,' I said, standing up and placing Monty on the floor. I needed to cut the fight off before it got any further, and I needed to end the conversation with Mum. Monty walked beside me as I went to follow Maja, who wore a relieved smile, down the stairs.

'We'll talk later,' Mum said to me, still sitting on the couch as I nodded to her before I disappeared down the stairs with Maja.

There's something cathartic about helping someone when you feel like your insides are falling apart. A distraction from what's happening in your mind and soul. Maja and I sat at the dining room table and worked through a practice exam. Through the entirety of her schooling, it had always seemed like Maja struggled academically, but from working through the questions with her, there was no reason for her to struggle. She grasped all the concepts perfectly if they were patiently and properly explained to her. Mum and Maja ended up in shouting matches when it came to school, and no one else had taken the time to sit down with her. *'She has so much potential, I just hope she can start to see it,'* I thought, watching Maja work.

'That's brilliant. You're doing so well,' I said, as Maja smiled broadly at getting another correct answer. I could feel the pride radiating off her as she began to read the next question aloud.

'This is the start of the second section of the exam which you have forty-five minutes to finish. Why don't I set the timer on your phone, and come back at the end, and we can go through the answers together? It can be like a real exam. You know all the content; you just need to be ready for the pressure of exam conditions,' I said, leaning back in my chair and looking at Maja.

Maja looked at me uneasily. Clearly, she still lacked confidence. The only way her confidence was going to grow was by doing it on her own and seeing the results. 'I don't know,' Maja said slowly.

'You're ready. Then I'll come back, and we can go through it together.'

'Okay, I'll try,' Maja said, pulling out a highlighter to establish the key information in each question.

I set the timer on Maja's phone and pressed start to begin her time. 'Trust yourself. You're killing this. I'm really proud of you,' I said as I stood up, put my phone in my pocket and patted her encouragingly on the shoulder.

'Thanks,' Maja said, smiling at me as if she was about to say something heartfelt. 'Now get out of here, I'm trying to focus.' I laughed shaking my head as Maja returned to her normal personality.

Picking up my guitar as I sat on my bed, I began to throw together random chords to see what would come out. A slow and emotional progression materialised, and I started to hum a melody along with it. I grabbed my song notebook that always sat on my amplifier next to my bed, writing everything that came into my mind. Coherent or not, I didn't care, it went on the page.

I randomly sang those lines in the melody I was humming until my door cracked open, and I saw Dad's head pop through it. 'That sounds good. Is that a new one?' Dad asked, not yet fully committed to coming into my room.

'Yeah, just started messing around with it now,' I said, standing my guitar up between my feet.

'I like it. So, how are you?' Dad asked uncomfortably.

'Mum sent you up here, didn't she?' I said, picking up my guitar and beginning to play again.

'No, she didn't. What makes you think that?' Dad asked, his voice going up an octave trying to conceal his lie. A salesman would normally be a better liar, but obviously that was saved for when fruit arrived, not lying to his son.

'Well, because through my entire life you've never come into my room and asked me, how I am? It feels too much to be coincidental that the first time comes just after I was interrogated by Mum.'

'She's worried about you, mate. You didn't see her constantly stressing about you when you were miserable every day before you met Nina. She was always asking me if she was a bad mother? Did she do something wrong? Now you two aren't together anymore, she's stressing that you'll revert to how you were before. She could see it before you two broke up. She loves you more than you understand,' Dad said, finally coming into my room and taking a seat on the end of my bed.

'First of all, I didn't say that Nina and I aren't together anymore. Secondly, she's a great mum so she shouldn't stress. I'm fine.' It was my turn to tell a bad lie.

'A mother not worry about her child? Yeah, that's not happening. Okay then, if everything's fine, I'll see you later,' Dad said, standing up, and leaving my room. I put my guitar down between my feet again.

'Dad,' I said, bringing him immediately back. I had never been hurting like that before, and I needed every possible trick to make the pain stop.

'Umm, how do you get over someone?' I mumbled in a voice that I was surprised he could hear. He returned to sitting on my bed, but this time halfway up the bed.

'Time. There's no easy, quick fix, I'm sorry. Time heals all wounds is a lie, but it does heal this wound. For me it was to surround myself with people even when I wanted to be alone, and to keep busy all the time, so I wasn't sitting around and thinking about it. If you're focused on something, then your mind isn't allowed to think about her.'

'The hardest thing for me is that I feel like I've lost my best friend. Every morning when I woke up, I would reach for my phone to see if she was thinking about me, or sent me a picture, but now I'm disappointed when I wake up. Not because I don't want to wake up anymore, but because I know that I have an entire day to get through with my favourite part of life gone,' I said, spinning the guitar between my feet.

'It's like trying to break an addiction. It takes a strong mind and time. I'm sorry I didn't get to meet her. If she's so special to you then she must be amazing,' Dad said, wrapping his right arm around my shoulder and pulling me into a half hug.

'Me too. It feels like our relationship's always going to be a big question. A big what if?' I didn't fight the hug from Dad. I allowed him to pull me into his comfort.

'Do you want to be friends with her? Maybe you weren't suited to be a couple, but you could be suited to being friends. Then who knows what the future could hold,' Dad said before pausing. I still wanted Nina in my life. I missed the connection with her.

'Maybe we just need some time to take the pressure off,' I thought.

'Luka, if someone adds value to your life, then you keep them in it. If they don't, then you remove them. I don't want to answer for you, but it seems like she adds value to your life,' Dad said, speaking in a soft tone that I had never heard from him before.

'She definitely does. What if she doesn't want to be friends though?' I asked, feeling the fear of that question being answered rising in my chest.

'Then you're in the exact same position as you are now. There's only one way to find out. Say hi,' Dad said, and for the first time in living memory, he kissed me on the forehead. He stood up, and once again walked towards the door.

'Hey Dad,' I said, once again, stopping him from leaving.

'Yeah?'

'Thanks,' I said smiling. He returned my smile and left my room.

Picking up my phone and opening my conversation thread with Nina, my hands began to tremble. 'Hey, how are you?' I typed out, and there was a rising nervousness in me that resembled the feeling of fearing the worst, similar to what I felt nearing the end of our relationship. *What if she doesn't reply?'* I wondered, my thumb hovering above the send button.

'Only one way to find out,' I said aloud to my empty room, as I lowered my quivering thumb to hit the send key. It's better to have an answer, rather than be left paralysed by the 'what if?'. At least it was one question I could get an answer to.

CHAPTER FIFTEEN
The Scrapbook

Early on Monday morning, the day after having dinner with Marko, I was sitting at the tennis courts with a coffee in hand, watching Andjela practise. The sun was barely poking its head above the horizon, and there was fog on my breath. Stefan was feeding Andjela backhands that were being sent with ferocity and precision down the line, cutting through the early morning fog. Požega is the fog city of Serbia, so it was the perfect time for Andjela to train as the poor lighting required her to focus at a higher intensity on the ball to be able to strike it with the appropriate timing.

I spent the previous night hugging my Luka pillow, unable to stop thoughts of him from swirling around my mind. Images of us together could not be chased from my brain, and I didn't want them to be. It felt good picturing us together. And then there was Marko hovering in the background. I was still in love with Luka, but I needed to stop being in love with him for my mental health. 'It can't work. It can't work,' I repeated aloud to myself. The mental merry-go-round made me get out of bed and come to the courts to watch Andjela train.

I was very physically attracted to Marko, and it felt amazing that the boy every girl in school swooned over, apart from Andjela, seemed to be interested in me. *Well, I think he's interested in me. It felt like he was going to kiss me last night, but he didn't, so maybe I'm wrong. He's a great distraction for me to get over Luka, but does that make me a bad person? To use someone to get over the man. Do you ever really get over your soulmate?'* I wondered, as I took another sip of my coffee. Marko was the type of guy you date for a summer. Luka was the type of man you marry.

'Bravo, Andjela,' Stefan shouted in the silent morning, as he began to pick up the tennis balls all laying together in the forehand corner at the opposite end of the court. 'Twenty sit-ups, twenty push-ups!' Stefan demanded. Andjela ran to the towel lying on the side of the court to begin her exercises, sweat dripping off her perfectly shaped brows.

Andjela was aware that I was there but was so focused on her training that she didn't acknowledge my presence. Her only objective at that moment was to be better than she was at the start of the session. She texted me back at two-am that she was going to bed, which meant she was only working on four hours sleep.

Exams started Monday and lasted for three school weeks. Andjela had her exams condensed into two weeks though, so the day after her final exam she would fly back to Melbourne with the Serbian Federation Cup team to play against Australia. *'In two weeks' time Andjela will have met Luka twice, and me, the one in love with him, would still have never met him in person. Life really can be cruel,'* I thought, trying to stop myself from becoming bitter.

My phone vibrated in my hand so I turned it over to see who could possibly be trying to contact me at stupid o'clock. It was Luka. I opened my phone to find Luka's smiling face gazing into my soul as he was still my wallpaper, and a text from him. 'Hey, how are you?'

Confusion made my mind feel like there were bumper cars driving around my brain. Was I happy or annoyed he texted me? *'I so desperately want to talk to him. I miss him so much, but I've just been dragged out of the deepest depression of my life, and if I start talking to him again, will I be sent right back there? What does he want? Should I ignore him and feel like a terrible person, or should I reply and risk all the progress I've made in the last ten days?'* I wondered, feeling very conflicted. I didn't know what to do.

Andjela and I walked into the Sunshine Café when school had finished for the day to have lunch. 'You look like a zombie. You need a nap,' I said after we each ordered pljeskavica and fries.

'Nap? No, I need a six-month coma to recover from what I've been doing lately. I'm texting Aleks all the time, studying, and training. I just need to make it through two and half weeks. That's all I keep telling myself. Do you even wake up from a coma feeling rested?' Andjela asked, as she closed her eyes and exhaled loudly to try and relax.

'I'm not sure. If I ever fall into one, I'll be sure to let you know when I come out of it. How are you feeling about exams?'

'Please do. I don't know. I feel like I'm doing as much as I can. I know my future is in tennis so I can't just forget that, but I can't forget school because I made a promise to my parents. It's tough, but I'm glad I have Aleks to take my mind off things,' Andjela said, opening her eyes, stretching them wide to try and get them to focus. Her eyes looked like Christmas, green and red.

'I don't think I could handle doing all that. My brain would explode,' I said laughing, and drinking a mouthful of the water sitting in front of me.

'Well, you are dealing with a lot now as well. The breakup and having to get through exams. It can't be easy to focus on studying when you have that stuff playing in your mind all the time,' Andjela said, as our lunch was laid in front of us by the waiter. We both thanked him and tore into our meals.

'Yeah, I'm not really sleeping because of it,' I said in a blasé fashion, as if sleep didn't matter. I didn't want to tell her that I had dinner with Marko the previous night, and that was playing a part in keeping me up. Neither of us needed the stress of her reaction to hearing about that. If I spent any more time with

Marko, I would need to tell Andjela when she got back from Australia though.

I was still trying to figure out what to do with the Luka message. It was sitting in my notifications taunting and tempting me every time I opened my phone. 'Luka texted me this morning,' I said casually out of nowhere, as Andjela had a mouthful of pljeskavica. Andjela hurried to swallow her food before her jaw hit the floor in shock.

'What did he say?' Andjela asked, reeling her jaw back off the floor.

'Just, 'Hey, how are you?' That's all. I haven't replied yet,' I said, looking intently over her left shoulder until I could see that she had swallowed her food.

'Why?'

'I don't know what to say, or if I should say anything at all.'

'Do you not want him in your life? He could just want to be friends with you,' Andjela said, finally swallowing her pljeskavica.

I looked at her suspiciously. 'Have you spoken to Luka again?' I asked.

'No, I only saw him the time I already told you about. I did say to him then though that he should text you if he wants to talk to you. That it would be a shame if you two were lost to each other,' Andjela said, picking up her pljeskavica once more. 'Do you think you could be friends with him?'

'I don't know. I still have feelings for him because my feelings were so strong. They are so strong. I miss him all the time, but I'm scared that if I start talking to him, I'll never be able to get over him. How am I supposed to ask him about girls when I know hearing about that's going to be like a knife through my chest? How am I supposed to tell him about guys I like or I'm dating? Friends talk about those things, and I don't think I could with him. I don't know what to do,' I groaned, putting my head in my hands.

'Maybe you need to have a way of acknowledging your time together and try to move past it. Why don't you make a Luka scrapbook? You can put photos in it and write about each one. Treat it like a diary, release all those romantic feelings. Like therapy, just a lot cheaper,' Andjela said, picking up several fries. She annihilated lunch like she would never eat again. I wasn't even halfway through my lunch and Andjela was finished.

After finishing the last of my meal, we paid and left the Sunshine Café. 'I need to give you the invitation to my birthday. Can you come back to my place now for a minute?' I asked Andjela.

'Your birthday's in three months. Why do you already have invitations?'

'You know what mamas are like. They need to be prepared.' I said shrugging. Andjela nodded and we walked back to my house so I could give her the invitation.

'I better take two. You know I'll lose one,' Andjela said, picking up two invitations and reading them before putting them in her backpack. 'Back at the Sunshine Café? Let's wipe out the bad memory of the last birthday we went to there. I can't wait for it.'

I pulled my phone out as Andjela left and clicked on the notification from Luka. 'Hey, I'm okay. How are you?'

I was sitting at my desk with my open schoolbooks laying in front of me. They stared at me, mocked me as I held a pen and had no academic thoughts flow from my brain to my hand. There were exercise questions on the page, but I couldn't comprehend what they were asking me to do. I felt anxious and my mind was cloudy, as if now that Luka wasn't my boyfriend, my brain didn't know how to operate properly. The only thought I had was Luka. Nothing specific about him. Just Luka.

I thought of Andjela's idea of a scrapbook and looked up at the shelf above my desk to see the pretty notebook I bought when I got Luka his Christmas present. I stood up and pulled it from the shelf; I flicked through the empty pages and ran my fingers over them. The pages were brown and felt rough, they felt like old parchment. I raised the book to my nose and took in the scent of old paper, closing my eyes to let it wash over me. It was begging to be written on, to be filled with something worthy.

'I'm okay. Just trying to keep myself busy. School, work, and gigs. What have you been up to?' Luka texted, pulling my attention away from the notebook.

'Same. Just studying and trying to survive exams. Hope I make it out with my sanity,' I replied. It felt weird. Like I was texting a stranger. I had all this knowledge about Luka, but it was like we were back to square one. Maybe I just had boyfriend knowledge and not friend knowledge. *Was our relationship built on friendship or romance?'* I wondered. I wasn't sure. I felt my anxiety melt away seeing his name on my phone. He needed to be in my life. In some way, shape or form; I couldn't lose him completely.

Scrolling through my Luka photo file I selected my favourites. Our first photo together, our first date, his first concert, the time he asked me to be his girlfriend, Luka and Andjela together, and myself in his hoodie, our hoodie. I emailed them to the closest printing shop and headed there to collect them.

An hour later I returned to my room with my printed photos. I glued each photo to its own page. Picking up my favourite blue pen, I looked at the first photo in the book, our first photo together, the one Luka took of us on the computer screen. I closed my eyes and let myself remember. Breathing deeply, I travelled back to that moment, and felt those feelings come rushing back. I didn't want to plan what I would write and try to craft it. I wanted it to be genuine with how I felt, no filter.

The pen caught on the slightly uneven parchment like paper of the notebook, and I began to write.

'I didn't think I needed anyone until I met you. A man to restore my faith in love and make me believe that I am worth something. I can still remember how my heart beat against my chest with nerves hoping that I wouldn't say the wrong thing, because I was immediately drawn to you. Not because of how handsome you are, or because of your accent. It was because of your eyes. A depth in them that made me know that I was looking into a soft soul. A genuine soul. The man that I had always heard about in fairy tales. My knight in shining armour didn't come on the back of a horse, he came on a computer screen from fifteen thousand kilometres away. Now that I think about it, I was in love with you as soon as I saw you.'

I read what I wrote hoping that I didn't make any spelling mistakes. I gently blew on the ink to make sure it was dry before moving onto the next page.

My phone buzzed and there was another text from Luka. 'You're the smartest person I know. Try not to stress too much. Those exams don't stand a chance against you.' His words carried more weight than other people's and gave me confidence. Those words had a cost too. They made my soul smile like nothing else could, but I couldn't let him make me feel like that anymore. 'He is your ex-boyfriend, Nina. Your ex,' I said aloud to myself.

I looked upon the next photo. The photo of our first date and I couldn't help but laugh. Luka was there in a nice blue shirt, holding a glass of wine to the camera saying cheers to me, and I had my hand covering my mouth laughing. We looked so happy. We were happy. I repeated the same step as before and closed my eyes to time travel to our first date, trying to remember that feeling. With little effort, all those feelings spread through my body.

'I was so nervous getting ready for our first date. Andjela and Milica were in my room helping me. I remember sitting down and thinking, I hope he can't see how sweaty I am, and it just looks like I'm glowing with happiness to be on a date with him. As soon as I saw you smile at me, all those nerves drifted away. It was just comfortable. It felt like we had known each other our entire lives. I was addicted to learning everything I could about you. All it took was one date for me to feel a love for you that I have never felt for anyone before. When we first met, I thought I was in love with you, by our first date I knew. I knew you were special. You are special. We were special.'

Writing just those two pages was emotionally exhausting. I felt completely drained as if I needed a nap, so I left the rest for later. I picked up my phone and replied to Luka. 'Thanks, I hope so. How's work and uni going?'

I put the Luka scrapbook back on the shelf and pulled my schoolbooks towards me. I had some mental clarity after writing, so I put my head down and began studying. The only time I left my room was for dinner.

My phone vibrated with a text from Marko. 'Hey, how's study going? I was wondering, do you want to hang out by my pool this weekend? I just looked at the forecast and it's going to be warm, so I'm inviting a couple of people around. Want to come?'

He clearly wasn't interested in how my study was going, so I ignored that question. I had a great time with him at dinner so I thought it could be fun to hang out at his pool. It would be a good circuit breaker a couple of days before exams. 'Sure,' I replied, and turned my attention back to my study.

'Work is work. Nothing interesting. I'm just trying not to fail any exams. I don't want to disappoint my mum,' Luka texted.

'I'm sure she's proud of you. I know I am. I need to study. We'll talk soon. Thanks for texting me,' I replied immediately.

'Thanks for replying,' Luka texted. I put my phone in my drawer and turned my full attention to my books.

I knocked on Marko's door and waited for an answer by turning around and taking in his family's garden. We were deep into spring, so the garden was in full bloom. Lily of the valley, Phoenix plant, and Banat crocus, amongst others. I noticed there wasn't a car in the driveway, as I took in every detail of the front yard trying to busy myself. They had a white fence bordering the street that matched the colour of the house. It was a similar design to my house from the front but significantly larger. Marko's family was one of the upper-class families of Požega.

I was thirty minutes late because I was sitting at home deciding on whether to come or not. Being basically naked in front of Marko was a scary proposition. Especially when he looked like he was hand sculpted by God. *'He has other people coming so he won't really notice if I come or not. There's still time to leave, but I did put all that sunscreen on so it would be a waste not to come,'* I argued with myself.

Footsteps approached, growing louder, and I saw Marko's large frame coming closer through the frosted glass in the front door. I started to pick my fingers as he was just on the other side of the door. I busied myself by continuing to stare at the plants when he opened the door. Even when I knew the door was open, I didn't look at him, I continued to be fascinated by the garden, particularly the Lily of the Valley.

'Hey, I'm glad you came,' Marko said, forcing me to turn and look at him. Obviously, he had to answer the door without a shirt on. I would judge him, but if you looked like an eighteen-year-old Zeus who could blame you for wanting to show off? All he had on were a pair of dark blue shorts, which felt like a flex.

'Well, I did think about not turning up, but the attraction of a pool in this weather is just too much for a girl to say no to,' I said, continuing to unconsciously pick at the end of my fingers.

'Is that the only thing you find attractive here?' Marko asked, leaning against the frame of the door.

I rolled my eyes and pushed past him, crossing the threshold of the house. There was a long hallway with multiple rooms lying off it. As I reached the end of the hallway it opened into a large family room. There was a staircase to the right, and a kitchen on the left. An enormous television was mounted on the wall with a couple of family photos and many of just Marko. Marko playing football, Marko receiving an award at school, Marko as a baby, Marko at Christmas. The so-called family room was dedicated almost entirely to him, as if it was a shrine. The entire back wall of the house was glass so you could see into the spacious backyard, including a pool. No one else had arrived yet.

'Where is everyone?' I asked, turning around and finding Marko right behind me.

'Umm, they're just running late,' he said, checking his phone while walking past me. He collected a towel lying on the back of the couch and exited the house towards the pool.

I stood there for a moment confused. *I'm thirty minutes late, so surely they aren't later than me. I guess it's not school, so there's no rush for them to be here at a certain time,'* I thought. I shook my head to knock the confusion from my mind and followed Marko towards the pool.

The sunlight danced off the surface of the pool, and the water rippled at the slightest of spring breezes. There were two sunbeds lying next to each other with an umbrella and table in between. I threw my bag onto the left sunbed as Marko had already laid his towel over the right.

I wasn't nervous anymore about being alone with Marko, but the nerves of revealing the bikini hiding beneath my shirt and shorts were worse than ever. It was different than when you're at a public pool because you aren't the sole focus of someone like I was there. I took a seat on the sunbed and busied myself in my bag, pulling my towel out and carefully spreading it across the lounger. I looked down at it, picking at my fingers, making sure that it was evenly spread.

There was a loud splash behind me that I felt against the back of my leg, causing me to turn and find Marko reappearing from below the water. He flicked his hair back and the water ran off his large chest and shoulders. 'Getting in?' Marko asked, splashing water in my direction.

'Yeah,' I said nervously, taking one more look through my bag before I couldn't delay it anymore. I unbuttoned my shorts and let them fall to the ground to unveil my orange high waisted bottoms. Like a band aid, I ripped my shirt off as quickly as possible to reveal a strapless matching orange bikini top. My back was to the pool, but as there was no sound of water moving, I assumed Marko was staring at me. I felt his eyes, burning a hole in me.

I prayed that the tie in my bikini top stayed strong, and turned quickly, leaping into the pool. The surface of the pool had been warmed by the sun, but as I fell deeper, the cool refreshing water surrounded my body. I held myself below the surface for as long as I could, using the time to adjust my bikini, making sure my top was covering everything it had to, before I was forced to the surface for oxygen. I slicked my hair back flat behind my ears, straining the excess water from my hair.

'Quite an impressive entrance,' Marko said, with the water from my dive dripping from his face. He leaned back and floated away from me in the water towards the deep end of the pool. They had high fences surrounding the backyard with flowers blooming on the attached trellis, giving the backyard a lot of privacy.

I floated on my back, drifting around the pool for a few minutes, closing my eyes and enjoying the peace of having the water gently wash over my body. The stress of my looming exams, and the Luka breakup had been eating away at me. Water gave a feeling of serenity.

I sat on the top step of the pool at the shallow end and saw Marko with his sunglasses on, sitting on the sunbed texting someone. 'Is that the others? Are they nearly here? Who's coming?' I asked. Marko put his phone down and then slipped back into the pool.

'Umm, yeah. I don't think they're going to make it. They all said they needed to study for exams,' Marko said, swimming towards me, careful to keep his head above water.

'So how are you feeling about the breakup? Still struggling, or it's getting a little easier?' Marko asked, sitting next to me on the top step in the pool.

'It's getting easier, but I think that's mainly because I've been so busy trying to get ready for exams. Then as soon as results come back, I have to apply for the Biology Faculty at university. If I didn't have that distraction, then I'd probably still be in bed,' I said, forcing an uncomfortable chuckle.

'It's good to have something to focus on. I was going to apply for that too, but maybe I'll travel for a year and then go to university,' Marko said, casually running his hands through his hair.

'Oh, that's so cool. I really want to travel one day,' I said, taking my attention from his handsome face and watching my legs kick through the water gently.

'I bet he's doing a lot worse than you,' Marko said softly, placing his hand on my shoulder for a moment, before letting it fall into the water. His soft touch sent a shiver through my body, I couldn't believe how attractive he was becoming to me.

'I hope he's not doing worse than me. I'm sure he's fine with his music, study, and work. He has just as much to keep himself busy as I do.' I ran my hands through the water. Continuously moving them back and forth, making small waves in the water.

'He obviously made a big mistake letting you go. Any person that does that will regret it for the rest of their lives,' Marko said, turning to face me.

I didn't want to look back at him, so I continued to focus on the waves I was making in the water. *They looked like waves at the beach. An Australian beach. No. A Hawaiian beach. Yes, that's better,'* I thought, chastising myself for thinking about anything Australian.

'He didn't let me go. I broke up with him.'

'Yeah, obviously he didn't break up with you. If it were me though, and I was the one you broke up with, I'd do everything I could to get you back. Someone as amazing as you has to be fought for. Whatever it takes,' Marko said. I looked down at his leg and saw it was considerably closer than it was before. His knee was almost touching mine. I pushed my knees together to create some more space between our legs.

'You really think so?' I asked, finally giving in and looking up at his face. He had taken his sunglasses off so I could see his eyes. They were dark brown, the same colour as his hair. Little beads of water sat on his wide chest, joining together until they were too big, and began to fall down his body. I watched as one ran all the way from his right pectoral, over his glistening abs and disappeared into the waistband of his blue shorts.

'Definitely. If you really love someone then you do whatever it takes to get them. If you do everything you can, and they still don't want you, then okay, but at least you tried, and you can walk away knowing that. What could he have done to fight for you?'

I sat in silence for a moment trying to think of anything Luka could have done to show me that it was worth the pain. That one day it would all be okay, and that we would share every day in person. 'I don't know. He didn't do anything to try and get me back,' I said bowing my head. *I thought he deeply loved me, and just hadn't said it, but maybe Marko's right. If he did love me, he didn't love me enough to fight for me. Maybe he didn't love me at all,'* I thought, feeling a knot tie in my chest.

'I would have got on the next plane and come to your door. Maybe I'm crazy though,' Marko said, and I returned my knees to where they were sitting before. Our legs were so close I could almost feel his leg hairs tickle me, and I noticed his arm was touching mine. My heart started to race, and there was a tingling feeling in my stomach that pushed the knot from my chest. I was glad we were in the pool because he couldn't tell that I was beginning to sweat.

'You think so?' I asked quietly, and I nudged my body into his so I could feel his warm, wet skin on mine.

'Without hesitation,' Marko whispered. I could see he was looking at my lips. Our faces were edging closer to one another. Marko gently bit his lower lip.

'You didn't invite anyone else. You only invited me, didn't you?' I asked, our faces were so close I could feel his hot breath tickling my lips. I knew what was about to happen, and I wasn't going to stop him. *If he doesn't kiss me then I'm going to do it,'* I thought, wanting to feel lips on mine.

'Sorry, I wanted to be alone with you. Is that bad?' he whispered. I shook my head with a smile. He closed the tiny space separating our lips and kissed me, placing his hand on my hip and pulling my body into his. Eyes closed, my skin on his skin. I could feel his hand rise from my hip, and up my back. His hand was so large it felt like it covered my entire upper back. My hand lightly ran down his arm, feeling the muscle definition in his bicep and forearm.

All thoughts of anything apart from Marko's lips on mine were pushed from my mind. For the longest time I was always wanting to be somewhere else. Whether that be in Australia with Luka, or just to disappear completely, but finally I felt absolutely present in the moment.

He wasn't the world's best kisser by a long stretch. It almost felt like he was trying to eat my mouth, but it felt nice to be wanted; to be desired. He made me feel pretty. *We can work on his technique through the summer,'* I thought.

We broke apart with his hand falling down my spine, finding a resting place on the small of my back. 'How was that?' Marko asked, a cheeky grin on his face.

Ignoring his fishing for a compliment question, that I couldn't honestly give, I stood on the step and dived into the pool, swimming to the opposite end. Marko placed his sunglasses down on the edge of the pool and followed. As he got near me, I splashed him, so he dived low and picked me up, launching me above the surface before I crashed back down into the pool. I squealed in shock as I felt like a great white shark launching at a seal on the surface and flying above the water. The pool, the pleasant table manners, his intelligence, and all that muscle. It's exactly what I needed in that moment.

I hadn't kissed a boy since I was with my cheating ex. Every day I was with Luka I thought about what it would feel like to have his lips touching mine, but it never happened. It was nice to feel wanted after my ex cheated on me, and Luka didn't fight for me. *'He never loved me enough to make this happen. He kept waiting for my birthday, and I couldn't wait any longer,'* I thought, feeling the excitement of kissing Marko.

Sneaking up behind him, I jumped onto his shoulders and dragged him underneath with me. He turned around and pulled me close to him underwater. We broke through the surface and kissed again. We floated there kissing, Marko holding me to his chest. His lips were soft, and his grip was strong around my body, so I was willing to tolerate the occasional tooth clash.

I extricated myself from his grip and pulled myself out of the pool. Marko followed. I wrapped myself in my towel and Marko rubbed his hands over the towel to help dry me. 'Thanks for coming,' he said, smiling and looking into my eyes.

'His eyes don't sparkle, but maybe that's just the shade of the umbrella. Yeah, that must be it,' I thought, searching for an explanation.

'Thanks for inviting me to your try and kiss Nina trap,' I said, pushing him back playfully. I could hear my phone vibrating from a phone call. I assumed it was Mama, so I let it ring out. *'I'll call her back soon,'* I thought.

'You don't seem too upset about it,' Marko said with a wry grin.

'Just trying to make the best out of the situation,' I whispered, shrugging.

'I must admit, I'm a bit surprised this has happened, after the, you know…' Marko said, trailing off.

'Look, I'm not going to stand here and say what happened was okay, because it wasn't. I guess I'm just the kind of woman that will give someone a second chance. You're a good person, you just did a bad thing,' I said, not breaking eye contact with Marko.

'Thank you for forgiving me, and giving me a chance.'

'I better get going. Like all the friends you didn't invite, I need to study.' Marko leaned down and put another kiss on my lips, causing me to go to my toes to make the height difference work.

I broke away, threw my shirt and shorts on, collected my bag, and headed for the door. Turning back, I saw Marko laying on the sunbed. It looked like I would be seeing myself out.

Even though it felt exciting to be wanted, I didn't feel happy while being with Marko, I just didn't feel awful. I was tired of being in a constant pit of despair and craved a break from that misery. A break from missing Luka, a break from thinking about Luka. While I didn't feel on top of the world with Marko, at least I didn't feel like I wanted to be buried beneath it.

Opening my phone, I saw it wasn't Mama that called me at all. It was Luka. I wanted to call him back, but I couldn't. I couldn't talk to him after just kissing someone he despised. I couldn't talk to him after kissing any boy. I wasn't ready to hear his voice again.

Two weeks later I walked to answer my door to find Andjela standing there. 'Hey, come in,' I said, standing aside and letting her walk past me to take off her shoes and sit at the table. 'All packed?'

'Yeah. The flight is at twelve-fifteen, so I'm going to have to leave here by seven tomorrow. Wanted to come by and see you before I left. How are your exams going?' Andjela asked. I poured the just boiled water into a cup to make her coffee, and placed it in front of her, carrying mine along with it.

'I think I've done okay so far. Still have a couple left next week. If you didn't come and drag me out of bed after my breakup, I think I'd still be in there,' I said, stirring my coffee.

'Nah, you would have pulled yourself out to get ready for exams. I just expedited the process. If you say you think you did okay, that really means you crushed it.' Andjela methodically stirred her coffee, carefully watching its clockwise revolutions.

'I hope so. Just have to wait and see, I guess. So, how are you feeling about the trip?' I asked, keen to deflect the attention from myself.

'I'm barely even thinking about tennis. All I'm thinking about is how it's going to be spending two weeks with Aleks and his family. And stressing about stupid things like whether I take them a gift or not, will they like having me there or will they want me to leave. I just hope I make a good impression,' Andjela said. I could hear the stress in her voice and saw her hand holding the cup was shaking slightly.

'Remember, you've met them before. If they didn't like you and weren't comfortable with you being around, then they wouldn't have asked you to stay with them. You should take a gift to his mama though. Pick something up that has to do with Požega. She'll love it,' I said, resting a hand on her arm to reassure her. I could see her exhale gently and her arm relax.

'Yeah, that's a good idea. I just can't wait to see him. I'm going to see him play basketball and they'll be able to show me around the city. Apparently Luka has a gig while I'm there, so I'm going to watch him play as well. Have you two been talking?' Andjela asked. I thought I wouldn't see her more excited than when she left for the Australian major tournament, but spending time with the Robertson family had her on a whole other level.

'Yeah, we've been talking a little bit. I'm trying to keep my distance though because I can't fall back in love with him. It's nice to see his name on my phone though. I'm not ready to talk to him as much as I used to. I'm too scared. I need to take baby steps, and hopefully we can be friends.' I didn't want to tell her that I still had feelings for him, that I was still in love with him, but she probably knew anyway.

'At least you guys are talking, and who knows what could happen in the future. Maybe our dream of marrying brothers is still alive,' Andjela said, drinking a mouthful of coffee and raising her eyebrows at me.

'Or I can just be the fun fake aunt that gets drunk at family events and has everyone whispering behind my back wondering why I'm there? That's a fun dream too.'

'So, are you looking at any boys to kill time with before you come to your senses and get back together with Luka?'

'Do celebrities count? I'm just going to focus on getting into uni. I don't have the mental strength to even try to deal with boys now. My emotions can't handle those creatures at the moment,' I said, leaning back and exhaling loudly.

'Who said anything about emotions? I was talking about a rebound guy or summer fling. It might be fun to have a boy to kiss for the summer.'

'Maybe. As you saw when you came in, there is an endless line of boys waiting at the door for me. Hey, number three, you've got thirty seconds to present your summer boyfriend case,' I shouted at the door. Andjela laughed shaking her head. I couldn't tell her about what happened with Marko. *I think I'll wait. A few decades feels like the right amount of time,'* I thought.

'I better get going. I need to get that gift for Mrs Robertson. Any ideas?' Andjela asked, as we walked towards the front door.

'It doesn't matter what you get. It's about the gesture.' Andjela was fidgeting, not her usual smooth self. It showed how important the trip was to her. 'Hey, just relax. They'll love you,' I said, as she put her shoes on, and I opened the door.

'Thanks. I'm so nervous. Hopefully, I can still punish a forehand,' Andjela said, as we hugged.

'You could pound a forehand in your sleep. I've seen you do it in some of those morning sessions. I'll be watching all your games. I won't miss a shot.'

'Try not to wake your family when you're watching,' Andjela said, as we broke apart and she walked backwards through the door.

'If they get woken up it's their own fault for not being up watching already. Love you,' I said, waving and blowing a kiss to her.

'Love you too. Call me,' Andjela shouted, making a hand phone sign, and holding it to her ear.

I nodded and closed the door. I heard my phone vibrate on the kitchen table, so I walked to see who it was. It was a text from Marko. 'Hey, I've been thinking about you. Would you like to go on a date with me?'

'*A date? An actual planned date with Marko,*' I thought in shock. I had enjoyed spending time with him, and Andjela's summer boyfriend idea was a good one. Plus, Andjela would be away, so the risk of her seeing us together was zero for three weeks. It still felt too soon after breaking up with Luka, but if I waited five years, it would still feel too soon.

'Okay,' I replied.

CHAPTER SIXTEEN
The Invitation

'Urgh. Why did I do that?' I groaned aloud to myself, throwing my phone to the far side of the bed. *Now I'm actually going to find out she doesn't want to talk to me. At least before I could ask myself what if? At least before I had hope. Now that I've texted her it's going to get ignored and my hope will be gone,'* I thought regretfully.

I reached for my guitar and continued to play, looking at the time on my bedside clock so I knew when to go downstairs to see Maja. I couldn't seem to hold the guitar properly. My fingers were on the wrong strings, and I couldn't play a basic G chord. My voice was cracking on even the moderate notes.

'Is that something vibrating? It must be my phone,' I thought panicking. I reached out quickly and snapped my phone up, praying it was a reply from Nina. Opening my phone, I saw the notification bar was empty. I didn't think my nervous system was so cruel that it would do that to me, but apparently it had jokes.

I put my guitar down, giving up on it for the day and laid flat on my bed staring at the roof. A small spider scurried across the ceiling heading towards a miniscule gap in the light fixture. Just as the little spider arrived at the gap another spider appeared, and they entered the roof through the light fixture together. *'Even that spider could get his Nina,'* I groaned.

I rolled over and buried my head into my unmade bed, lying there face down without moving. My mind was normally alight with fake conversations or speaking to myself, but not then. There was no conversation in my head. Just an image. Nina sitting underneath a tree with Monty on her lap, patting him. So graceful, so beautiful. My mind taunting me with what I had let slip away.

My phone vibrated, and with the reaction time of a martial arts expert, my hand reached out and grabbed it. I rolled onto my back and held it in front of my eyes. As I attempted to open it, my hand slipped and my phone fell, landing hard just under my left eye. I swore loudly and put my hand immediately to my face.

'Do you mind? I'm trying to play a game here,' Aleks yelled through the wall.

'I'm sorry my broken cheekbone is ruining your afternoon,' I screamed, taking my hand from my cheek and scrunching my face up to help ease the pain. I walked to the bathroom and looked at my eye closely in the mirror. There was already a red mark, which would look a lot worse in the morning. Picking up a face towel, I dampened it with cold water under the tap and put it on my cheek.

I walked back into my room and picked up my phone to see the message. 'Hey Luka, I'm going with Michael to the driving range in an hour. Do you want to come?' James' text read. After all that it wasn't even from Nina. I was getting myself so worked up I was starting to get hurt. Some stress relief at the driving range sounded like it might help. I could go and beat the hell out of some golf balls.

'Pick me up,' I replied, and walked downstairs to see how Maja was going with her exam.

'Hey, I was just coming to get you. I've finished,' Maja said, as I turned the corner at the bottom of the stairs. We walked into the dining room to go over the practice exam.

'Wow. This is impressive. You got twenty-three out of twenty-five correct. I'm so proud of you. Do you see what you can do? All you need to do is focus and you'll kill it. Doesn't it feel good?' I asked, patting Maja on the shoulder.

She stared down at her work, and I watched as a small smile, radiating with pride, broke across her face. Maja nodded and turned to me. 'Can we do some more work tomorrow?'

'Of course,' I replied. I stood up and kissed her on the top of her head, before walking through the front door to meet James.

An hour later Michael, James and I stood on the second level of the Albert Park driving range, golf clubs in hand. It was our favourite driving range because for three very limited golfers, it gave us the illusion that we were hitting the ball much further than we were. The sun had set, but the flood lights illuminated the driving range. It was filled with people, mainly middle-aged men looking like they had just come from work. Fog emanated from our mouths in the cold night, as we tried to hit the cover off every golf ball.

'Wow, look at that one go,' James said, holding his finishing position as the ball trickled away in front of him and dropped over the edge.

'Okay, so we have a new leader for the worst shot of the night. As it stands, you're buying dinner,' Michael said, teeing up a ball.

'I think the only way for someone to beat that is if they miss the ball completely,' I said, hitting my driver with a wicked slice that looked in danger of going out of bounds of the driving range.

'Can we agree that if I hit the cart picking up the balls that we split the bill?' James asked.

Michael and I looked at each other in consultation before nodding. 'The way you're going, I don't think there's much danger of that happening. Unless you're trying to miss it, then you have a chance,' I said, switching back to a six iron for the health and safety of the people walking in the park next to the driving range.

'So, how are you handling the Nina situation?' Michael asked.

'Can we talk about someone succeeding instead of failing? Ask James how he's going.'

'I have a date with Emma, one of the girls Michael and I were talking to while you were hooking up,' James said, as he connected well with a ball finally that looked to be perfectly on track to hit the cart. 'Ooooooh.' At the last moment the cart turned left and avoided James' ball.

'It looks like you're running out of balls, James,' Michael said, looking over the partition separating us.

'Plenty of chances. So yeah, we're just going to a pub and having a couple of drinks,' James said. He seemed to be taking much greater time over each shot. It wasn't helping him though, as none had been close to the cart apart from that one ball.

'So, I'm succeeding with girls, and Michael is doing nothing with girls. I think it's time we hear about some failing with girls. You're up, Luka,' James said.

'I'm okay. I mean she made her decision, and I have to accept that. Am I happy about it? No, but sometimes life just sucks. Oh yeah, and I texted her,' I said nonchalantly. I didn't want to bring down their mood by telling them the truth that I wasn't sleeping. That I lay awake at night feeling that crushing pressure on my chest that only Nina seemed able to alleviate. I knew I needed to find a way to release it on my own, but I wanted her to be the primary thought on my mind, I wasn't ready for her not to be.

I swung my club as hard as I could, finally connecting flush with a shot, sending it soaring into the floodlights down the middle until I heard it clang into the one-hundred-and-seventy-five metre sign.

Michael and James stared after the ball, to see it ricochet off the sign. 'I'm guessing she hasn't replied if that shot has anything to do with it,' James said, and he began to laugh with Michael.

'I'm glad me losing her is giving you two so much enjoyment,' I said in a huff, throwing the six iron down and picking up the driver again. I wasn't in the mood to take mercy on the people walking around the park any longer. *Look out, I'm swinging as hard as I can,'* I thought with a scowl on my face.

'Come on, mate. You know we're always here for you, but if we can get you to joke and laugh about it, then you're halfway to getting over her. She's your first love. You'll have another, and another, and another. Just give it time,' Michael said, as he struck a driver as hard as he could which hooked so viciously, I thought I saw it put its indicator on. He then sat down on the bench behind James and me with his empty bucket.

'Yeah maybe,' I said, hitting my last ball with so much top spin it fell rapidly and hit the roof of the cart seventy metres into the driving range. I wanted to tell them I didn't want to have to love another woman, ever. I just wanted Nina. That no woman would ever be as perfect for me as she was, and I couldn't give up on her, but I wasn't interested in continuing the discussion with them.

'If my date goes well with Emma, then maybe she can organise a double date for us with you and Tayla. You were an absolute shambles that night and she was still into you. I think she'd give you another shot even though you ran out on her,' James said.

'Why don't you organise a double date with the other girl who was there that Michael was talking to? What was her name again? Madison?' I asked, trying to keep the attention off me dating anyone else.

'She didn't like Michael,' James said, laughing as he placed another ball carefully on the tee.

'Why not?'

'She told him about her weekend trip to Sydney, so Michael went on a twenty-minute play by play of his European trip. She thinks he's a snob,' James said, focusing on the ball in front of him.

'I don't think it was that. I think the issue was me saying that I would never date a smoker, and then saw a packet in her purse,' Michael said.

'Looks like the double date is back on you, Luka,' James said.

I didn't reply because I didn't want to give the idea air. It would be good for me, but I didn't want a quick fix with a random girl. I wanted to think about Nina and no one else because no other woman existed in my mind.

'Okay, so here it is. Last ball to avoid paying for dinner,' James said, kissing it and placing it gently on the ground. The cart was only around fifty metres from James, so he picked out a sand wedge. Looking at the cart and then focusing on the ball, he took his club back and gave a half swing.

'Ahhchoo,' I fake sneezed, and James wickedly shanked the ball off the hosel of the club as the cart drove in the opposite direction, missing by fifty metres. Michael and I burst out laughing as James slowly turned around to face me with his arms out wide looking incredulous.

'Sorry, you know how bad my hay fever can get,' I said, rubbing my nose.

'You don't even get hay fever, and it's almost bloody winter,' James shouted, outraged.

'I don't know about you Luka, but I'm feeling like tonight is a lobster kind of night,' Michael said, standing up and collecting his clubs.

'I feel like it's a wagyu steak kind of night,' I replied, picking up my clubs and walking next to Michael heading towards the car.

'Why not both?' James suggested, sarcastically.

'Great idea,' Michael and I said together, looking over our shoulders laughing.

I felt a vibration in my back pocket. After being burned earlier by my nervous system, I took it from my pocket with an element of scepticism. It wasn't a joke this time, it was Nina. At once, all the pressure on my chest was released. *I guess I can change her name to Nina in my phone now,'* I thought.

Three weeks later I was sitting at the table eating dinner with Mum, Dad, and Maja, when we heard movement at the front door. Monty was lying asleep at my feet and was roused awake for a moment, lifted his head, and looked in the direction of the front door before realising he cared more about sleeping than seeing what was causing the noise. With a huff of frustration, he put his head back on my feet and started to snore.

'You're such a gentleman. Your mother taught you well,' a Serbian accent said, accompanying the footsteps that grew louder, making their way down the hall. A soft thud hit the carpet and the door separating the hall from the living room and kitchen opened. Through it walked Andjela, with Aleks closely following like a puppy.

'Sorry, we would've waited but we didn't want to,' Maja said through a mouthful of pasta.

'Stop it, Maja. Welcome back,' Mum said, getting up immediately and rushing over to Andjela, embracing her. Dad followed suit, giving Andjela a welcoming hug. I stood up and felt Monty's head slide off my feet and hit the ground, but he just continued to snore.

'Hi Luka, how are you?' Andjela asked, hugging me. We broke apart and she looked at me with a sympathetic half smile, as if to say, I know, you don't have to answer.

'Congratulations on the win. You killed us,' I said, as we all took a seat around the table. Maja never left her seat; she continued to eat her pasta.

'Aleks, come and grab these,' Mum said, serving two bowls of pasta. Aleks came to collect them immediately, placing one in front of Andjela and the other in front of himself, taking his seat next to me.

'Thanks. The team played well, and I'm so happy with how I performed. I feel like I'm getting more comfortable at the level every time I play. Oh Mrs Robertson, I have a gift for you,' Andjela said, jumping up and racing into the hall.

'You need more petrol,' Aleks said, as he mixed the Bolognese sauce through his penne pasta.

'So, did you fill it up?' Dad asked.

'If I did then I wouldn't say you need petrol. I'm not John Robertson, I'm not made of money,' said Aleks, not even looking up from his pasta. Dad shook his head and looked as though he was about to reply when Andjela came back into the room.

'Here. I heard you like tea, so I got you this handmade mug. They make them just outside of Požega in the mountains,' Andjela said, handing the mug over to Mum. She turned it over in her hands, making sure she took in every detail. Mum gently ran her hands over the outside of the rough, terracotta mug.

'I love it. Thank you,' Mum said, standing up and hugging Andjela again.

'One more thing. I stopped by Nina's grandparents' place the day before I left and picked this up,' Andjela said, handing over a jar of honey. 'Aleks said you love to have honey on your toast in the morning. Her grandparents' make it, and a million other things, so I thought I'd bring you some.'

'Tomorrow morning I'm going to have toast with this honey, and my tea in this mug. You shouldn't have got me anything,'

Mum said, placing them both delicately on the kitchen counter. 'Sit down, eat.'

'Sorry guys, I would have got you something as well, but I thought if I could win her over, then the rest of you would just fall into line,' Andjela said, shrugging and beginning her pasta. 'This is delicious. Thank you!'

'I think you've won her over. It's fine, we'll all fall into line now. We know our place,' Dad said.

'So, what are you wanting to see here?' I asked Andjela, finishing the last of my pasta.

'I want to see an Australian football game at the MCG, go to the botanical gardens, drive the Great Ocean Road, and of course see Aleks play basketball. It's only fair after he spent three days watching me play tennis,' Andjela said, grinning at Aleks and placing her hand on top of his. 'Oh Luka, I hear you have a concert in the city Saturday night. We're definitely going too.'

'Why don't we all go? Luka, ask Sam if he can make an exception and let Maja into the bar to see you play. I'm sure he won't have a problem if you get permission from him first. Aleks is eighteen now so he's fine. We should have been to see you long before this. It'll be fun,' Mum said, beaming.

'Hopefully it's a happier atmosphere than the last time you heard me play,' I said, taking the empty plates from the table, rinsing them, and putting them in the dishwasher.

'Hey Luka, are you ready to go?' Andjela asked, finding me lying down on the couch staring at the television that wasn't on. I had been lying there for what felt like an hour staring at my phone, opening the chat thread with Nina, seeing her status turn from online to offline repeatedly. My earlier text to her just sitting there unread, ignored.

'Is Nina dating someone?' I asked Andjela, ignoring her question. I knew I had to leave for my gig soon, but it felt like the least important thing in the world. I felt paralysed and sick at the thought my mental bully was putting in my brain of her dating someone else. Nina seeing my text but returning another guy's texts instead, smiling at his messages, telling him that he had beautiful eyes and sending him selfies. I pulled my protesting body up and sat on the couch.

'No way. If she was dating someone I would know. She told me about you the day after you met, so there's no way I wouldn't know. Why?' Andjela asked, sitting on the television stand so that she was in my eye line.

'She wouldn't tell you if it was that Marko guy because you'd be angry with her. I texted her and even though she hasn't read the text, it says she's online and isn't replying to me. So, I can't help but think she's texting a guy and ignoring me. Maybe I'm crazy, it just sucks is all,' I said, rubbing my eyes and letting out a low groan.

'There's no way in a million years she would date that crumb. Not after what he did.' She was so confident it put me at ease, but there was still that little voice in my head saying it might be someone else.

'It's out of your control so there's no point worrying about it. Whenever I feel like you're feeling now, I leave my phone at home and go do what I love. I go to the tennis courts and play someone at the club, or practise with my coach, or just smash as many serves as I can. Put your phone down because I'm really excited to watch you do what you love doing,' Andjela said, standing up and walking towards me with an extended hand to help me up. I accepted Andjela's hand and put my phone on flight mode, sliding it into my back pocket.

Since I started playing at One Note, I had added more of my originals and reduced the number of covers. I wanted to find my own way on stage, and when I played too many covers, I felt like I was hiding behind someone else's story. It seemed to be working because I was seeing a lot of people regularly, and I loved to see their reactions when I played my own songs. Some things worked, some things didn't, but I was slowly finding my own way. Each time I walked onto stage I felt more comfortable. My confidence had grown since that first night and I felt like I belonged. I belonged on stage. I belonged to the crowd.

That night wasn't just any gig; it was the first time my family had seen me play since Nana's funeral. 'Hey everyone, I want to say a big thank you to you all. It means the world to me that I see so many smiling faces that have accepted me here. Tonight's special because it's the first time my family has come to see me play. So, if everyone can please be on their best behaviour for my mum, I'd appreciate it,' I said, with my pick in my hand, pointing towards her seated at a two-person table on my left with Dad.

The entire bar burst into applause, and I could hear a couple of drunks yell, 'Hi Mum,' through the applause.

'I've been waiting all week to get here in front of you, so I hope you all have as much fun as I will playing for you,' I said, looking down lovingly at my guitar hanging from my shoulder, my safety net, running my hand gently over its curves. For the ten seconds I stood on stage before putting it on I felt naked, vulnerable, but the moment I hung it over my shoulder those feelings were gone. It was my armour. I felt strong and confident, like the most interesting thing in the room. Michael, James, Maja, Aleks, and Andjela all stood in the front row looking up at me waiting for me to begin.

A gentle hush came over the bar as they waited for me to strike the strings. Even though I felt supremely confident on stage, the thought of Nina with another guy floated back into my mind. It made me feel sick. It returned the elephant to my chest and radiated anxiety throughout my body. Through the day I tried to avoid thinking about it, focusing intently on something else, anything else, but she was always hovering over it, casting a shadow upon everything I did. One Note was the antidote. I decided the best way to start was to play the first song I wrote for her. If she wouldn't leave my mind then I was going to sing for her; I was going to sing to her, as if she was standing next to Andjela looking up at me lovingly. The moment I hit that first note, all that negativity washed away. It was released into the atmosphere and nothing else mattered. It was just Nina and I, alone in a room as I sang to her. The stage with my guitar was my paradise, my sanctuary, my haven. I felt free.

As soon as I started playing, I felt like the person that wrote it. Head over heels in love with Nina. There was no other guy, there was no Tayla, there was no distance. There was just a love that I had never felt before her, flowing from my soul through my guitar and voice into her heart.

I looked over to the table my parents were sitting at and saw Dad extend a hand to Mum. They began dancing with each other next to their table and I couldn't help but laugh through a line of the chorus. I pictured Nina and I dancing like that on our wedding day. I knew that world only existed in my delusional mind, but I didn't care. It made me happy to think about.

By the time the final chorus came around most of the bar were singing along. Andjela held her phone aloft in one hand, her other hand was held by Aleks. She turned her phone around to film the bar, and I could see that she was broadcasting live on social media.

I didn't want the song to end. I didn't want the joy or the warm feeling the song gave me to end. 'And again!' I shouted, as I played through the chorus once more. Having so many people I knew there, and feeling so deeply about Nina, allowed me to connect with the audience on a level I hadn't engaged with them before. They could feel the emotion in my lyrics. You read words and think you understand what they mean, but you can't know until you feel them. I understood the word euphoria that night. *This is what I want to do for the rest of my life,'* I thought, smiling, looking at my parents dancing.

'Wow. Thank you. Thank you for making tonight so special. I just want to point out that my family aren't the only special guests tonight. We have the future number one tennis player in the world here. All the way from Serbia, Andjela Marjanović.'

Andjela jumped on stage and waved to everyone, taking a dramatic bow while holding her phone up, before jumping off the stage to stand next to Aleks. I watched him take her hand, Andjela turned towards him, and they kissed. They broke apart and she rested her head on Aleks' shoulder for a moment. I felt so envious of them. They got to meet and were perfect for one another, while I never got to meet Nina.

Scanning the room continuously I saw another familiar face. James had left the front of the stage and was standing next to three girls. One of them was Emma, who he had been on a couple of dates with, her friend Madison, and Tayla. She was making direct eye contact with me, but I couldn't figure out what kind of eye contact it was. I didn't know if she was upset at me for running out of the bar or deeply feeling what I was playing. To be honest, I didn't really care either way.

'So, I wrote this one in the last couple of weeks. I'm still working on it, so please, lower your expectations,' I said, smiling down at my guitar. While I felt upset and hurt that I wasn't with Nina anymore, I also felt grateful that our paths crossed. Even if it was just for a short period of time, she had made me a better person. When I was in my darkest times, where the cruel voice in my head started to viciously attack me, I could remind myself

that if she was at one stage my girl, then I couldn't be everything
that bullying voice in my head said I was.

I don't know what I did right to meet you.
You had my heart,
Right from the start.
You were a gift straight from heaven.
You restored my belief,
It happened quickly.

I put my heart on the line,
To forever call you mine.
To live in the divine,
You chance that hell may arrive.
You opened my eyes,
To my bully's poison lies.
So instead of the end,
My soulmate is now a friend.

I don't know what I did wrong to lose you,
But I watched you float away.
You couldn't stay.
I couldn't love you the way you needed.
When you looked, I was found nowhere.
Life's just not fair.

I put my heart on the line,
To forever call you mine.
To live in the divine,
You chance that hell may arrive.
You opened my eyes,
To my bully's poison lies.
So instead of the end,
My soulmate is now a friend.

You saw in me,
What I could never see.
If you were never mine,
I never would have found my light.

I put my heart on the line,
To forever call you mine.
To live in the divine,
You chance that hell may arrive.
You opened my eyes,
To my bully's poison lies.
So instead of the end,
My soulmate is now a friend.

As I finished my set, I looked at Andjela's phone and placed my hand on my heart. I had a strong sensation that I was being watched by Nina, but that was probably just wishful thinking. I walked off stage and immediately went to the change room to put away my guitar. Locking my case, I walked back to the main room of the bar and saw my parents. Mum was the first one to reach me, greeting me with a crushing bear hug. 'I'm so proud of you. We had the best time,' Mum said, poking Dad to prompt him to agree.

'It was great, mate. I didn't even feel like falling asleep,' Dad said, looking at Mum as if to ask her if that was good enough. Obviously, Dad kept the heartfelt stuff for when others weren't listening. 'So, time to go?'

'Hold on, I need to find Maja. Oh no, she's talking to some guy. He looks like he's thirty! Come on, let's grab her and go,' Mum said, quickly kissing me on the cheek before chasing after Dad, who was already on his way to save Maja.

I stood there scanning the bar. People were breaking off into their social groups, and a DJ walked onto stage to begin his set.

On one side of the bar were James and Michael with the three girls. On the other side of the bar were Andjela and Aleks.

'Hey! That was amazing. I had the best time,' Andjela said, bringing me into a one arm hug while holding her phone in the other hand. 'I just live streamed your entire set. Everyone commenting loved your songs. She hasn't said anything about the show yet, but I saw Nina watched the entire time.'

I couldn't help but break into a big smile, which I tried to hide by looking down at my feet. All but one of the original songs I played was about her, and she would have known that.

'Don't you get nervous when you're up there?' Aleks asked. I saw his hand reach down and once again take Andjela's. She accepted his and angled her body in to touch his.

'Not really. If I hit the first note I'm okay. It's just fun. It's nowhere near as scary as if I had gone to meet Nina in Serbia, or you know, be in any social situation,' I said, laughing awkwardly.

Andjela looked down at her phone and smiled before showing me her screen. It was a text from Nina. 'I watched the entire show. He's so good. He doesn't know how talented he is.'

I didn't even try to hold back my smile. Everything meant more coming from her. I could feel my hands shaking as I reached for my phone in my back pocket. I wanted to see if Nina texted me directly, so I turned my phone off flight mode. Opening my text thread with Nina, I saw she was online, and my unanswered text turned from delivered to read. I looked at it with anticipation, my heart rate increasing, waiting for her to tell me that she loved the show.

As quickly as the warm feeling of happiness spread to my extremities, the constricting feeling in my chest hit, as I saw her status change from online to offline. 'Hey, how are you?' was all I texted her, and I got ignored. Compliments meant more from her, but being ignored hurt more too. I felt like she had just broken up with me all over again. I felt nauseous. I needed the bathroom because I was about to throw up. There wasn't an escape though, I couldn't just run away from Andjela and Aleks.

I wanted to disappear. The sadness and hurt were swallowing me up. I needed the ground beneath me to open so I could disappear into it and never return. Leaving and entombing myself in my blankets in bed wouldn't be enough, it would just begin the soul crushing over thinking about why she hated me so much. *'What did I do wrong?'* I thought, desperately wracking my brain searching for an answer. I couldn't think of anything. All I wanted to do was talk to her. I missed Nina being my friend more than I missed her being my girlfriend. I didn't feel like I missed her like I missed my guitar; I missed her like there was a piece missing from me. A piece that I couldn't find anywhere else aside from in her love. I needed to be important to her again, and it shattered my soul that I wasn't worthy of a reply. *'I'm worthless,'* I thought, trying to keep the outer shell of myself composed.

I slipped my phone back in my pocket and hoped that I was hiding the heartbreak from my face. I took a deep, silent breath in through my nose and out through my mouth to try and relax myself.

'Is everything okay? You're really white,' Aleks said.

'Yeah, just had a notification that I'm almost out of data for the month. Not really sure how that's possible when it's only seven days into the month and I live on Wi-Fi.' I looked to my right and saw Michael and James still talking to the three girls. Tayla looked my way and smiled. 'I'll catch up with you guys later, okay?' They both nodded and I walked towards Michael and James.

'Hey, we were just talking about you,' James said, as he embraced me, smelling like beer. I extricated myself from his hug with great difficulty and shook Michael's extended hand.

'Hello, superstar,' Tayla said, looking me up and down.

'How are you?' I asked Tayla, hoping the gut-wrenching disappointment of being left on read by Nina wasn't apparent in my voice.

'Pretty good. We were just talking earlier today about what we were going to do tonight, and Emma suggested we come and see you play. Hard to say no to that idea. Luka, this is Emma and Madison. You probably don't remember them you were so drunk. For that matter, you might not even remember me. I'm Tayla,' Tayla said, sarcastically, pointing to her two friends and then herself. I shook both of their hands ignoring Tayla's attitude.

'Do you guys want to get a booth?' James asked, looking around the group.

'Great idea,' replied Emma. James placed his hand on the small of her back, guiding her towards the booths. Emma was the tallest with bushy red hair, blue eyes, and a joyful face. Madison was the shortest with shoulder length black hair, a round face, and big lips.

I attempted to follow but Tayla stopped me, placing a hand firmly on my chest. I stepped back and gave her a quizzical look. 'Where did you go?' Tayla asked sternly, crossing her arms holding her clasp purse. She was wearing a pair of high waisted blue jeans and a white crop top. Her blonde hair fell purposely and elegantly over her right shoulder. Tayla was extraordinarily pretty.

'I just went to put my guitar away,' I replied, pointing towards the dressing room, slightly confused as to why she would care where I went when I finished my set.

'No, no. That night in the bar. I thought we were having a good time, and you just disappeared without even a goodbye. I thought you would at least ask for my number. What happened?'

'Sorry. On the way to the bathroom, I started to feel sick, so I needed to leave and get some fresh air. Then they wouldn't let me back in,' I said, my eyes looking everywhere but meeting her direct and searching gaze. Her smoky mascara made her blue eyes pop. It felt like she was Medusa, and if I made eye contact it would be the end for me.

'You needed fresh air? Luka, we were at a rooftop bar. Please don't lie to me. If you're not interested in me then just be a man and tell me. I'm not a child,' said Tayla, her cadence increasing.

'It was more that I was feeling claustrophobic, and I needed space. I'm sorry for being rude. I was too drunk, and I could barely process putting one foot in front of the other. Can you forgive me?' I asked, putting my hands in my pockets and daring to make direct eye contact. She analysed my eyes for a moment, not blinking as she thought about what to say next.

'Under one condition. I want to take a photo with you,' Tayla said, showing me her phone.

'Umm, yeah. That's fine, I guess. Why do you want a photo with me?' I asked, confused. *If I had been so rude to her, why would such a basic thing be all it took for her to forgive me?* I thought, taking her phone.

'So that when you're a big star you won't forget the girl who you took your first fan photo with. Not that you would ever be able to forget me anyway,' Tayla said, batting her eyelids.

Tayla stood next to me, leaning in firmly to my body. I placed my hand around her waist, and she rested a hand gently on my chest. I forced a lip closed smile and snapped two photos. I handed her phone back and she looked at the pictures. I attempted to walk towards the booth where the others waited, but Tayla grabbed my wrist. 'I'm not happy with these. One more try,' she said, and pulled me back towards her.

I looked to my right and saw Aleks and Andjela laughing. Andjela had got her phone out to film, and Aleks was mocking me pretending to take selfies. I glowered at them before snapping my head back quickly to look at the camera to make it end. I felt so awkward and uncomfortable standing there while she continued to take photos. Once again Tayla scanned through the photos she took, and I didn't dare walk away for fear of being dragged back because of another unsatisfactory set of pictures.

'Oh, that's a cute one. We make a good-looking couple, don't you think?' Tayla asked, showing me the photo on her phone. She looked stunning, and I looked like I wanted to be a million kilometres away. Maybe fifteen thousand four hundred and ten kilometres away, but who's measuring?

'Yeah, it's great,' I said, attempting to walk towards the booth, but she was still blocking my path.

'Here, put your number in,' Tayla said, opening new contacts in her phone and handing it to me.

She was incredibly pretty, but she was starting to annoy me. It would be hard to put a fake number in because she had access to me with James dating Emma. Plus, she had already shown she wasn't afraid to turn up to my show even after I had run away. I decided to put in my real number and let future Luka deal with it. *This Luka's had enough,* ' I thought.

'Come on, let's go and sit with the others,' Tayla said, taking my hand and leading me to the booth.

A few days later after multiple sleepless nights, I was sitting next to Andjela, droopy eyed, watching Aleks at basketball training. 'Watch how he moves, he's such a natural, elegant athlete. Amazing. Our kids will be very talented. Are you even watching?' Andjela asked, nudging her elbow into my ribcage.

'Yeah, he's great,' I said, rubbing my ribs, and trying to stifle a yawn that looked like the king of the jungle roaring.

'Are you okay? You look terrible,' Andjela said, dragging her eyes off Aleks to look at me.

'I've barely slept the last few days. I'll be fine though. At some point I have to fall asleep, right?' I asked, hoping more than believing what I said.

'You seem really stressed. Maybe you need to get away for a little bit. A change of scenery,' Andjela suggested, turning her head back to watch Aleks walk towards the bench for a drink.

The look on her face was something to behold. *This is love. There could be one thousand people in here and she would be able to find Aleks immediately. I wonder if that's how Nina would have looked at me,'* I thought.

'I am, but where would I even go? I have to go to work for Dad, exams are in a couple of weeks, and I don't want to give up the one thing that's really getting me through this right now which is playing at One Note. If I go away, he'll find someone much better than me, and then I won't be able to play there anymore.'

I don't know if it was because I wasn't sleeping or because I wasn't with Nina, but my chest constantly felt tight. Ever since Nina stopped answering my calls it had been growing worse. I thought even though it would hurt when she broke up with me, at least it would take away the stress of me wondering why she wasn't treating me the same as when we first met, but I was wrong. The 'what if?' was a picnic compared to what I was feeling. The elephant was back sitting on my chest and had no interest in moving, ever. I had no idea how to get him to leave me alone. I felt hopeless.

'Did you see the bar on Saturday night? The place was going crazy, and that was because of you. The owner spoke to Aleks and I after your set saying he's worried what will happen to the bar when you leave because you've brought so much to it. Don't sell yourself short. Nina's right, you don't know how good you are. You even had that pretty, blonde girl all over you afterwards. What's happening there?'

Practice had finished so Aleks and the team were walking towards the change rooms to shower. Andjela pulled her legs up and crossed them on the seat, turning to face me, palms placed on her chin.

'I met her in a bar a few weeks ago. She's okay, I guess. I'm just not really interested, but don't want to hurt her feelings. I can't put my finger on it. It's just…it's just not the same,' I mumbled, dropping my head, and taking a deep breath trying to fight off the exhaustion and the elephant.

'You mean she's not Nina?' Andjela asked softly. I didn't feel like I could talk about it with James or Michael again. I thought I would be annoying them, but it was different talking to Andjela about Nina. Andjela was sitting in front of me. Nina's best friend was right there. I felt like I could reach through her and touch Nina.

'Yeah. As soon as I saw Nina, I could feel it. It's not fair. Why Andjela? Why? I'm so angry. I thought my nana sent me Nina as a way of looking after me, but then she was taken away. Why would this angel be sent to me and get taken from me before I got to meet her? Why does the most incredible woman I've met in my life have to be the woman I can't meet? I know I'm sounding like a whiny spoiled child right now, but she's all I can think about. I can't sleep because I can't shake her from my mind. I don't know what to do,' I said, my breathing becoming rapid, trying with all my might not to completely break down. The lack of sleep had worn my patience down to nothing.

'Then why don't you meet her? Why don't you come to Požega and meet her?' Andjela asked, smiling as if it was like driving to the next suburb.

'What are you talking about?' I asked, bewildered.

'You're sitting here and complaining about not meeting her, but you're not actually doing anything about it. Yes, it's a long way, but you could get on a plane tonight if you wanted. She doesn't want words Luka, she wants actions. She doesn't want you to tell her that you love her, she wants you to show her that you love her. Here,' Andjela said, reaching into her purse and pulling out an envelope.

'What's this?'

'Open it.'

I carefully undid the blue envelope and pulled out the piece of blue and silver cardboard inside. Scrawled upon it with black cursive writing was an invitation.

Nina's Birthday
August 23rd 21:00
Sunshine Café

'She invited me?' I asked, feeling shocked, holding the invitation up in my quivering hand. My heart started pounding at the idea of going to Nina's birthday. I wanted hope, I just didn't want false hope. It had to be a big, cruel practical joke. Andjela was about to burst out laughing and rip the invitation from my hand. It would be incredibly mean and massively out of character for her, but still more likely than Nina inviting me to her birthday.

'She didn't, but I know she wants you there. I've known her since I was six. I know her, and I know she needs to meet you. Organising this is going to be my birthday present to her. We're going to surprise her,' Andjela said, bouncing in her seat with the excitement of a child on Christmas morning.

'So, this is real? It isn't a joke? I'm not going to turn up to a bar and see six Serbian guys that don't speak a word of English wondering what I'm doing there?'

'Don't be stupid. Luka, this is real. Her birthday is in less than three months. This is real if you want it to be. Here's your opportunity, but if you don't take this chance then you don't deserve her. If you want her, then go and get her.' Andjela was leaning forward urging me on, like she was urging herself to find that last effort in a long three-set match. My eyes were wide staring at the invitation. Adrenalin coursed through my body. My heart was pounding with excitement like I was about to go to the airport.

Does Nina really want me there though? I don't want to ruin her birthday and be there when I'm not welcome,' I thought, unable to stop butterflies springing to life, chasing the elephant from my chest. The despairing hopelessness was gone, and the euphoria of possibility had returned.

'I need to think about this,' I said, tapping the invitation on my knee. I could feel every possible scenario running through my head simultaneously. I was terrified, excited, happy, and nervous, all at the same time. I didn't feel tired anymore but knew I would sleep easily and deeply that night.

'You won't regret coming. You'll only regret not coming, Luka,' Andjela said, standing up and shooting a spare basketball that had rolled to us. Air ball.

'I hope that's not a sign,' I thought.

CHAPTER SEVENTEEN
The Birthday Party

I dragged my body from my bed to lay on the couch while my brain loaded for the day. I had been awake earlier that morning texting Marko but fell back asleep. It was a warm Saturday morning, and I found I was alone in the house. I assumed Milica and Jovan were out with friends, and Mama at Baka's house. She loved to visit her for a coffee and sit in the garden on a sunny morning. We were in the twilight of spring with summer reminding us every few days it was just around the corner.

Usually at that time of the year after school had finished, Andjela and I would be at the pool, or finding different nature walks to go on. Sadly, those days were most likely gone because she was in Melbourne with Aleks and would soon be on the WTA tour full-time.

I laid on the couch and opened my phone to see a picture text from Andjela. She was in the bar where Luka played every week. I was in disbelief she got to see him play in person. 'Can you stream his concert for me please? I want to watch him play,' I texted Andjela.

'Of course. He's going on in a couple of minutes,' she replied immediately.

I bounced off the couch and quickly organised myself a coffee knowing I wouldn't be able to drink that piping hot wake up juice until about three songs into his set.

With my breakfast ready in my cup, I sat on the couch and leant my phone against the cushions so I could watch without getting a sore arm. Luka began to play, and I instantly recognised the song. It was the first song he ever played for me. Something was awakened in me. I didn't feel like the woman that broke up with him, nor did I feel like the woman who was his friend. I felt like the woman who was his girlfriend again. I was transported to sitting at my desk hearing him play the song to me for the first time from his bedroom. The feelings I was trying to push away since we broke up burst from me like a phoenix from the ashes. Butterflies exploded into life inside me and I craved to be his again, for Luka to be mine. To finally touch him, to feel his loving embrace.

I had a front row view of Luka playing but I didn't feel like I was in the front row. I felt like he was on the couch playing for me. Only for me. Repeatedly he looked into the camera as if he knew I was on the other end. I could feel in my chest that he was looking into my soul. *'How is it possible to feel like someone is staring into your soul when you're watching him play on your phone from the other side of the world, and he doesn't know you're watching?'* I wondered.

I was entranced by his play. The way he tapped his foot to keep his timing. The way his body swayed and moved in perfect unison with the melody. His facial expressions showed the emotion of what he was singing about. I thought he would look hurt singing about me, but the only way to describe the look on his face as he performed was joyous.

He began to play a song I had never heard. *'He said he never had feelings for anyone that he has for me. Sorry, had for me. So maybe this new song is about me too,'* I thought. Maybe I was wrong, and it wasn't about me at all, but the guilt I felt was inescapable. In my soul I could feel he was singing about me. I felt a stabbing pain in my chest that I caused him the kind of pain that I could feel in his lyrics and saw etched on his face. In the end, there is no escaping hurting those you love.

His lyrics weren't angry though, they were grateful. Grateful for our time, and that I was in his life. Even though I was glad he was grateful, I desperately wanted to be a bigger part of his life. To be his every day, within arm's length, not a day on a plane away. *'Is it even possible? I guess it could be if we want it enough, but maybe he's moved on?'* I wondered.

Where just a moment before there was a stabbing in my chest, there was now a hollow feeling of sadness that I couldn't make a future with the love of my life work. A silent tear ran down my left cheek, and I could see its streak reflected in my phone, but I refused to wipe it away. I deserved the sadness. I deserved the pain.

I carried my phone to my room and got my Luka hoodie from my closet. I didn't care that it was a warm morning. I pulled it over my head and walked back to the couch, once again sitting down, and leaning my phone against a cushion. I bowed my head to smell the hoodie, to smell Luka. His scent had long been washed away but that smell was burned in my memory. His scent wafted from my memories, up through my nostrils and I closed my eyes to take it in, wanting to focus all my energy on that scent. My body yearned to bury my head in his chest and drift off to sleep with his arms wrapped around me tightly.

Through the concert, Andjela turned the camera around so I could see the rest of the bar. I saw his friends and family having a great time together, laughing and dancing. The cruel teasing questions started to roll around my mind. Did I do the right thing? Did I give up too quickly? Andjela and Aleks were making it work, so why couldn't I make it work with Luka? Maybe I just didn't deserve him.

I found myself singing along and even clapping after he finished a song as if I was in the crowd myself. It would have been embarrassing if anyone came home and saw me clapping to a guy singing on my phone. The guilt and pain of not being with him anymore was replaced with enjoying watching him do what he loved. It was infectious. I could only have enjoyed it more if I was standing right in front of him in person.

Andjela was lucky she got to be there, and more so because she was there in person with the guy she loved. If I hadn't met Luka that night, then she never would have met Aleks. While I could have been resentful, I wasn't. It was beautiful that my love with Luka could birth another romance. I was having too much fun watching Luka to have a negative thought in my mind.

The concert ended and four words accidentally slipped from my lips. 'I love you, Luka,' I said to my phone, as I spun my hair around my finger. As if he heard me, a huge smile broke across his face as he tapped his right hand on his heart, looking directly into the camera of Andjela's phone. My fingers stopped twirling my hair and fell to my chest, where I put my hand on my heart so I could feel him.

Luka walked off stage and the feed fell dead on my phone. I sat for a couple of minutes processing what I just watched, then texted Andjela to tell her how good he was, and he had no idea how talented he was yet. My body collapsed back onto the couch to try and emotionally recover from the last forty-five minutes. *'He must still love me if he played all those songs he wrote about me, knowing that Andjela was there,'* I thought, beaming. There was no wiping the smile from my face.

Opening my phone, I read the text that Luka sent me the previous day. I stared at it for a moment and saw Luka's status change from offline to online. He asked me the most basic of questions, yet my fingers had frozen. They sat above the keys on my phone unable to come up with any kind of coherent response. *How am I? I don't know. How am I supposed to tell him I feel amazing, miserable, hopeless, and hopeful all at once, because I'm still head over heels in love with the most amazing man I could ever not meet?'* I thought, feeling nauseous with all those emotions swirling around inside me. It was too much to deal with, I felt overwhelmed, so I exited the chat thread without replying.

'Am I a terrible person for not replying?' I wondered, sitting in silence, staring at the wall. I didn't want to lie and just give the generic response, 'Hi, I'm good thanks, you?' I wanted to tell him that I was in love with him. That I wanted to be his, and whatever the hurt I would feel while waiting for him, it would be worth it to be in his arms one day. *What if he doesn't feel the same? What if he's moved on, and all the emotion he was singing with was coming from a different source?'* I asked myself. He could have met someone else, and she was bringing that beauty out in him. I couldn't risk not hearing him respond with the words I so desperately craved him to say to me. I love you too, Nina. That's all I wanted to hear. *It was probably best to say nothing at all. For now,'* I thought.

Even though I just saw him, I already missed his face. I missed the way he moved. I missed those eyes. My gosh, how I missed those eyes. Opening my phone, I headed straight to his social media and scanned through all the photos I had seen a bajillion times before. He didn't post very often, so I didn't have a lot of photos to gaze upon. I wanted to see if there were any that I hadn't seen before, so I opened his tagged photos.

There she was. A blonde bombshell named Tayla, going by the name on her profile. She had a very pretty face, beautiful blonde hair flowing over her shoulder with a perfect hourglass figure. Standing in tight to Luka with his arm around her, her body touching his body, her hand on his chest. The description read, 'My Star'. My blood was boiling. *How dare she touch him? How dare she call him 'My Star'?'* I thought, as my hands started to shake with rage. I hated her. I wanted to hurt her. She was touching my Luka. *He's not yours anymore, remember?'* I told myself. I didn't know anything more about her aside from her name, but I hated her more than I had hated anyone in my life. I wanted to burst into painful tears. To punch something. To break something. Anything to assuage the pain. The pain radiated through my body, emanating from my soul. A deep pain that I had never felt before. I was immobilised, all I could do was continue to stare at the photo, letting the knife be plunged into my soul over and over again. I should have been the woman that he had his arm around, not her.

I felt disgusting, ugly, and stupid. For a moment I was foolish enough to believe that there could be a way to make things work with Luka. I was so naïve. There was a beautiful Australian woman that Luka could see whenever he wanted, could kiss whenever he wanted, whereas all I could do was send him a kissing emoji. *'I bet he's kissing her right now. I'm going to be sick,'* I thought, running to the bathroom. I knelt in front of the toilet wanting to throw up the image from my body. To purge myself of the disgusting thought of Luka kissing another woman. The image wouldn't leave me. It was tattooed on my mind, and I knew that it would be haunting my dreams.

I wondered who he would pick. *'If Tayla and I were standing in front of him, who would he walk towards? I bet he would pick her. She didn't hurt him like I did. If I hadn't left him, then he never would have met her. It's all my fault. I deserve the pain. I hate myself,'* I thought with disgust.

I thought of them laughing together, cuddled together watching movies, her telling him how much she loved his soulful eyes, and falling asleep together. Him writing songs about her. Her meeting his family, them getting married, having children. Having the children I dreamed I would be having with him. It wasn't her fault; it was my fault that my future had faded away.

I walked to my room, ripped my Luka hoodie off, threw it into my closet and I burst into tears. I laid down and held the Luka pillow close to me, crying painfully into it. The tears felt like they were coming from a place deep inside me. They weren't sadness tears from my heart; they were tears from a shattered soul. I clung tightly to the pillow praying that it would turn into Luka. I would have given anything to have him laying with me, or to be in that bar with him. I knew he wouldn't want me to be though. He didn't want me anymore. I sobbed loudly and didn't care who could hear my cries. I wanted to scream but couldn't scream loud enough to rid the pain from my body. I had ruined everything.

She didn't do anything wrong and neither did he. I broke up with him, and he was doing what he should be doing, moving on. To see it hurt much more than thinking he would find another girlfriend though.

I thought the destruction of my heart when we broke up was as bad as it could get, but that pain was a whole new level I didn't know I could feel. I fell into a deeper pit of despair than I had ever fallen before. I had broken my own heart again. I wanted him to be happy, but really, I wanted him to be happy with me.

After what felt like an eternity of sobbing into my Luka pillow, I got my breathing and tears under control. Last time I broke my heart it was days before Andjela dragged me out of my hole, but Andjela wasn't there to do it again. I had to do it myself. I couldn't be on my own. I needed to move on like Luka had, even if I wasn't ready. Picking up my phone, which was bounced from my bed in my emotional breakdown, I texted Marko. 'So, when are we going on this date?'

A couple of weeks had passed since the night Andjela was at Luka's concert. I took a seat in the town centre waiting for her to arrive. I was wearing a short black dress sitting in the summer sun watching children run through the fountain laughing. Andjela got home the previous night, and I couldn't wait to hear everything about her trip.

'Hey,' Andjela said, running up to me. I jumped up and hugged her as we swayed side to side trying to squash each other.

'This is a cute dress.' Andjela stood back to admire it. She wore a white sundress with flowers on it.

'I just bought it last weekend,' I said, posing for a moment to show it off. It was a cheer up Nina present for self-care.

'You look amazing. We need to take a picture together.' Andjela reached into her purse and pulled out her phone to take a photo. 'Love it. I'm posting this. You look so good; Luka will definitely be commenting on it. Oh, not Luka, umm, random Australian guys not called Luka,' Andjela said, winking, as we took a seat under the trellis full of blooming flowers giving us shade from the sun.

'I doubt he's thinking about me anyway. So how was the trip?' I didn't want Andjela to know I was creeping around on social media and found that photo of Luka with that girl. That girl, I couldn't even bring myself to say her name.

'Oh Nina, it was amazing. I didn't want to leave. Aleks and I were crying at the airport when he dropped me off. I guess it's what I've signed up for though. We'll keep having to say airport goodbyes, but I know that one day we won't have to anymore,' Andjela said, her voice cracking. Andjela's eyes were glassy, like she was back in the airport with Aleks.

'Wow, you're really smitten.'

'No, I'm not smitten. I'm in love with him. Doesn't it show how fragile things are? All of this happened because Marko is a vile pig. If he didn't do that to you at his party, then you don't leave early. If you don't leave the party, then you don't meet Luka, and in turn, I don't meet Aleks. It's crazy how close we were to never meeting at all,' Andjela said, with her eyes now back in focus. She leaned back on the bench and little beams of sunlight broke through the flower covered trellis to shine upon her in her flowery white sundress.

'Well, if it meant you met the love of your life, I would go through all of it again,' I said, forcing a smile.

'Are you saying if it wasn't for that, you wish you hadn't met him?' Andjela asked, with her carefree expression turning serious.

'What do you mean?' I asked.

'I can see it Nina, you're still in love with him. Whether you admit it to me or not. Do you ever wish that you hadn't met Luka? If you had the chance to go back in time and not go on that website, would you? Then you wouldn't have gone through the heartache that you have the last couple of months.' She had turned her body to face me, crossing her right leg over her left, those green eyes staring into me.

'I just said yes, because it meant you met Aleks so…' I began to say before Andjela cut me off.

'Take me out of it. Just answer about you. Do you regret meeting Luka?'

I sat there thinking for a moment before I answered. Andjela sat and silently watched me ponder her question. She was looking for any little physical tell to make sure I was telling her the truth. I had never thought about it like that before. Sure, it would have caused me less pain, but would I rather have never met him and give up all those feelings, and those amazing memories?

'No. I'm happy I met him. Yeah, it hurts a lot, and it almost feels cruel that we live so far away, but being in love with Luka was the best I've ever felt. I felt things I had never felt before. Emotions that I thought only existed in books. He set a standard that I know I need to find if I'm going to be with someone else. If I never feel that again, then I'm grateful I was able to experience that with him, because not everyone gets to have those feelings.'

'Do you really think you won't feel that again? I mean you're about to turn eighteen and you're already thinking you might not feel love again. It's kind of sad.'

'Life is sad. It's hard. Not everyone gets their fairy tale happy ending. I'm not saying it won't happen, but it's hard to believe that someone else can make me feel the kind of love I have for him. It just seems like every relationship I have will be a little disappointing because it won't be with Luka. I don't think you ever truly get over losing your soulmate,' I said with a grimace. Even though it hurt to think about not being with Luka, the thought of him still made my soul smile.

'Have? As in current? Look at those eyes twinkle,' Andjela said, a smile spreading across her face.

'Whatever, it doesn't matter. I blew it anyway,' I said, shrugging.

'I don't think you blew it with him. Maybe you just needed some time apart to fully understand how much he means to you. If you really are meant to be together then I'm sure you'll find a way. I bet he would visit if you asked him to,' Andjela said, extending a hand and placing in on my arm.

'No one is insane enough to fly from Melbourne to Belgrade, then get a bus three hours just to see their ex-girlfriend,' I said, scoffing at her ridiculous idea.

'You might be surprised,' Andjela said, turning away to watch the children playing in the fountain.

Andjela's eyes left me and moved to look behind me, her face turned from a smile, to a look of revulsion. I felt a large hand lay upon my shoulder and my heart ceased beating as I recognised who it belonged to. Immediately I began to nervously pick at my fingers. I looked up as Marko leant down and kissed me directly on the lips. There was a clatter on the ground as I broke the kiss with Marko and saw Andjela's keys lying beside her feet. She was staring from Marko to me, her mouth hanging open in complete shock.

'What the hell was that? Get away from her. What are you doing? What's happening?' Andjela yelled in a high-pitched voice, jumping up from the bench. She stood with her left foot forward, looking like she was getting ready to punch Marko again.

'Didn't you tell her? You told me you were going to tell her,' Marko said to me, and I could hear the disappointment in his voice.

'Good job Nina, you are the gold standard of ruining things with everyone,' I thought, ashamed of myself. Trying to save everyone's feelings had led me to hurt everyone's feelings.

'Yeah, but she was away, and I wanted to tell her face to face. I was going to tell her today, but you came before I got the chance,' I attempted to explain to Marko.

'Tell me what?' Andjela asked, hoping that the one percent chance it was all a sick joke came to fruition. She was still standing in a fighting stance ready to uncoil at a moment's notice.

'Marko and I have been spending time together,' I said, diplomatically.

'Spending time together? Nina, tell her the truth. Andjela, we're dating,' Marko said directly to Andjela.

'Hold on a second. You go from Luka to this muscled up virus? Seriously? Tell me this is a joke, Nina. Tell me this is all a big joke, and we can move on with our lives,' she said, waving her hands animatedly. She closed her eyes forcefully, then opened them again widely, trying to make her nightmare end.

'It's not a joke, Andjela. I like hanging out with him. We've moved past that night,' I said, as Marko placed his hand on my shoulder. I pushed it away; it was no time for affection.

Andjela stared open mouthed at a loss for words. Her disgust was written all over her face. I had never seen her look like that before.

'I just want us to be friends. That we can hang out together and have a fun summer. Can we do that Andjela?' Marko asked, extending his hand towards her.

'Luka set a standard, a standard for how you should be treated, you literally just said that, and then you drop your standards to the gutter. How long has this been going on? How long have you been lying to me?' Andjela asked, looking from Marko's extended hand to his face with contempt. I could hear her blood boiling. Marko withdrew his hand and put it in his pocket.

'About six weeks.'

'Six weeks!?' I can't even look at you right now. Nina, I love you, but I watched this germ force himself upon you, which had you feeling as low as dirt. I'm not going to spend one minute of my last summer in Požega around him. I'm so disappointed in you,' Andjela said, as she glowered at me, then picked up her keys, and shot a final look of disgust at both Marko and me, before walking away.

It felt like someone had cut open my chest and punched my heart each step she took away from me. I thought it would be bad, but I never thought it would be that bad when I told her. I sat there staring after her as she turned the corner out of sight. I wanted to burst into tears. I had already lost Luka; I couldn't lose Andjela too. *What am I going to do?* I thought, panicked.

A couple of days passed and all my attempts to communicate with Andjela went ignored. I thought she would be upset, but I didn't think she would react as strongly as she did. If she wasn't going to reply to my calls or texts, then I would go to her house.

Andjela's house was on the other side of town. Usually, I would get a taxi there, but I had no obligations for the day, so I felt like a long walk in the fresh mountain air would give me some time to think about what I was going to say to her.

I loved the vibe of summer. There were always people congregated out the front of their houses with friends, while their children played in the front yard. Children are always outside playing in summer in Požega. I could have done without having to say hello five hundred times a day, but it was nice seeing people happy. Maybe when you have winters as cold as ours, you truly appreciate when the sun comes out. When we were little, Andjela would be at my house first thing every morning. We would go out and not come home until it was time for dinner. We wouldn't do anything interesting apart from walk around town and talk. Sitting in the train museum eating chips and laughing with each other. Those are some of the happiest memories of my life. I couldn't lose my most important and treasured friend.

I walked through the front gate of Andjela's house and up the steps that led to her front door. The blinds were covering the windows either side of the front door, so I couldn't look into the living room to see if she was home. I knocked on the faded white front door with chips of paint missing, and heard the scuffing of a chair moving, followed by slow footsteps. 'Oh, hey,' Andjela said, with a mixture of disappointment and shame in her voice, making momentary eye contact before looking at the ground behind me.

'Hey, can I come in?' I asked. Normally when I arrived at Andjela's house, I opened the door myself and walked in, but that day I made sure to knock. Andjela stood in the middle of the door frame, her eyes still focused behind me. She nodded her head after a moment and stood aside so I could cross the threshold into her house. There was a small entrance room that had a hallway leading to the bedrooms, a door to the left led to a study, and the door to the right led to the kitchen and living room. We went through the open door on the right into the kitchen.

'Sorry I didn't reply,' Andjela mumbled, taking a seat at the kitchen table, looking intently at the fake flower centrepiece, on top of a delicate lace placemat, in the middle of the table. It was a combination of white and red roses. I waited for her to offer an explanation as to why she didn't reply, but none was forthcoming. She was wearing a white singlet with black shorts and her face was red, so I assumed she had just got home from tennis practice.

'Why didn't you?' I asked quietly, taking the seat next to her. Andjela got up from the table, filled two glasses with water and dropped a lemon slice in each, placing one in front of me, and clinging onto the other herself.

'I didn't know what to say. I was mad at you and embarrassed. Disappointed in myself for how I reacted,' Andjela said, turning her attention from the centrepiece to the lemon slice in her glass. It floated gently in the water, with the lemon flesh starting to fray. It was very hot in Andjela's house, so the glass already had drops of condensation.

We sat in silence, and I had no idea how long it lasted. It was almost a contest of who would speak first. It wasn't a normal friend argument, it was about something much deeper, so I didn't know the best way to handle the makeup conversation with her. I didn't know if I should talk about something random to get the conversation flowing, or dive right into the reason I was there. The only thoughts I had the last couple of days were about talking to her, not what I would say. On the walk over my mind was a blank. The entire walk was filled with thoughts about whether she would even let me in, or would she slam the door in my face, or worse, not open the door at all.

'Why him?' Andjela whispered, still staring at her lemon slice, she looked like if she focused on it hard enough, she would be able to make it levitate.

'Umm,' I said, completely unprepared for the most obvious answer she would want.

'I watched him completely disrespect you. He showed that you're only a conquest to him. If you watched me be with someone who had done that to me, then you would be so disappointed in me, and here you are with Marko. Please help me understand,' Andjela said, finally dragging her eyes from her glass and making eye contact with me.

'Well, he's smart, hot, has like a bajillion pack,' I began to say, before she cut me off with a laugh filled with venom.

'Seriously? That's it? I watched a boy cheat on you and felt sick to my stomach, as if he'd cheated on me. You go from that and meet this beautiful man who is perfect for you. Who treats you like his queen, and that ended. Trust me, I feel it every day, I understand why. But then you drop your standards to this. Back to a boy who sexually assaulted you and his explanation is, sorry, I had too much to drink. Why don't you respect yourself?' Andjela asked, her venom turning to frustration, causing her eyes to begin to well with tears.

'I'm not you, Andjela. I'm not a mentally strong elite athlete that can fly around the world and see her boyfriend. I don't have the money to get on a plane and visit Luka. So that just means I have to find a guy here,' I said, shrugging with a pained smile on my face. Droplets began to fall from Andjela's eyes, causing my eyes to start burning with painful tears.

'I'm not saying get on a plane and go to Luka. I'm saying there are lots of great guys here, and Marko definitely isn't one of them,' Andjela said, wiping the tears streaking down her red cheeks.

'He's been nice to me since that night. Maybe you just need to give him a chance like I have,' I said. My tears began to slow as I spoke about Marko.

'When you were with Luka it was the happiest I've ever seen you. Since you broke up, I've barely seen that sparkle in your eye. You say you've been hanging out with Marko for six weeks, and your eyes have been dead unless we've been talking about Luka. Whether you want to keep lying to yourself or not, Marko isn't going to bring out that sparkle in you,' Andjela said.

'I don't know what you want from me.'

'You don't owe me an explanation, but you owe yourself one. If you can't at least be honest with yourself, then I don't see the point in talking about this anymore,' Andjela said, standing up from the table.

'Stop. Can you please sit down? Can we keep talking? Please?' I begged her, grabbing a hold of her arm. Andjela stared at me for a moment in thought, considering whether she should pull her arm away or sit back down. I didn't dare break eye contact, not even to blink. I wasn't strong enough to have the conversation with myself; I needed to have it with her.

'Okay,' Andjela whispered, and took her seat, so I let go of her arm. She was sitting on the edge of her seat, ready to get up at any moment.

'You want to know why him? It's because I'm sad. I'm sad, Andjela. Even though we broke up and I'm with Marko now, Luka is still the first thing I think about when I wake up, and the last thing I think about before I fall asleep. I know he's perfect for me, more so than any other man on this planet, but I'm stuck here. And he's stuck there. Every day was hurting more and more because I just wanted to be with him, but I wasn't. I thought that if I broke up with him, then the pain would stop. This pain would stop,' I said. I could feel something constricting my chest, it was becoming hard to breathe. I placed both my hands on my chest, as if to fight off whatever was preventing my lungs from taking in air. The tears started to roll down my cheeks again, and I knew I wouldn't be able to stop them. 'It hasn't stopped though. Maybe it will one day, and maybe it won't. So yes, I'm still in love with Luka, and I know even in fifty years part of me will still be in love with him, but at least I can hold Marko's hand. We can go on dates. I can kiss him.' Andjela had tears flowing from her green eyes at the same speed as mine. She wiped them away with her palm to be instantly replaced by fresh tears.

'You know I understand that because I'm with Aleks. I know how hard this distance is for me, and I imagine it's just as hard for you,' Andjela whispered, her crying eyes looking into mine.

'Yeah and now imagine if you hadn't been able to see Aleks at all. You know that build-up of pressure in your chest when you haven't seen him in a while?' I asked Andjela, and she nodded. I leaned forward in my chair almost pleading for her to understand me. 'Well imagine if you didn't have the release of actually seeing him. That moment where you didn't realise how hard it was to breathe until you finally hugged him. That pressure just built and built until it was too much for me. I love him more than I could love anyone, more than I love myself, but I couldn't breathe anymore.'

'I'm sorry you're hurting so much. I wish you talked to me about this. Maybe I could have helped,' Andjela said, taking my hand in hers and squeezing it.

'I'm tired of being sad. No, we aren't going to live happily ever after, and that's okay, but at least I don't feel sad when I'm with Marko. He's been a perfect gentleman to me since that night. No, he isn't Luka. No other man ever will be Luka, but please Andjela, I need you to understand me. The last two days I've been out of my mind scared that I was going to lose you.

I've already lost the love of my life; I can't lose my best friend too,' I said, squeezing her hand, our tears still flowing.

'You will never lose me. You're my sister. I won't tell you what to do, because you need to do what's best for you. Just be careful with him. Please,' Andjela said, leaning forward in her seat. We both stood and pulled each other into a strong, loving hug.

'I invited him to my birthday. Marko. I'm not asking you to like him, I'm just asking you to not break his nose again,' I said, laughing through my tears, still hugging Andjela.

'I hope your tata doesn't get to him at the party.'

'Or worse, my mama,' I said, and we broke our hug laughing at the thought of Mama chasing Marko out of my birthday party.

It had been about three months since hanging out with Marko at his pool. Things were fine between us, and he and Andjela were civil with one another, but there was something missing. There were no butterflies with Marko, he just helped me avoid feeling sad about Luka. That shouldn't be a reason to be with someone, but it was the best strategy I had to avoid falling back into that pit of despair.

I had applied to university and been accepted into the biology program. I would be going to Belgrade to study in September. That meant a lot of down time with nothing to do apart from hang out. Marko decided to travel for a year before coming back to study. We both knew our summer fling was just that, and we had no future. It would be impossible for me to see a future with anyone as long as my heart belonged to Luka. No matter how hard I tried, my heart continued to yearn for him.

While I wasn't in complete despair not being with Luka, I wasn't able to shake the thought of him from my mind. Even if it was just a summer fling, I couldn't stay with Marko any longer.

I didn't want to be that type of person. *'I need to end things with him,'* I thought.

'Hey honey, are you almost ready to go?' Tata asked, sticking his head into my bedroom. It was my birthday. My eighteenth birthday. Tata came home the day before from work just to celebrate with me. Andjela told me for weeks there was going to be a birthday surprise, and having Tata there was the best present I could ask for.

'Yeah, just finishing getting ready,' I replied, as I did the final touches on my makeup. I straightened my hair and parted it to the right. It fell over the front of my right shoulder, while the left side was behind my ear and down my back.

I stood up and examined myself in my full-length mirror that was attached to the front of my closet. Mama and I bought a new dress just for my party a few days earlier. It was a figure hugging, light pastel blue, one shoulder mini dress. I ran my hands down my front to iron out a small crease.

Opening my closet, I looked through my shoes to find the perfect pair of heels to go with my new birthday dress. I found a pair of gold toe post tie leg heeled sandals. I took a seat on my bed and put them on. I walked back to my closet mirror and examined the finished product. Placing my hands on my hips, I tilted my head and while I was ready to go, something was missing. Luka. I picked up my phone and took a picture, sending it to him. 'Ready for my party. Wish you were here for it.'

Luka and I had been talking more. I felt lucky to have him in my life, even if it wasn't in the way I wanted him to be. My phone vibrated in my hand, so I looked down at it to see an immediate reply. *'It's the weekend. Why is he replying to me in the middle of the night?'* I wondered.

'You look so beautiful, sunshine. I wish I could be there too. Happy birthday.' Sunshine. I loved when he called me sunshine.

I felt a rush of dopamine, serotonin and oxytocin run through my body. I read the message back multiple times with a big smile on my face. Immediately I replied with a red heart emoji. *'Shouldn't the butterflies become milder the further you are from your breakup?'* I wondered, staring down at the word with a smile painted on my face.

I was about to walk from my room when my Luka scrapbook caught my eye. I had been working on it intermittently and only had one photo left to write about. *'Maybe if I write the final entry then it will feel like Luka is with me at the party,'* I thought.

Tata and Mama would be annoyed for making them wait, but it was my birthday, so they would just have to deal with a five-minute delay. I took a seat at my desk and opened the scrapbook to the last photo I had. It was from our last date before we broke up. I had accidentally woken him, but he was still happy for me to call. We spoke long into the Williamstown night.

'Nina! Are you ready?' Tata yelled through the door beginning to sound impatient.

'Give me five minutes. I'm almost done,' I yelled back. I began to write.

This date was somehow my happiest memory, yet one of my saddest with you. I asked if you had time for a video call, and even though you were sleeping, you said yes. You always made time for me. You still always make time for me. For three hours I felt butterflies constantly in my stomach, unable to stop myself from staring into your eyes. I knew in that moment that I could stare into those eyes for the rest of my life. When our date ended, I sat there gazing at this picture I had taken. I took it just as you called me your girl. Both of us feeling immeasurable happiness. Then a sadness took over. That all I wanted to do was fall asleep in your arms, but I couldn't. I wanted to be waking up next to you every morning, but I couldn't see that happening in the next four years. Going through that craving pain in my stomach of missing you so

deeply became stronger constantly. I loved you more every day. Still,
I think often about what life would be like if I never let you go.
What our life would be like. I'm still in love with you, Luka.

I took a deep breath and sat for a moment staring into space.
'Why couldn't he just live next door? Why does life have to be
so hard sometimes?' I groaned, desperate for him to be with me
for my birthday.

'Nina! Let's go! We're late!' Tata screamed through the door
again, knocking hard upon it.

'Coming!'

I stood up, collected my phone and purse, and walked
through the door to find Tata red faced in a suit on the other
side, leaving my scrapbook open on my desk.

'Sorry,' I said, walking straight by him.

'What were you doing in there?' he asked, frustrated,
following me towards the front door.

'Just finishing a book. I only had a little to go and I wanted
to finish it before the party,' I said, as he followed me through
the front door to the car which was already running.

'A book?! We're running late to your birthday because you
were reading a book?' Tata asked incredulously.

The sun was setting on the warm, still, August evening. It
was a perfect summer night. Mama, Milica, and Jovan were
waiting in the car for us.

'It's alright you two. We can call off search and rescue, we've
found Nina,' Mama said sarcastically to my siblings, as I put on
my seatbelt.

'Okay, let's go,' Tata said, putting the car into reverse and
backing out of our driveway at a speed like we were escaping a
wildfire.

It was almost nine so people would be arriving soon. I was
expecting around one hundred people, including family, friends,
and then obligatory invitations for friends of my parents.

Five minutes later we walked through the front doors of The Sunshine Café. There were high, small round tables surrounding the dance floor. A stage was set up to the left of the main entrance, opposite to the platformed area, next to the side door which led to the outside seating area. A large cake reading 'Happy Eighteenth Birthday Nina' sat on a table on stage where people had started to place presents. All around the café were balloons with '18' on them, and there were streamers on the walls. *I wonder how many I'll be able to take home,'* I thought, looking around at all the tempting balloons.

Mama and Tata broke off immediately and started talking to our family. Jovan and Milica saw my little cousins and ran off with them. As I walked around the café, people came up to hug me and wished me a happy birthday. With every happy birthday wish, I seemed to feel a little bit worse. There were so many people there, but there was one person who wasn't. I didn't want to think about what was missing, but I couldn't shake those perfect eyes from my mind.

'Hey, sorry I'm a little bit late,' Andjela said, embracing me and kissing me on the cheek. 'Happy birthday. Sorry I didn't bring your present, it's better that I give it to you later.' Andjela was wearing a black, strapless bodysuit with red heels. She wore red lipstick, and her blonde wavy hair was down to the small of her back.

'That's okay. I'm just glad you're here. You look amazing. I love your hair. I bet Aleks loved this look,' I said, stepping back to check out Andjela.

'Look at what he sent me after I sent him a photo,' Andjela said, showing me her phone. It was a video of Aleks' jaw opening and then him pretending to pass out on the floor. 'Isn't he just too cute?'

'You're both very lucky,' I said, hoping I didn't sound jealous.

'Obviously we've saved the best for last. Look at you. Look at this dress. This is outrageous,' Andjela said, twirling her finger to make me spin around. 'I almost reacted like Aleks when I walked in here and saw you. Excuse me, can you take a picture please?' Andjela asked the waiter walking past.

Andjela and I posed for a moment as the waiter took our photo, at first standing up, then he proceeded to crouch down to get one from another angle. *He's really putting in a strong effort here,'* I thought.

'Thank you,' Andjela said with a smile, taking her phone back from the waiter. 'You really do look extraordinary.'

'Thanks,' I said, and I could feel the heat rising in my face.

Andjela looked down at her phone to scroll through the pictures. 'Oh, this one is cute. I'll send it to you,' she said, showing the photo to me.

'Is Marko here?' Andjela asked in a monotonous tone, looking towards the bar to see if he was anywhere around.

'Oh. No, he isn't here yet. He said he was coming when I spoke to him earlier today. He's just running late, I guess. Probably caught in traffic or something,' I said, looking at my phone to see if he had texted, but just finding the photo from Andjela.

'Traffic? Nina, this is Požega. The only traffic that boy is experiencing is being caught in a video game. Well, I'm glad he's not here yet. Let's get a drink.'

'Two rakija's please. Are you excited for you first ever drink, Nina?' Andjela asked very loudly, so the bartender and all my family within earshot could hear. Mama looked over at us and rolled her eyes.

'Andjela, I've served both of you a million times before,' the bartender said with a wry grin. Andjela shrugged and passed me one of the glasses.

'Happy birthday!' Andjela said, as she raised a glass and took a sip of her rakija. I followed her lead and took a sip of mine.

'Can I have some?' Jovan asked, dodging past Mama who was yelling at him to calm down and stop running.

'Are you sick?' I asked.

'No.'

'Then you can't have any. Have a cola,' I said, before turning to the bartender and asking him to pour one.

'Hi Andjela, how are you?' Tata asked, as he and Mama walked up to stand next to Andjela and me. 'One rakija, and one white wine please,' Tata said, turning his attention to the bartender.

'Good, sir. Happy to be home?' Andjela asked, taking another sip of rakija.

'So happy. I can finally be with my girls and my little troublemaker,' Tata said, as Jovan started flying around the café again, holding his cola. 'So where is this Marko? I've heard, well I wouldn't say good things, let's say I've heard about him.' Tata had a scowl on his face and stood a little taller with his shoulders back as he spoke, puffing out his chest.

'He's coming,' I said, quickly pulling out my phone to text Marko. 'Where are you?'

'I think it's very rude that he's late. Your mother and I were looking forward to having a chat with him. We'd like to get to know him seeing as your mother says you never bring him to the house.'

He wasn't super late, but I was a little surprised that he hadn't texted me since the morning. Stopping to think about it, it didn't really bother me if he came or not. It had been months since my devastating break up, and even though I was with someone else, I couldn't stop thinking about Luka. I wanted him back, but he was with that girl in Australia. *What a bitch trying to say she owns him. Calling him her star. I guess if he has her in his city, why would he want to be with me?'* I thought, as I couldn't stop the image from floating into my mind of the two of them standing close with each other. That image had never left me alone and still made me feel nauseous every time I thought of it. I took another sip of rakija and gently shook my head to try and knock it from my mind.

'I'm sure he'll be here soon. Oh look, the DJ is starting. Come on Andjela,' I said, drinking the rest of my rakija like it was a shot before grabbing Andjela by the arm to drag her away to the dance floor.

My phone vibrated and I opened it feeling already annoyed at the stupid excuse Marko would be giving me for being late, except it wasn't Marko at all. It was Luka. Instantly a smile broke across my face from ear to ear reading his text. 'I hope you're having an amazing time at your party.'

'Who is it that has you smiling like that? I haven't seen you smile at your phone like that since you were with Luka. Please tell me it isn't Marko,' Andjela groaned, looking at me with dread.

'It's Luka,' I replied.

'Come on. Let's dance,' Andjela said beaming. I put my phone away and began to dance with Andjela. I didn't know if it was Luka's text or the alcohol, but I felt like I was floating. As soon as Andjela and I started, I saw Tata take Mama's hand and lead her onto the dancefloor. In no time, half of the people who were at my party were dancing. Even Milica was dancing with Jovan.

'Can I have a dance with my daughter?' Tata asked, extending his hand towards me as Mama watched glowing with happiness.

'Of course,' I said, accepting his hand.

'Are you enjoying your party?' Tata asked, as he led me swaying to the fast pace of the music. I looked over and saw

Mama dancing with both Jovan and Milica. Milica was laughing and Jovan looked like he might, possibly, be enjoying it too.

'I am. Thanks for spending so much money on it. I would have been just as happy with a dinner at home.' I was with my family, dancing with my tata, having a great time. There was just one thing that was preventing the night from being magical.

'You don't need to thank me. Just being here and seeing everyone have a great time is all the thanks I need. So where is this boy? He's still not here,' Tata said, attempting to sound casual, but unable to hide his irritation.

'I don't know. He's always late.' For every one of our dates Marko had been there before me. He either got sucked into a black hole, or he just wasn't coming. If there was a tiny corner of my mind that thought there could be something with Marko in the future, then him being late answered that question. I wasn't his priority.

'You deserve someone who treats you like a queen, not someone who can't be bothered to tell you he's running late,' Tata said, as he spun me around as the song ended.

'I had someone who treated me like that, but I let him go. I broke his heart. So, no Tata, I don't deserve someone like that because if I did, I would still have him. After breaking his heart, and breaking my own, what I really deserve is for the guy that I'm dating to not turn up to my birthday party,' I said, trying to suppress the feeling that I had ruined my entire life. I wasn't sure what had come over me to spill this to Tata. It felt good to tell him though.

Tata pulled me into him and hugged me. It was the kind of hug you get when you're little and fall over on the pavement scraping your knee. He's there to pick you up and hold you. Telling you it will all be okay while hugging you, and you really believe it will be. The kind of hug that made the pain go away. He didn't say a word, and he didn't have to.

'So, is everyone having a great time?' Andjela asked the room through the microphone on stage.

'Yes!' the mass of people responded to her. Tata and I broke our hug and turned our attention towards Andjela.

'Good. I'm having a great time too. How could I not be? It's Nina's eighteenth birthday! Now Nina, what can I say? I'm so lucky to call you my best friend. Your butt better be coming to some of these tournaments with me, because without your support, I couldn't have got this far, or through school. I know you're going to do amazing things at university and make us all proud.' Andjela paused and everyone joined in a round of applause. I felt uncomfortable being the centre of attention. The sooner she finished, the better.

'I told you before that I didn't have your present with me, but it just got here. I hope it's everything you ever dreamed. Happy birthday. I love you,' Andjela said, with a sparkle in her eye. She walked off stage to the door leading to the outside seating area and opened it, sticking her head out. Her voice carried into the silent café, as I waited for her surprise.

Andjela spoke in English, which piqued my interest. 'Hey, are you ready?' she asked someone just beyond the door.

CHAPTER EIGHTEEN
The Journey

Two months had passed since Andjela gave me the invitation to Nina's birthday. I had been mulling whether I should go or not the entire time, barely going an hour without thinking about it. I had time and time again decided to go, and not to go. Rushes of enthusiasm at the prospect of surprising Nina on her birthday, on a wild adventure to the other side of the world and visiting the city where my grandparents and mother came from was tantalising. Life isn't like a movie though, if I put myself out there and it didn't go to plan, then that could have been a humiliation I never recovered from.

It was August twenty-first, and I was sitting at the table on the back deck watching the sun slowly disappear into the large trees far beyond the backyard fence. The extraordinary beauty of the red, orange, and yellow, perfectly shaded from one to the other slowed my mind. I took in deep breaths of the winter twilight as two parrots sat on a branch of the cherry plum tree, which was starting to show signs of life with its little white flowers beginning to blossom. I watched the birds interact with one another as I mindlessly turned the invitation in my left hand while with my right, I stroked Monty's fur as he lay by my side.

'Hey, do you want to go to dinner with me Saturday night?' I read Tayla's text in the preview bar of my phone. We had been talking politely, but she had asked me the same thing several times and each time I had declined her invitation.

I'll reply to her later,' I thought, turning my attention back to the invitation.

'Hey, are you okay?' James asked, taking a seat beside me.

'Yeah. Where did you come from?' I asked, confused, looking around. I didn't even notice his presence until I heard the scrape of the chair being pulled out next to me at the table.

'Through the magic portal that is your side gate. So, are we thinking about footy or girls?' he asked, leaning back in his chair and looking upon the sunset with me. I handed him the invitation without taking my eyes off the sunset. I was entranced by it.

'Ahh, *the* girl. Wait, this thing's in two days! Why am I just finding out about this now?' James asked, his voice almost squeaking, taking the invitation and reading it.

'I didn't tell anyone.'

'Why not? This is massive!'

'I wanted to make my own decision. I knew if I told people about it then they would try to convince me to do one thing, or the other. Then it wouldn't be genuinely my decision. It really is gorgeous, isn't it?' I asked, as the sun continued to set.

'Yeah, it is, but Luka, you can watch a sunset every day of your life. You can even watch it in Požega, they'll have them there too. The woman you're in love with doesn't send you an invitation to her birthday every day,' James said, turning towards me and leaning forward in his chair. 'Just because it's your decision doesn't mean it's going to be a good one. People make their own awful decisions all the time. Just look at me. It was my decision to go out with that crazy girl Emma, and then she keyed my car. My own bad decision.'

'It was also your decision to bail on meeting her parents for dinner and instead you came and saw me play at One Note for the millionth time,' I replied smirking, finally dragging my eyes off the sunset to face him.

'And that was an example of me making a good decision on my own. People always show you sooner or later who they really are. Emma decided to key my car, Nina decided she wants you at her birthday,' James said, pointing at the invitation held in his hand.

'She didn't invite me. Andjela gave it to me when she was out here last time.'

'And? What difference does it make if she mailed, emailed, or gave it to Andjela to give to you? The main point is that she wants you to have it. She wants you there,' James said, brandishing the invitation in the air like it was the vital piece of evidence and he was showing it to the accused in the witness box.

'It might not be a real invitation,' I said.

James smacked me on the nose with it. 'Does it feel real now?'

'Thanks. I mean Andjela invited me, Nina didn't. I don't know if she just wants us to meet, or if she's hoping for something bigger to happen.'

'What did Nina say when you spoke to her about it?' James asked, leaning back in his chair again. I felt like I was on the witness stand because I immediately felt myself relax now that he had sat back, like when the lawyer walked back to their table. I knew it was just a momentary respite though. The next assault was coming soon.

'Nothing. We haven't spoken about it,' I said, turning my gaze back to the sunset.

'What!? How is that even possible?' James asked in disbelief. I could hear people walking around in the kitchen. Mum was preparing dinner and Dad had just got back from the shops.

'Andjela wants it to be a surprise. Plus, there's been this nagging voice in the back of my head saying maybe Nina doesn't want to meet me. That Andjela doesn't really know what Nina wants,' I said, voicing the question I had been asking myself repeatedly the last two months.

'Why would she ever put you in a position like that?' James asked, scoffing at the idea. He threw the invitation onto the table, and I watched it spin until I answered him.

'I don't know. She's probably very confident she knows Nina wants me there, but she couldn't be certain unless she asked Nina outright,' I suggested, shrugging my shoulders and leaning forward onto the table. The sun had almost completely set, disappearing behind the large trees far beyond the back fence.

'Well, here's another idea. Take a chance. There are some regrets in this life you can deal with, but this isn't one of them. Do you want to be wondering for the rest of your life if you let go of the woman you're meant to marry? You have to try.' James stood up and began to pace back and forth on the other side of the table, urging me to get on the plane. Mum saw James and gave him a smiling wave. 'Hi Aunt Milena.'

'I can't go,' I said softly, staring down at my feet in disappointment. 'It's too big of a risk.'

'Look at me, Luka,' James said, sitting back down and tapping me on the knee. I looked up and met his eyes and felt them pierce me. 'You are so full of crap. You went on and on about how special she is. That you could marry her one day, and this is your decision? If you really wanted her then you would go and get her. If you sit here and don't go, then you don't deserve a woman like that. Happiness doesn't just come knocking on your door, you have to go and take it. Go and get her, Luka,' James said, passionately.

'I don't know.'

'That's exactly my point. You can't know. That's why you need to go. This is your chance to be there in person with her. To finally meet the woman of your dreams. It's time, Luka. You have to know,' James said, feeling the indecision in me and pushing forward.

Monty nudged at my hand reproachfully because I had the audacity to stop patting his stomach for a moment. I returned to my service to appease the head of the household.

'Okay,' I whispered. Adrenaline pumped through my body as soon as those two syllables left my lips. *I'm going to do it. I'm really going to meet her,'* I thought, my decision finally made. James was right. Andjela was right. If I didn't take this chance, then I didn't deserve Nina.

'Yes!' James shouted with a fist pump, drawing curious looks from Mum and Dad inside.

'I'll have to fly out tomorrow night, which would get me to Požega the day of the party,' I said, picking up the invitation and looking at the date, as if I hadn't already memorised every possible detail of it long ago, including the small bend in the top right-hand corner.

'Well…what are you waiting for? Go and get ready,' James said, flicking his hands at me to prompt me into action.

'What do you think this is? A Hollywood romantic comedy? The main character comes to an epiphany and goes rushing off to the airport immediately? I'll just book the ticket on my phone now. Actually, I do need my passport to book,' I said, and ran inside to find my passport.

Sitting back down at the outside table, I picked up my phone and within five minutes I had booked my flight to leave the next night at nine-thirty from Tullamarine airport to Belgrade via Doha. A surreal feeling of euphoria, greater than playing to a crowded bar took over. I felt so light that I could float away. *I can't believe it. I'm going to meet Nina. Well, unless the plane crashes,'* I thought perversely.

'Okay. Tickets are booked. I guess I better tell my family now that I'm going to Požega tomorrow.'

'Yeah, that's probably a good idea. You can't just disappear to another country. They might worry. Can you just promise me one thing?' James asked in a serious tone, as if he was about to ask me for a kidney.

'What?'

'If it all goes horribly wrong, and it's an experience that scars all your future romances leading to unhealthy relationships for the rest of your life, will you please tell Michael and I the full story? All the details? All the horrible, humiliating details that'll keep you awake in thirty years so I can make fun of you for the rest of our lives?' James asked, unable to keep a straight face any longer, breaking into a wide smile.

'Of course. Hey, thanks for waiting until after I booked the ticket before putting that into the universe. Very considerate of you,' I said, shaking my head as my phone vibrated with the email confirmation of my tickets.

'How long are you going for?' James asked.

'I've booked a return ticket for two weeks later, but I'll see what happens,' I said, shrugging. I peeked down at my shirt to see my heart beat was visible. The excitement at the prospect of meeting Nina had my hands shaking. It didn't feel real yet.

'Don't you have uni?' James asked.

'Yeah, but this is more important,' I said, and we both laughed.

'Luka, dinner's ready. James, do you want to stay for dinner?' Mum asked, walking onto the back deck and standing next to the table, careful not to tread on Monty.

'I'd love to, Aunt Milena.' Mum smiled and walked back inside. 'I have to be here for when you tell them,' James said, clapping me on the shoulder and walking inside to take a seat at the kitchen table.

'James!' Maja yelled, as she saw him walk into the house. She ran up to him and launched herself at him like the leopard attacking the kudu in Kruger National Park.

'How are you?' James asked Maja, as he tried to recover the breath he lost when Maja knocked the air out of him.

'Good. Why are you here?' Maja asked. Aleks walked in and shook James' hand before taking his usual spot at the kitchen table.

'Can't a guy just come and see his favourite people?' James asked, sitting down at the bottom of the table between Maja and Aleks. Dad put a plate of roast pork and vegetables in front of him. James gave me a sideways glance and gestured his head towards Mum as if to tell me to get his entertainment going.

'Well, we don't care why you're here, we're just glad that you are,' Mum said, kissing him on the top of his head. Dad continued to put the plates on the table.

'So, Luka, how was your day? Any news?' Mum asked, as she poured gravy over her pork, waiting to pour hers until last to make sure everyone else at the table had as much as they wanted. She always started with me because mine was normally the quickest and least interesting life update to hear. The longer I waited to tell them, the harder it was going to be. Band-aid action was needed.

'Not too much,' I said, and as Mum went to ask Aleks about his day, I ripped the band-aid off. 'I bought a ticket to Belgrade five minutes ago. Oh, and I'll be flying out tomorrow night.' The entire table stopped like someone hit the pause button, apart from James, who was bent over laughing at the end of the table. 'Oh yeah, Dad, that reminds me. I won't be able to work tomorrow night. I have something on.' I began to casually eat my potato and pumpkin mash as my family continued to stare at me.

'Are you tolling us?' Mum asked, finally finding her voice as the person with the remote hit play.

'Trolling, Mum,' Maja chimed in to help Mum with her modern-day vernacular. Mum must have overheard Maja use the word on the phone. 'Well, are you?'

'Nope. I have an invitation to Nina's birthday, so I decided to go. I better text Andjela to let her know I'm coming,' I said, pulling my phone out and messaging Andjela.

'Why though? Didn't she break up with you?' Dad asked, sounding confused.

'Yeah, but she's my friend. Can't I go to my friend's birthday?'

'Don't try and act like you've got friendship on your mind,' James said, before cutting off a piece of roast pork with gravy and crackling atop.

'Thank you, James. What a fine contribution you have made to this evening's meal,' I said, scowling at him.

'You are welcome,' James said with a cheeky smile, enjoying the entertainment like it was his favourite television show.

'Look, Luka, do what you have to do. No one here is standing in your way. I understand the birthday part of it, but you've had nine months to visit her, why now?' Dad asked, putting his knife and fork down.

'I have to know,' I whispered.

'Have to know what?' Dad asked, urging me to give more information.

'I have to know if there's anything there. I can't stop thinking about her. I have to know if I'm in love with her, or some fantastical idea of her. I have to find out if she has any feelings for me. I have to meet her. I have to,' I said, without breaking eye contact with Dad.

'Well, sweetie, I can tell you this. No Serbian woman is going to like you if you treat your dinner like that. Eat,' Mum said, pointing her knife at my full plate.

'We all already know he eats like a baby bird. Just look at those arms,' Aleks said, filling his plate with his second serving.

'I just hope you know what you're doing. I'll support you all the way if you feel you need to do this,' Mum said, putting her cutlery down.

'I need to.'

'Then do it. Just make sure you go and visit the house your grandparents and I lived in. I hope I can get there too one day,' Mum said, recommencing her dinner.

'You might be able to get there twice when these two marry those girls,' Maja said, through a mouthful of food like the delicate little flower she could be. She proceeded to pick up a piece of steamed carrot, and shoot it into my glass of water, splashing it all over my plate, continuing to hold her follow through. Aleks, James and Maja burst into uncontrollable laughter. Mum and Dad admonished her through spurts of their own laughter. Even I began to laugh. Nothing could spoil the mood I was in. I was going to meet Nina.

'Great form, Maja,' Aleks said, as she started to hand out high fives.

My phone was lying face down on the table when it vibrated. Trying to look at it without anyone noticing, I saw a text from Andjela. 'I think you should bring your guitar.'

I had been lucky to travel overseas with my family several times, and always the most exciting part was the day we left. The anticipation of the adventure awaiting us and all the possibilities to come. While my parents stressed about packing and making sure to remember all the passports, nothing could ruin that Christmas Eve feeling for me.

It was my first time flying alone. I had a feeling of anticipation building inside me that something incredible was about to happen. I didn't even want to acknowledge that things could go badly. I had the feeling that bully was speaking, he was just drowned out by the overwhelming excitement.

Night had fallen over Melbourne as the end of winter approached. Mum was driving me to the airport cautiously as rain pounded against the car. We cut through the sheets of rain as the windshield wipers moved so quickly they looked like they could fly off into the night at any moment. We travelled over the Bolte Bridge passing the lit-up city on our right, onto Citylink before hitting the Tullamarine freeway on route to the airport. I said my goodbyes to Dad, Aleks and Maja at home, before leaving for my surreal adventure.

After checking in my bag and guitar, Mum and I wandered around the departure terminal. She wasn't going to leave until I went through the customs gate. We looked through overpriced souvenirs before sitting down in a restaurant to have a cup of tea together.

'I don't know why I ever order tea. They either give it to you so you can assemble it like build-a-bear, or they make it and completely ruin it. I'm paying for a tea bag and boiling water. What's the point?' Mum asked rhetorically, as she put a splash of milk into her tea and stirred. I counted them out, fifteen stirs exactly before taking a careful sip. 'Not as good as yours. With you being gone for two weeks your father will be making tea for me. Lord help me.' She made the sign of the cross and took another sip of her tea.

'Would you like me to stay so I can make you tea, Mum?' I asked, raising an eyebrow as I raised my cup to my lips.

'You can make anything sound stupid, Luka. So how are you feeling? Are you nervous?'

'You know what? I'm not. This might sound stupid seeing as I have a plane ticket here with my name on it saying, destination Belgrade, but it doesn't feel real. Even though I'm about to get on a plane it doesn't feel like it's going to happen,' I replied. I was wearing my most comfortable hoodie and tracksuit pants for the twenty-two hours of travel. *Hopefully Nina doesn't steal this hoodie. Actually, it would be a good sign if she did,'* I thought.

'Do you want to be nervous?' Mum asked, holding her cup in two hands to warm them.

'No, but I thought I would feel something sitting here. I was so excited last night and this morning, but now I don't feel anything. My bags are being carted towards the plane and I'm travelling to the other side of the world to see her, but how I feel doesn't match the magnitude of what my brain is telling me I'm doing. My mind and body aren't in concert. It feels as though I'm about to drive around the corner to the supermarket to pick up a bottle of milk,' I said in a disappointed tone. Being excited and feeling the anticipation was half the fun, so I felt like I was being deprived of that.

'You will feel it. Trust me. When you get on the plane, you will feel it. When you get to Belgrade, and then to Požega, you will feel it. And Luka, trust me, everything that you felt before is nothing compared to what you will feel when you see her.' I hoped she was right. I was worried that if I didn't feel anything then that was a sign, but maybe I was just protecting myself. Time would tell. 'Come on, you have to go now,' Mum said, looking down at her watch. We stood up and she picked up my passport with my tickets inside it as I threw my carry-on bag over my shoulder, and we walked towards the customs control gate.

I had struck the economy class jackpot by having no one in the three seats next to me. Poor man's business class. Soothing music of a flute played gently through the cabin as I buckled myself in and waited for the plane to depart. As soon as I buckled my seatbelt, I felt a pinch of anxiety, as a baby elephant settled himself on my chest. I smiled knowing that I was starting to feel the emotion of my journey. There was no turning back.

The plane accelerated along the runway and as it gathered speed, my nervous, excited energy increased. The tyres left the tarmac, and I was on my way. I felt relieved I was starting to feel the excitement again. It was mixed with a level of anxiety, either the bully was getting louder, or the positive voice was getting quieter. All the possibilities of what could happen were playing out in my mind.

I stared at the back of the seat in front of me, waiting for the seatbelt sign to turn off, thinking, imagining. Trying to imagine what it would feel like when I saw Nina. I knew Mum was right, I wouldn't be able to come close to imagining that feeling. I felt tense as I tried to fight off my bully's negativity by screaming positive thoughts in my mind. The elephant grew bigger, constricting my breathing as I tried to ignore any negative possibility.

I raised all the armrests, put my hood up and my noise cancelling headphones on. I laid down and tried to sleep through as much of the flight as possible. *'Hopefully I haven't wasted all my luck on this trip by getting these four seats together,'* I thought, drifting off to sleep.

I had spent so much time looking at my phone, stressing over the actions or inactions of Nina, I was finally in a place where I could turn my phone off for fourteen hours and drift off to another place. It was a kind of meditation where you were detached from the outside world, which was exactly what I needed. The positive and negative voices in my head took their turns, but while I slept, I only saw the perfect scenario. My internal bully wasn't present in my dreams.

As I boarded the flight in Doha heading for Belgrade, I made sure to remove my writing book from my bag before I stored it in the overhead compartment and took my place in my window seat. As soon as the seatbelt light turned off next to the ever glowing no smoking sign, I pulled down my food tray and laid my book open upon it. While travelling towards Nina, I had one image lodged in my mind. I kept picturing us dancing together to an Ed Sheeran song. She was pressed against me with my right-hand holding her left, my left hand on her waist, and her right hand on my shoulder. Dragging my eyes from staring out the window picturing my paradise, I began to write.

For five and a half hours I wrote, scribbling out lines and re-writing them, craving the presence of my guitar in my hands. I felt inspired by one picture that was tattooed to my mind. I pictured what it would be like to dance with Nina. To hold her close to me and move as one to the music at her birthday, forgetting there was anyone else in the room. We were the only two people to exist in our world. I tore out sheets of paper and shoved them in frustration in the pocket in front of me to accompany the safety guidelines for the flight. Searching for the perfect lyrics to do my feelings justice. I sang the words in my head hoping what I was hearing in my mind would be what I heard aloud. *That our hearts beat together, never alone. Two souls entwined, we are home,'* I sang in my mind, repeatedly.

'Hello everyone, this is your captain speaking. We have begun our descent into Belgrade. It is a still morning with a current temperature of twenty degrees. There is light cloud cover which will clear leaving you with a perfect day reaching a top of twenty-eight degrees. Thank you for choosing Qatar Airways, and we hope to see you again soon,' the captain said, cutting through the constant roar of the old Airbus A-320.

'I don't think they've put their best aircraft on the Doha-Belgrade route,' I thought, looking around the old fuselage.

Realising that I was approaching Belgrade made my insides feel like they twisted into a tight ball. *I've really travelled from Williamstown to Belgrade,'* I thought in disbelief. My anxiety stepped up another level as the elephant on my chest had matured from a baby to an adolescent. It was becoming harder to breathe every metre I got closer to Nina. I embraced the anxiety. I embraced the excitement. For the first time I welcomed the difficulty to breathe, because I knew when I saw Nina, I would feel the ultimate high.

I snapped my head from my song book to look out the window and saw the fields of Serbia below. It looked like a patchwork quilt with the different colours of the farms, ranging from yellow wheat, to green corn, to brown blocks recently ploughed ready to be planted. The skinny roads separating the blocks gradually drew closer until I could make out the cars being driven. *What would they think of a guy flying from Australia to surprise his ex-girlfriend at her birthday party? They'd have to think I'm insane. I probably am,'* I thought with a smile, as we continued our descent into Belgrade.

Fields turned to a forest of buildings as country became city. Where before there were small streets dividing blocks of land, there were now freeways, buildings both short and tall spread widely with two rivers, Danube and Sava, flowing through the heart of the city and meeting at Ušće. A set of buildings looked like stairs as the plane closed in on Nikola Tesla airport. Coming to Serbia was no longer an idea. It may not have felt real sitting in Melbourne airport, but the reality was setting in as I looked upon the Serbian capital. I could feel sweat between my fingers and toes as I saw the runway from the window. My entire body clenched as we approached the runway until I felt a gentle bump as the plane hit the tarmac. *I'm in Serbia, Nina. I'm here,'* I thought, exhaling.

Even though I had come all the way from Williamstown, and it was beginning to sink in, it still felt like I was a million miles away. The excitement was growing but the anticipation of what lay ahead that night was taking over my mind. I was so close, yet there was still so far to go. The time was eleven-thirty, so I had nine and a half hours until Nina's party. I had waited nine months, but it still felt like a lifetime away.

Checking my seat pocket several times to make sure I left nothing behind apart from bad lyrics, I stood up and collected my bag from the overhead compartment, delicately sliding my song book inside. I foraged around until I found my passport. I stared at the door of the plane, begging them to let us disembark, longing to be sent on my way. *'What's taking so long?'* I screamed in my head, urging them to open the door. Waiting impatiently, finally I saw the people in business class disappear. Slowly the plane emptied, and I counted down the number of rows until it was my turn to race into Serbia. *'Seven, six…hurry up, man!'* I felt envious of the people that I watched disappear from the plane. The anxiety continued to build inside me, desperate to be moving towards Požega. *'Finally,'* I thought, as it was my rows turn to disembark. I looked to my left and saw people from rows behind me trying to force their way ahead of me, but I stepped into the aisle and blocked their path while flashing them a dirty look. *'We are supposed to move row by row, we're not savages, learn the etiquette, animals,'* I thought, outraged.

I politely nodded to the stewardess as I stepped off the plane, and I was on my way. I tried to walk as casually and quickly as possible, managing to move past several old ladies, a woman with a baby, and a middle-aged man on crutches. It probably wasn't the greatest athletic achievement of a member of my family, considering my brother's talents, but I took it as a win for what I was trying to achieve. Get to Nina.

There wasn't any line to speak of at customs due to my magnificent athleticism getting past those people. I passed customs quickly, surviving a long stare from the customs officer before she stamped my passport and granted me entry to Serbia. In no time I had collected my bag and guitar, withdrawn Serbian dinars from the ATM, and walked to the outside world. I walked through the doors that felt like they separated some in between place that didn't belong to any country and Serbia. I stood in the busy arrival terminal for a moment trying to get my bearings. I began to walk aimlessly, not sure where to go next to get to the bus terminal, hoping a solution would present itself to me. *'I really should have researched this before leaving,'* I thought frustratedly. Turning left for no particular reason, I found my path blocked, and I thought someone had turned off the lights.

An enormous man was standing in my path, barrel chested and soaring above me. He looked thirty centimetres taller and double my width. *'Am I about to get robbed in the middle of the airport with all these people around?'* I wondered, swallowing with great difficulty, looking up into his hard face.

'Excuse me, sir, do you need a taxi?' he asked in a very polite tone with his heavy Serbian accent. Either my Serbian had improved dramatically since walking off the plane twenty minutes earlier, or he was speaking English. The latter seemed the most likely.

'Umm, yes, yes I do,' I replied nervously, trying not to be overwhelmed by the entire experience.

Without uttering another word, his frying pan sized hands swooped down and scooped my bag and guitar from what I thought was my strong grip and led me from the terminal. He was so big and intimidating that he could be kidnapping me, and I would just go along with it. People moved from his path like he was an ice barge in the Antarctic. As soon as we stepped through the doors to the outside world I took in the smell of Serbia. It smelled like a mix of fresh air, farming and burning wood. We walked by the taxi rank, and I felt immeasurably stupid for not seeing the large sign and the line of twenty taxis just outside the terminal door waiting to take people to their next destination.

'Not far,' he said over his shoulder, as he continued to lead the way, thundering along with each step. Finally, we arrived at his unmarked Mercedes that he claimed was a taxi. He loaded my luggage into the boot and opened the rear door for me to get inside. Everything I had read and been told about travel said don't get into an unmarked taxi, so within twenty-five minutes of arriving I had made my first travel mistake. A good start. 'Where to?' he asked, looking at me in the rear-view mirror with his dark brown eyes staring a hole through me.

'Belgrade bus station, please,' I said, my voice breaking from a combination of nerves, and it barely being used in almost a day. He nodded and accelerated quickly out of the car park. He was the perfect taxi driver, even if I broke the first rule of travel. He didn't ask me one question and just focused on the road.

Our path from the airport was surrounded by open fields with trees lining the side of the road. Lying behind those trees on the left was a corn field, and on the right empty fields as far as the eye could see. Our road curved slightly to the right and joined the main freeway which the bear like driver merged onto, joining many cars flying along, using the one hundred and twenty km/h speed limit as a mere suggestion.

I stared from the window trying to take in every little bit of the Serbian landscape I could as we sped past. The fields engulfed my vision, and I tried to comprehend how far I had come. I felt an immediate level of comfort coming back to the country of my grandparents and mother, like I was where I belonged. The rains must have been good as the ground was lush with green. Trees every shade of green stood guard over the freeway and showed us the path to Belgrade. They didn't stand alone for long before apartment buildings joined them, and they mingled together in a mixture of city and country.

I thought with every moment I spent in Serbia, moving closer to Nina, that my nerves would gradually increase, but I was wrong. An odd calmness was engulfing my body, and I wasn't sure how I should interpret it. *'Is it because my family is from here? Does it mean I feel at ease moving towards where I need to be? Does it mean that meeting Nina still doesn't feel real? Or does it mean that my heart and soul feel at home?'* I wondered. Whatever the answer was, I would have it by the end of the night.

Over the Sava River on Savski Most took me from New Belgrade into Old Belgrade. Taking in the stunning buildings of the old city, Stari Grad, with its rich history. Some buildings were still showing the signs of previous conflicts, and rather than knock those buildings down, they were left standing as a constant reminder of their history. Of the history of my family's country. I hoped Nana would be smiling down with pride, seeing her grandson return to the old country.

I saw street signs indicating that we were nearing the bus station. The traffic was beginning to build, and we came to almost a crawl as we neared my next stop.

A busy street full of trams, cars and buses, passed the bus station as many different people walked in and out. Businessmen walking with purpose in their stride, grandmas with handbags, young people with big suitcases coming and going. A smile broke across my face watching them, wondering where they were going. *'What exciting thing is happening in their life that is bringing that look of possibility and hope to their eyes,'* I wondered.

Whether they were fat or skinny, all the men were very tall. If I saw anyone short, I immediately thought they were a tourist. The women were beautiful and elegant. They walked smoothly with their shoulders back and head held high. All the women were dressed nicely like they had somewhere important to be.

'Four thousand five hundred dinars,' the driver said, extending his hand, attempting to turn his enormous body in the tight confines of his seat with great difficulty. I reached into my wallet and gave him the money.

'That seems like a lot,' I thought, looking at the remaining cash in my wallet. He extricated himself from his seat, opened my door and placed my bags and guitar on the curb before disappearing into the chaotic Belgrade traffic. I stood there for a moment thinking about the currency conversion and dropped my head. About seventy Australian dollars. He was definitely heading back to the airport to find his next English-speaking idiot.

I shook my head before I picked up my bags and guitar and walked into the bus station. I felt like everyone was staring at me, like they could smell that I was a foreigner, and could see the trepidation written all over my face. Their looks brought back my anxiety as I tried to figure out which way to go to buy my ticket. People buffeted me, saying things I didn't understand as my head was on a swivel trying to find the ticket window. On the left of the bus terminal as I walked were the individual gates for the departing buses. People formed orderly lines waiting to hand over their tickets and get onto the bus. There were several kiosks on the left selling snacks, newspapers, cigarettes, and gum, with an attendant that looked like they would rather be anywhere else in the world. On the right there were a series of glass doors, and I saw above one of them a sign reading 'Tickets'. Grateful the sign was in English, I veered right through the doors to tackle my next challenge. Buying my bus ticket.

There were five different people at windows looking like bank tellers, with each window saying something different above it. As I didn't speak Serbian, I had no idea which was the right line to go with, so like in any multiple-choice question, if in doubt, go with C. Joining the back of the third line, I waited and prayed that the dour, surly looking middle aged woman selling tickets spoke English. Practising over and over in my mind the two words I needed to say, *Požega, please. Požega, please. Surely that would be enough,'* I thought, anxiously.

As the line dwindled my anxiety grew, my heart was beating ever faster, rattling against my ribcage. Every other thought had been pushed from my mind other than the singular goal of getting the ticket. If someone asked me for my name, I would need a minute to collect the information from the deep recesses of my mind. Nothing else in my world existed apart from those two words. Požega, please.

The person in front of me walked from the teller with their ticket leaving me face to face with the surly looking woman. She looked like she had spent the last fifty years perfecting her resting bitch face and had it down to an art form. She gestured me to move towards the window, staring a hole through me over her glasses that sat on the end of her long nose. As I reached the window, she looked away from me and turned her attention to the computer, not saying a word. I had no idea if she was doing something else, or if she was waiting for me to speak. *Why can't she just say something, or even look at me to ask, hey idiot, where do you want to go?'* I thought, nervously. I felt the sweat running down my sides and prayed I would find the hotel before the party so I could shower away the travel and stress. Throwing caution to the wind, I put into practice the two words I had been practising the last fifteen minutes standing in line. 'Požega, please,' I said, fighting through the lump in my throat.

'Okay, that will be two thousand dinars,' she replied in perfect English, not taking her eyes off the computer screen. I slid a two thousand dinars note to her through the small gap at the bottom of the glass separating us. She typed at the speed of one hundred words a minute and printed off my ticket, sliding it through the same hole in the glass, and I began to walk away.

Before I could take two steps, I turned back to her. 'What time is the bus arriving in Požega?' I asked. If I couldn't speak Serbian, then I wouldn't know when to get off the bus. I could end up going past Požega, get completely lost and miss Nina's party. It sounded like the kind of stupid thing I would do after coming so far.

'Five-thirty, dear. Have a pleasant journey,' she said, breaking her resting bitch face to flash me a kind smile. I returned her smile feeling more relaxed than I was a few minutes earlier and looked down at my ticket. I was grasping it so tightly my knuckles had turned white. It read that the bus was departing from gate eighteen, so I walked from the counter to find my gate. I slipped the ticket into my pocket before picking up my bag and guitar.

I didn't have to go far as it was directly in front of me as I walked back through the glass doors of the ticket office. I handed my ticket to the station attendant, and he granted me access to where the bus was lying in wait. A sign reading 'Užice' was stuck to the buses front window. I gave my guitar and bag to the large, balding man loading luggage onto the bus. He wore a shirt and tie, but his neck was too large to do up the top button. He was so enormous his arms were on a forty-five-degree angle. 'Two hundred dinar, please,' he said after placing my bags into the storage compartment. I handed him the money, and he gave me a luggage receipt in return. Clambering onto the bus, I found a seat halfway down the aisle on the left. I sat on the aisle seat and placed my carry-on bag on the window seat. After travelling so far, it was in everybody's best interest that they didn't sit next to me, no one needed their nose subjected to that.

The adolescent elephant was stirring on my chest, pressing his powerful legs into my lungs, forcing the limited oxygen from my body. I took a deep breath and exhaled another lungful of anxiety from my body, being another step closer to Nina. I stared through the window watching people slowly climb the steps onto the bus. Looking down at my ticket grasped tightly in my hand, I saw the bus wouldn't be departing for another hour for my three-hour trip. I pulled my headphones from my bag and connected them to my phone, pressing play on my Ed Sheeran and John Mayer playlist. After twenty-two hours on a plane, an extraordinarily expensive taxi ride, and then getting the ticket to Požega, I felt completely exhausted. Taking my hoodie off, I folded it to form a makeshift pillow and swapped seats with my bag to rest my head against the window. *'Send me to sleep Ed and John,'* I thought, as my breath fogged up the window.

I found myself awake but refused to open my eyelids. I could tell that it was late in the afternoon and had a terrible sinking feeling that I had gone past Požega. I was the only person on this planet dumb enough not to set an alarm to make sure I didn't miss my stop. Begrudgingly, I lifted my eyelids to face the brutal reality that I had missed my stop. The late summer sun was blocked by the valley we were driving through, so I moved my eyes to above the driver to find the digital clock. Five-twenty. I exhaled loudly, relief washing over my body. I hadn't missed my stop.

I closed my eyes for a moment to reset and rub them to force myself to wake up. Opening my eyes again I looked out the window to see trees of deep green completely covering the mountains to both my left and right. On my right the mountains were just beyond a stream running the same direction as the bus, and on the left was a sharply rising mountain. Looking back at the clock, I saw another two minutes had passed and I felt my heartrate start to increase. I couldn't pull my eyes from the clock to enjoy the stunning scenery. I stared at the clock as if I could make time speed up if I concentrated hard enough. As it turned out, it had the opposite effect. Time felt like it was standing still.

Ever so slowly the clock ticked towards five-thirty. I counted out the beats of the colon to try and aid my countdown to Požega. The time reached five-thirty and passed it. With each beat of the colon, I felt the tightness in my chest build and my heart beat a little harder. My right leg started to bounce, and I looked through the window searching for a sign that said Požega. *'Surely it can't be far away,'* I pleaded to myself, as if the cruel voice in my head was holding the answer. At least I had one answer, I didn't feel anything before I left, but I certainly did approaching Požega. It was all beginning to feel real, with my anticipation and nervous energy constantly growing. There was an electrical pulse of excitement surging through my body. With every passing second, I was the closest I had ever been to Nina.

Through the window appeared a sign pointing left that read 'Požega'. The bus obeyed the sign and as we followed the road, I felt my heart leap into my throat beating at hyper speed causing me to search for breath. Open fields on our right turned into buildings, both businesses and homes. On our left we passed a corn field and a mechanic before a yellow metal fence materialised that looked like it had spears atop. Behind this fence was the bus station. Taking a sharp left, the bus pulled into the old station that looked like it hadn't had maintenance work done on it since it was first built.

'Požega,' the bus driver said over the PA system, as he came to a complete stop and opened the doors. The bus was three quarters empty but out of fear of not getting off in time, I jumped up, shoved my hoodie and headphones into my bag, and walked quickly from the bus, jumping the last step to finally feel the ground of Požega below my sweating feet. Another bubble of anxiety left my body as the adolescent elephant on my chest calmed. I had made it.

'I'm here, Nina,' I thought, closing my eyes and breathing in the pure Požega air.

Standing at the front of a short line beside the bus bouncing on my toes, the man who took my ticket and put my bags under the bus raised the door of the bag storage compartment. I spotted my bag and guitar immediately and needed to stop myself from reaching for them. I pointed to them with too much enthusiasm, and the man handed them to me with a 'calm down boy' look on his face. I raced towards the exit of the bus station which sat on the main street leading to the centre of town. I looked up the directions to the hotel before I left Williamstown, so I knew that it was left from the bus station on the same street. I watched the bus take a right out of the station along the main street, which I saw was called Nikole Pašića, and headed in the direction it came. I turned my attention in the direction my map was sending me and continued towards what I hoped was Hotel Požega.

Never had I breathed air so clean. There was not a cloud in the sky, and I knew that at night, the sky would be littered with an uncountable number of stars. As I walked towards the hotel, there were high green bushes on my left hiding a park, and on my right double storey buildings that looked like a business on the ground floor, and a residence on the upper floor. Buildings made of brick and concrete. Hairdressers and cafes, busy with clients as the locals went about their day in the glorious afternoon mountainside sun. Perfectly manicured trees were planted in the sidewalk, about five metres apart on both sides of the road. I passed a statue of a bronze woman which looked gold where people had touched her for good luck.

The only thing stopping me from breaking into a run were my heavy legs. My feet raced along as quickly as they could, as if getting to the hotel quicker would make nine o'clock come sooner. It was only a short walk, and within five minutes I came across a car park with a tall building sitting behind it with 'Hotel Požega' in huge letters above it. *'At least I didn't get lost,'* I thought, amazed that I had managed to find my way from Williamstown to my hotel in Požega. Wheeling my suitcase along with my left hand and carrying my guitar in my right, I walked into the lobby of the hotel and checked in. A large lobby with several different businesses operating in offices located on the left side, such as a travel agent and a souvenir shop. Off to the right, behind the check in desk was the hotel restaurant.

Check-in went smoothly and I raced up the stairs in no time to find my room, the numbers three-zero-seven on the door. My right arm was aching by the time I walked into my hotel room, placing my phone on the desk, and guitar and bag at the foot of the bed before I collapsed upon it. The room contained a queen-sized bed, couch, television, mini bar, and a small desk. The bathroom was just inside the door, and a mirror was on the wall opposite the bathroom, so you could get a great look at yourself leaving the bathroom. All I wanted to do was take a shower and refresh myself before the party.

Throughout the entire trip I spent so much energy focusing on making it to Požega, I hadn't yet taken the time to process the magnitude of what I was doing. Before that moment I had let myself think about meeting Nina, but not how it would happen, and what would happen. I only had thoughts of success or failure, not what those two things would look like. Williamstown was so far from Požega, I wasn't sure I ever really believed that I would step foot in Nina's hometown, even when I was on the bus and held a ticket that said Požega.

It was six-thirty, and I was going to need every second of the next two and a half hours. Andjela said she knew Nina wanted me there, but that we should keep it a surprise. I hoped she was right or else it would be an expensive humiliation. *I'm not sure how I'll recover if Nina doesn't want me here. No, I won't think about that. Only positive thoughts,'* I urged myself, determinedly. I shook my head to knock the negative thoughts from my mind. Going into something with a positive mindset wasn't normally in my personality, but if I went in with a defeatist attitude, then I didn't stand a chance. I needed to make sure she knew I belonged there, that I belonged with her. If I acted like I didn't belong, then she would feel like the chemistry wasn't right between us.

I closed my eyes and visualised what it would feel like to see her smile in person; what it would feel like to touch her hand; what her skin would feel like; the shape of her body; what she smelt like; what her lips would feel like pressed against mine. I felt my body yearn for all of it. I could feel it in the deepest recesses of my body, inside my soul. I opened my eyes and walked into the bathroom to shower. The time would pass very quickly, and I needed to get ready.

I laid all my clothes out on the bed trying to figure out what I was going to wear. Her favourite shirt of mine was the light blue buttoned up, collared shirt. It was what I wore on our first date. I put that on a coat hanger as decision one was made. Tossing up between my tan chinos and black jeans, I settled on the former and laid them neatly over the back of the chair sitting at the desk to keep them crease free. I didn't think a pair of runners would be a good way to complete the outfit, so I pulled from my bag a pair of immaculate white high-top shoes. I looked at them for a moment and was content with what I had picked. As I felt another step closer to seeing Nina, the excitement increased again with my skin feeling like it was on fire.

I threw the rest of my clothes in my bag and closed it. I didn't want to put on my clothes for the party yet, because I knew I would somehow find a way to drop Bolognese sauce on them without having pasta within one hundred metres of me. I dragged a pair of sweatpants and a t-shirt from my bag and put them on for safety.

Removing my guitar from its case, I hung it over my shoulder and paced my room back and forth repeatedly, playing the song I wrote on the plane. I walked to the window of my third-floor room and peered out over the homes of Požega, wondering where Nina was. I turned and walked towards the door, going past the bathroom, catching a glimpse of myself in the mirror singing my new song. Staring at myself while I played, I couldn't help but break into a smile. The electricity and adrenaline coursing through my body made me start jumping up and down. *'I'm going to meet her. I'm really going to meet Nina tonight,'* I thought.

My phone buzzed on the desk, so I rushed to it, breaking off the song in the middle of the chorus. It was a picture from Nina of her in a short blue dress. 'Wow,' I said aloud, before my hand covered my mouth. A warmth spread to my fingers and toes looking at her. *'How is she so beautiful? This will all be worth it, even if I only get to see her for one moment,'* I thought, trying to control my emotions while gazing upon her beauty. I replied to Nina and continued to pace the room which almost turned into a skip. I should've been passed out on the bed from the marathon trip, but I felt like I had just drunk four shots of espresso in succession.

I repeated the song until just before nine. I couldn't get the picture of Nina from my mind as I played. It was our song. Intermittently I opened my phone just to look at the picture of her in that dress, each time I did, it caused a kaleidoscope of butterflies to explode in my soul. I put my guitar down on the bed with shaking hands because it was time to get dressed. Before I could get dressed though, there was a fast, loud, knock on the door. *'Did I leave something at the front desk?'* I wondered, crossing my room quickly. I walked towards the door with a furrowed brow, curious as to who would be needing to see me.

Andjela jumped through the doorway and engulfed me in an enormous hug. 'You came!' she screamed, as she squeezed me as if I was an almost empty toothpaste tube. 'I can't believe you're here.' My brain struggled to compute that Andjela was standing in my hotel doorway, so I squeezed her back trying to make her feel how excited I was to be there, as I smiled from ear to ear. I felt my body relax at seeing her friendly face. There wasn't a shred of anxiety in my body, and if there was, Andjela's excited hug squeezed it out of me and into the atmosphere.

'How did you know I was here?' I asked confused, yet jubilant as we broke our hug, and she walked into my room looking around and taking a seat on the bed.

'Well, there's only one hotel in Požega, so that part wasn't challenging. Then I just asked reception what room they had you in. Let's not act like I just solved the Jack the Ripper case,' Andjela said, standing up and walking over to the window. Night had fallen over Požega, and the main street of the quiet mountain side town was lit up.

'Do you think this will be okay to wear?' I asked, showing Andjela my shirt and chinos which I had laid out neatly on the bed.

'Yeah, I think it will look great on you. Nina's going to love it,' she said. I tried to get my smile under control, but the fishhooks in my mouth were pulling my smile as wide as it could go.

'I just can't believe I'm here. It feels real, but it doesn't feel real. Does that make sense?'

'Not even a little bit,' Andjela said laughing, and shaking her head.

'Well, I know that I'm here and looking at you. I can feel how close I am. Something that I've imagined every day for the last nine months is finally here, but for it to actually happen is still beyond my comprehension,' I explained. 'I'm in the town where my grandparents are from. Where my mother was born. My family's story begins here, and I've been brought back. It feels like there's a bigger power at play, like Nana is pulling the puppet strings.'

Andjela nodded in understanding. 'Yeah, I get it. It feels like it's meant to be, but meant to be can only present you with the opportunity. After that it's for you to accept meant to be or reject it.'

'I'm here to take my shot. I guess we'll find out soon if it is or not.' We looked at each other for a moment, disbelief reflected in both of our expressions. 'It's even bizarre seeing you here. I'm so happy I came.'

'Honestly, I didn't think you were going to come. You did leave it to the last minute to decide,' Andjela said, sitting on the bed shaking her head and picking up the guitar. She tried to play a note but didn't hold the string down firmly enough, so it just vibrated in a nothing sound.

'Yeah, I probably could have given myself a couple more days.'

Andjela stood up and took a step forward so there was barely a metre separating us, placing her hands on my shoulders. 'The main thing is that you're here now. Okay, now listen. I have to go in a second, I'm already late. You need to get there at ten. Don't come in the front door, wait by the side door. At ten I'm going to make a little speech, and then I'll announce that I have a gift for Nina. I'll open the door for you and bring you in. Then play whatever song you want on stage. Okay?' Andjela said, making fierce eye contact with me to make sure I understood the plan.

'Perfect. Got it,' I replied, nodding my head. The anticipation that I felt before in my stomach had moved up to my chest. My excitement was exploding, so I felt glad that I would be able to play a song; it would settle me.

'I have to go now. I'm so happy you're here though. This really is incredible. I can't believe it,' Andjela said, kissing me on the cheek with a gleam in her eye, before disappearing through the door.

The next hour of waiting was unbearable. Nine months earlier we met, but that final hour felt even longer. I couldn't sit still. I felt like a puppy that had boundless energy and no idea what to do with it all. I continued to practise the song while pacing my room, trying to be productive and make time speed up. I hoped the rooms next to me were empty because they would have been getting sick of the song if they weren't.

Checking on my phone how long it would take to walk to the café, it said I was only four minutes on foot away. *'Nina would be there now. She's just a four-minute walk from where I'm standing,'* I thought, starting to jump on the spot. The anticipation rose from my chest to my throat. I was so excited I wanted to scream. I felt like my hair was tingling. I set an alarm on my phone for nine-fifty, so I knew when to get ready and to stop me looking at my phone. I was sweating profusely with excitement as the time drew nearer. *'I'm not going to look at the time for thirty minutes,'* I thought. Once I was sure thirty minutes had passed, I checked the time on my phone. *'Only five minutes?!'* I thought incredulously, tossing my phone onto the bed. It was torture.

I was wearing out the carpet with my stress pacing for the time to come. I had sweated so much I needed to take another shower to clean the excitement off myself. I could barely hold onto the bar of soap because my hands were shaking so much. Multiple times it slipped from my grasp, and I had to fight to collect it from the shower floor. Drying myself with a fresh towel, I hung it over the bathroom door handle and began to dress. I dressed in my light blue shirt, tan chinos, and white shoes. I packed my guitar and checked the time on my phone. Nine fifty-five. 'It's time,' I said aloud to the empty hotel room.

I walked to the door, turned, and examined myself in the mirror. Looking from head to toe with my guitar case clenched in my tight right-hand grip, I felt the adrenaline rush through my body like it was trying to escape. Taking a deep breath, I turned and walked through the door. I bounced down the stairs just short of a run as my legs weren't capable of moving any slower.

I had complete tunnel vision as I turned right out of the hotel and then took another right at a street called Francuska.   I consulted the map on my phone that said to take the first left, and then right, along the continuation of Francuska street. My breathing was becoming quick and shallow with each step I took closer to my destination. With each step I took closer to Nina. I reached an intersection where Vuka Karadžića ran perpendicular to Francuska. Directly across the street was a building that resembled a hut with its sharp sloping tiled roof and walls made from large slabs of painted concrete. I could hear music blasting from the door that swung open as people arrived carrying gifts.

I adjusted the guitar case in my sweating hand as I crossed the road to the café. I stopped in my tracks and stared at the building, listening to the laughter, singing, and joy that radiated from the café. My excitement and sense of anticipation built with each step I took towards the door Andjela told me to wait at, to a level they had never reached before, still unable to comprehend that Nina was just through that door. It was a ridiculous and insane idea, and yet, I was jubilant that I was there. I didn't want to be anywhere else on the planet. For the entirety of the time I had known Nina, I had only once been exactly where I needed to be, and that was on that computer to meet her. Since then, I had always been in the wrong place, until I looked upon the Sunshine Café.

I rounded the café, walking past a painting of a little prince under a beaming sun to find the side door Andjela spoke of, with a collection of tables and chairs on paved bricks, in the area in front of it. In the corner, leaned up against the building were several large umbrellas. It was a glass door, so I walked to it and peered through. My heart felt like it was going to beat out of my chest as I craned my neck trying to get my first glimpse of Nina in the flesh through the crowd of people. The music stopped suddenly, and Andjela began to speak, but I didn't understand one word of her Serbian. Her voice stopped and there was a round of applause.

Looking at my phone, I saw the time was five past ten, so I pulled my guitar from its case, and hung it over my shoulder waiting for Andjela to usher me inside. My entire body was clenched, wracked with anxiety, nerves, anticipation, and excitement, as each second felt like it dragged on for an eternity. I could barely breath. No matter how deep the breath I took, it wasn't enough oxygen. I wouldn't be able to breathe normally until I saw Nina.

I stared up at the cloudless sky and the full moon shining. It looked like every star in the universe was on display. They looked so bright that streetlights wouldn't be necessary. Looking at all those stars lighting up the night sky, it was impossible not to think about how small I was, yet I didn't think there was any living being doing anything more important in the entire vast universe, than what I was doing at that moment.

'Come on,' I said quietly, hoping Andjela would hear. My shirt was rising and falling with the beat of my heart as it bruised my ribs. I sat down and breathed slowly, in an attempt to calm myself. My right leg bounced on the ball of my foot, and I silently screamed at the door trying to get Andjela to hurry up. There was a huge pressure on my chest, but it wasn't just an elephant anymore. It had been joined by an infinite number of butterflies that felt like they were going to explode from my body at any moment. The anticipation was killing me.

The door opened and Andjela stuck her head through. 'Hey, are you ready?' she asked, with a huge smile on her face. I nodded, feeling both relieved and terrified that the moment I had been waiting for was finally upon me. With a final deep breath, I stood up and walked towards the door.

I stopped dead in my tracks on the precipice of the café. On the precipice of finally seeing Nina in the flesh. 'Wait. Is she taller than me?'

'What?' Andjela asked, her mouth hanging open at my timing.

'Is she taller than me? I need to be taller than her or else it'll be weird,' I said. Andjela's hands were on the door frame and her head was hanging through.

'Are you kidding me? Don't be ridiculous. Come on,' Andjela said, shaking her head with a grin, before standing back against the door frame so I had a clear path through.

There are moments in your life where things change forever. Rarely are you aware before they happen that your life will never be the same again. I knew that when I walked over that threshold, I wouldn't be able to remember what life was like before I did. A time before I saw her. My body was shaking, and my heartbeat felt like it only had a few minutes left, as if it was trying to get a lifetime of beats out before it was too late.

Staring at the threshold for a moment, aware that as soon as I crossed, I would leave behind a time where I had not seen Nina in person. After nine months it was time. I was ready. I walked through the door that Andjela was standing just inside of, holding it open for me, and tried to make eye contact with no one. I didn't know if the café was completely silent or if my hearing wasn't working. I focused on what was directly in front of me, taking a sharp right as I stepped through the door and took just two strides before reaching a step, walking onto stage, and standing behind the microphone. A murmur came over the room. *I guess they know who I am,'* I thought, looking down at my feet. I couldn't wait to get there and see Nina; it had been all I had thought about for nine months, but standing there it was like I was trying to avoid seeing her. I couldn't ever live the moment of seeing her for the first time again. My anticipation just before I saw her for the first time felt like the butterflies had reproduced to a level that my body wouldn't be able to tolerate for much longer. I turned and plugged my guitar into the amplifier and stood tall with my shoulders back. I couldn't wait any longer. I thought my search for her would take some time in the sea of people, but that wasn't the case.

The butterflies in my soul paused, as if waiting for the moment Nina appeared to me. *'I see her. She's there. Right there,'* I thought, and felt the butterflies explode from my chest to the tips of my fingers and toes, and the end of my hair. The butterflies chased the elephant from my body. I could feel them dancing in my eyebrows. She was the first face I found in the room. Only a few metres away from me, slightly to the right, with her hand over her mouth in complete shock. Nina looked how I felt. She looked like she had no idea what she should do. I didn't know if I should speak, start to sing, or drop my guitar, run and hug her. Since the moment I met Nina, I thought she was the most beautiful woman in the world, but I still managed to be wrong. There could be nothing more beautiful in our universe. I was in awe looking upon her. She radiated elegance and grace just standing there and staring at me in a way that I could never fully appreciate through video chat or pictures. Her eyes smiled as they glistened in a moment that I could tell she still didn't believe was happening. *'She is sunshine. She is my sunshine,'* I thought, as I smiled at her from ear to ear.

There were a million things I wanted to say, but I wanted to say them just to her. To hold her hand, look into her eyes and tell her everything I felt in my soul. To finally tell her that I loved her. It wasn't for a crowd of people I didn't know though. I hoped there would be time later to tell her everything I had been feeling since I met her that November morning. *'For now, I hope she can feel it with what I play. I love you, Nina,'* I thought, placing my hand on my heart. Nina moved her hand from her mouth to her heart, and I knew she was feeling what I was feeling.

Everyone else in the room disappeared. There was only Nina and me. All the nerves, anxiety and negative possibilities about going to Požega were gone. I only felt one thing. Love. For every one of our video calls, I knew I loved her more each time, but that feeling was nothing in comparison to standing in Nina's presence; to look upon the beautiful soul that I knew to be the perfect partner for mine. In her presence, I was finally home.

I said I'd fought, gave all I could.
Soulmates don't exist; you'll still find your bliss.
I've realised the truth before my eyes.
I can't face this life with another by my side.
If you love someone, you have to show them.
Not just words, give them action.
So here I am, my eyes on you,
Telling you facts your heart always knew.

If you find yourself, in the arms of another,
Know he'll never love you better.
Our hearts beat together, never alone.
Two souls entwined. We are home.

Life is hard, but love is harder,
So let me sing you a picture.
Me on one knee, you crying yes,
You at the altar in a white dress.
Tears in your eyes and a beaming smile,
Telling me we're expecting a child.
Til the end of days, you'll have me,
My sunshine, I want our family.

If you find yourself, in the arms of another,

Know he'll never love you better.
Our hearts beat together, never alone.
Two souls entwined. We are home.

Take my hand, we'll do this life together.
Finding peace in one another.
Our elephants are waved goodbye.
Living our life with butterflies.

If you find yourself, in the arms of another,
Know he'll never love you better.
Our hearts beat together, never alone.
Two souls entwined. We are home.

I couldn't take my eyes off her. In sweats and a hoodie, or a dress, Nina was poetry in human form. I didn't even want to blink because that felt like a wasted moment. All I could think about the entire time I was playing was running over and hugging her. To finally feel her body touching mine. I had craved it since the moment I met her, and after nine long months, I couldn't believe I was so close to finally holding her.

I hit the last chord of the song, and everyone remained silent except for Andjela who applauded loudly. The rest of the café followed her lead and politely clapped while the people who recognised me stared in disbelief. Nina stared open mouthed until she politely clapped with the rest of the café, looking grateful to have something to do with her hands.

My feet were stuck to the floor. I didn't know if she wanted me to go to her, or if I should walk off the stage and put my guitar away. Her hanging mouth changed from shock to a smile, the one I had seen so many times before on our cyber dates, the one with the sparkle in her eye. It looked like her eyes were beginning to well up as she covered her face with both her hands. That look told me exactly what I needed to do. I needed to go to her. Taking my guitar off, I leaned it against the amplifier. I turned around to walk towards her, and just as I did, a tall, very handsome, and muscular man who looked like his shirt would split over his biceps walked up behind her. *'I know him. That's Marko,'* I thought, panicking. I remembered his face from the picture Nina sent me months ago, before my first gig. He tapped Nina on the shoulder, and she turned to see who it was. He leant down and kissed her on the lips. Her eyes widened in shock, and her lips stayed closed as his lips pressed to hers.

Something shattered inside me. I felt like I had just been punched in the stomach by Mike Tyson. A poison sprayed all over the butterflies, killing every last one inside me. The self-loathing part of myself roared into life, cackling with laughter. I was feeling like he was stomping on the dead butterflies. I couldn't seem to look away from a moment that felt like it would never end. *'Would the person that's hit slow motion on the remote here please press play? Or fast-forward? Or stop? Anything, please,'* I begged.

I was so confused. *'Why is she kissing him?'* I thought. She wasn't pushing him away, so he must be her boyfriend. I felt like the dumbest person alive.

The people you love the most always have the potential to hurt you the most. You trust them with your most prized possession, your heart. The greatest falls can only happen when you're at your greatest height. Playing a song to Nina and seeing her reaction in person to something I wrote from my heart for her was the greatest moment of my life. I was about to walk over and embrace her for the first time, but no, instead came my greatest fall, the worst moment of my life, and I was left a shell of a human. I no longer felt like a man, I felt about three centimetres tall. Humiliated.

'I can't stay here,' I thought desperately. Tearing my eyes away from her being kissed by Marko, I turned quickly and felt a hand touch my arm, but I brushed it off like I didn't notice it, before

walking through the door I entered. I walked through that door four minutes earlier full of hope, I walked back through it completely broken.

As soon as I got outside, I broke into a run. I ran as fast as I could. I felt like my legs were about to fly off but still I urged them to move quicker, to take me from that place as quickly as possible. It felt like my body was going to split from the stitch in my side, but I didn't care. I crossed through the open door of the hotel, tore through the lobby and up the stairs, opened my room and locked the door behind me. I paced my room trying to understand what I just witnessed. I had a three-hour bus ride and a twenty-two-hour flight in front of me back to Australia to let it all sink in. *'At least I'd be locked in a place where I'd be able to put some serious overthinking into what just happened,'* I thought.

The devastation turned to rage. *'How could Andjela do that to me? How could she not warn me about what I was walking in to? I thought she liked me. She loves my brother, and she sets me up like that? What did I do to her to deserve that?'* I thought, feeling my anger boil inside me.

I collapsed onto the bed and felt the elephant return. He had brought the entire bachelor herd with him, and I could feel all that weight and pressure upon my chest. I fought for breath, heaving in deeply but still not getting enough oxygen. The pressure on my chest was too great.

The moment played on repeat in my mind. I watched this strong, huge, handsome man kissing the woman I was head over heels in love with through my mind's eye. *'Why would I ever believe that a woman like Nina could want me when she could have a man like that? You're a fool, Luka,'* I thought self-loathingly.

Before I met Nina, I thought that I wasn't good enough and she changed that. She made me realise there wasn't anything wrong with me. That I wasn't the disgustingly ugly boy that I saw staring back at me in the mirror with his skin crawling the night of Nana's funeral. That feeling was back though. I was once again that disgusting boy standing in front of his mirror feeling an electrical pulse of revulsion for himself.

The kiss continued to play on a loop in my mind, no matter if my eyes were open or shut. Each time the scene played, a stabbing pain in my chest became deeper and sharper. I struggled to stand up and began to try and fight off the elephants on my chest. I traced the same steps I had less than an hour before when I was so hopeful, catching a glimpse of myself in the mirror as I did. I turned to look at myself. The look I saw on my face was one of pure hatred. 'You deserve this. This is what you get for being such a pathetic loser. You deserve this pain. Look how ugly you are. Look at those skinny arms. Look at your skin. Do you really think she would ever want you? You are so stupid. Look how much more handsome he is than you. I bet he's smarter than you, and kinder than you are too. You could never have her. You disgust me,' I spat aloud to the person staring at me from the mirror, with a mixture of fury and repulsion. I felt the electrical pulse course through my nervous system telling me how disgusting I was.

A nauseousness rose in me. I rushed to the bathroom kneeling in front of the toilet, feeling like I was about to throw up. *'I want to go home,'* I thought, desperately heartbroken.

I needed a circuit breaker. It was very early in Melbourne, but I needed to talk to someone to release the extraordinary pressure crushing my chest. I couldn't breathe; I needed a release. My shaking hand grabbed my phone and called James. 'Please pick up,' I pleaded aloud, as the phone continued to ring.

'Hello,' a very groggy James said on the other end of the phone.

'She has a boyfriend,' I whispered.

'What? What happened?' James asked, suddenly alert.

'I saw her there. She was right there in front of me. I was about to walk to her when I saw some Adonis walk up behind her and kiss her,' I said, feeling the tears well up.

'Oh, mate. I'm so sorry. Are you okay?' he asked.

That was it. The one question I didn't want to hear. That question opened the flood gates on my tears. They flowed painfully and freely from my eyes, and I watched them hit the bathroom floor. I wasn't okay, but I didn't want to say that aloud.

'I don't know. I'll be okay,' I squeaked, trying to hide my flash flooding of tears from him.

'What's going on?' I heard Michael's voice ask.

'He saw Nina kissing another guy at her birthday,' James explained to Michael. 'Michael's here too, mate. We went out last night and he crashed at mine.'

'Hey Luka, what're you going to do?' Michael asked.

'I have no idea,' I mumbled, my forearms resting on the toilet seat, ready for me to throw up at any moment.

'Pack your stuff and come home,' James said.

'Yes, come home, mate. Just come home,' Michael echoed.

I nodded my head, forgetting that they weren't in the bathroom with me. 'Are you still there? Luka!?' James asked in a panicked voice.

'Yeah. Okay. I'll get on the first flight tomorrow,' I said, wiping the tears from my cheeks with my sleeve.

'If you need anything, just call,' Michael said.

'Hey James?' I asked.

'Yeah, mate?'

'I did it. I did everything I could. Fought with more than I ever knew I had. I guess at the end of the day, I'm just not good enough,' I said, and the tears streamed faster and harder. I had never cried like that before; I had never hurt like that before.

'You are good enough, mate,' James said, passionately.

'You are. Just because she's with someone else doesn't mean you're not good enough,' Michael said emphatically. I could feel how upset they were.

'Thanks, guys. Thanks for answering. I'll see you soon. I love you guys,' I said, sniffing loudly.

'I'm sorry we didn't go with you,' Michael said.

'Yeah, Luka. We should be there with you. Remember, we love you too. Hey Luka, we're proud of you, mate. You went for it. You did everything you could,' James said. Without being able to utter another word, I hung up the phone.

I sat back on the bathroom floor, leaning against the cabinet beneath the sink. Weeping silently, I watched the tears fall from my cheeks onto my tan chinos. They quickly dried but through my blurred vision I felt like I could still see them. The tears were the butterflies leaving me. They died the moment Nina kissed him.

I heard a quiet knock on the door. It sounded nervous. 'Go away, Andjela!' I shouted, snapping my head in the direction of the door, sniffing loudly. Again, with trepidation there was a knock. I stood up with every bit of strength I could muster and walked towards the door, wiping away my tears. 'I said go away,' I shouted, as I turned the door handle and ripped it open.

'You forgot this.' It wasn't Andjela. Nina stood in the doorway with my guitar case in her hand.

CHAPTER NINETEEN
The Hotel

Who is she talking to?' I wondered, as Andjela walked off the stage and spoke to someone just through the side door. I craned my neck to try and get an angle to see who it was but couldn't see. She seemed to be coaxing the person in, so that removed the chance of it being Marko, the only person that had not arrived. Andjela dragged her head back inside the café with a huge smile on her face and beckoned the person in. I saw a guitar neck appear through the door, soon followed by... no. *'No way. It can't be him. He can't be here. How did Andjela find such a perfect Luka doppelganger?'* I thought in complete shock.

I saw a nervous smile on the doppelganger's face as he turned and walked onto stage. The same nervous smile I saw when I first started dating the real Luka. The nervous look on his face was adorable. I didn't know how he nailed all Luka's mannerisms so perfectly, but his impression was starting to get scary. I wasn't sure why Andjela thought it would be a good present, it almost felt cruel.

It felt like he was intentionally avoiding my eyes as he busied himself on stage, plugging his guitar into the amplifier and setting himself behind the microphone. I looked at Andjela still standing by the door, and she began to laugh and nodded when she saw me staring at her. *'Why did she nod? Is it really him? Nope, it can't be,'* I thought, refusing to believe that Luka could be standing in front of me.

The doppelganger closed his eyes for a moment and then his eyes found mine. *'It's him! Those eyes,'* I thought, and felt my knees buckle and joyous butterflies exploded inside my chest. I would recognise how they made me feel when they locked with mine anywhere. My heart skipped several beats before springing back to life. Everyone and everything in the room disappeared apart from Luka. We may as well have been back on a video chat with him about to share a song with me. I wanted to run to him and touch him, to jump into his arms, but my feet felt as though they were stuck in concrete. My dream had come true. Luka was finally in front of me.

Without saying a word, Luka began to play a song that I hadn't heard before. My brain couldn't register anything he was singing, but I could feel every note that he sang and played. *'I could listen to this man sing every day for the rest of my life, but can he please finish this song so I can be next to him, talk to him, touch him,'* I begged the time Gods, craving the distance between us to finally disappear.

My brain started to register what he was singing. *'These aren't the words someone sings to a friend. Maybe, just maybe…,'* I thought, refusing to let myself really believe there could be hope. The longer the song went on, the more deeply I fell in love. He was pouring his soul out to me. The deep connection I could feel when we spoke on video chat was dwarfed by the instant connection I could feel being in his presence. A bolt of electricity from his voice shot straight into my soul, waking every cell in my body. Even my toenails were aware of the magnitude of the moment. My entire body was buzzing.

I was stuck in between not wanting the song to end, and for it to end immediately so I could get to Luka. I had waited long enough. He must have been feeling the same because he didn't take his eyes off me for a moment. *'No man would do this for a woman he wasn't in love with,'* I thought, trying to convince myself that it was finally happening. What I had been dreaming of; a world of Luka and I together had finally arrived.

I didn't know where to put my hands. *'What do I even normally do with these things?'* I thought, as I balled them up into tight fists and then spread my fingers wide apart, wiping them on my dress.

'My gosh, Luka, finish your beautiful song so I can kiss you!' I screamed in my head.

Endorphins rushed through my body watching the way he swayed from side to side, how he tapped his left foot to keep his song in time, and the love I heard in his voice. *'How could any woman ever let this man go? Obviously, you would have to be certifiably insane, but if he ever gives me another chance, then I'll show him every day how much I love him. Whatever it takes to make us work. We belong together,'* I thought, determinedly. Memories of wearing our hoodie and having Luka's scent waft through my nostrils had me craving to be near him, near the source of my favourite smell. I wanted to be dancing with Luka to his new song.

Luka played the final chord of the song and the smile that spread across his face sent a kaleidoscope of butterflies through my body. He looked incredibly uncomfortable as a few people clapped, but the people who knew who he was stood there in shock. Andjela applauded loudly until the room came to its senses and applauded Luka's song. I finally woke the neurons to send the message to my hands to applaud with everyone else. They felt exceptionally weak and the most I could muster was a light, polite clap.

He was looking directly at me, not breaking eye contact for a second. Not through a screen, but right in front of me with his real, perfect eyes. My hands moved to my mouth as I still couldn't fathom that Luka was standing there. *'He is real,'* I thought, still in shock as my hand rose to my hair that fell over my shoulder, twirling it around my finger. Luka removed the guitar from his shoulder and turned around to lean it against the amplifier. I tried to again rouse my inactive neurons to get my feet to move towards him, but they refused to move.

Suddenly I felt a tap on my shoulder and was spun around. Someone kissed me. My eyes stayed wide open and saw the person kissing my tight, pursed lips was Marko. His timing couldn't have been worse. Seeing Luka made me forget that Marko even existed, and now Luka was seeing the guy that he hated more than anyone kiss me in front of a room full of people. *'His heart must be breaking,'* I thought, trying to wake my mind into action and break the kiss. I was stuck in shock. Every one of the butterflies in my soul fell to the floor of my stomach and were squashed by my heart falling on top of them.

In the space of four minutes, I went from being attracted to Marko, to being as attracted to him as I was to a jaguar. I mean they look good, but I don't want them to ever kiss me. I didn't know if it was a quick peck on the lips, or a prolonged kiss because time seems to stand still when you can feel your world falling apart. I thought I wanted Luka before I saw him, but after finally seeing his perfect eyes for myself, I knew I didn't want to ever be with anyone else. For those four minutes I thought I was about to be back with the man of my dreams, and somehow, I had managed to break his heart all over again. *'Why didn't I at least tell him about Marko?'* I thought, furious at myself. Marko pulled away and I turned to the stage immediately to see it vacant, and the side door slowly closing. Luka had gone.

I spun my head in every direction hoping that Luka hadn't been the one that walked through that door. I needed to find him. I needed to explain why I didn't tell him about Marko. I tried to walk towards the side door that I assumed Luka had exited from, when my arm was grabbed from behind. 'Where are you going? What's wrong?' Marko asked, as I tried to pull my arm from his vice like grip.

'Where did he go? I need to find him,' I said, panicked. 'You're hurting me. Let go,' I growled at Marko. 'Never touch me like that again. I go where I want, when I want, and right now I want to get away from you to find Luka,' I said, finally prising myself free from his grip that left a red mark on my arm, adrenaline pumping through my body.

'Wait a minute. Was that singing boy your ex?' Marko asked, beginning to laugh with derision.

'That man is Luka, who I'm going to find right now. You might be taller and have bigger arms than him, but you could never be the man he is. You could never have the heart or soul to write and sing something like he did. Now leave me alone,' I scalded Marko, and tried to walk away again to recommence my search for Luka.

'Don't you dare walk away from me,' Marko said furiously, grabbing my arm again and pulling me back towards him.

I had never hated anyone more in my life. What I felt towards that girl with her arm around Luka was nothing compared to the hatred that filled my entire being at that moment. It became clear then from the look on his face that he didn't care about me, I was just a conquest to him. His eyes didn't sparkle when he looked at me for a reason.

A fist flew past my left ear out of nowhere and hit Marko on his previously broken nose. Andjela stood next to me panting after mustering all her power like an overhead smash into a punch through Marko's face. A loud thud echoed through the café as Marko's huge body thundered to the floor. Andjela and I looked down and surveyed the damage as Marko stared at the ceiling, hands covering his nose, blood flowing from his face like a faucet.

Marko jumped up and spat blood on the ground. 'I didn't do anything last time, but I'm not going to let it go again, you bitch,' Marko spat, looking like he was about to lunge. Before he could get to Andjela or me, Tata stood in between us and looked Marko in the eye with disdain.

'Unless you want me to put you on the floor, I suggest you leave. Now,' Tata said quietly, but his fury was obvious, balling his right hand into a fist, as Marko looked around him at Andjela, then at me, trying to make his decision.

'Whatever. I was just trying to sleep with you anyway. Have your loser,' Marko said to me around Tata, spitting on the ground in front of me, and turning towards the front door, slamming it behind him as he exited.

'I'm kind of glad you got together with him now. It meant I got the chance to punch him again,' Andjela said, putting a hand on my shoulder.

'Did you see where Luka went? I need to find him,' I said desperately to Andjela. My head was on a swivel between the side and front doors, hoping that Luka would reappear.

'I tried to stop him when he left, but he walked straight past me through the door when Marko kissed you. I assume he went back to his hotel room though. He doesn't really have anywhere else to go,' Andjela said, taking her hand off me and pulling out her phone. 'I'll text him.'

'No. Do you know what room?' I could feel tears welling up behind my eyes. *If I've lost him forever because of a pig like Marko, I'll never be able to forgive myself,'* I thought. I didn't expect a conversation with Luka to go well, but I had to talk to him. I had to try.

'I'll walk you to his room. You can get him back. He came all this way just to see you for your birthday. He loves you, Nina,' Andjela said softly, placing her powerful right hand gently on my arm.

'You really think so?' I asked, with hope shining in my eyes.

'I know so. Did that song sound like a man that just wants to be your friend?' Andjela asked, smiling.

'Okay, let's go. He left his guitar here too,' I said, with a newfound steely resolve.

We walked towards the stage, and I picked up his guitar. We found his case on a table just through the side door, so I placed it inside, sealed the case, and we walked as quickly as our heels would allow towards the hotel.

'I really wish I wore flats. These heels are slowing me down way too much,' Andjela said, as we crossed the road in front of the café and took a left-hand turn with Luka's guitar held tightly in my right-hand.

Navigating our way towards the hotel and walking through the carpark, I couldn't help but feel grateful Andjela was beside me. I would be a complete wreck walking towards Luka if she wasn't by my side. Andjela led the way through the foyer and up the stairs. We got to the third floor and took a right turn. With each passing door I felt the anxiety rise in my chest, knowing I was walking towards Luka. My eyes scanned from left to right, wondering which door Luka was hidden behind. Finally, we stopped in front of the fourth door on the right side of the corridor. My lungs had forgotten how to breathe, and my heart had forgotten how to beat. I bent over, placed the guitar by my side, and put my hands on my knees, oxygen finally granted passage to my lungs. Taking breaths like I was a thirty-year smoker with emphysema, I let in as much air as I could before standing upright and closing my eyes.

I felt scared of how poorly it could go, but I was determined to get into that room and talk to Luka. If he had no interest in talking to me then I had to live with that, but I couldn't live with not trying at all. The prospect of talking to Luka in person gave me courage, even if I was terrified.

'This is it,' Andjela said in a voice barely above a whisper. 'How do you feel?'

'Absolutely terrified. Look at my chest. I didn't know hearts could beat this fast,' I said, looking down and placing a shaking hand on my chest.

'Staring at your chest seems like more of a job for Luka. Plus, he has the excuse of saying he's looking at your heart.' I couldn't help but shake my head and laugh which relaxed me. 'I have to ask; did I do the right thing bringing him here?' Andjela asked nervously, standing between the door and me.

'I wish with every fibre of my being that he didn't see what he saw tonight,' I whispered. Andjela looked down at her feet and a silent tear fell from her left eye. *It must be breaking her heart thinking that she hurt Luka and me,* I thought.

'I'm sorry. I thought I was doing something great for you guys, but in reality, I just hurt you both,' Andjela said, still paying close attention to the floor.

'You brought Luka here. Watching him walk through that door and sing to me was the greatest moment of my life. No matter what happens, whether he lets me into his room or not, I'm so grateful you brought him here. I'll remember my greatest ever gift for the rest of my life. Thank you.' Andjela looked up and hugged me. I embraced her with both my arms. 'I love you,' I whispered in her ear, and kissed her on the cheek.

'I love you too. Now go and get your man,' Andjela said, kissing me on the cheek and walking back down the hall. I waited until I saw her disappear down the stairs and then turned my attention back to the door. I picked up Luka's guitar, closed my eyes, and took a deep breath. With fear and excitement fighting for dominance, I knocked on the door with my shaking left hand.

'Go away, Andjela!' I heard his Australian accent yell from behind the door. I was worried he didn't come back to his room and was wondering around Požega, but thankfully I was in the right place. I knocked again. 'I said go away,' Luka said again, the pain dripping from his voice. I watched the door handle turn before being wrenched open.

'You forgot this,' I said, holding up Luka's guitar with my aching right arm. He stared at me with his mouth hanging open. I thought he had the most beautiful eyes I had ever seen in photos and on video, but it was nothing compared to what I was looking into when he opened the door. While there were no tears in his eyes, they were red and glistened as if he had just wiped them away and they could begin falling again at any moment. *Why do eyes look more beautiful when filled with tears? Why is there such beauty in sadness?'* I wondered, looking into his glistening blue eyes. I felt a stab to my heart that I put that hurt in his eyes by not being honest. The hurt was mixed with shock seeing me stand in front of him. Behind that I could see how kind and loving they were, with a glimmer of hope. I thought before, but at that moment I knew, they were the most beautiful eyes in the world.

'Can we talk?' I asked nervously, as Luka continued to stare at me open mouthed, praying he would let me into his room. I was willing to sleep on the hallway floor if I needed. I was determined that he at least hear me out, if after that he never wanted to see me again, I would just have to live with that.

'Okay,' Luka said in a cracking voice, standing aside to let me in. 'Here, let me,' Luka said, reaching for the guitar and holding the door open as I walked over the threshold into his room. I heard a sniff from behind me as I entered. Even in heartbreak he was a perfect gentleman.

Every possibility as to how it would go was running through my mind. *Will he yell at me and tell me to leave while I try to explain? Will we talk everything through and get back together? Will he listen to everything I have to say, understand me, and still ask me to leave? At least he's giving me a chance to talk to him,'* I thought, hoping I would be able to put together an articulate sentence.

Out of the million times I played the scenario out in my head of meeting Luka in person for the first time, it never happened like that. It was always a movie moment where we would see each other from a distance, leaving our bags behind and running to embrace each other. Life never plays out how you plan; you just have to make the best decisions you can in the moment with the information you have.

I turned around and looked at Luka, not sure where, or how to begin, whether to sit or stand. Luka took a seat on the edge of the bed and looked up at me nervously pacing in front of him. 'Do you want to sit?' he asked, looking from me to the space next to him on the bed.

'Umm, yeah okay, thanks,' I said, my voice breaking, as I sat down next to him and crossed my right leg over my left. I couldn't believe I was so close to him, that I could touch him. I so desperately wanted to hold his hand in mine, but I didn't. I didn't know if he wanted me to touch him at all, so I would have to wait and see how the conversation went. I hadn't earned that privilege yet.

Faintly I noticed his scent. There was no hint of cologne, it was all Luka. It was intoxicating, drawing me nearer. I needed to get closer to the source. He smelled like happiness.

'Your eyes are so beautiful.' The words escaped my lips before I could pull them back. I couldn't help but lose myself in them, I was entranced. I was putty in his hands, and he had no idea. Andjela said that when I saw his eyes in person I wouldn't stand a chance, and she was right. Just a look was all it took for my soul to do a somersault. It had found home.

'Thanks. I love your smile,' Luka replied, blushing and looking very intently at his shoes. We sat in silence waiting for the other to break it.

I didn't know how to process or verbalise what I was feeling. Just a few hours earlier I was sending Luka a photo thinking he was in Australia, but really, he was in Požega. My body was consumed with shock that the man of my dreams who had previously only existed in my phone and on my computer, was sitting less than a metre away from me. Close enough for me to touch. *'Oh, I so badly need to hold his hand,'* I thought, looking down at his musical fingers.

I could feel his nervous energy and looked down at his leg to see it bouncing. *'He must be just as nervous as me,'* I thought, as I began to absentmindedly twirl my hair. We sat there in silence for a moment with neither of us sure how to begin.

'Did you have any idea you'd be seeing me today?' Luka asked, and I was grateful that he had finally broken the silence.

'Andjela said she had a surprise for me, but I never would've guessed it would be you. When did you get here?' I asked. I wanted to look straight into those magical blue eyes, but I dared to only take glances. I continued to twirl my hair, waiting for the pleasantries to end and the real conversation to start.

'A few hours ago. It's funny how us meeting are polar opposite experiences. For me this anticipation has been building for a couple of days from when I knew I was coming, and for you, it's a big surprise. Are you glad I'm here?' Luka asked, his leg now bouncing higher like he was trying to settle an upset baby on his knee.

'I bet our babies would be adorable. Come on, Nina, get through this conversation before worrying about having his babies,' I thought, ever so gently shaking my head, trying to conceal a wry smile.

'It was the happiest I've felt in my entire life. So no, I wasn't glad, I was ecstatic. Why didn't you tell me though?' I asked, risking a glance into those beautiful, soulful eyes, and then looking away like I was looking into a solar eclipse, and needed to protect my eyesight.

'I wanted it to be a surprise. Also, if I told you I was coming then there was a chance you would tell me not to come, that we were better off being friends from afar. If I just turned up then at least I got to see you, even if it was just for a moment, then it was worth it,' Luka said, looking at my hand twirl my hair.

'I would never tell you not to come. I might not believe that you were actually coming though, even if you said you were. Even if you sent me a photo in front of Hotel Požega. Even if you sent me a photo from outside my house, I wouldn't believe it until I actually saw you. I just might have done some things differently though,' I said, trailing off and hanging my head.

'A photo in front of your house sounds a bit stalky,' Luka said, and we both laughed. 'What would you have done differently?' Luka leaned forward and looked directly into my eyes. I dared to only meet his gaze for a moment before looking away.

'The Marko situation….' I said, trailing off.

'Oh, yeah. That…' Luka said, turning his attention back to my hand twirling my hair. He looked like he wanted to grab my hand to stop me but thought better of the idea.

'I'm sorry.'

'You don't have anything to be sorry for. I mean I thought we were friends so you probably should have told me as a friend, but you don't owe me anything. We're not together so you didn't do anything wrong. I guess it just wasn't great seeing you kiss someone else is all,' Luka said, looking into my eyes and giving me a weak, hurt smile.

Everything was more intense with Luka. The love I felt was more intense than I had ever felt before. The disappointment I felt in myself when I knew I had hurt him or let him down was more intense too. I wanted to protect him from all bad feelings that could come his way, but I was probably the person who had hurt him the most. I promised myself that if he gave me another chance that I would make sure I protected his immaculate heart from everything that could hurt it. I wanted to be his shield, and him to be mine. I would bring him happiness, not sorrow.

'We are friends, Luka. Well, at least I hope we are. I'm sorry I didn't tell you.'

'Are we friends? Or do we just call each other that so we can feel like we're still a real part of each other's lives?' Luka asked.

'Umm, I don't know,' I said softly, staring at the wall. His question hit me hard. I had never considered the possibility that we weren't really friends.

'I mean we don't talk very often. When we do it's superficial small talk, never about real things like if you're dating someone or life plans or feelings. And you often leave me on read when I text you. I don't think that's real friendship,' Luka said. He didn't sound angry, just being honest. Like releasing his inner most thoughts for the first time, to the only person in his life who would really understand him.

'You're right. I guess…. I guess I was just scared,' I said, trying to work through in my mind what he had said.

'Scared about what?' Luka asked, prodding me for more information.

'I was scared that if we talked too often then I would want you back. There was a time I left you on read just after I watched your concert when Andjela was there. I wasn't trying to be mean, I so badly wanted to be with you after watching you sing, but I was worried that if we talked then I would tell you that. And that you either wouldn't want to, or that we would get back together, and I would lose you again. Losing you the first time was the hardest thing I've ever gone through; I couldn't handle doing it again,' I finished, my breathing getting short and my heart beating quickly. I saw Luka's hand move slightly towards me, as if to console me, before pulling back and placing it on his knee.

'Is that when you got together with Marko?' Luka asked.

'We had our first date just after that, but it's a long story that goes back before then.

'Can you tell me the whole story?' Luka asked softly. His soft tone had a way of making me feel comfortable enough to tell him anything, to want to tell him everything. I told him the entire story of the assignment, through to what happened at my birthday party.

'It's just, on one hand I don't understand why you're with him because of what he did to you. On the other hand, I understand why you would be with him. The guy looks like a Greek god. I think the part that upset me the most when I saw you kissing him was, well is, that I know I don't stand a chance with you. I always thought you were out of my league and then that kind of confirmed it. At least I got to meet you, to sit here and talk to you. I guess it just sucks when you know you tried as hard as you could, did everything in your power and it still wasn't enough, because I wasn't enough. I'm not enough. I just hope you two are happy together,' Luka said, looking at me with those hurt eyes, cutting through me like a hot knife through butter.

'What are you talking about? Luka, I broke up with him. I decided earlier tonight I was going to break up with him. The moment I saw you tonight I forgot he even existed. Yeah, he's a good-looking guy, but he isn't half the man you are. He doesn't have your heart, and he doesn't look at me the way you do. When he looks at me, I just see him in that moment. When you look at me, I see an entire life in front of me. He wouldn't have travelled halfway around the world to play a song at my birthday. I mean you came from Australia and still managed to arrive at my party before him. Don't you remember what I said when we first met? I'm not out of your league. You can put yourself down, but I think you're really handsome. You have the most beautiful eyes I've ever seen. No one could ever have my heart like you do. He could never have feelings for me like you do....' I said hopefully, trailing off. I wanted to hear it. That one short sentence. I wanted to hear those three words leave his lips and remove all doubt. The words Luka had never said to me before.

I thought he felt it, but I needed to hear the words. *'He has to love me to come all this way, doesn't he?'* I asked myself.

Luka sat up and I noticed that his leg stopped moving mid bounce. He placed his hand on mine, and I immediately stopped twirling my hair. I had been craving the touch of that hand since November thirteenth, the day we met. It sent a shock through my body like a defibrillator. That simple touch of his hand on mine. For the first time in my life, I could consciously feel my heartbeat in my ear lobes.

'Feelings? No, I don't think that's strong enough to describe what I'm experiencing. Didn't you listen to my song? I'm in love with you, Nina,' Luka said, staring deeply into my eyes. I dared not look away. I felt like my heart was going to explode with happiness. There didn't exist a better feeling on this planet than when the one you love tells you they love you too.

'You are?' I said jubilantly. 'I love you too, Luka. I thought it was going to go away when we broke up. I didn't want the love to go away, but I wanted the pain to stop. I distracted myself to stop the hurt for a little while, but it was only temporary. What I was really doing was ignoring my true feelings. You were the one I wanted to show my outfit. You were the one I wanted there tonight more than anyone, I just thought it wasn't possible. I never stopped loving you and somehow, I love you more now than I did before we broke up.' I sat staring back into his perfect blue eyes. I leant in slightly hoping that he would notice my body language and lean in the rest of the way. I looked down at his lips wondering if they would be a perfect match for mine like our hearts were. Luka broke into a huge smile and took his hand off mine. *'No, don't take away your hand,'* I thought, disappointedly. A moment later he slid his fingers in between mine. Finally, I was holding hands with Luka. I couldn't help but match Luka's smile looking down at our fingers intertwined, in disbelief that they were finally together. We were finally together.

'I feel the exact same way. I mean, I have been ever since I first saw you, and every day since then it's grown stronger. I tried everything to get over you, but nothing worked, and it all just made me feel disgusting. Even though we weren't together, if I even talked to another woman, I felt like I was cheating on you,' Luka said, his voice began to race, and his leg started to bounce again. I placed my free hand on his bouncing leg to ease his anxiety. His leg stopped bouncing at my touch.

'I have to admit, I did see a photo online of you with a girl. She said you were her star, so I thought you had moved on from me,' I said, trying to be casual and not bring up the whole mental breakdown over a photo thing.

'Oh damn, I forgot about Tayla. She asked if I wanted to have dinner with her tonight, but I forgot to text her back. We were talking but we never hung out together. I just met her a couple of times when I was out. I always avoided going out with her because I wasn't feeling it. It wasn't the same,' Luka said.

'What do you mean, it wasn't the same?'

'Didn't feel the same as when I would talk to you. I didn't think about her during the day, but I never stopped thinking about you. I don't want to date anyone.'

I looked down at our hands entwined and smiled, feeling bittersweet. *How stupid am I?* I thought. I could have just asked him how it was going with the Australian girls rather than making my mind up from one photo online. To hear him say he didn't want to date anyone though, felt like a punch to the stomach, but I couldn't blame him. I held his hand a little tighter worrying it would be the last time, not wanting him to let go.

'Is that when you started hanging out with him? You thought I'd moved on so you decided you should too?' Luka asked.

'We had hung out before then, but we didn't have a first date until I saw that picture. So, you don't want to date anyone now?' I asked nervously, terrified of hearing his answer. If he wasn't ready to date anyone yet, I would understand, but I would wait for him until he said he didn't want to date me. I wasn't going to be the one to end it a second time. *I'm not making that mistake again,'* I thought, determination rising inside me.

'Sorry, I misspoke. Nina, I don't want to date anyone else. As in, I only want to date you,' Luka said, a huge beaming smile breaking across his handsome face.

The butterflies exploded back into life in my stomach, dancing with joy. I wanted to jump up and do a cartwheel except I didn't know how, and my dress wasn't a cartwheel kind of dress. *He wants to be with me!'* I screamed in my head. *I'm not going to let him go ever again. If we're to start again then I need to be completely honest so there's nothing that can stand in our way.'* I steeled myself to talk to him about my lie and put that behind us.

'I'm sure you're upset about the age thing.'

'What age thing?' Luka asked, furrowing his brow quizzically at me.

Somehow, I had cleared one impossible hurdle, so time for the other. It was like clearing the Great Wall of China and then finding another one behind it. I needed to do it though.

'You didn't see the eighteens all around the café?' I asked.

'I was a bit distracted seeing you for the first time and trying to remember the lyrics. What are you talking about?'

'Umm, you're going to be really mad at me, so I hope you'll let me explain. I know I should have told you the first time we spoke, but I was scared. I lied to you. I told you I was eighteen when we met, but really, I was seventeen. Tonight, was my eighteenth birthday party, not my nineteenth,' I said nervously, trying to keep the strength in my voice.

'I did think it was a little odd that you would have such a big birthday party for your nineteenth,' Luka said slowly, taking his beautiful gaze off me, staring at the wall in front of us with his eyes wide in contemplation. He pulled his fingers entwined with mine from my grip. My hand followed his like a magnet, wanting it back.

'He hates me,' I thought, bowing my head. 'I'm really sorry. I just thought that if you knew I was seventeen then you wouldn't talk to me. The moment I saw you I liked you, and I wanted to keep talking to you. I should have told you the truth. I'm so sorry. Can you forgive me? Please?' I pleaded with him, speaking more quickly with every syllable. I lifted my head to look at Luka, trying to meet his gaze, tears lining up at my tear ducts.

Luka stood up and walked away to the window and back. He stopped in front of me, and I grabbed both of his hands to stop him from walking away again, looking up into his disappointed face.

'Why do you have to make things so much harder than they have to be? You should have told me the truth from the beginning,' Luka said in a tired voice, as he fought to avoid my eyes which I was so desperate for him to meet.

'I know, but if you knew I was seventeen, would you have kept talking to me?'

'Probably. Maybe. I don't know,' Luka said, his eyes looking at everything apart from me.

'Exactly. You don't know.' I stood up and looked eye to eye with Luka in my heels. 'So yes, I should have told you the truth, but that lie means that you are here, and I am here, and we love each other. Can it really be a bad thing if it results in this?' I asked, touching his chest and then mine, moving closer to him. Luka couldn't avoid my eyes any longer; we were separated by less than thirty centimetres.

'The ends don't justify the means, Nina. It was my decision to make with the truth,' he whispered.

'Do you want me to leave?' I asked, unable to hold my tears in anymore. They charged through my ducts like the rampaging wildebeest that killed that lion in that cartoon movie. I wouldn't have blamed him if he said yes, but I didn't know how I would ever be able to walk through the door away from him.

He stared silently into my eyes, and I had no idea what he was about to say. Time stood still as I swung back and forth between thinking Luka was about to tell me to leave or tell me to stay. My anxiety built, waiting for him to answer. Ever so gently he shook his head. Relief washed over me and the panic that was radiating through my body, waiting for him to answer was released.

'No way. I never want you to leave. Nina, if this is going to work though, we have to be honest with each other. The good things, and the things that are hard to say. It can't work any other way.'

'I know. No more secrets, Luka. I promise,' I said, squeezing his hands to reassure him.

Taking his hands from my grip, Luka walked over to the desk and picked up his phone. *Who could he possibly need to text now? Maybe he's texting Tayla that he's with his soulmate,'* I thought. 'What are you doing?' I asked, wanting him back next to me so I could hold his hand again.

Music started playing from his phone, and within two seconds I recognised it was my favourite Ed Sheeran song. 'I hate dancing, but the entire trip here I was thinking about dancing with you at your nineteenth birthday. While we know that wasn't possible for several reasons, now that you're here, I was wondering if I could dance with the woman I'm in love with on her eighteenth birthday?' Luka asked, walking towards me with his hand extended.

My heart jumped up and down like a Doberman excited that it had just been praised. I extended my right hand to take his left, and he pulled me into his body, my chest on his, placing his right hand on my waist. I placed my left hand on his shoulder, with our faces separated by just a few centimetres. He led me slowly, swaying back and forth to the rhythm of the song. I could feel his heartbeat on my chest, and knew he could feel mine also, as they beat in concert.

I was so excited I felt like jumping on the spot, yet also felt completely relaxed. I was where I was meant to be. My body was pressed against his and I felt myself being pulled even closer, like a black hole and I didn't have any way to resist the gravity. I took my hand from his and wrapped both of my arms around his neck, standing in front of him, body to body, face to face. Luka wrapped his arms around my waist and pulled me as close to him as he could. Finally, after nine months Luka was holding me like I had craved to be held the entire time. Ed continued to croon in the background, and I was exactly where I wanted to be. Where I needed to be. I held onto Luka and never wanted to let him go. My soul had found its perfect mate. His scent washed over me, and I felt my knees weaken, grateful that I was holding onto him for support. I searched my mind for an answer as to what he smelled like; then it came to me, he smelled like home.

'What?' I asked self-consciously, as Luka stared into my eyes without saying a word.

'You are so beautiful.' He continued to look into my eyes and nervously smiled. I felt excited because I could read his mind. He was thinking what I was thinking; that our lips needed to meet. We were only separated by a few centimetres. I gently bit my lower lip and looked at his, feeling myself drawn to him like the most powerful magnet. I saw his eyes looking at my lips, begging to feel mine upon his. Luka closed the space between us and touched his lips to mine. I felt my toes curl in my heels as we kissed tentatively. Our lips began to dance with each other, Luka leading the slow, deep, and passionate pace of our very first kiss. The euphoria was indescribable. My soul and heart leapt in unison, celebrating as dopamine, serotonin and oxytocin flowed through me. I felt like I was high. *If this is what a kiss can feel like, then I've never really been kissed before. I am truly, head over heels in love with this man, my man, and never want to kiss another set of lips again,'* I thought.

Our lips finally separated, and he started smiling widely looking into my eyes. 'Do you want to stay tonight?' Luka asked, as we continued to sway to the sweet melodic sounds of Ed.

'Yes,' I said nodding, and I rested my head on Luka's shoulder.

'You better tell your mama that you won't be home tonight. I don't need her sending out a search party because you didn't come home,' Luka said, as we broke our close dancing embrace.

He leaned in and kissed me again, making the butterflies in my stomach do backflips. *The butterflies are going to be very tired from all this exercise,'* I thought, wiping my bottom lip after our kiss.

'I'll tell Mama I'm staying at Andjela's. I'm not sure how happy she'll be if I say I'm staying in the hotel for the night with the singer from the party,' I said, walking towards my phone and crafting messages to both Mama and Andjela.

'If it was our daughter who said that, I'd be speeding to the hotel right away to drag her butt back home,' Luka said.

'Our daughter?' I thought excitedly, as my fingers shook trying to type the messages to Mama and Andjela. He took his cute white shoes off and slipped himself under the covers. He looked so handsome lying there, I couldn't believe he ever thought he was ugly.

I turned the lights off, took off my heels, pulled back the covers, and nervously laid down on the bed next to him. My eyes adjusted to the lack of light, with a small amount slipping into the room from the streetlights behind the blind which allowed me to see I was looking into Luka's eyes. Even in the dark, Luka's eyes were extraordinary.

'Thank you for coming all this way to see me. You're the best present I've ever received,' I said, gently touching his cheek. I could see him close his eyes at my touch, and wrap his left arm around me, pulling me closer.

'Thank you for coming here to see me. To come and talk through everything. I thought when I left your party, I wasn't going to see you again,' Luka whispered, opening his eyes. He kissed me deeply on the lips. Each time he kissed me it was the best kiss of my life. The butterflies continued their dance, but every other part of my body was at peace. Even my heart had slowed to a relaxed level. The elephant that spent so much time sitting on my chest had finally disappeared into the African savanna.

'Let's get some sleep. You must be completely exhausted,' I whispered in a tone a couple of octaves higher than my usual voice. He nodded and I turned around to lay on my side, my back against his chest. Luka slid his right arm under my neck and wrapped his left arm over my body, intertwining his fingers with mine. I pushed back against his warm body and could feel his slow, gentle heartbeat against my back.

'So, does this mean you're my girlfriend again?' Luka asked, planting a tender kiss on my neck. It sent a shiver down my spine, causing me to push back into his body involuntarily. He squeezed his arms around me a little tighter.

'If you want me to be,' I whispered.

'Of course. I don't want to be with anyone else,' Luka said in my ear, and I could feel his hot breath against my ear and neck.

'Did you really mean it? All the things in your song?' I asked, unsure whether it was how he really felt or there was some creative license.

'Every word of it,' Luka said, then kissed me gently on the back of my neck.

'I love you, Luka.'

'I love you too, Nina. I feel like I'm home.'

'Me too. We are home,' I said gently, knowing that I was truly where I belonged. In no time, we both drifted off to sleep in each other's arms, deeply in love.

I slept deeply and dreamlessly that night. I was living my dream. Wrapped in Luka's warm embrace was all I had wanted for the previous nine months, even though I tried to run from it. Finally, being with him, I knew it was all I wanted long before I even met him.

Stirring as the morning sun broke through the blinds of the hotel room, I turned myself around and saw that Luka was already awake. 'Good morning, handsome,' I said, sleepily kissing him. 'Have you been awake for long?

'A little bit,' Luka said, running his hands gently up and down my back. His easy, soft touch sent a tingle all the way to my toes. I didn't know the touch of another person could do that to me. I wish he woke up at the same time as me because I had missed out on the cute morning voice. I had been cheated.

'Why didn't you wake me up?' I asked, kissing him again. I needed to somehow squeeze nine months of kisses into the time he was with me. I wasn't sure if it was possible, but I was going to give it my best effort.

'You were so peaceful sleeping I couldn't disturb you. Plus, I was happy just lying here holding you,' Luka said, and he moved my hair from my eyes placing it behind my ear. Without even trying he did things that put my stomach into a twist. I put my head into his chest like a puppy curling up in its bed.

'How long are you going to be here?' I asked, hating myself for already thinking about Luka having to leave.

'Two weeks, then I have to go back because I'm missing uni being here,' he said, kissing my fivehead. I could feel the sadness in his voice as he told me. I didn't know how I was going to handle watching him leave. Closing my eyes tightly, I pushed the idea of him leaving from my mind. 'Let's not worry about that. Let's just enjoy the time we have together.'

I nodded into Luka's chest and could see that I had got makeup all over his nice blue shirt.

'So, I was thinking, and I'm not sure if you'll be able to, but I'll ask anyway.' Luka sounded nervous, as if he had been working up the courage to ask a particular question the entire time he was waiting on me to wake up. I looked up into those perfect blue eyes, my interest piqued to hear what idea had him so nervous. 'I know I told you me visiting was your birthday present, but what if it wasn't?'

'What do you mean?' I asked, a curious expression on my face.

'What do you think about taking a trip somewhere? We could leave this afternoon. I can pick a city if you trust me,' Luka said, his voice slightly shaking.

'Really? I love that idea!' I exclaimed, sitting bolt upright as if an electric current just got shot through the bed. 'I don't start uni for a few weeks, so I have some time. We just have to go and talk to my parents about it first.'

'Of course. Want to go now?' I nodded my head with a big smile on my face. I threw the covers off and bounced out of bed, barely able to stop myself from dancing on the spot.

'I think you better change your shirt, or else my parents will know that I spent the night with you and not at Andjela's.' Luka took off his shirt and threw a navy hoodie on over a white t-shirt. *'Seeing as I'm his girlfriend again, that makes it our hoodie and it will be staying here when he leaves,'* I thought, seeing a little bit of his stomach as he struggled to get it over his head. He went into the bathroom and within a couple of minutes we were on our way.

The sun was already high in the sky as we walked through the front door of the hotel. Luka was walking with a small gap between us, his hands in his pockets, and that was just unacceptable. I glimpsed down and saw Luka take his hands from his pockets, our hands now separated by barely a couple of centimetres. I could almost feel a breeze as his hand moved past mine. We turned right, in the direction of the bus station, and I grazed my hand against his to see if he would create more space between us or take hold of my hand. Our hands brushed against each other again, sending a tingle to my stomach as I craved to hold him. As his hand moved past mine again, I took it, sliding my fingers between his. Luka looked over at me and smiled. I couldn't help but return his smile before shyly looking at the ground, hoping I wasn't stepping on any cracks in the pavement.

As we walked in comfortable silence towards my house, basking in the summer sun, it was slowly sinking in that we were finally together as a couple. If I knew what was at the end of those nine months, I would have waited for him, because nothing could ever compare to being in his presence. I knew I sounded like a love crazed teen, but that's just because I was a love crazed teen. I knew I had found my soulmate. Luka was my man, and I didn't want to hold the hand of another man again. He looked over at me and smiled. Luka looked like he couldn't believe that he was walking down the street in Požega hand-in-hand with me.

I wanted as much physical contact without being one of those gross public display of affection couples. I could feel his palm get sweaty, so I squeezed his hand reassuringly, and placed my left hand on his arm to tell him he had nothing to worry about. He was safe with me.

We walked along the underpass below the train tracks, greeting all my neighbours who were enjoying the sun on their front porches as we walked past. Finally, we turned into my driveway and closed in on the front door of my house. My heart was beating quickly from the excitement of introducing Luka to my family. Once he met my family it would make our relationship one-hundred percent official. When you're in a relationship, you're not just with that one person, you are integrating them into your life, integrating them into your family.

I looked over at Luka and saw a nervous expression on his face. Beads of sweat appeared on his forehead, his palm feeling clammy. *This must be a lot for him to handle in twenty-four hours,'* I thought, struggling to fathom how strong he was for travelling so far to surprise me. *'I don't think I could do it.'*

Just before we got to the door we stopped, and I turned to Luka. 'Are you okay?'

'Yeah, I'm alright. Just never met the parents before,' Luka said, and I could see his Adam's apple bulge as he swallowed.

'Just be you, they're going to love you. As long as you take your shoes off, you'll be fine. There's no coming back from wearing shoes in the house.' Luka smiled and I could see his shoulders relax.

I watched Luka try and untie his shoes by standing on one leg, but he lost his balance and almost fell. His hands were shaking so he crouched down and slowly untied his shoes, holding them together neatly as I ripped off my heels feeling the kind of relief I felt when I took my bra off after a long day. Opening the door, I walked through first, thinking it was best for me to lead the way into the house. I watched Luka hold onto his shoes, standing just inside the front door uncomfortably, unsure what he should do next, as I placed my heels neatly next to the door. 'Put them down there,' I said, pointing at the pile of shoes next to the door. He gently placed them together against the wall.

'Mama? Tata?' I yelled and walked into the living room.

'You don't need to yell. We're right here. Who's this?' Tata asked, dragging his eyes from the television to look at Luka and me entering the room.

'That's Luka, you literally saw him on stage last night. Try and keep up. How are you? Welcome to our home. Please, take a seat,' Mama said, walking to Luka and kissing him three times on the cheek, alternating with each kiss.

'Nice to meet you,' Luka said in a quivering voice, shaking Tata's hand and taking a seat on the couch.

'So, you came all the way from Australia for our girl. You can't get a girl in Australia? You must be crazy to come all this way,' Tata said. Luka looked at me, unsure how to respond to my father's baiting.

'Or maybe he just really loves me, Tata,' I said, jumping in to help Luka and taking a seat next to him. I touched his hand and could feel it was cold. *He must be so nervous,* I thought. Luka's hand clenched mine as soon as I touched his, like a drowning man grabbing hold of a life preserver ring.

'A distinction without a difference,' Tata said, chuckling to himself. He raised his right hand for a high five with Mama, who glared daggers at him.

'Stop it, Milan,' Mama said sternly. 'Would you like a drink, Luka?'

'Water, please.' A moment later Mama handed him a glass of water. 'Thank you,' Luka said, and looked grateful for something to do with his free hand.

'So, what do you think of our town?' Mama asked, taking a chair from the table and turning it to face him, then sitting down.

'I love it. It's a bit surreal actually. Not just to meet Nina and all of you, but because my mum's side of the family came from this town, so it's special to see where they came from. I have a couple of weeks until I have to go back to Australia, so I'm hoping to explore a bit more of the area,' Luka said, and I could feel his hand relax and warm up as he spoke. The initial shock of meeting my family was wearing off.

'Oh, a Serbian man. Why didn't you tell me, Nina? You must have a rakija with me,' Tata said, jumping up to get the glasses.

'Tata, it's not even midday. Luka you don't have to if you don't want to.'

'What's your point? And look at the guy. He looks like he could use a rakija,' Tata said, pouring a glass and handing it to Luka. Luka placed his water down and took the glass from Tata. He poured another and offered it to Mama and me, but we both rejected it. 'Živeli,' Tata said, clinking his glass with Luka's and taking a sip, Luka following suit.

'What do you think?' I asked, looking at Luka, trying to see how well he handled homemade rakija.

'It's burning my insides. I'm just glad I didn't cough it up,' Luka whispered to me as he took another sip.

'So, what's the story here?' Mama enquired, gesturing to us holding hands, sitting against one another.

'He's my boyfriend,' I said, and could feel Luka squeeze my hand in approval.

'You've raised an incredible woman, and I can't imagine being with anyone else. I wanted to make sure that I came and met you in person, so you know the man your daughter is with,' Luka said, and I saw his right leg was bouncing. I placed my free right hand on his thigh to reassure him. His leg rested and I heard a deep exhale from him as he finished the rakija. I began to stroke my thumb along his hand, and I could see him smile at the floor.

'I appreciate that. Some people would avoid our house completely, so if you're man enough to come here and shake my hand, then I know you must be okay,' Tata said, and he walked over to Mama, standing by her side and placing an arm around her shoulder.

'I have heard a lot of great things about you so I'm very excited you've come. Would you like to have dinner with us tonight? I'm making burek. I know it won't be as good as your mother's, but I would love for you to try it,' Mama said, beaming at Luka and me.

'Well, I would love to, but there is something that we wanted to talk to you about,' Luka said, before looking at me, as if to check if it was the right time. I nodded to urge him on. 'I want to take Nina on a trip for a few days, so I've come to ask your permission if I can. I understand if you aren't comfortable with that, but you should know that I love your daughter very much, and would never let anything happen to her,' Luka said with a kind authority.

I loved how he was talking to my parents. He was becoming more comfortable and taking control of the situation. He wasn't scared anymore. I looked at him and unconsciously bit my lower lip. *I hope no one saw that,'* I thought.

Mama and Tata exchanged a silent look. I knew they were going to say no, but I was proud of Luka for asking them anyway. 'Teodora and I need to talk about it. We need to know where you're going and how long you will be gone,' Tata said, staring at Luka. Luka didn't break eye contact with him until Tata looked at Mama. 'So, where are you going?'

'I want it to be a surprise for Nina, so I'm going to whisper it to you,' Luka said, standing and walking across to Mama and Tata. He leaned down and whispered while I tried with all my might to overhear what he said, before sitting next to me again and taking my hand.

Mama and Tata exchanged looks and Tata could barely stifle a laugh. 'You're really going all out, aren't you?' Tata asked rhetorically.

Jovan and Milica walked into the room. 'Hi,' Luka said, taking his hand from mine, standing and shaking hands with them. All the nerves from before had gone. He looked at home.

'Okay, so all of you need to get out of here for a bit so we can talk about this,' Tata said, standing up and herding us from the living room.

'Do you know how to play football?' Jovan asked, grabbing Luka's hand, and leading him outside. I could feel my heart melt seeing Jovan and Luka hold hands talking to each other.

'I do. I hear you're a great player. You're going to have to play with me and show me how it's done,' Luka said, slipping on his shoes and running after Jovan out the door. Milica and I walked behind them outside.

'Where did you learn English,' I asked Jovan in shock.

'Video games,' Jovan said, smiling.

Jovan set up his toy trucks on the ground at each end of the yard to be the goals. 'I start,' Jovan said, trying to catch Luka unawares, dribbling the ball towards my boyfriend, who was looking at me. Milica and I took a seat at the table just outside the door and watched them play.

My heart swelled watching Luka play with Jovan. Jovan was shouting out the score after each one of his goals to make sure we all knew that he was winning. It was incredibly sweet of Luka to let Jovan win, and he looked like he was genuinely having fun. He wasn't doing it for me; he was doing it because he wanted to be part of my family. Luka was doing it for Jovan. Marko didn't even want to come to my house, and here was Luka playing football with my brother. With every passing minute watching them play, I fell deeper in love with him. *'How am I going to feel in another year, five years, twenty years' time if I feel like this now?'* I wondered.

'They are so cute together,' Milica said. I nodded and pulled out my phone and started to film them play. We both broke out in hysterics as Luka picked up Jovan, took the ball from him, then dribbled the ball while carrying Jovan and kicked a goal.

'No foul! No foul!' Luka shouted, as he continued to carry Jovan around the yard. Finally, Luka put a laughing Jovan down and proceeded to take off his hoodie and spin it around his head in celebration. Jovan tackled Luka around the legs to the ground, both laughing wildly.

'I'm so lucky,' I said to Milica, as they finally got up, covered in dirt, panting, and laughing.

'Jovan! What did you do?' Mama asked angrily, walking outside and looking at the state of Jovan and Luka. Tata followed closely behind her and stood surveying the scene. I pressed stop on the video. Luka and Jovan playing together was the kind of video I would need to watch every night before I went to sleep after Luka left.

'He's okay. We're just playing,' Luka said, they stood up and Luka put a hand on Jovan's shoulder. Jovan looked up at him adoringly, as if he just found his long-lost older brother.

I couldn't help but pull out my phone again and take a photo of them together. *'I think I've got my new wallpaper,'* I thought.

'Luka, give me your shirt and pants. I'll wash them for you,' Mama said, holding her hand out.

'No, it's okay, but thank you,' Luka laughed, dusting himself off. It would have been a funny sight to have Luka in Tata's tracksuit while Mama washed his clothes.

'So, we spoke about it,' Tata said, wrapping an arm around Mama's shoulder.

My heart started to beat very quickly. *If the answer's going to be no, then they wouldn't have taken so long to talk about it, would they?'* I thought, hopefully. The idea of travelling somewhere with Luka was a dream to me. After all that time apart, to be able to spend all day and night with him was what I wanted more than anything.

'Nina, you're eighteen and about to go to university. Your mother and I are comfortable with you two going on a trip together. If you call every day and give us the address of the hotel where you're staying. Are we understood?' Tata asked in Serbian, puffing his chest out and taking it in turns to stare at Luka and me.

'Really? Thank you,' I squealed, jumping up with excitement barely believing what I just heard. I ran up to my parents wrapping my arms around them. Luka would have understood the answer from my reaction.

'We have always trusted you, Nina, and there's something about you, Luka, so I know you won't let any harm come to our daughter. Those aren't just words to you. They're a promise and we believe you,' Tata said, returning to English. I turned to look at Luka wanting to kiss him, but I needed to control myself until we left on our trip.

'You need to look out for him as well,' Mama said to me.

'Thank you so much, sir. Your trust means a lot to me. I won't let you down,' Luka said. Luka then walked to my father and shook his hand, before hugging my mother. He stood next to me taking my hand, and unable to wait until the trip, he planted his lips softly on my cheek. I felt my adductors spasm, knocking my knees together.

'We both need to get ready. I'm going to go and pack a bag for our trip, and I'll let you pack. It's midday now. Can you meet me at the bus station at four?' Luka asked softly, standing in front of me, holding both of my hands like we were at the altar.

I nodded and kissed him on the lips. If I was going to have to wait four hours to see him, then I needed to make sure I got one kiss in before he left to get ready, even if my parents had to see. After all, they did see one forced upon me last night, at least on this occasion, I consented to the kiss.

'Oooo, gross,' Jovan yelled, covering his eyes.

'Thank you for the dinner invitation. If you'll have me, I'll be here the first night we get back,' Luka said, smiling at Mama.

'You are always welcome here,' Mama said, beaming at him.

My family are going to be almost as upset as me seeing him leave,' I thought. After a kiss on the cheek and a hug with his hands stroking my back, Luka waved to all of us and walked back towards his hotel.

'You better get packing,' Mama suggested. I waited for Luka to be out of sight, then ran inside to get ready for our mystery trip.

'It's ridiculous how quickly three hours disappears,' I thought, as I continued to rush around my room. Spending thirty minutes on the phone debriefing Andjela on everything that had happened since she left me at Luka's hotel door definitely put a hole in my packing time.

Luka had just sent me a photo of his bag packed ready for our trip. I had been rifling through my closet trying to pick several perfect cute outfits. It was almost impossible to pack when I had no information about where we were going. *I know it will be close, so the climate has to be similar to Serbia, but what will we be doing on our trip?'* I wondered, trying to decide between my floral sundress and my plain green one, before folding them and neatly placing them both inside my suitcase.

I made sure there were outfits for us to go on a hike, for a day in a romantic European city, and dinner date. Finding my white jeans and low-cut black shirt, the same as I wore when we first met, I folded them into my suitcase. Dresses, jeans, tights, and different kinds of shoes. If I wasn't going with Luka, then being given such little preparation time with a mystery location would be a kind of cruel punishment.

Dropping my makeup bag into my suitcase, I looked at the time and saw that I had one hour before I had to meet Luka. An hour to have a shower, get dressed and get to the bus station. Normally a shower was a twenty-minute experience of singing and mentally placing myself in fake scenarios, but that shower was a race against time. The water normally took a minute to warm up, but I didn't have the luxury to wait. I jumped into the freezing cold shower with a steely resolve to grin and bear it to make sure I wasn't late. By the time the temperature hit its perfect, scolding my skin point, I had to get out.

I put on my fancy, matching underwear and bra for once. I was unsure whether Luka would be seeing them, but I wanted to be prepared if the scenario arose. *Damn, I'm not going to have time to do my makeup. Well, if this is going to work, he has to get used to seeing me without it on,'* I thought, trying to comfort myself.

'You're more beautiful without makeup than with it,' I heard Luka's voice lying to me in my mind. I was so lucky to have such a supportive man that always hyped me up. 'Stop it, Nina,' I scalded myself aloud, shaking my head to drive that cute man's sweet words from my mind. I had wasted enough time daydreaming about our trip, especially as the real thing was waiting for me. I didn't have to daydream anymore.

'Everything okay in there? You're talking to yourself,' Mama said through the door.

'Yeah. I'm just getting dressed,' I shouted in reply, trying to squeeze myself into my tight blue jeans that made my butt look good. I picked up the white long-sleeved shirt on my bed and put it on, thankful that Mama ironed everything before folding it and delivering it to my room. Glancing at the time to make sure minutes hadn't disappeared into the abyss, I saw that I had enough time, but it was becoming too close for comfort. I checked my bag, hoping I had remembered everything.

'Can I come in?' Mama asked.

'Yes,' I said in a stressed voice.

'How's it going in here?' Mama asked, watching me rifle through my packed bag.

'Umm, yeah okay, I guess,' I replied, getting down on all fours looking for my black boots that I thought I had left underneath my bed. 'Just looking for my black boots.'

'They're at the front door. Nina. Stop for a second. Just breathe,' Mama said, grabbing a hold of my shoulders to get my attention.

'Mama, I don't have time to stop for a second. I don't have long, and I'm just stressed. I need to leave soon. My gosh,' I said panicked, putting my hand on my fivehead, knowing I would feel better once I got to the bus station.

'You just need to make sure you have one thing, and you can buy anything else you need when you get there.'

'What's that?' I asked, my eyes still darting around the room trying to see if I had forgotten anything.

'Your passport.'

'Oh no. I don't know where it is. I don't even know where I put it last. Luka won't have Wi-Fi at the bus station so I can't even text him to tell him if I'm late. No, it's all falling apart. He's going to be so mad at me. What if I'm late and he gets on the bus without me?' I ranted in hysterics, on the verge of panic tears that I could feel burning my eyes as I tried to hold them in. *Can eighteen-year-olds have heart attacks? If they can, then I'm about to have one,'* I thought.

'Nina, stop it. Here,' Mama said, pulling my passport out of her back pocket and handing it to me as the stress tears began to fall from my eyes in relief.

'Thank you,' I said, throwing myself into my mother's arms. 'At least when I go to Australia, I'll have more than an afternoon to get ready.' I wiped the stress tears from my eyes, feeling relieved that I didn't have time to put makeup on.

'Take this too,' Mama said, putting something in my hand and closing my fingers around it. I looked down to see she had put three hundred euro in my hand.

'No, Mama. This is way too much,' I said, feeling fresh tears come back, and I offered my hand with the money back to her. *'I just need to get to the bus station, I'm way too emotional now,'* I thought, a cheek splitting smile breaking across my face in gratitude of my mama.

'Take it. I hope this trip is everything you've been dreaming of, and he is the man you really want. You're going to make each other very happy,' Mama said, as her eyes began to glisten with tears of joy seeing through the stress of preparing, to the excitement and joy I felt for my trip with Luka. I tucked the money into my wallet.

'I love you,' I said, hugging Mama. I was lucky to have my family, Andjela and Luka in my life. I had everything I would ever need with them.

'Come on. Close your bag and let's go,' Mama said, breaking the hug and walking through my bedroom door. I put my passport into my backpack along with my phone charger, wallet and lip balm. I took my suitcase and walked towards my bedroom door. 'Forget something?' Mama asked, with raised eyebrows, looking over my shoulder. My phone was sitting on the bed. 'I hope Luka is good under pressure because it definitely isn't a state you thrive in.' Mama shook her head and walked to the front door. I would have loved to say she was wrong, but it was hard to make any counter argument to that after how I had handled the last few minutes.

Sliding my phone into my back pocket, I followed Mama to the front door. Slipping on my black boots, I collected my jacket from the hook next to the front door before opening it. Jovan came running from the living room and launched himself to hug me. My eyes glanced up at the clock just behind him and saw that I had twenty minutes to get to the station. It was only a five-minute drive, so I had plenty of time. 'Thanks. I needed that, Jovan,' I said, kissing him on the cheek. Milica appeared in the doorway to the living room, as did Tata.

'Do you think he'll play football with me when you get back?' Jovan asked, shyly.

'He already told me that he needs a rematch against you after you beat him earlier today,' I said, giving him an extra squeeze. Jovan kissed me on the cheek, and having got the answer he wanted, ran back into the living room to continue watching a re-run of a SpongeBob episode he would have watched that morning.

'Bring me back something,' Milica said, hugging me.

'I'll find the cheapest keyring I can. Nothing but the best,' I said, laughing and kissing her goodbye on the cheek.

'Have a great time. You picked a good man,' Tata said, giving me his stress relieving bear hug and kissing me on my fivehead.

'He's the best. How long will you be here, Tata?' I asked. I hadn't even thought about how long Tata would be home for, so I was worried he would have to go back to work before I got home.

'Don't worry. I'll be here when you get back. Now go, he'll be wondering where you are,' Tata said, pushing me towards the door. He picked up my bag and dragged it to the car, heaving it into the boot. 'Geez, are you taking rocks with you?' I jumped into the front passenger seat where Mama was waiting in the driver's seat with the car already running and ready in reverse.

'Love you!' Tata shouted and waved goodbye, as Mama hit the accelerator and reversed down the long driveway.

'Buses don't normally come early, do they?' I asked, looking at my phone to make sure I still had lots of time. We drove under the train track underpass and fortunately the road was clear, so we didn't have to stop at the stop sign. Mama took a left onto Železnička and put her foot down hard. Another left and we were racing down Nikole Pašića, with the bus station just a little further up on the left.

'Is that Luka there?' Mama asked, pointing at a man sitting on the edge of the bus bench. He looked adorable in his blue jeans, white t-shirt, and black jacket.

'Yes,' I yelled in excitement, pointing at him. He was craning his neck, searching, looking in every direction for me.

'Hang on, we're almost there,' Mama said. I was bouncing in my seat in anticipation, taking off my seat belt, my hand on the doorhandle, waiting for the car to stop so I could jump out. The car came to a halt just by the entrance gate. I jumped from the car and easily pulled my bag from the boot with the adrenaline of seeing Luka again coursing through my body.

'Bye, Mama. I love you,' I said, kissing her on the cheek through her lowered window.

'Nina, take this. It's burek for you and Luka,' Mama said, handing a container to me through the window. I rolled my eyes smiling, before I turned to walk through the gates. 'Love you!' Mama yelled after me, as I took long strides with my backpack over my shoulder, pulling my suitcase with one hand, and carrying the burek in the other towards my waiting soulmate.

CHAPTER TWENTY
The Bus Station

'Why is she here? Is she here to apologise, or yell at me for coming to her party without her inviting me and ruining it,' I wondered, as I tried to read her next action from the look on her face. I was trying not to let my emotion show, but that ship might have sailed by me yelling through the door for Andjela to go away, and while I had wiped away my tears, Nina would still be able to see the evidence of my heartbreak in my eyes. *'She is so beautiful. Stop, Luka! You're supposed to be angry!'* I scalded myself, not being able to shake the thought that she looked majestic.

I looked at Nina's face and could see that she was upset, but I wasn't sure if it was because of me or the situation. Nina asked if she could come in, and even though she just tore my heart out and stomped on it with her heels, I wanted to at least have one in person conversation with her.

Nina gracefully walked over the threshold, and I made sure to take the guitar from her. Taking the guitar case, I could feel that the handle was sweaty. After what just happened, I was sure it wouldn't have been easy for her to come to my room, so I had to give her credit for talking to me face to face instead of settling for texting me. Or even worse, never contacting me again. Either of those things would have broken my already shattered heart.

I didn't know what to expect. I was hurt and humiliated. While I was on stage singing there was something in the way Nina looked at me that said she shared my feelings, but after seeing her kiss Marko, I knew I must have been seeing what I wanted to see. I had put myself on the line in a way I never had before. The only thing that would have helped me recover was to have a completely open conversation, otherwise I would be asking myself what if, for the rest of my life.

Nina looked skittish, nervous, as if she didn't know where to look or what to do with her hands. She put her hands together and then by her side, as if it was her first day with them. Her eyes found mine and then looked away quickly, barely holding each other's gaze for longer than a second. I thought I was going to be the uncomfortable one. Well, the more uncomfortable one.

I offered Nina a seat next to me and she took it, sitting nervously on the edge of the bed with her eyes scanning the room as if she was looking for something. Having her next to me had my nerves jangling more than they were before I walked onto the stage in the café, and my leg couldn't help but start to bounce. Nina looked down at my leg, and I could see her extend a hand slightly towards me, as if to calm me, but thought better of the notion. We sat in silence for a moment, neither of us sure how to begin the conversation. It had been a disaster of the highest order, but at least James would have his entertaining story.

I needed to break the deadlock. I needed to tell her everything that I had been holding in because I couldn't let the opportunity go. It would never come again. It was my chance to tell her the words bouncing around my heart. I felt so nervous that my right leg continued to bounce, trying to rid my body of the nervous energy, but it wasn't working.

Before I could mount the courage to speak, Nina's voice squeaked saying how she thought my eyes were beautiful. Hearing that and seeing her smile relaxed me. I sheepishly told her how much I loved her smile, and the awkward silence returned.

She began to twirl her hair, which I knew she did when she was nervous, but excited. I was happy to see that she was excited to be next to me.

I had waited to be in her presence for nine months; I had to begin the conversation or else we would sit in silence until she decided it was a waste of her time and left. *'Come on, Luka, you can do it. Just something simple to get the ball rolling. It's Nina, you know her,'* I urged myself.

I asked Nina if she knew I was coming, and things began to flow. It felt like a first date, an excited energy but an undertone of nerves knowing things could go horribly wrong. Neither of us seemed sure what to say, but at least we were talking. It was hard for my brain to process that it was the same woman who I fell in love with over a computer sitting next to me. I couldn't believe she was within touching distance. I looked down at her hand and so desperately craved to grasp it. *'I can't, not yet anyway,'* I thought, trying to maintain my composure.

As the conversation continued, I became more and more comfortable. The nerves and anxiety of being face to face with Nina dropped with every passing moment I was in her company.

When you fall in love with someone over a computer screen you can't be sure if you're in love with the person or with the idea of the person. You can't know that, until you're with them and feel their energy wrapped with your own. That if the picture they displayed of themselves is their true self, a caricature, or a fictional character. It's hard to put into words how you can know which is which, you just have to feel it, and I knew by looking into Nina's eyes as she spoke, as she poured her heart out to me, and listened to me, that every feeling we shared was real. We didn't fall in love with the idea of one another, we fell in love with one another.

I was completely entranced by Nina. Every word, every movement of her head, of her body, even the way she was sitting was drawing me into her. All the hurt that I was feeling was washed away hearing her apologise for the situation. I could hear in her voice that she didn't want that to happen. By the time Marko arrived, she didn't want him there. She didn't want to be with him anymore.

My heart jumped into my throat, the butterflies in my stomach were roaring back to life. I couldn't believe what I had heard. *They broke up. Nina is single. Do I actually have a chance here?'* I thought, hope beginning to swell.

I tried to swallow my smile, not to let her see I was happy she broke up with her boyfriend. I wanted to tell her that I loved her. That she should be with me, but I needed to hold my run. I needed to keep listening to her and wait for the perfect moment to tell her everything that I was feeling. Most of my life I had been the quiet one, not saying what I really felt, but Nina had changed that for me. She had given me the confidence to believe that I should be heard, and what I had to say was important. *'She may regret giving me that confidence when I tell her that she's the only one I want to be with,'* I thought, covering my mouth to hold in a chuckle.

I wanted to touch her. Just feel her skin for the first time. Her hands were next to mine, pressed into the mattress. Looking at them, I wondered if Nina would pull her hand away if I moved mine towards hers. Even though she had poured her feelings out to me, she might not be ready for physical contact. It was a gamble, but one I was willing to take.

My nerves returned with a vengeance. Looking deep into her brown eyes with flecks of green, I moved my hand towards hers, hoping that my aim was on target, and I didn't miss her hand. I didn't miss. Her hand muscles contracted slightly upon my first touch but then relaxed. Her skin was soft and warm. An electricity shot through my body with senses being awakened I didn't know existed. They say when you know, you know.

Looking into Nina's eyes while she spoke of her feelings for me and we touched each other for the first time; there was no doubt. I knew.

I couldn't hold it in any longer, I had to tell Nina how I truly felt. My heart was about to beat out of my chest from the excitement of telling her the three most powerful words in the English language for the first time. The thing that I wanted to tell Nina for months. I just hoped that she would tell me the same. Nina was the first thing on my mind in the morning, and the last thing on my mind at night. That I could barely go an hour without thinking about her in some way. That I wanted her to be my wife, and me, be her husband. That I wanted to have a family with her one day.

Nina looked in shock, in complete disbelief at hearing me tell her that I loved her for the first time. Shock mixed with relief on Nina's face. She broke into a huge smile and told me she loved me too.

'Did she really say those words? Did Nina really say she loves me too?' I wondered in disbelief. Those beautiful words coming from that beautiful woman. The words I so desperately wanted her to utter. Nina truly loved me. We could finally be together.

My hand on hers wasn't enough. I needed my fingers wrapped in between hers. For us to be connected. I took my hand off the top of Nina's and saw her look down at it. There was a momentary look of disappointment on her face that I wasn't touching her hand anymore. I slid my hand underneath, and then my fingers in between hers. She had long, elegant fingers, like a piano player. Nina accepted my hand and gripped it back. The look on her face changed from disappointment to one of comfort. I was craving intimacy with Nina. I needed to be closer to her.

The thought of every other human apart from Nina had been pushed from my mind. I was shocked when she reminded me of Tayla, and I felt bad that I had forgotten about replying to her invitation. I had no idea that she even knew about Tayla, that she cared enough at that time to look through my tagged photos. Even though I knew I shouldn't have, it felt good to know that when we had broken up, she felt strongly enough for me to not want me to be with someone else. Nina never truly let go of me. She needed to know that I didn't want to date anyone but her though. I understood why she thought I was in a relationship after seeing that photo, but there was no one else. There was only Nina.

Just when I thought we were through the worst of it, battling through the chaos of the night, and thinking we were back together, Nina dropped a bombshell on me. Nina had lied to me about her age. I knew I picked the hardest kind of relationship, but why did it have to be so hard? I couldn't believe I didn't see the eighteens around the café. Stupid isn't a word strong enough to describe how I felt.

I pulled my hand away like it was on a hot stove. She was apologising profusely, and I understood why she did it, but that didn't mean I was happy. I honestly wasn't sure if I would have kept talking to her if I knew she was seventeen. Looking into her eyes, I could see the tears welling up. She was so upset and scared. Scared that she might lose me. She needed to know that she wouldn't lose me, but lying to me wasn't okay, and it couldn't happen again. Neither of us should stand for lying. If we weren't open and honest, then our relationship didn't have a chance. I wanted a clean slate and a promise to each other that we wouldn't hide anything else.

Nina asked if I wanted her to leave. Never. Never in a million years would I want her to leave. I was already scared of the mess I was going to be when I had to drag myself from Požega and head back to Australia. I needed to make sure I made the most of every second I spent with her. Often you don't fully appreciate how special a moment is while you're in it, but I knew how special every second in her presence was.

I didn't get the chance to dance with her at her birthday, so being together in my hotel room was the perfect time. I stood up and walked to my phone, then pressed play on my favourite Ed Sheeran song. Nervously I walked back towards her and extended my hand to ask if she would dance with me. Seeing the look on Nina's face go from sadness at me walking to my phone, to joyous when I extended my hand, sent a feeling of euphoria through my body. *'I put that smile on her face, and that twinkle in her eye. I love seeing sunshine smile,'* I thought, looking into her smiling eyes.

When people meet in person, they take for granted seeing the person they love move. The way they walk. The way they use their hands when they're nervous. The way their body listens to what you're saying. Why wouldn't they? They've seen it ever since they met. When you meet someone online you don't get to see how their body moves. Those little things are exciting and just watching Nina take my hand and move with me to the tender melody had my heart racing with excitement, but also, I felt at ease. I pulled her body into mine and could feel her warmth against me. Her hand shook slightly, but I could tell she was more comfortable with me as each moment passed. Our bodies were pressed against one another, and I could feel our hearts beat together in perfect harmony. My body told me what my mind knew, I had found my soulmate.

Staring into Nina's eyes I knew I had never considered another woman beautiful before. I couldn't believe that for the entire time she had been in my room I hadn't told her. She looked at me with concern, wondering why I was silently staring into her eyes while our bodies swayed perfectly together. I told her what was on my mind, I didn't think, I knew that she was the definition of beautiful. Her face relaxed and lit up. *'I can't wait to tell her how beautiful she is every day for the rest of our lives,'* I thought. I was aware how corny my thoughts were, but I didn't care, I was in love.

From the moment I saw her on our first video chat I wanted to kiss Nina. Even when I opened the hotel room door and I was heartbroken, I wanted to kiss her. Through our entire conversation I wanted to kiss her, even when I was hurting at being lied to. If it wasn't on the forefront of my mind, then it was in the back of my mind. *This is the moment,'* I thought, our faces were barely separated. I saw her glance at my mouth, gently biting her lower lip, as if she was asking me to kiss her. No, telling me to kiss her. Nina moved her head slightly towards mine. It was time. *I'm going for it,'* I thought, tired of waiting. I could feel her heart rate increase to the same speed as mine as I moved towards her lips. She knew what was about to happen.

Without even thinking about how I would kiss her, I laid my lips on hers. Fireworks exploded through my entire body, from my lips to my soul. My hands were on her waist, and her arms were wrapped around my neck. Nina's soft and tender lips worked in perfect time with mine. There is kissing, and then there is kissing the one you love. There is no comparison between the two. When you kiss the one you love, your entire being comes alive, causing the lion in your soul to roar. My eyes were closed but my mind's eyes showed me the picture I was missing. Nina and I kissing in the middle of the hotel room to what I'll always remember as our song.

Reluctantly I broke the kiss. It was getting late, and her family would be worrying, but I didn't want her to leave. I knew she wouldn't be able to stay but I had to ask. The worst she could say was no, but I was going to try because I was tired of missing her. Tired of wasting time because that's what time was when I was away from her. The Nina pillow would no longer do; I needed the real thing. I asked the question and waited with bated breath for her answer.

'*Yes!*' I screamed in my head. Nina said she would stay with me, and I couldn't have been happier. I was going to have to see a cardiologist because all the acrobatics my heart was performing couldn't be healthy.

I suddenly felt exhausted. It had been a draining day, or two, or three. I wasn't even sure anymore. It felt like an eternity, and also just a moment ago that I left my family's house. I wanted to lay with Nina in my arms and sleep. I took off my shoes and laid on my side of the bed, unsure whether Nina had a side. Nina took off her heels and turned off the lights, laying down next to me. '*I guess I picked the right side,*' I thought, smiling gently at the figure of Nina laid next to me.

The emotion of the day and the adrenaline of being in Nina's presence for the first time had carried me all the way to lying next to her, but the second my head hit the pillow, I could barely keep my eyes open. The weight of the day was in them, and it felt like they weighed five tonnes. I was just grateful that I was there with her. Nina turned her back to me and pushed her body into mine. I wrapped my arms around her and felt completely safe. She was protecting me from my worst enemy. Myself.

Before we fell asleep, I had to ask one final question. I needed to find out if we were back together. I couldn't have any doubt. She was lying peacefully in my arms, but I needed to hear the words. Asking Nina the question, I kissed her tenderly on the neck and squeezed her a little tighter, as if to dispel any doubt she may have had. Getting the only thing I wanted since the day she broke up with me; to have Nina be my girlfriend again, I felt a big exhale of anxiety leave my body. My exhaustion from the long, emotional day caused me to forget it was there. It had been there since we broke up. My anxiety was finally gone.

I told Nina I loved her before closing my eyes. I listened to her breathing and tried to match my rhythm with hers. In no time at all, I drifted off to sleep. Comfortable, relaxed, and happy. I was exactly where I was supposed to be. I was home.

Waking to the sounds of chirping birds, I opened my eyes and saw the sun poking through the blinds. I rubbed my aching cheeks. I must have been smiling all through the night. My right arm was numb, so I pumped my fist to try and get some circulation going without rousing Nina awake, as it was pinned beneath her peaceful body. I wasn't sure what the time was, but I didn't care. I was completely content lying with Nina in my arms.

As I was lying there, while Nina peacefully slept, an idea occurred to me. I wanted to make the most of my time with Nina, and one great way to do that was to take a trip together. Create memories that would last a lifetime. Special memories we could talk about when we're old and grey, and I knew the perfect place. It seemed unlikely she would be able to go, but I also thought that when I asked her to spend the night. *'Our entire relationship is improbable, why would we stop beating the odds now?'* I wondered, optimistically.

It could have been minutes; it could have been hours. I had completely lost track of time, but Nina finally grumbled awake and turned around immediately to kiss me. I loved waking up with her. It felt surreal. There is no better way to start the day than to wake up with the one you love.

The excitement of my idea had my body buzzing. I wasn't sure if the feeling in my arm was the circulation returning, or the excitement of my idea. I wanted to start the trip as soon as possible. Asking Nina was the easy part. She was over the moon to go away together. Next was the hard part. Asking her parents.

Agreeing to go immediately worked on two fronts; one, to get an answer as soon as possible; two, so I could introduce myself to her family.

I took off my shirt covered in Nina's makeup and put on a hoodie that I had no doubt wouldn't be making the return trip to Williamstown. I walked into the bathroom and brushed my teeth quickly, so I didn't have bad breath meeting her family for the first time.

My phone read ten-thirty, so we left the room, walked downstairs and through the hotel doors. As we walked into the Požega sunshine, the smell of the crisp, clean country air filled my nostrils. There wasn't a cloud in the sky, but there were puddles and the smell of rain. I could smell grass in the air as well. Breathing in the country air was cleansing for my sinuses.

My lack of boyfriend experience had me overthinking every action or inaction. There we were, walking along the street to meet Nina's parents, in the glorious sunshine, but instead of enjoying the picture-perfect serenity of the setting, I was stressing about whether I should be holding her hand. My parents always held hands when walking down the street, so I supposed it was the thing couples did. Her hand accidentally grazed mine as we walked in the direction of the bus station. I shook my head in disbelief at the thought of only arriving there less than a day before. So much had happened, it felt like it was a previous life.

Waiting for her hand to swing past my side again I tried to grab it but missed. *'Damn it,'* I thought in frustration. I was glad I grasped thin air, because if I touched her hand and let it slip, that would've been embarrassing. Before I could try another attempt to take her hand, Nina took mine. We were completely on the same page.

In most situations my mind would be going a million miles an hour over thinking every possible situation, and while I was a little edgy because of meeting Nina's family, I knew everything would be okay because I was with her. I was trying to focus on my surroundings, the look of the houses, the smiling faces we passed, and Nina's company. No matter how hard I tried, I couldn't stop my hand from sweating. She must have noticed because she gave me a little squeeze and placed her free hand on my arm as we walked.

I tried to take in every detail of my family's hometown. I loved the open fields on our left and corn fields on our right as we walked towards a curve in the road. *'What would this place look like from those mountains?'* I wondered, looking off to my right to see the glorious mountainous landscape covered in green. We walked past a basketball court that must have had ten boys and girls running around playing and another ten waiting to play. The laughter I heard made me smile as I saw a girl running around celebrating a made shot.

We turned left into a long driveway and approached what I thought must surely be Nina's house. I couldn't help but stare in awe of the stunning open spaces. Fields of lush green surrounded her house, and I wondered how great a childhood would be with those surroundings. To be able to go outside and run around with your friends all day in those fields until it was time to go home for dinner. Living outside and not through a screen.

We reached the door of Nina's house. I began to take off my shoes, but it was very difficult as my nervous hands were shaking. Standing on one leg like a flamingo, I attempted once again to undo my double knotted laces but lost my balance and stumbled. My racing heart and shaking hands were throwing off my balance, so I bent my knees and undid my laces. Holding my shoes together nervously, I followed Nina over the threshold of the house with great trepidation. I didn't want to do the wrong thing in someone else's home, especially when I was trying to make a strong first impression. I stood in the entrance room to the house waiting to follow Nina's lead. The shower was running, and I could hear a video being played in another room. Nina instructed me to leave my shoes just inside the door and shouted out to get the attention of her parents. Walking into the living room I saw her parents look up at us with beaming smiles from the couch. Family photos were spread around the room spanning all three kids lives. Clean dishes sat in the drying rack on the sink, and a beautiful centre piece of flowers was sitting on the table.

The colours of the room complemented each other perfectly, with the walls a cream colour and the couch an inviting navy blue. Her parents stood up to welcome me. I kissed her mother three times, alternating each cheek, and I shook hands with her father. They looked incredibly pleased to meet me, but there was a noticeable level of dominance asserted in the strength her father put into our handshake. Her father looked like he was always the life of the party, making jokes at anyone's expense, even mine. Her mother was the Serbian version of my Serbian mother. I could see in her face she was a warm woman, and because I had come into her home with her daughter, I was already a special person to her. They made me feel at home and in turn, my nerves faded away.

I was offered a glass of rakija from her father and I accepted. Drinking rakija with Mr Draganić felt like a rite of passage and helped lower my nerves to an almost unnoticeable level.

I should have been nervous to ask if I could take their daughter on a trip, but for some strange reason I wasn't. My nerves had dissipated, and they were all linked to meeting Nina's family, hoping to be accepted. I felt like I belonged there. They were an extension of my family. I walked to the table where Mrs Draganić sat, and Mr Draganić stood next to her, and whispered as quietly as possible where I wanted to take Nina. They said they would discuss it which was the best result I could have hoped for.

Milica and Jovan entered the room, so I walked over immediately to introduce myself. Milica looked quiet and reserved, speaking in a tone barely above a whisper. Jovan had a joyful look on his face and was immediately dragging me outside to play football with him. I was very surprised he spoke any English at all; it was far from perfect, but impressive nonetheless. I hadn't even finished tying my shoes when I looked up and saw him standing in the middle of the yard with the ball at his feet. Milica and Nina followed us outside, taking a seat to watch.

The field Jovan set up was approximately twenty metres long. There were patches of dirt that looked like they had just dried out from the rain overnight. Undulations in the grass and dirt made the ball difficult to control for a novice like me, but not for Jovan. He knew the pitch like the back of his hand, expertly navigating the uneven field.

It was a difficult balance between letting him win and not making it so obvious that he got mad at me for not trying. It was like playing with a dog; if you let them win playing tug, they run back to you immediately wanting to play again.

'Wow! Great move, Jovan!' I yelled, as he manoeuvred around me, and I dramatically lunged the wrong way to let him in for another goal. I put my hands on my knees and panted as Jovan kicked the ball back to me to restart the game. He could play all day and not get tired. *Is this kid a cyborg?*' I wondered. I was ready for a nap.

'Six-three,' he said, as he took a defensive stance, readying himself for my attack. I looked over to Nina and smiled. Nina returned my smile and pulled her phone out and looked like she was recording our game. *I'm going to try and make Nina laugh with this next play,*' I thought, thinking of an idea. I dribbled towards

Jovan and let him take the ball from me. As he was about to score, I picked him up and dribbled the ball the length of the field with him under my arm.

'Ne, ne, ne!' Jovan yelled, laughing as I gently kicked the ball between two of his tractors which were playing the part of goal posts. I ran wildly around the yard celebrating, removing my hoodie, and swinging it around my head. Jovan ran up to me and tackled me around my legs, dragging me to the ground. We both laughed hysterically covered in dirt.

Obviously, Nina's parents had to choose that moment to come outside to see Jovan and I lying in the dirt. *If they had decided to allow Nina and I to go on the trip, surely seeing me roll their son in the dirt like crumbed chicken would change that,'* I thought. Jovan and I saw them standing on the edge of where the pavement turned to grass. We stopped immediately and stood up as if we had just been caught misbehaving by the principal. Mr Draganić broke into a smile, and Mrs Draganić asked something of Jovan in Serbian. From her tone, she was not happy. I put my arm around Jovan and reassured them it was okay. She wanted to wash my dirty clothes there and then, but I didn't particularly want to sit around in my underwear while she washed them.

I looked to Nina and could see she was staring at her parents while twirling her hair, waiting to hear their decision. If I was sitting down my leg would be bouncing like a paint can shaker in a hardware store. Even though my mind was telling me repeatedly the answer would be no, I continued to hope. You can't live life without hope.

I didn't understand the words as they left her father's lips, but from the smile on his face and the squeal of joy emanating from Nina, it must have been the answer we wanted. Nina rushed to her parents and embraced them with sheer elation and gratitude. As with us meeting in person, neither of us genuinely believed it would happen until Nina heard the words and I saw her reaction, especially with where I was planning on taking her.

Struggling free from his daughter's embrace, Mr Draganić turned to English and addressed me directly. He had put an incredible amount of trust in both Nina and I, and I wouldn't take that trust for granted. I knew that when I returned with his daughter, she would be just as healthy, and even happier than when we left from the bus station that afternoon.

Walking to Mr Draganić, I shook his hand to assure him that the trust and faith he had put in me was well placed; I wouldn't let him down. He shook my hand with a lighter grip, saving my knuckles from being punished again.

Turning my attention quickly to Nina, I took both her hands in mine, so glad to be touching her again. I placed a gentle kiss on her cheek, trying to control the affection I displayed for her in front of her family. I would have lots of opportunities to be overly affectionate on our trip. Nina wrapped her arms tightly around my body and placed her head on my shoulder.

We agreed that we would meet at the bus station at four, so I needed to go back to the hotel to pack. Nina must not have had the same qualms about kissing in front of her parents, as she took her head off my shoulder and kissed me on the lips. I was very aware her family had their eyes on us, so my lips stayed tightly shut. I opened one eye to look at her parents and saw her father looking at the dirt, kicking it. Jovan was covering his eyes and Milica looked like she was laughing. While Mrs Draganić looked at us with a big smile.

Bidding the family farewell, I turned from the Draganić house and walked back towards my hotel. Even though I knew I was going to see Nina in four hours, it was hard to walk away. I snuck a look over my shoulder as I neared the end of the driveway and saw that Nina was standing outside the house watching me. *How pathetic is it that she's been gone from my company for two minutes and I already miss her? Maybe I should think of it as sweet instead,'* I thought, unable to believe just how in love I was with her. With a wave and blowing a kiss, I turned the corner and continued my way back to the hotel.

My bag was packed sitting next to the hotel room door ready to go. I had finished a sweep of my room to make sure that I had everything I needed. My wallet and phone were in my jeans pockets, my passport in my jacket pocket. The time was three-thirty, and I was getting antsy. Nervously I got down on all fours and checked under the bed to make sure my passport didn't leap from my pocket and slide under the bed. Nope, just a cheeky spider scurrying away at the sight of my stressed face.

I stood up and brushed myself off. Standing in front of the mirror that was insulting me only the night before, spitting all the awful things that I had ever thought about myself, I stared at myself again. Wearing blue jeans, high top tan boots, a white t-shirt, and a black jacket, I looked myself up and down.

'The only beautiful woman I have ever laid eyes on thinks I'm handsome. I am not ugly. The smartest woman I have ever spoken to thinks I have an interesting mind. I am not stupid. The woman I am in love with wants to be with me; she loves me. I am not a loser. I am winning,' I thought, smiling at myself, finally silencing the bully in the back of my mind.

Closing my eyes, I took a deep breath and saw Nina's smile drift through my mind. I could feel her hands on my body, and an electric warmth spread through my being. I could feel her lips pressed to mine, her warm body against me, and her heart beating in perfect timing with mine. With my eyes closed it felt like she was with me. I was craving her touch. To sit and talk to her while holding her hand was all I wanted, and I was counting down the seconds until I could have it again.

I took a photo of my bag and sent it to Nina to let her know I was on my way. Picking up my bag, I threw it over my shoulder and left my large suitcase and guitar in my room; I would be returning. My walk from the hotel room became a jog as I hit the stairs. I didn't want Nina to be waiting on me to arrive. Looking at the time, I saw I had fifteen minutes until we were due to meet. *'Fifteen minutes of standing in the room daydreaming. Really? Welcome back to the real-world Luka,'* I thought. I shook my head smiling at the realisation that my real world was walking to meet my girlfriend Nina for our trip.

I walked through the hotel's front door and the sun shone brightly in my eyes. It felt warm on my skin and any sign of rain had long disappeared. A group of chatting middle-aged men stood in front of the pub across the road from the hotel. There must have been eight of them all wearing different coloured tracksuits. A group of young girls walked past me in the direction of the town centre laughing amongst themselves. Two boys around Jovan's age ran past me carrying a basketball. *'They must be heading for the basketball court that I walked by on the way to Nina's house. This must be a great place to live,'* I thought serenely.

I stopped at Vuka Karadžića, the street that led to the Sunshine Café, which I needed to cross to get to the bus station. I checked several times for cars, not wanting to look the wrong way because they drove on the right side, as opposed to the left in Australia. A Yugo car stopped and gestured for me to cross. I gave a courtesy wave and broke into the awkward half jog in reciprocity for letting me cross.

I walked into the bus station and saw a small group of people milling around on the other side of the gate where the bus would depart. I was on the arrivals side, not wanting to buy the tickets until Nina arrived. There was a ticket box next to the gate with an elderly man wearing glasses and a Šajkača, a Serbian folk hat. Another man was checking tickets and letting passengers through the gate. The group of people waited patiently for the bus to arrive, several looking up the street to see if it was approaching. I craned my neck trying to see Nina in the pack, but I couldn't find her.

The old Luka would be stressing, wondering where Nina was, and why she wasn't at the bus stop already. Wondering if something had happened, or if she just changed her mind about coming on the trip. I felt completely at ease though. I took a seat on the bus station bench and laid my bag to rest next to me on the ground, staring in the direction of the gate, waiting to see Nina arrive.

Absentmindedly I looked at my phone to see if there was a text from Nina, before realising I had no data. Sitting peacefully, I wondered if Nina would be happy about the destination I had chosen for our first trip. The future I laid out for her during our first conversation was coming to pass. *'I truly do have the Sight,'* I thought, unable to stop the smile from spreading across my face.

I wondered if I should go and buy tickets, but there was still no bus, or Nina in sight. *'It's probably best to just wait for Nina to arrive,'* I thought.

'Luka!' I heard a voice yell. I turned to see my beautiful girlfriend approaching me with a bag over one shoulder, a container in that hand, and dragging a suitcase with the other. A euphoria washed over me seeing Nina floating towards me. She looked incredible with a smile spread across her face. I was addicted to seeing that smile. I bounced off the bench and met her as quickly as I could. Taking the suitcase from Nina, I kissed her and wrapped my arms around her in an embrace that said it's been too long. Her head rested on my shoulder, and I breathed in every particle of her scent. She smelled like apple shampoo, burek, and the smell in the air just before it rained. She smelled like love.

I released my hug and took her suitcase towards where my bag waited. We leaned into each other sitting on the bench, desiring the closeness we had missed for the last nine months. Nina placed her bag on the ground, and the plastic container on the bench next to her. 'We're only going for a few days, sunshine. You look packed for a round the world trip,' I joked, feeling the weight in her suitcase.

'Ha ha, very funny. I didn't know what to pack so I had to be cautious and pack for all scenarios,' Nina said.

'Are you okay? You seem a bit out of breath,' I asked, noticing her cheeks were flush, as I put my arm around her shoulder. Nina leaned down and rested her head on my shoulder.

'Yeah, I was just stressing because I was worried that I'd be late. Did we miss it?' Nina asked, looking over at the group of people waiting for the bus to arrive.

'It hasn't come yet. I'm not sure what's going on,' I said, looking towards the place the bus would depart. 'What's that?' I pointed at the container sitting next to Nina on the bench.

'Oh yeah, Mama sent this,' Nina said, handing me the container. I opened it and the smell of the freshly made burek wafted through my nostrils, smelling just like my mum's.

'She really wants me to try her burek. It smells incredible,' I said laughing, and picking up a piece and taking a bite. The light pasty had a crunch, and the meat inside was as soft as velvet. 'This is amazing,' I said after swallowing my first mouthful.

'I think it's so we don't eat anything unhealthy tonight. Mama hates any kind of fatty food,' Nina said, taking a piece herself and eating it.

'This taste's too good to be healthy,' I said, wiping my hands on the bus bench.

'So, are you going to tell me where we're going, or are you going to continue to torture me?' Nina asked, lightly hitting me on the leg.

'Well, I guess I can tell you now. I've tortured you enough with that packing challenge,' I said, sticking my tongue out at her. 'Do you remember when we first met, and I told you your future?' I asked, kissing her head through her beautifully flowing brown hair.

'Yes...' she said slowly, sitting up straight and turning towards me so she could look me directly in the eye.

'I told you I could tell the future. We're going to Paris. Happy birthday, sunshine.' Nina's face lit up like Paris at night, and she climbed on my lap to embrace me.

'Oh, thank you. I'm so lucky I found you,' Nina said, kissing me on the lips.

'I'm the lucky one. I feel so grateful that I'm the only one who gets to love you like I do, and I know that will never change because I'm going to earn your heart every single day. I don't want to be anywhere without you,' I whispered into her ear.

'We are special together, Luka,' Nina said, and I kissed her again, deeply on the lips. The shiver that radiated through my body was something only she could make me feel. It was emanating from our souls combined, knowing I had found my soulmate. It was my soul celebrating. It was magic.

'Thank you for choosing me,' I said, unable to stop the smile in my heart from spreading across my face.

'Thank you for coming to get me,' Nina said, as I stared into her sparkling eyes.

An announcement came over the loudspeaker in Serbian. 'What did they say?' I asked Nina. She leaned back and I wrapped my arms around her midriff, her hands resting on my shoulders.

'It said that the bus broke down and another will be here in an hour,' Nina said. 'You don't mind waiting with me?'

'I don't want to wait with anyone else,' I said, kissing Nina on the lips again. Nina climbed off my lap and sat tightly against me.

We sat on the bench together waiting for the bus. Both content, engulfed with butterflies, without an elephant in sight. Happy together.

About the Author

This is the first published work by AMJ Dykes, a mind that constantly invents fictional scenarios and finally decided to stop keeping them to himself. Somewhere along the way, he fell in love with writing, became obsessed with it, and basked in the levity it brought him. He hopes this story gives readers even a fraction of the joy, escapism, and late-night overthinking that writing it gave him.